The JUNIOR CLASSICS

VOLUME TWO · STORIES OF WONDER AND MAGIC

Warren Chappell

The dragon came nearer and nearer.

[See page 151]

The JUNIOR CLASSICS

Edited by MABEL WILLIAMS *and* MARCIA DALPHIN.

With Introduction by WILLIAM ALLAN NEILSON, LL.D.,

President Emeritus, Smith College; Introduction to First Edition

by CHARLES W. ELIOT, LL.D., *Formerly President of Harvard*

University. WILLIAM W. BEARDSLEY, *Editorial Director*

Popular Edition

ILLUSTRATED

VOLUME

TWO

STORIES OF

WONDER

AND MAGIC

P. F. COLLIER & SON CORPORATION

CONTENTS

FUN AND NONSENSE

CONTENTS

CONTENTS

STORIES BY HANS CHRISTIAN ANDERSEN

Illustration by V. Pedersen

(The sources of the stories in this volume will be found listed on page 368.)

Fun and Nonsense

THE MAGIC FISHBONE

By *CHARLES DICKENS*

With Illustration by F. D. BEDFORD

T HERE was once a king, and he had a queen; and he was the manliest of his sex, and she was the loveliest of hers. The king was, in his private profession, under government. The queen's father had been a medical man out of town.

They had nineteen children, and were always having more. Seventeen of these children took care of the baby; and Alicia, the eldest, took care of them all. Their ages varied from seven years to seven months.

Let us now resume our story.

One day the king was going to the office, when he stopped at the fishmonger's to buy a pound and a half of salmon not too near the tail, which the queen (who was a careful housekeeper) had requested him to send home. Mr. Pickles, the fishmonger, said, "Certainly, sir; is there any other article? Good morning."

The king went on toward the office in a melancholy mood; for quarter-day was such a long way off, and several of the dear children were growing out of their clothes. He had not proceeded far, when Mr. Pickles's errand-boy came running after him, and said, "Sir, you didn't notice the old lady in our shop."

"What old lady?" inquired the king. "I saw none."

Now the king had not seen any old lady, because this old lady had been invisible to him, though visible to Mr. Pickles's boy. Probably because he messed and splashed the water about to that degree, and flopped the pairs of soles down in that violent manner, that, if she had not been visible to him, he would have spoilt her clothes.

Just then the old lady came trotting up. She was dressed in shot silk of the richest quality, smelling of dried lavender.

"King Watkins the First, I believe?" said the old lady.

"Watkins," replied the king, "is my name."

"Papa, if I am not mistaken, of the beautiful Princess Alicia?" said the old lady.

It instantly flashed upon the king that she must be a fairy, or how could she know that?

"You are right," said the old lady, answering his thoughts. "I am the Good Fairy Grandmarina. Attend! When you return home to dinner, politely invite the Princess Alicia to have some of the salmon you bought just now."

"It may disagree with her," said the king.

The old lady became so very angry at this absurd idea, that the king was quite alarmed, and humbly begged her pardon.

"We hear a great deal too much about this thing disagreeing and that thing disagreeing," said the old lady, with the greatest contempt it was possible to express. "Don't be greedy. I think you want it all yourself."

The king hung his head under this reproof, and said he wouldn't talk about things disagreeing any more.

"Be good, then," said the Fairy Grandmarina, "and don't! When the beautiful Princess Alicia consents to partake of the salmon—as I think she will—you will find she will leave a fishbone on her plate. Tell her to dry it, and to rub it, and to polish it, till it shines like mother-of-pearl, and to take care of it as a present from me."

"Is that all?" asked the king.

"Don't be impatient, sir," returned the Fairy Grandmarina, scolding him severely. "Don't catch people short, before they have done speaking. Just the way with you grown-up persons. You are always doing it."

The king again hung his head, and said he wouldn't do so any more.

"Be good, then," said the Fairy Grandmarina, "and don't! Tell the Princess Alicia, with my love, that the fishbone is a magic present which can only be used once; but that it will bring her, that once, whatever she wishes for, *provided she wishes for it at the right time*. That is the message. Take care of it." The king was beginning, "Might I ask the reason?" when the fairy became absolutely furious.

"*Will* you be good, sir?" she exclaimed, stamping her foot on the ground. "The reason for this, and the reason for that, indeed! You are always wanting the reason. No reason. There! Hoity-toity me! I am sick of your grown-up reasons."

The king was extremely frightened by the old lady's flying into such a passion, and said he was very sorry to have offended her, and he wouldn't ask for reasons any more.

"Be good, then," said the old lady, "and don't!"

With those words, Grandmarina vanished, and the king went on and on and on, till he came to the office. There he wrote and wrote and wrote, till it was time to go home again. Then he politely invited the Princess Alicia, as the fairy had directed him, to partake of the salmon. And when she had enjoyed it very much, he saw the fishbone on her plate, as the fairy had told him he would, and he delivered the fairy's message, and the Princess Alicia took care to dry the bone, and to rub it and to polish it, till it shone like mother-of-pearl.

And so, when the queen was going to get up in the morning, she said, "Oh, dear me, dear me; my head, my head!" and then she fainted away.

The Princess Alicia, who happened to be looking in at the chamber door, asking about breakfast, was very much alarmed when she raw her royal mamma in this state, and she rang the bell for Peggy, which was the name of the lord chamberlain. But remembering where the smelling-bottle was, she climbed on a chair and got it; and after that she climbed on another chair by the bedside, and held the smelling-bottle to the queen's nose; and after that she jumped up again and wetted the queen's forehead; and, in short, when the lord chamberlain came in, that dear old woman said to the little princess, "What a trot you are! I couldn't have done it better myself!"

But that was not the worst of the good queen's illness. Oh, no! She was very ill indeed, for a long time. The Princess Alicia kept the seventeen young princes and princesses quiet, and dressed and undressed and danced the baby, and made the kettle boil, and heated the soup, and swept the hearth, and poured out the medicine, and nursed the queen, and did all that ever she could, and was as busy, busy, busy as busy could be; for there were not many servants at the palace for three reasons: because the king was short of money, because a rise in his office never seemed to come, and because quarter-day was so far off that it looked almost as far off and as little as one of the stars.

But on the morning when the queen fainted away, where was the magic fishbone? Why, there it was in the Princess Alicia's pocket! She had almost taken it out to bring the queen to life again, when she put it back, and looked for the smelling-bottle.

After the queen had come out of her swoon that morning and was dozing, the Princess Alicia hurried upstairs to tell a most particular secret to a most particular confidential friend of hers, who was a duchess, though nobody knew it except the princess.

This most particular secret was the secret about the magic fishbone, the history of which was well known to the duchess, because the princess told her everything. The princess kneeled down by the bed on which the duchess was lying, full-dressed and wide-awake, and whispered the secret to her. The duchess smiled and nodded. People might have supposed that she never smiled and nodded; but she often did, though nobody knew it except the princess.

Then the Princess Alicia hurried downstairs again to keep watch in the queen's room. She often kept watch by herself in the queen's room; but every evening, while the illness lasted, she sat there watching with the king. And every evening the king sat looking at her with a cross look, wondering why she never brought out the magic fishbone. As often as she noticed this, she ran upstairs, whispered the secret to the duchess over again, and said to the duchess besides, "They think we children never have a reason or a meaning!" And the duchess, though the most fashionable duchess that ever was heard of, winked her eye.

"Alicia," said the king, one evening, when she wished him good night.

"Yes, papa."

"What is become of the magic fishbone?"

"In my pocket, papa."

"I thought you had lost it?"

"Oh, no, papa!"

"Or forgotten it?"

"No, indeed, papa."

And so another time the dreadful little snapping pug-dog, next door, made a rush at one of the young princes as he stood on the steps coming home from school, and terrified him out of his wits; and he put his hand through a pane of glass, and bled, bled, bled.

When the seventeen other young princes and princesses saw him bleed, bleed, bleed, they were terrified out of their wits, too, and screamed themselves black in their seventeen faces all at once.

But the Princess Alicia put her hands over all their seventeen mouths, one after another, and persuaded them to be quiet because of the sick queen.

And then she put the wounded prince's hand in a basin of fresh cold water, while they stared with their twice seventeen are thirty-four, put down four and carry three, eyes, and then she looked in the hand for bits of glass, and there were fortunately no bits of glass there. And then she said to two chubby-legged princes, who were sturdy though small, "Bring me in the royal rag-bag: I must snip and stitch and cut and contrive." So these two young princes tugged at the royal rag-bag, and lugged it in; and the Princess Alicia sat down on the floor, with a large pair of scissors and a needle and thread, and snipped and stitched and cut and contrived, and made a bandage, and put it on, and it fitted beautifully; and so when it was all done, she saw the king her papa looking on by the door.

"Alicia."

"Yes, papa."

"What have you been doing?"

"Snipping, stitching, cutting, and contriving, papa."

"Where is the magic fishbone?"

"In my pocket, papa."

"I thought you had lost it?"

"Oh, no, papa!"

"Or forgotten it?"

"No, indeed, papa."

After that, she ran upstairs to the duchess, and told her what had passed, and told her the secret over again; and the duchess shook her flaxen curls, and laughed with her rosy lips.

Well, and so another time the baby fell under the grate. The seventeen young princes and princesses were used to it; for they were almost always falling under the grate or down the stairs; but the baby was not used to it yet, and it gave him a swelled face and a black eye. The way the poor little darling came to tumble was, that he was out of the Princess Alicia's lap just as she was sitting, in a great coarse apron that quite smothered her, in front of the kitchen fire, beginning to peel the turnips for the broth for dinner; and the way she came to be doing that was, that the king's cook had run away that morning with her own true love, who was a very tall but very tipsy soldier. Then the seventeen young princes and princesses, who cried at everything that happened, cried and roared. But the Princess Alicia (who couldn't help crying a little herself) quietly called to them to be still, on account of not throwing back the queen upstairs, who was fast getting well, and said, "Hold your tongues, you wicked little monkeys, every one of you, while I examine baby." Then she examined baby, and found that he hadn't broken anything; and she held cold iron to his poor dear eye, and smoothed his poor dear face, and he presently fell asleep in her arms. Then she said to the seventeen princes and princesses, "I am afraid to let him down yet, lest he should wake and feel pain; be good, and you shall all be cooks." They jumped for joy when they heard that, and began making themselves cooks' caps out of old newspapers. So to one she gave the salt-box, and to one she gave the barley, and to one she gave the herbs, and to one she gave the turnips, and to one she gave the carrots, and to one she gave the onions, and to one she gave the spice-box, till they were all cooks, and all running about at work, she sitting in the middle, smothered in the great coarse apron, nursing baby.

By and by the broth was done; and the baby woke up, smiling

like an angel, and was trusted to the sedatest princess to hold, while
the other princes and princesses were squeezed into a far-off corner
to look at the Princess Alicia turning out the saucepanful of broth,
for fear (as they were always getting into trouble) they should get
splashed and scalded. When the broth came tumbling out, steam-
ing beautifully, and smelling like a nosegay good to eat, they clapped
their hands. That made the baby clap his hands; and that, and his
looking as if he had a comic toothache, made all the princes and
princesses laugh. So the Princess Alicia said, "Laugh and be good;
and after dinner we will make him a nest on the floor in a corner,
and he shall sit in his nest and see a dance of eighteen cooks." That
delighted the young princes and princesses, and they ate up all the
broth, and washed up all the plates and dishes, and cleared away,
and pushed the table into a corner; and then they in their cooks'
caps, and the Princess Alicia in the smothering coarse apron that
belonged to the cook that had run away with her own true love that
was the very tall but very tipsy soldier, danced a dance of eighteen
cooks before the angelic baby, who forgot his swelled face and his
black eye, and crowed with joy.

And so then, once more the Princess Alicia saw King Watkins
the First, her father, standing in the doorway looking on, and he
said, "What have you been doing, Alicia?"

"Cooking and contriving, papa."

"What else have you been doing, Alicia?"

"Keeping the children light-hearted, papa."

"Where is the magic fishbone, Alicia?"

"In my pocket, papa."

"I thought you had lost it?"

"Oh, no, papa!"

"Or forgotten it?"

"No, indeed, papa."

The king then sighed so heavily, and seemed so low-spirited, and
sat down so miserably, leaning his head upon his hand, and his
elbow upon the kitchen table pushed away in the corner, that the
seventeen princes and princesses crept softly out of the kitchen, and
left him alone with the Princess Alicia and the angelic baby.

"What is the matter, papa?"

"I am dreadfully poor, my child."

"Have you no money at all, papa?"

"None, my child."

"Is there no way of getting any, papa?"

"No way," said the king. "I have tried very hard, and I have tried all ways."

The king sighed heavily and seemed low-spirited.

When she heard those last words, the Princess Alicia began to put her hand into the pocket where she kept the magic fishbone.

"Papa," said she, "when we have tried very hard, and tried all ways, we must have done our very, very best?"

"No doubt, Alicia."

"When we have done our very, very best, papa, and that is not enough, then I think the right time must have come for asking help of others." This was the very secret connected with the magic fishbone, which she had found out for herself from the good Fairy Grandmarina's words, and which she had so often whispered to her beautiful and fashionable friend, the duchess.

So she took out of her pocket the magic fishbone, that had been dried and rubbed and polished till it shone like mother-of-pearl; and she gave it one little kiss, and wished it was quarter-day. And immediately it *was* quarter-day; and the king's quarter's salary came rattling down the chimney, and bounced into the middle of the floor.

But this was not half of what happened—no, not a quarter; for immediately afterwards the good Fairy Grandmarina came riding in, in a carriage and four (peacocks), with Mr. Pickles's boy up behind, dressed in silver and gold, with a cocked hat, powdered hair, pink silk stockings, a jeweled cane, and a nosegay. Down jumped Mr. Pickles's boy, with his cocked hat in his hand, and wonderfully polite (being entirely changed by enchantment), and handed Grandmarina out; and there she stood, in her rich shot silk smelling of dried lavender, fanning herself with a sparkling fan.

"Alicia, my dear," said this charming old fairy, "how do you do? I hope I see you pretty well? Give me a kiss."

The Princess Alicia embraced her; and then Grandmarina turned to the king and said rather sharply, "Are you good?" The king said he hoped so.

"I suppose you know the reason *now* why my god-daughter here," kissing the princess again, "did not apply to the fishbone sooner?" said the fairy.

The king made a shy bow.

"Ah! but you didn't *then?*" said the fairy.

The king made a shyer bow.

"Any more reasons to ask for?" said the fairy.

The king said, No, and he was very sorry.

"Be good, then," said the fairy, "and live happy ever afterwards."

Then Grandmarina waved her fan, and the queen came in most splendidly dressed; and the seventeen young princes and princesses, no longer grown out of their clothes, came in, newly fitted out from top to toe, with tucks in everything to admit of its being let out. After that, the fairy tapped the Princess Alicia with her fan; and the smothering coarse apron flew away, and she appeared exquisitely dressed, like a little bride, with a wreath of orange-flowers and a silver veil. After that, the kitchen dresser changed of itself into a wardrobe, made of beautiful woods and gold and looking-glass, which was full of dresses of all sorts, all for her and all exactly fitting her. After that, the angelic baby came in running alone, with his face and eye not a bit the worse, but much the better. Then Grandmarina begged to be introduced to the duchess; and, when the duchess was brought down, many compliments passed between them.

A little whispering took place between the fairy and the duchess; and then the fairy said out loud, "Yes, I thought she would have told you." Grandmarina then turned to the king and queen, and said, "We are going in search of Prince Certainpersonio. The pleasure of your company is requested at church in half an hour precisely." So she and Princess Alicia got into the carriage; and Mr. Pickles's boy handed in the duchess, who sat by herself on the opposite seat; and then Mr. Pickles's boy put up the steps and got up behind, and the peacocks flew away with their tails behind.

Prince Certainpersonio was sitting by himself, eating barley sugar, and waiting to be ninety. When he saw the peacocks, followed by the carriage, coming in at the window, it immediately occurred to him that something uncommon was going to happen.

"Prince," said Grandmarina, "I bring you your bride."

The moment the fairy said those words, Prince Certainpersonio's face left off being sticky, and his jacket and corduroys changed to peach-bloom velvet, and his hair curled, and a cap and feather flew in like a bird and settled on his head. He got into the carriage by the fairy's invitation; and there he renewed his acquaintance with the duchess, whom he had seen before.

In the church were the prince's relations and friends, and the Princess Alicia's relations and friends, and the seventeen princes and princesses, and the baby, and a crowd of the neighbors. The marriage was beautiful beyond expression. The duchess was bridesmaid, and beheld the ceremony from the pulpit, where she was supported by the cushion of the desk.

Grandmarina gave a magnificent wedding-feast afterwards, in which there was everything and more to eat, and everything and more to drink. The wedding-cake was delicately ornamented with white satin ribbons, frosted silver, and white lilies, and was forty-two yards round.

When Grandmarina had drunk her love to the young couple, and Prince Certainpersonio had made a speech, and everybody had cried "Hip, hip, hip, hurrah!" Grandmarina announced to the king and queen that in future there would be eight quarter-days in every year, except in leap-year, when there would be ten. She then turned to Certainpersonio and Alicia, and said, "My dears, you will have thirty-five children, and they will all be good and beautiful. Seventeen of your children will be boys, and eighteen will be girls. The hair of the whole of your children will curl naturally. They will never have the measles, and will have recovered from the whooping-cough before being born."

On hearing such good news, everybody cried out "Hip, hip, hip, hurrah!" again.

"It only remains," said Grandmarina in conclusion, "to make an end of the fishbone."

So she took it from the hand of the Princess Alicia, and it instantly flew down the throat of the dreadful little snapping pug-dog, next door, and choked him, and he expired in convulsions.

THE STORY OF THE FOUR LITTLE CHILDREN WHO WENT AROUND THE WORLD

By EDWARD LEAR

With Illustrations by THE AUTHOR

ONCE upon a time, a long while ago, there were four little people whose names were

VIOLET,   SLINGSBY,   GUY,   and LIONEL.

They all thought they should like to see the world. So they bought a large boat to sail quite round the world by sea, and then they were to come back on the other side by land. The boat was painted blue with green spots, and the sail was yellow with red stripes: and, when

they set off, they only took a small Cat to steer and look after the
boat, besides an elderly Quangle-Wangle, who had to cook the dinner and make the tea; for which purposes they took a large kettle.

For the first ten days they sailed on beautifully, and found plenty

to eat, as there were lots of fish; and they had only to take them out
of the sea with a long spoon, when the Quankle-Wangle instantly
cooked them; and the Pussy-Cat was fed with the bones, with which
she expressed herself pleased, on the whole: so that all the party
were very happy.

During the daytime, Violet chiefly occupied herself in putting
salt water into a churn; while her three brothers churned it violently,

in the hope that it would turn into butter, which it seldom if ever
did; and in the evening they all retired into the tea-kettle, where they
all managed to sleep very comfortably, while Pussy and the Quangle-
Wangle managed the boat.

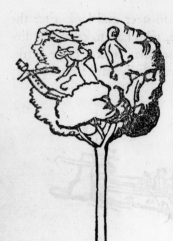

After a time, they saw some land at a distance; and, when they came to it, they found it was an island made of water quite surrounded by earth. Besides that, it was bordered by evanescent isthmuses, with a great gulf-stream running about all over it; so that it was perfectly beautiful, and contained only a single tree, 503 feet high.

When they had landed, they walked about, but found, to their great surprise, that the island was quite full of veal-cutlets and chocolate-drops, and nothing else. So they all climbed up the single high tree to discover, if possible, if there were any people; but having remained on the top of the tree for a week, and not seeing anybody, they naturally concluded that there were no inhabitants; and accordingly, when they came down, they loaded the boat with two thousand veal-cutlets and a million of chocolate-drops; and these afforded them sustenance for more than a month, during which time they pursued their voyage with the utmost delight and apathy.

After this they came to a shore where there were no less than sixty-five great red parrots with blue tails, sitting on a rail all of a row, and all fast asleep. And I am sorry to say that the Pussy-Cat and the Quangle-Wangle crept softly, and bit off the tail-feathers of all the sixty-five parrots; for which Violet reproved them both severely.

Notwithstanding which, she proceeded to insert all the feathers

—two hundred and sixty in number—in her bonnet; thereby causing it to have a lovely and glittering appearance, highly prepossessing and efficacious.

The next thing that happened to them was in a narrow part of the sea, which was so entirely full of fishes that the boat could go on no farther: so they remained there about six weeks, till they had eaten

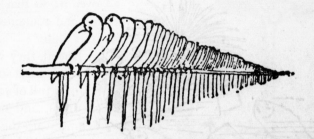

nearly all the fishes, which were soles, and all ready-cooked, and covered with shrimp-sauce, so that there was no trouble whatever. And as the few fishes who remained uneaten complained of the cold, as well as of the difficulty they had in getting any sleep on account of the extreme noise made by the arctic bears and the tropical turn-spits, which frequented the neighborhood in great numbers, Violet

most amiably knitted a small woolen frock for several of the fishes, and Slingsby administered some opium-drops to them; through which kindness they became quite warm, and slept soundly.

Then they came to a country which was wholly covered with immense orange-trees of a vast size, and quite full of fruit. So they

all landed, taking with them the tea-kettle, intending to gather some of the oranges, and place them in it. But, while they were busy about this, a most dreadfully high wind rose, and blew out most of the parrot-tail feathers from Violet's bonnet. That, however, was

nothing compared with the calamity of the oranges falling down on their heads by millions and millions, which thumped and bumped and bumped and thumped them all so seriously, that they were obliged to run as hard as they could for their lives; besides that the sound of the oranges rattling on the tea-kettle was of the most fearful and amazing nature.

Nevertheless, they got safely to the boat, although considerably vexed and hurt; and the Quangle-Wangle's right foot was so knocked about, that he had to sit with his head in his slipper for at least a week.

This event made them all for a time rather melancholy: and perhaps they might never have become less so, had not Lionel, with a most praiseworthy devotion and perseverance, continued to stand on one leg, and whistle to them in a loud and lively manner; which diverted the whole party so extremely that they gradually recovered their spirits, and agreed that whenever they should reach home, they would subscribe toward a testimonial to Lionel, entirely made of gingerbread and raspberries, as an earnest token of their sincere and grateful infection.

After sailing on calmly for several more days, they came to another country, where they were much pleased and surprised to see a countless multitude of white Mice with red eyes, all sitting in a great circle, slowly eating custard-pudding with the most satisfactory and polite demeanor.

And as the four travelers were rather hungry, being tired of eating nothing but soles and oranges for so long a period, they held a council as to the propriety of asking the Mice for some of their pudding in a humble and affecting manner, by which they could

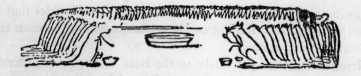

hardly be otherwise than gratified. It was agreed, therefore, that Guy should go and ask the Mice, which he immediately did; and the result was, that they gave a walnut-shell only half full of custard diluted with water. Now, this displeased Guy, who said, "Out of such a lot of pudding as you have got, I must say, you might have spared a somewhat larger quantity." But no sooner had he finished speaking than the Mice turned round at once, and sneezed at him in an appalling and vindictive manner (and it is impossible to imagine a more scroobious and unpleasant sound than that caused by the simultaneous sneezing of many millions of angry Mice); so that Guy rushed back to the boat, having first shied his cap into the middle of the custard-pudding, by which means he completely spoiled the Mice's dinner.

By and by the four children came to a country where there were no houses, but only an incredibly innumerable number of large bottles without corks, and of a dazzling and sweetly susceptible blue color. Each of these blue bottles contained a Blue-Bottle-Fly; and all these interesting animals live continually together in the most copious and rural harmony: nor perhaps in many parts of the world is such perfect and abject happiness to be found. Violet and Slingsby and Guy and Lionel were greatly struck with this singular and instructive settlement; and, having previously asked permission of the Blue-Bottle-Flies (which was most courteously granted), the boat was drawn up to the shore, and they proceeded to make tea in front

of the bottles: but as they had no tea-leaves, they merely placed some pebbles in the hot water; and the Quangle-Wangle played some tunes over it on an accordion, by which, of course, tea was made directly, and of the very best quality.

The four children then entered into conversation with the Blue-Bottle-Flies, who discoursed in a placid and genteel manner, though with a slightly buzzing accent, chiefly owing to the fact that they each held a small clothes-brush between their teeth, which naturally occasioned a fizzy, extraneous utterance.

"Why," said Violet, "would you kindly inform us, do you reside in bottles; and, if in bottles at all, why not, rather, in green or purple, or, indeed, in yellow bottles?"

To which questions a very aged Blue-Bottle-Fly answered, "We found the bottles here all ready to live in; that is to say, our great-great-great-great-great-grandfathers did: so we occupied them at once. And, when the winter comes on, we turn the bottles upside down, and consequently rarely feel the cold at all; and you know very well that this could not be the case with bottles of any other color than blue."

"Of course it could not," said Slingsby. "But, if we may take the liberty of inquiring, on what do you chiefly subsist?"

"Mainly on oyster-patties," said the Blue-Bottle-Fly; "and when these are scarce, on raspberry vinegar and Russian leather boiled down to a jelly."

"How delicious!" said Guy.

To which Lionel added, "Huzz!" And all the Blue-Bottle-Flies said, "Buzz!"

At this time, an elderly Fly said it was the hour for the evening-song to be sung; and, on a signal being given, all the Blue-Bottle-Flies began to buzz at once in a sumptuous and sonorous manner, the melodious and mucilaginous sounds echoing all over the waters, and resounding across the tumultuous tops of the transitory titmice upon the intervening and verdant mountains with a serene and sickly suavity only known to the truly virtuous. The Moon was shining slobaciously from the star-bespangled sky, while her light irrigated the smooth and shiny sides and wings and backs of the Blue-Bottle-Flies with a peculiar and trivial splendor, while all Nature cheerfully responded to the cerulean and conspicuous circumstances.

In many long-after years, the four little travelers looked back to that evening as one of the happiest in all their lives; and it was already past midnight when—the sail of the boat having been set up by the Quangle-Wangle, the tea-kettle and churn placed in their respective positions, and the Pussy-Cat stationed at the helm—the children each took a last and affectionate farewell of the Blue-Bottle-Flies, who walked down in a body to the water's edge to see the travelers embark.

As a token of parting respect and esteem, Violet made a courtesy quite down to the ground, and stuck one of her few remaining parrot-tail feathers into the back hair of the most pleasing of the Blue-Bottle-Flies; while Slingsby, Guy, and Lionel offered them three small boxes, containing, respectively, black pins, dried figs, and Epsom salts; and thus they left that happy shore forever.

Overcome by their feelings, the four little travelers instantly jumped into the tea-kettle, and fell fast asleep. But all along the shore, for many hours, there was distinctively heard a sound of severely-suppressed sobs, and of a vague multitude of living creatures using their pocket-handkerchiefs in a subdued simultaneous snuffle, lingering sadly along the walloping waves as the boat sailed farther and farther away from the Land of the Happy Blue-Bottle-Flies.

Nothing particular occurred for some days after these events, except that, as the travelers were passing a low tract of sand, they perceived an unusual and gratifying spectacle; namely, a large number of Crabs and Crawfish—perhaps six or seven hundred—sitting by the water-side, and endeavoring to disentangle a vast heap of pale pink worsted, which they moistened at intervals with a fluid composed of lavender-water and white-wine negus.

"Can we be of any service to you, O crusty Crabbies?" said the four children.

"Thank you kindly," said the Crabs, consecutively. "We are trying to make some worsted mittens, but do not know how."

On which Violet, who was perfectly acquainted with the art of mitten-making, said to the Crabs, "Do your claws unscrew, or are they fixtures?"

"They are all made to unscrew," said the Crabs; and forthwith they deposited a great pile of claws close to the boat, with which Violet uncombed all the pale pink worsted, and then made the loveliest mittens with it you can imagine. These the Crabs, having resumed and screwed on their claws, placed cheerfully upon their wrists, and walked away rapidly on their hind-legs, warbling songs with a silvery voice and in a minor key.

After this, the four little people sailed on again till they came to a vast and wide plain of astonishing dimensions, on which nothing whatever could be discovered at first; but, as the travelers walked onward, there appeared in the extreme and dim distance a single object, which on a nearer approach, and on an accurately cutaneous inspection, seemed to be somebody in a large white wig, sitting on an arm-chair made of sponge-cakes and oyster-shells. "It does not quite look like a human being," said Violet doubtfully; nor could they make out what it really was, till the Quangle-Wangle (who had previously been round the world) exclaimed softly in a loud voice, "It is the co-operative Cauliflower!"

And so, in truth, it was: and they soon found that what they had taken for an immense wig was in reality the top of the Cauliflower; and that he had no feet at all, being able to walk tolerably well with a fluctuating and graceful movement on a single cabbage-stalk—an accomplishment which naturally saved him the expense of stockings and shoes.

Presently, while the whole party from the boat was gazing at him with mingled affection and disgust, he suddenly arose, and, in a somewhat plumdomphious manner, hurried off toward the setting sun—his steps supported by two superincumbent confidential Cucumbers, and a large number of Waterwagtails proceeding in advance of him by three and three in a row—till he finally disappeared on the brink of the western sky in a crystal cloud of sudorific sand.

So remarkable a sight, of course, impressed the four children very deeply; and they returned immediately to their boat with a strong sense of undeveloped asthma and a great appetite.

Shortly after this, the travelers were obliged to sail directly below some high overhanging rocks, from the top of one of which a par-

ticularly odious little boy, dressed in rose-colored knickerbockers, and with a pewter plate upon his head, threw an enormous pumpkin at the boat, by which it was instantly upset.

But this upsetting was of no consequence, because all the party knew how to swim very well: and, in fact, they preferred swimming about till after the moon rose; when, the water growing chilly, they sponge-taneously entered the boat. Meanwhile the Quangle-Wangle threw back the pumpkin with immense force, so that it hit the rocks

where the malicious little boy in rose-colored knickerbockers was sitting; when, being quite full of lucifer-matches, the pumpkin exploded surreptitiously into a thousand bits; whereon the rocks instantly took fire, and the odious little boy became unpleasantly hotter and hotter and hotter, till his knickerbockers were turned quite green, and his nose was burnt off.

Two or three days after this had happened, they came to another place, where they found nothing at all except some wide and deep pits full of mullberry-jam. This is the property of the tiny, yellow-nosed Apes who abound in these districts, and who store up the mulberry-jam for their food in winter, when they mix it with pellucid pale periwinkle-soup, and serve it out in Wedgwood china-bowls, which grow freely all over that part of the country. Only

one of the yellow-nosed Apes was on the spot, and he was fast asleep; yet the four travelers and the Quangle-Wangle and Pussy were so terrified by the violence and sanguinary sound of his snoring, that they merely took a small cupful of the jam, and returned to re-embark in their boat without delay.

What was their horror on seeing the boat (including the churn and the tea-kettle) in the mouth of an enormous Seeze Pyder, an aquatic and ferocious creature truly dreadful to behold, and happily, only met with in those excessive longitudes! In a moment, the beautiful boat was bitten into fifty-five thousand million hundred billion bits; and it instantly became quite clear that Violet, Slingsby, Guy, and Lionel could no longer preliminate their voyage by sea.

The four travelers were therefore obliged to resolve on pursuing their wanderings by land: and, very fortunately, there happened to pass by at that moment an elderly Rhinoceros, on which they seized; and, all four mounting on his back—the Quangle-Wangle sitting on his horn, and holding on by his ears, and the Pussy-Cat swinging at the end of his tail—they set off, having only four small beans

and three pounds of mashed potatoes to last through their whole journey.

They were, however, able to catch numbers of the chickens and turkeys and other birds who incessantly alighted on the head of the Rhinoceros for the purpose of gathering the seeds of the rhododendron-plants which grew there; and these creatures they cooked in the most translucent and satisfactory manner by means of a fire lighted on the end of the Rhinoceros's back. A crowd of Kangaroos and gigantic Cranes accompanied them, from feelings of curiosity and complacency; so that they were never at a loss for company, and went onward, as it were, in a sort of profuse and triumphant procession.

Thus in less than eighteen weeks they all arrived safely at home, where they were received by their admiring relatives with joy tempered with contempt, and where they finally resolved to carry out the rest of their traveling plans at some more favorable opportunity.

As for the Rhinoceros, in token of their grateful adherence, they had him killed and stuffed directly, and then set him up outside the door of their father's house as a diaphanous doorscraper.

LIVING IN W'ALES

By *RICHARD HUGHES*

Illustrations by GEORGE CHARLTON

ONCE there was a man who said he didn't like the sort of houses people lived in, so he built a model village. It was not really like a model village at all, because the houses were all big enough for real people to live in, and he went about telling people to come and Live in W'ales.

There was also living in Liverpool a little girl who was very nice. So when all the people went off with the man to live in W'ales, she went with them. But the man walked so fast that presently some of them got left behind. The ones who were left behind were the little girl, and an Alsatian dog, and a very cross old lady in a bonnet and black beads, who was all stiff, but had a nice husband, who was left behind, too.

So they went along till they came to the sea; and in the sea was a whale. The little girl said, "That was what he meant, I suppose, when he talked about living in W'ales. I expect the others are inside: or, if not, in another one. We had better get in this one."

So they shouted to know if they might come in, but the whale didn't hear them. The nice husband said that if that was what living in W'ales meant, he would rather go back to Liverpool; but the horrid old lady said, "Nonsense! I will go and whisper in its ear."

But she was very silly, and so instead of whispering in its ear she went and tried to whisper in its blowhole. Still the whale didn't hear; so she got very cross and said: "None of this nonsense, now! Let us in at once! I won't have it, do you hear? I simply won't stand it!" and she began to stir in his blowhole with her umbrella.

So the whale blew, like an enormous sneeze, and blew her right away up into the sky on top of the water he blew out of his hole, and she was never seen again. So then the nice husband went quietly back to Liverpool.

But the little girl went to the whale's real ear, which was very small and not a bit like his blowhole, and whispered into it, "Please, nice whale, we would so like to come in, if we may, and live inside." Then the whale opened his mouth, and the little girl and the Alsatian dog went in.

When they got right down inside, of course, there was no furniture. "He was quite right," said the little girl. "It is certainly not a bit like living in a house."

The only thing in there was a giant's wig that the whale had once eaten. So the little girl said. "This will do for a door-mat." So she made it into a door-mat, and the Alsatian dog went to sleep on it.

When he woke up again he started to dig holes: and of course it gave the whale most terrible pains to have holes dug by such a big dog in his inside, so he went up to the top of the water and shouted to the Captain of a ship to give him a pill. On board the ship there was a cold dressed leg of mutton that the Captain was tired of, so he thought, "That will make a splendid pill to give the whale." So he threw it to the whale, and the whale swallowed it; and when it came tobogganing down the whale's throat, the Alsatian dog, who was very hungry, ate it, and stopped digging holes; and when dog stopped digging holes the whale's pain went away. So he said "Thank you," to the Captain. "That was an excellent pill."

The Captain was very surprised that his pill had made the whale well again so soon: he had really only done it to get rid of the cold mutton.

But the poor little girl wasn't so lucky as the Alsatian dog. *He* had a door-mat to sleep on, and something to eat. But there was no bed, and the little girl couldn't sleep without a bed to sleep on possibly, and had nothing to eat, and this went on for days and days.

Meanwhile the whale began to get rather worried about them. He had swallowed them without thinking much about it; but he soon began to wonder what was happening to them, and whether they were comfortable. He knew nothing at all about little girls. He thought she would probably want something to eat by now, but he didn't know at all what. So he tried to talk down into his own inside, to ask her. But that is very difficult: at any rate *he* couldn't do it. The words all came out instead of going in.

So he swam off to the tropics, where he knew a parrot, and asked him what to do. The parrot said it was quite simple, and flew off to an island where there was a big snake. He bit off its head and bit off its tail, and then flew back to the whale with the rest of it. He put most of the snake down the whale's throat, so that one end just came up out of its mouth.

"There," he said, "now you have got a speaking tube. You speak into one end of the snake, and the words will go down it inside you."

So the whale said, "Hallo!" into one end of the snake, and the little girl heard "Hallo!" come out of the other. "What do you want?" said the whale. "I want something to eat," said the little girl. The whale told the parrot, "She wants something to eat. What do little girls eat?"

"Little girls eat rice pudding," said the parrot. He had one, in a big glass bowl; so he poured it down the snake, too, and it came down the other end and the little girl ate it.

When she had eaten it she caught hold of her end of the snake, and called "Hallo!" up it.

"Hallo!" said the whale.

"May I have a bed?" said the little girl.

"She wants a bed," the whale said to the parrot.

"You go to Harrod's for that," said the parrot, "which is the biggest shop in London," and flew away.

When the whale got to Harrod's, he went inside. One of the shop-walkers came up to him and said, "What can I do for *you,* please?" which sounded very silly.

"I want a bed," said the whale.

"Mr. Binks, BEDS!" The shopwalker called out very loud, and then ran away. He was terribly frightened, because there had never been a whale in the shop before.

Mr. Binks, the Bed Man, came up and looked rather worried.

"I don't know that we have got a bed that will exactly fit you, sir," he said.

"Why not, silly?" said the whale. "I only want an ordinary one."

"Yes, sir," said the Bed Man, "but it will have to be rather a large, ordinary one, won't it?"

"Of course not, silly," said the whale. "On the contrary, it will have to be rather a small one."

He saw a very nice little one standing in a corner.

"I think that one will just about fit me," he said.

"You can have it if you like," said the Bed Man. "But I think it's you who are the silly to think a little bed like that will fit you!"

"I want it to fit me *inside,* of course," said the whale, "not *outside!*—Push!" and he opened his mouth.

So they all came and pushed, and sure enough it just did fit him. Then he ate all the pillows and blankets he could find, which was far more than was needed really, and when it all got down inside, the little girl made the bed and went to sleep on it.

So the whale went back to the sea. Now that the little girl and the Alsatian dog both had had something to eat and somewhere to sleep, they said:

"The man was right, it really is much more fun living in W'ales than living in houses."

So they stayed on.

P.S.—The parrot went on feeding them, not always on rice pudding.

THE GARDENER AND THE WHITE ELEPHANTS

By *RICHARD HUGHES*

Illustrations by GEORGE CHARLTON

THERE was once a gardener who had to look after such a big garden that he had to get up at one in the morning, and didn't get to bed till twelve at night. In fact, he only got one hour's sleep each night. And working so hard made him get thin and old and rheumaticky and lame long before he should.

One day he planted out a beautiful bed of sweet peas; but when he came in the morning something had been and eaten them up.

"Slugs!" said the gardener; and when he planted out a fresh bed he made slug-traps out of orange peel and set them among the sweet peas. But when he came in the morning the sweet peas were all eaten up, but the slug traps weren't touched.

"Then it isn't slugs," he said. "I wonder what it is? There is only one thing to do: tonight I must miss my only hour of sleep and sit up and watch."

So at twelve o'clock he went and sat by the sweet pea bed to watch. And he got sleepier and sleepier, till at last, when it was just a quarter to one, he couldn't keep awake and fell fast asleep; and when he woke up all his sweet peas had been eaten again.

So the next night he went to watch again, and this time took with him his fountain pen; and each time he was just going to fall asleep he gave himself a jab with the nib and woke himself up again. And at five to one, what should he see but a very old rabbit, so old that its fur was all coming off, and its whiskers had turned white, and it hobbled as much as he did. But although it was so old, in a twinkling of an eye it had gobbled up all his sweet peas, and was hobbling away. Then the gardener got up and tried to chase it: but though the rabbit limped, he limped, too, and, though they both went so slowly, he couldn't quite catch it: but they hobbled and hobbled till they reached the rose garden; and when they got there the rabbit nibbled a rose leaf, and no sooner did it do that than all of a sudden it became a gay young rabbit again and galloped away at ever such a pace, while the poor old gardener was left rubbing his eyes.

"Well, well," he said: "well, well, well!"

So the third night he went to watch again, and again he kept awake by jabbing himself with his fountain pen, and again the rabbit came, old now as it had been before it ate the rose-leaf. It gobbled up the little sweet pea seedlings, and the gardener chased it; but though he went as fast as he could it was still ahead of him when they got to the rose garden. Then the rabbit nibbled a rose-leaf, and quick as lightning it was galloping away. But this time the gardener ate a rose-leaf too, and in a moment he was turned into a strong young man, and chased the rabbit as fast as ever he could.

This time the rabbit couldn't get quite away, but it was still ahead when it reached its hole. The rabbit dived into the hole, and the gardener dived in after it, and the rabbit burrowed and the gardener burrowed, but still he couldn't quite catch it nor the rabbit quite get away—no, not though it dug like mad. Then, all of a sudden, the rabbit dug its way through into a great black pit, and the gardener, following close behind, suddenly found himself falling head over heels. But he didn't have far to fall; only, when he sat up the rabbit was nowhere to be seen.

It was quite dark, but all the same he could just make out some huge white shapes. So he struck a match to see what it was, and found he was among twenty or thirty white elephants, all sleeping on the ground. Then one of them woke up, and asked him who he was, and what he was doing.

"I came in, chasing that rabbit," said the gardener. The white elephant looked most shocked.

"What!" he said. "You were chasing our terrible Lord and Master, the Rabbit Whom None Dares Disobey?"

"Indeed I was," said the gardener. "But do you mean to say all you great white elephants are the slaves of one silly old rabbit?"

"Of course we are," said the white elephant.

"And you do what he tells you?" asked the gardener.

"Of course we do," said the white elephant.

"But supposing you didn't?" said the gardener. "What would happen?"

"I don't know," said the elephant; "no one has ever dared to try."

"Then try!" said the gardener. "Nothing will happen! Do something disobedient and see!"

"But what is there disobedient we can do?" said the white elephant.

"Is there a way out of this cave?" asked the gardener.

"Yes, there is," said the elephant. "But the terrible rabbit has told us not to go out."

"Then come out!" said the gardener. "Show me the way, and we will all go out together."

So the first white elephant woke up the others and explained the idea to them. Then they all began to go up the tunnel that led out of the cave together. But they hadn't gone far when they found the rabbit blocking their way.

"Go back!" said the rabbit, and all the elephants were ready to turn around and do what they were told. But the gardener called out, "I'm not afraid of you! You're only a silly old rabbit!"

"Oh, I am, am I?" said the rabbit in a most wicked voice, and before their eyes he began to swell and grow, and his teeth grew sharp as a tiger's, and his eyes flashed fire. Then he sprang at the first elephant with a savage growl, and plunged his teeth in its trunk.

"That's what comes of disobeying ME!" he said.

But the gardener was not afraid, and, big and fierce though the rabbit had become, he sprang at it and seized it by the throat, and then began the most terrible fight between the gardener and the rabbit. Sometimes the gardener got the best and held the rabbit down on the ground, and sometimes the rabbit got the best and tried to bite the gardener's throat. But at last the gardener won, and managed to strangle the rabbit till it was quite dead; and then the other white elephants marched on up the tunnel till they reached the open air.

"Now, will you be my white elephants?" asked the gardener.

"We will, of course, we will," sang the white elephants all together.

Now that he had all these white elephants the gardener, of course, was rich, and didn't have to work in the garden any more. Instead he had a small but comfortable house for himself, and a perfectly enormous stable for all the white elephants; and there they lived happily together forever after. And this was the strange thing, that though when the rabbit had eaten the rose-leaf it had only made him young for one night, when the gardener ate his it made him young forever, so that he never grew old again at all.

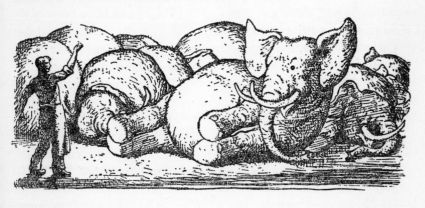

PRINCE RABBIT

By A. A. MILNE

With Illustrations by HUGH CHESTERMAN

O NCE upon a time there was a King who had no children.
Sometimes he would say to the Queen, "If only we had a
son!" and the Queen would answer, "If only we had!" And then
on another day he would say, "If only we had a daughter!" and the
Queen would sigh and answer, "Yes, even if we had a daughter, that
would be something." But they had no children at all.

As the years went on, and there were still no children in the
Royal Palace, the people began to ask each other who would be the
next King to reign over them. And some said that perhaps it would
be the Chancellor, which was a pity, as nobody liked him very much;
and others said that there would be no King at all, but that everybody would be equal. Those who were lowest of all thought that
this would be a satisfactory ending of the matter; but those who
were higher up felt that, though in some respects it would be a good
thing, yet in other respects it would be an ill-advised state of affairs;
and they hoped, therefore, that a young Prince would be born in the
Palace. But no Prince was born.

One day, when the Chancellor was in audience with the King,
it seemed well to him to speak what was in the people's minds.

"Your Majesty," he said; and then stopped, wondering how best
to put it.

"Well?" said the King.

"Have I your Majesty's permission to speak my mind?"

"So far; yes," said the King.

Encouraged by this, the Chancellor resolved to put the matter
plainly.

"In the event of your Majesty's death——" He coughed and began
again. "If your Majesty ever *should* die," he said, "which in any case
will not be for many years—if ever—as, I need hardly say, your

34

Majesty's loyal subjects earnestly hope—I mean they hope it will be never. But assuming for the moment—making the sad assumption—"

"You said you wanted to speak your mind," interrupted the King. "Is this it?"

"Yes, your Majesty."

"Then I don't think much of it."

"Thank you, your Majesty."

"What you are trying to say is, 'Who will be the next King?'"

"Quite so, your Majesty."

"Ah!" The King was silent for a little. Then he said, "I can tell you who won't be."

The Chancellor did not seek for information on this point, feeling that in the circumstances the answer was obvious.

"What do you suggest yourself?"

"That your Majesty choose a successor from among the young and highly born of the country, putting him to whatever test seems good to your Majesty."

The King pulled at his beard and frowned.

"There must be not one test, but many tests. Let all, who will, offer themselves, provided only that they are under the age of twenty and are well-born. See to it."

He waved his hand in dismissal, and with an accuracy established by long practice the Chancellor retired backwards out of the Palace.

On the following morning, therefore, it was announced that all those who were ambitious to be appointed the King's successor, and who were of high birth and not yet come to the age of twenty, should present themselves a week later for the tests to which His Majesty desired to put them, the first of which was to be a running race. Whereat the people rejoiced, for they wished to be ruled by one to whom they could look up, and running was much esteemed in that country.

On the appointed day the excitement was great. All along the course, which was once round the castle, large crowds were massed, and at the finishing point the King and Queen themselves were seated in a specially erected pavilion. And to this pavilion the competitors were brought to be introduced to their Majesties. And there were nine young nobles, well-built, and handsome, and (it was thought) intelligent, who were competitors. And there was also one Rabbit.

The Chancellor had first noticed the Rabbit when he was lining up the competitors, pinning numbers on their backs so that the people should identify them, and giving them such instructions as seemed necessary to him. "Now, now, be off with you," he had said. "Competitors only, this way." And he had made a motion of impatient dismissal with his foot.

"I *am* a competitor," said the Rabbit. "And I don't think it is usual," he added with dignity, "for the starter to kick one of the competitors just at the beginning of an important foot-race. It looks like favoritism."

"You can't be a competitor," laughed all the young nobles.

"Why not? Read the rules."

The Chancellor, feeling rather hot suddenly, read the rules. The Rabbit was certainly under twenty; he had a pedigree which showed that he was of the highest birth; and—

"And," said the Rabbit, "I am ambitious to be appointed the King's successor. Those were all the conditions. Now let's get on with the race."

But first came the introduction to the King. One by one the competitors came up . . . and at the end—

"This," said the Chancellor, as airily as he could, "is Rabbit."

Rabbit bowed in the most graceful manner possible; first to the King and then to the Queen. But the King only stared at him. Then he turned to the Chancellor.

"Well?"

The Chancellor shrugged his shoulders.

"His entry does not appear to lack validity," he said.

"He means, your Majesty, that it is all right," explained Rabbit.

The King laughed suddenly. "Go on," he said. "We can always have a race for a new Chancellor afterwards."

So the race was started. And the young Lord Calomel was much cheered on coming in second; not only by their Majesties, but also

Hugh Chesterman

Calomel, whirling his long sword, rushed upon Rabbit.

[See page 37]

by Rabbit, who had finished the course some time before, and was
now lounging in the Royal Pavilion.

"A very good style, your Majesty," said Rabbit, turning to the
King. "Altogether he seems to be a most promising youth."

"Most," said the King grimly. "So much so that I do not propose to trouble the rest of the competitors. The next test shall take
place between you and him."

"Not racing again, please, your Majesty. That would hardly be
fair to his lordship."

"No, not racing; fighting."

"Ah! What sort of fighting?"

"With swords," said the King.

"I am a little rusty with swords, but I daresay in a day or two—"

"It will be now," said the King.

"You mean, your Majesty, as soon as Lord Calomel has recovered
his breath?"

The King answered nothing, but turned to his Chancellor.

"Tell the young Lord Calomel that in half an hour I desire him
to fight with this Rabbit—"

"The young Lord Rabbit," murmured the other competitor to
the Chancellor.

"To fight with him for my kingdom."

"*And* borrow me a sword, will you?" said Rabbit. "Quite a small
one. I don't want to hurt him."

So, half an hour later, on a level patch of grass in front of the
pavilion, the fight began. It was a short, but exciting, struggle. Calomel, whirling his long sword in his strong right arm, dashed upon
Rabbit, and Rabbit, carrying his short sword in his teeth, dodged
between Calomel's legs and brought him toppling. And when it was
seen that the young Lord rose from the ground with a broken arm,
and that with the utmost gallantry he had now taken his sword in
his left hand, the people cheered. And Rabbit, dropping his sword
for a moment, cheered, too; and then he picked it up and got it
entangled in his adversary's legs again, so that again the young Lord
Calomel crashed to the ground, this time with a sprained ankle.
And there he lay.

Rabbit trotted into the Royal Pavilion, and dropped his sword in the Chancellor's lap.

"Thank you so much," he said. "Have I won?"

And the King frowned and pulled at his beard.

"There are other tests," he muttered.

But what were they to be? It was plain that Lord Calomel was in no condition for another physical test. What, then, of an intellectual test?

"After all," said the King to the Queen that night, "intelligence is a quality not without value to a ruler."

"Is it?" asked the Queen doubtfully.

"I have found it so," said the King, a little haughtily.

"Oh," said the Queen.

"There is a riddle, of which my father was fond, the answer to which has never been revealed save to the Royal House. We might make this the final test between them."

"What is the riddle?"

"I fancy it goes like this." He thought for a moment, and then recited it, beating time with his hand.

> "My *first* I do for your delight,
> Although 'tis neither black nor white.
> My *second* looks the other way,
> Yet always goes to bed by day.
> My *whole* can fly, and climb a tree,
> And sometimes swims upon the sea."

"What is the answer?" asked the Queen.

"As far as I remember," said His Majesty, "it is either *Dormouse* or *Raspberry*."

"'Dormouse' doesn't make sense," objected the Queen.

"Neither does 'raspberry,'" pointed out the King.

"Then how can they guess it?"

"They can't. But my idea is that young Calomel should be secretly told beforehand what the answer is, so that he may win the competition."

"Is that fair?" asked the Queen doubtfully.

"Yes," said the King. "Certainly. Or I wouldn't have suggested it."

So it was duly announced by the Chancellor that the final test between the young Lord Calomel and Rabbit would be the solving of an ancient riddle-me-ree, which in the past had baffled all save those of Royal blood. Copies of the riddle had been sent to the competitors, and in a week from that day they would be called upon to give their answers before their Majesties and the full Court. And with Lord Calomel's copy went a message, which said this:

"*From a Friend.* The answer is *Dormouse.* BURN THIS."

The day came round; and Calomel and Rabbit were brought before their Majesties; and they bowed to their Majesties, and were ordered to be seated, for Calomel's ankle was still painful to him. And when the Chancellor had called for silence, the King addressed those present, explaining the conditions of the test to them.

"And the answer to the riddle," he said, "is in this sealed paper, which I now hand to my Chancellor, in order that he shall open it, as soon as the competitors have told us what they know of the matter."

The people, being uncertain what else to do, cheered slightly.

"I will ask Lord Calomel first," His Majesty went on. He looked at his lordship, and his lordship nodded slightly. And Rabbit, noticing that nod, smiled suddenly to himself.

"Lord Calomel," said the King, "what do you consider to be the best answer to this riddle-me-ree?"

The young Lord Calomel tried to look very wise, and he said:

"There are many possible answers to this riddle-me-ree, but the best answer seems to be *Dormouse.*"

"Let someone take a note of that answer," said the King; whereupon the Chief Secretary wrote down: "LORD CALOMEL—*Dormouse.*"

"Now," said the King to Rabbit, "what suggestion have you to make in this matter?"

Rabbit, who had spent an anxious week inventing answers each more impossible than the last, looked down modestly.

"Well?" said the King.

"Your Majesty," said Rabbit with some apparent hesitation, "I have a great respect for the intelligence of the young Lord Calomel, but I think that in this matter he is mistaken. The answer is not, as he suggests, *wood-louse,* but *dormouse.*"

"I *said* 'dormouse,'" cried Calomel indignantly.

"I thought you said 'wood-louse,'" said Rabbit in surprise.

"He certainly said 'dormouse,'" said the King coldly.

"'Wood-louse,' I *think,*" said Rabbit.

"Lord Calomel—'*Dormouse,*'" read out the Chief Secretary.

"There you are," said Calomel. "I did say 'dormouse.'"

"My apologies," said Rabbit, with a bow. "Then we are both right, for *dormouse* it certainly is."

The Chancellor broke open the sealed paper, and to the amazement of nearly all present read out "Dormouse."

"Apparently, your Majesty," he said in some surprise, "they are both equally correct."

The King scowled. In some way, which he didn't quite understand, he had been tricked.

"May I suggest, your Majesty," the Chancellor went on, "that they be asked now some question of a different order, such as can be answered, after not more than a few minutes' thought, here in your Majesty's presence. Some problem in the higher mathematics, for instance, such as might be profitable for a future King to know."

"What question?" asked His Majesty, a little nervously.

"Well, as an example—what is seven times six?" And, behind his hand, he whispered to the King, "Forty-two."

Not a muscle of the King's face moved, but he looked thoughtfully at the Lord Calomel. Supposing his lordship did not know!

"Well?" he said reluctantly. "What is the answer?"

The young Lord Calomel thought for some time, and then said, "Fifty-four."

"And you?" said the King to Rabbit.

Rabbit wondered what to say. As long as he gave the same answers as Calomel, he could not lose in the encounter, yet in this case "Forty-two" was the right answer. But the King, who could do no wrong, even in arithmetic, might decide, for the purposes of the competition, that "Fifty-four" was an answer more becoming to the future ruler of the country. Was it, then, safe to say "Forty-two"?

"Your Majesty," he said, "there are several possible answers to this extraordinarily novel conundrum. At first sight the obvious solution would appear to be 'Forty-two.' The objection to this solution is that it lacks originality. I have long felt that a progressive country such as ours might well strike out a new line in the matter. Let us agree that in future seven sixes are fifty-four. In that case the answer, as Lord Calomel has pointed out, *is* 'Fifty-four.' But if your Majesty would prefer to cling to the old style of counting, then your Majesty and your Majesty's Chancellor would make the answer 'Forty-two.'"

After saying which, Rabbit bowed gracefully, both to their Majesties and to his opponent, and sat down again.

The King scratched his head in a puzzled sort of way.

"The correct answer," he said, "is, or will be in the future, 'Fifty-four.'"

"Make a note of that," whispered the Chancellor to the Chief Secretary.

"Lord Calomel guessed this at his first attempt; Rabbit at his second attempt. I therefore declare Lord Calomel the winner."

"Shame!" said Rabbit.

"Who said that?" cried the King furiously.

Rabbit looked over his shoulder, with the object of identifying the culprit, but was apparently unsuccessful.

"However," went on the King, "in order that there should be no doubt in the minds of my people as to the absolute fairness with which this competition is being conducted, there will be one further test. It happens that a King is often called upon to make speeches and exhortations to his people, and for this purpose the ability to stand evenly upon two legs for a considerable length of time is of much value to him. The next test, therefore, will be—"

But at this point Lord Calomel cleared his throat so loudly that the King had to stop and listen to him.

"Quite so," said the King. "The next test, therefore, will be held in a month's time, when his lordship's ankle is healed, and it will be a test to see who can balance himself longest upon two legs only."

Rabbit lolloped back to his home in the wood, pondering deeply. Now there was an enchanter who lived in the wood, a man of many magical gifts. He would (it was averred by the countryside) extract colored ribbons from his mouth, cook plum-puddings in a hat, and produce as many as ten silk handkerchiefs, knotted together, from a twist of paper. And that night, after a simple dinner of salad, Rabbit called upon him.

"Can you," he said, "turn a rabbit into a man?"

The enchanter considered this carefully.

"I can," he said at last, "turn a plum-pudding into a rabbit."

"That," said Rabbit, "to be quite frank, would not be a helpful operation."

"I can turn almost anything into a rabbit," said the enchanter with growing enthusiasm. "In fact, I like doing it."

Then Rabbit had an idea.

"Can you turn a man into a rabbit?"

"I did once. At least I turned a baby into a baby rabbit."

"When was that?"

"Eighteen years ago. At the court of King Nicodemus. I was giving an exhibition of my powers to him and his good Queen. I asked one of the company to lend me a baby, never thinking for a moment that—— The young Prince was handed up. I put a red silk handkerchief over him, and waved my hands. Then I took the handkerchief away. . . . The Queen was very much distressed. I tried everything I could, but it was useless. The King was most generous about it. He said that I could keep the rabbit. I carried it about with me for some weeks, but one day it escaped. Dear, dear!" He wiped his eyes gently with a red silk handkerchief.

"Most interesting," said Rabbit. "Well, this is what I want you to do." And they discussed the matter from the beginning.

A month later the great Standing Competition was to take place. When all was ready, the King rose to make his opening remarks.

"We are now," he began, "to make one of the most interesting tests between our two candidates for the throne. At the word 'Go!' they will——" And then he stopped suddenly. "Why, what's this?" he said, putting on his spectacles. "Where is the young Lord Calomel? and what is that second rabbit doing? There was no need to bring your brother," he added severely to Rabbit.

"I am Lord Calomel," said the second rabbit meekly.

"Oh!" said the King.

"Go!" said the Chancellor, who was a little deaf.

Rabbit, who had been practising for a month, jumped on his back paws and remained there. Lord Calomel, who had no practice at all, remained on all fours. In the crowd at the back the enchanter chuckled to himself.

"How long do I stay like this?" asked Rabbit.

"This is all very awkward and distressing," said the King.

"May I get down?" said Rabbit.

"There is no doubt that the Rabbit has won," said the Chancellor.

"Which rabbit?" cried the King crossly. "They're both rabbits."

"The one with the white spots behind the ears," said Rabbit helpfully. "May I get down?"

There was a sudden cry from the back of the hall.

"Your Majesty?"

"Well, well, what is it?"

The enchanter pushed his way forward.

"May I look, your Majesty?" he said in a trembling voice. "White spots behind the ears? Dear, dear! Allow me!" He seized Rabbit's ears, and bent them this way and that.

"Ow!" said Rabbit.

"It is! Your Majesty, it is!"

"Is what?"

"The son of the late King Nicodemus, whose country is now joined to your own. Prince Silvio."

"Quite so," said Rabbit airily, hiding his surprise. "Didn't any of you recognize me?"

"Nicodemus only had one son," said the Chancellor, "and he died as a baby."

"Not died," said the enchanter, and forthwith explained the whole sad story.

"I see," said the King, when the story was ended. "But of course that is neither here nor there. A competition like this must be conducted with absolute impartiality." He turned to the Chancellor. "Which of them won that last test?"

"Prince Silvio," said the Chancellor.

"Then, my dear Prince Silvio—"

"One moment," interrupted the enchanter excitedly. "I've just thought of the words. I *knew* there were some words you had to say."

He threw his red silk handkerchief over Rabbit, and cried "Hey presto!" And the handkerchief rose and rose and rose. . . .

And there was Prince Silvio!

You can imagine how loudly the people cheered. But the King appeared not to notice that anything surprising had happened.

"Then, my dear Prince Silvio," he went on, "as the winner of this most interesting series of contests, you are appointed successor to our throne."

"Your Majesty," said Silvio, "this is too much." And he turned to the enchanter and said, "May I borrow your handkerchief for a moment? My emotion has overcome me."

So on the following day, Prince Rabbit was duly proclaimed heir to the throne before all the people. But not until the ceremony was over did he return the enchanter's red handkerchief.

"And now," he said to the enchanter, "you may restore Lord Calomel to his proper shape."

And the enchanter placed his handkerchief on Lord Calomel's head, and said "Hey presto!" and Lord Calomel stretched himself and said "Thanks very much." But he said it rather coldly, as if he were not really very grateful.

So they all lived happily for a long time. And Prince Rabbit married the most beautiful Princess of those parts; and when a son was born to them there was much feasting and jollification. And the King gave a great party, whereat minstrels, tumblers, jugglers and suchlike were present in large quantities to give pleasure to the company. But in spite of a suggestion made by the Princess, the enchanter was not present.

"But I hear he is so clever," said the Princess to her husband.

"He has many amusing inventions," replied the Prince, "but some of them are not in the best of taste."

"Very well, dear," said the Princess.

THE PUMPKIN GIANT

By MARY E. WILKINS

A VERY long time ago, before our grandmother's time, or our great grandmother's or our grandmother's with a very long string of greats prefixed, there were no pumpkins; people had never eaten a pumpkin pie, or even stewed pumpkin; and that was the time when the Pumpkin Giant flourished.

There have been a great many giants who have flourished since the world began, and although a select few of them have been good giants, the majority of them have been so bad that their crimes even more than their size have gone to make them notorious. But the Pumpkin Giant was an uncommonly bad one, and his general appearance and his behavior were such as to make one shudder to an extent that you would hardly believe possible. The convulsive shivering caused by the mere mention of his name, and, in some cases where the people were unusually sensitive, by the mere thought of him even, more resembled the blue ague than anything else; indeed, was known by the name of "the Giant's Shakes."

The Pumpkin Giant was very tall; he probably would have overtopped most of the giants you have ever heard of. I don't suppose the Giant who lived on the Beanstalk, whom Jack visited, was anything to compare with him; nor that it would have been a possible thing for the Pumpkin Giant, had he received an invitation to spend an afternoon with the Beanstalk Giant, to accept, on account of his inability to enter the Beanstalk Giant's door, no matter how much he stooped.

The Pumpkin Giant had a very large yellow head, which was also smooth and shiny. His eyes were big and round, and glowed like coals of fire; and you would almost have thought that his head was lit up inside with candles. Indeed there was a rumor to that effect amongst the common people, but that was all nonsense, of course; no one of the more enlightened class credited it for an instant. His mouth, which stretched half around his head, was furnished with rows of pointed teeth, and he was never known to hold it any other way than wide open.

The Pumpkin Giant lived in a castle, as a matter of course; it is not fashionable for a giant to live in any other kind of a dwelling—why, nothing would be more tame and uninteresting than a giant in a two-story white house with green blinds and a picket fence, or even a brown-stone front, if he could get into either of them, which he could not.

The Giant's castle was situated on a mountain, as it ought to have been, and there was also the usual courtyard before it, and the customary moat, which was full of—*bones!* All I have got to say about these bones is, they were not mutton bones. A great many details of this story must be left to the imagination of the reader; they are too harrowing to relate. A much tenderer regard for the feelings of the audience will be shown in this than in most giant stories; we will even go so far as to state in advance, that the story has a good end, thereby enabling readers to peruse it comfortably without unpleasant suspense.

The Pumpkin Giant was fonder of little boys and girls than anything else in the world; but he was somewhat fonder of little boys, and more particularly of *fat* little boys.

The fear and horror of this Giant extended over the whole country. Even the King on his throne was so severely afflicted with the Giant's Shakes that he had been obliged to have the throne propped, for fear it should topple over in some unusually violent fit. There was good reason why the King shook: his only daughter, the Princess Ariadne Diana, was probably the fattest princess in the whole world at that date. So fat was she that she had never walked a step in the dozen years of her life, being totally unable to progress over the earth by any method except rolling. And a really beautiful sight it was, too, to see the Princess Ariadne Diana, in her cloth-of-gold rolling-suit, faced with green velvet and edged with ermine, with her glittering crown on her head, trundling along the avenues of the royal gardens, which had been furnished with strips of rich carpeting for her express accommodation.

But gratifying as it would have been to the King, her sire, under other circumstances, to have had such an unusually interesting daughter, it now only served to fill his heart with the greatest anxiety on her account. The Princess was never allowed to leave the palace without a bodyguard of fifty knights, the very flower of the King's troops, with lances in rest; but in spite of all this precaution, the King shook.

Meanwhile amongst the ordinary people who could not procure an escort of fifty armed knights for the plump among their children, the ravages of the Pumpkin Giant were frightful. It was apprehended at one time that there would be very few fat little girls, and no fat little boys at all, left in the kingdom. And what made matters worse, at that time the Giant commenced taking a tonic to increase his appetite.

Finally the King, in desperation, issued a proclamation that he would knight anyone, be he noble or common, who should cut off the head of the Pumpkin Giant. This was the King's usual method of rewarding any noble deed in his kingdom. It was a cheap method, and besides everybody liked to be a knight.

When the King issued his proclamation, every man in the kingdom who was not already a knight, straightway tried to contrive ways and means to kill the Pumpkin Giant. But there was one obstacle which seemed insurmountable: they were afraid, and all of them had the Giant's Shakes so badly, that they could not possibly have held a knife steady enough to cut off the Giant's head, even if they had dared to go near enough for that purpose.

There was one man who lived not far from the terrible Giant's castle: a poor man, his only worldly wealth consisting in a large potato field and a cottage in front of it. But he had a boy of twelve, an only son, who rivaled the Princess Ariadne Diana in point of fatness. He was unable to have a bodyguard for his son; so the amount of terror which the inhabitants of that humble cottage suffered day and night was heart-rending. The poor mother had been unable to leave her bed for two years, on account of the Giant's Shakes; her husband barely got a living from the potato field; half the time he and his wife had hardly enough to eat, as it naturally took the larger part of the potatoes to satisfy the fat little boy, their son, and their situation was truly pitiable.

The fat boy's name was Æneas, his father's name was Patroclus, and his mother's Daphne. It was all the fashion in those days to have classical names. And as that was a fashion as easily adopted by the poor as the rich, everybody had them. They were just like Jim and Tommy and May in these days. Why, the Princess's name, Ariadne Diana, was nothing more or less than Ann Eliza with us.

One morning Patroclus and Æneas were out in the field digging potatoes, for new potatoes were just in the market. The Early Rose potato had not been discovered in those days; but there was another potato, perhaps equally good, which attained to a similar degree of celebrity. It was called the Young Plantagenet, and reached a very large size indeed, much larger than the Early Rose does in our time.

Well, Patroclus and Æneas had just dug perhaps a bushel of Young Plantagenet potatoes. It was slow work with them, for Patroclus had the Giant's Shakes badly that morning, and of course Æneas was not very swift. He rolled about among the potato-hills after the manner of the Princess Ariadne Diana; but he did not present as imposing an appearance as she, in his homespun farmer's frock.

All at once the earth trembled violently. Patroclus and Æneas looked up and saw the Pumpkin Giant coming with his mouth wide open. "Get behind me quickly, O my darling son!" cried Patroclus.

Æneas obeyed, but it was of no use; for you could see his cheeks each side his father's waistcoat.

Patroclus was not ordinarily a brave man, but he was brave in an emergency; and as that is the only time when there is the slightest need of bravery, it was just as well.

The Pumpkin Giant strode along faster and faster, opening his mouth wider and wider, until they could fairly hear it crack at the corners.

Then Patroclus picked up an enormous Young Plantagenet and threw it plump into the Pumpkin Giant's mouth. The Giant choked and gasped, and choked and gasped, and finally tumbled down and died.

Patroclus and Æneas, while the Giant was choking, had run to the house and locked themselves in; then they looked out of the kitchen window; when they saw the Giant tumble down and lie quite still, they knew he must be dead. Then Daphne was immediately cured of the Giant's Shakes, and got out of bed for the first time in two years. Patroclus sharpened the carving-knife on the kitchen stove, and they all went out into the potato field.

They cautiously approached the prostrate Giant, for fear he might be shamming, and might suddenly spring up at them and—Æneas. But no, he did not move at all; he was quite dead. And, all taking turns, they hacked off his head with the carving-knife. Then Æneas had it to play with, which was quite appropriate, and a good instance of the sarcasm of destiny.

The King was notified of the death of the Pumpkin Giant, and was greatly rejoiced thereby. His Giant's Shakes ceased, the props were removed from the throne, and the Princess Ariadne Diana was allowed to go out without her bodyguard of fifty knights, much to her delight, for she found them a great hindrance to the enjoyment of her daily outings.

It was a great cross, not to say an embarrassment, when she was gleefully rolling in pursuit of a charming red and gold butterfly, to find herself suddenly stopped short by an armed knight with his lance in rest.

But the King, though his gratitude for the noble deed knew no bounds, omitted to give the promised reward and knight Patroclus.

I hardly know how it happened—I don't think it was anything intentional. Patroclus felt rather hurt about it, and Daphne would have liked to be a lady, but Æenas did not care in the least. He had the Giant's head to play with and that was reward enough for him. There was not a boy in the neighborhood but envied him his possession of such a unique plaything; and when they would stand looking over the wall of the potato field with longing eyes, and he was flying over the ground with the head, his happiness knew no bounds; and Æneas played so much with the Giant's head that finally late in the fall it got broken and scattered all over the field.

Next spring all over Patroclus's potato field grew running vines, and in the fall Giants' heads. There they were all over the field, hundreds of them; then there was consternation indeed! The natural conclusion to be arrived at when the people saw the yellow Giants' heads making their appearance above the ground was, that the rest of the Giants were coming.

"There was one Pumpkin Giant before," said they, "now there will be a whole army of them. If it was dreadful then what will it be in the future? If one Pumpkin Giant gave us the Shakes so badly, what will a whole army of them do?"

But when some time had elapsed and nothing more of the Giants appeared above the surface of the potato field, and as moreover the heads had not yet displayed any sign of opening their mouths, the people began to feel a little easier, and the general excitement subsided somewhat, although the King had ordered out Ariadne Diana's bodyguard again.

Now Æneas had been born with a propensity for putting everything in his mouth and tasting it; there was scarcely anything in his vicinity which could by any possibility be tasted, which he had not eaten a bit of. This propensity was so alarming in his babyhood, that Daphne purchased a book of antidotes; and if it had not been for her admirable good judgment in doing so, this story would probably never have been told; for no human baby could possibly have survived the heterogeneous diet which Æneas had indulged in. There was scarcely one of the antidotes which had not been resorted to from time to time.

Æneas had become acquainted with the peculiar flavor of almost everything in his immediate vicinity, except the Giants' heads; and he naturally enough cast longing eyes at them. Night and day he wondered what a Giant's head could taste like, till finally one day when Patroclus was away he stole out into the potato field, cut a bit out of one of the Giants' heads and ate it. He was almost afraid to, but he reflected that his mother could give him an antidote; so he ventured. It tasted very sweet and nice; he liked it so much that he cut off another piece and ate that, then another and another, until he had eaten two thirds of a Giant's head. Then he thought it was about time for him to go in and tell his mother and take an antidote, though he did not feel ill at all yet.

"Mother," said he, rolling slowly into the cottage, "I have eaten two thirds of a Giant's head, and I guess you had better give me an antidote."

"O my precious son!" cried Daphne, "how could you?" She looked in her book of antidotes, but could not find one antidote for a Giant's head.

"O Æneas, my dear, dear son!" groaned Daphne, "there is no antidote for Giant's head! What shall we do?"

Then she sat down and wept, and Æneas wept too as loud as he possibly could. And he apparently had excellent reason to; for it did not seem possible that a boy could eat two thirds of a Giant's head and survive it without an antidote. Patroclus came home, and they told him, and he sat down and lamented with them. All day they sat weeping and watching Æneas, expecting every moment to see him die. But he did not die; on the contrary he had never felt so well in his life.

Finally at sunset Æneas looked up and laughed. "I am not going to die," said he; "I never felt so well; you had better stop crying. And I am going out to get some more of that Giant's head! I am hungry."

"Don't, don't!" cried his father and mother, but he went; for he generally took his own way, very like most only sons. He came back with a whole Giant's head in his arms.

"See here, Father and Mother," cried he; "we'll all have some of this; it evidently is not poison, and it is good—a great deal better than potatoes!"

Patroclus and Daphne hesitated, but they were hungry, too. Since the crop of Giants' heads had sprung up in their field instead of potatoes, they had been hungry most of the time; so they tasted.

"It is good," said Daphne; "but I think it would be better cooked." So she put some in a kettle of water over the fire, and let it boil awhile; then she dished it up, and they all ate it. It was delicious. It tasted more like stewed pumpkin than anything else; in fact it was stewed pumpkin.

Daphne was inventive, and something of a genius; and next day she concocted another dish out of the Giants' heads. She boiled them, and sifted them, and mixed them with eggs and sugar and milk and spice; then she lined some plate with puff paste, filled them with the mixture, and set them in the oven to bake.

The result was unparalleled; nothing half so exquisite had ever been tasted. They were all in ecstasies, Æneas in particular. They gathered all the Giants' heads and stored them in the cellar. Daphne baked pies of them every day, and nothing could surpass the felicity of the whole family.

One morning the King had been out hunting, and happened to ride by the cottage of Patroclus with a train of his knights. Daphne was baking pies as usual, and the kitchen door and window were both open, for the room was so warm; so the delicious odor of the pies perfumed the whole air about the cottage.

"What is it smells so utterly lovely?" cried the King, sniffing in a rapture.

He sent his page in to see.

"The housewife is baking Giants' head pies," said the page returning.

"What?" thundered the King. "Bring out one to me!"

So the page brought out a pie to him, and after all his knights had tasted to be sure it was not poison, and the king had watched them sharply for a few moments to be sure they were not killed, he tasted, too.

Then he beamed. It was a new sensation, and a new sensation is a great boon to a king.

"I never tasted anything so altogether superfine, so utterly magnificent in my life," cried the king; "stewed peacocks' tongues from the Baltic are not to be compared with it! Call out the housewife immediately!"

So Daphne came out trembling, and Patroclus and Æneas came also.

"What a charming lad!" exclaimed the King, as his glance fell upon Æneas. "Now tell me about these wonderful pies, and I will reward you as becomes a monarch!"

Then Patroclus fell on his knees and related the whole history of the Giants' head pies from the beginning.

The King actually blushed. "And I forgot to knight you, O noble and brave man, and to make a lady of your admirable wife!"

Then the King leaned gracefully down from his saddle, and struck Patroclus with his jeweled sword and knighted him on the spot.

The whole family went to live at the royal palace. The roses in the royal gardens were uprooted, and Giants' heads (or pumpkins, as they came to be called) were sown in their stead; all the royal parks also were turned into pumpkin fields.

Patroclus was in constant attendance on the King, and used to stand all day in his antechamber. Daphne had a position of great responsibility, for she superintended the baking of the pumpkin pies, and Æneas finally married the Princess Ariadne Diana.

They were wedded in great state by fifty archbishops; and all the newspapers united in stating that they were the most charming and well-matched young couple that had ever been united in the kingdom.

The stone entrance of the Pumpkin Giants' castle was securely fastened, and upon it was engraved an inscription composed by the first poet in the kingdom, for which the King made him laureate, and gave him the liberal pension of fifty pumpkin pies per year.

The following is the inscription in full:

> "Here dwelt the Pumpkin Giant once;
>   He's dead, the nation doth rejoice,
>   For, while he was alive, he lived
>   By e——g dear, fat, little boys."

The inscription is said to remain to this day; if you were to go there you would probably see it.

HOW THEY BROKE AWAY TO GO TO THE ROOTABAGA COUNTRY

By *CARL SANDBURG*

GIMME THE AX lived in a house where everything is the same as it always was.

"The chimney sits on top of the house and lets the smoke out," said Gimme the Ax. "The doorknobs open the doors. The windows are always either open or shut. We are always either upstairs or downstairs in this house. Everything is the same as it always was."

So he decided to let his children name themselves.

"The first words they speak as soon as they learn to make words shall be their names," he said. "They shall name themselves."

When the first boy came to the house of Gimme the Ax, he was named Please Gimme. When the first girl came she was named Ax Me No Questions.

And both of the children had the shadows of valleys by night in their eyes, and the lights of early morning, when the sun is coming up, on their foreheads.

And the hair on top of their heads was a dark wild grass. And they loved to turn the doorknobs, open the doors, and run out to have the wind comb their hair and touch their eyes and put its six soft fingers on their foreheads.

And then because no more boys came and no more girls came, Gimme the Ax said to himself, "My first boy is my last and my last girl is my first and they picked their names themselves."

Please Gimme grew up and his ears got longer. Ax Me No Questions grew up and her ears got longer. And they kept on living in the house where everything is the same as it always was. They learned to say just as their father said, "The chimney sits on top of the house and lets the smoke out, the doorknobs open the doors, the windows are always either open or shut, we are always either upstairs or downstairs—everything is the same as it always was."

After a while they began asking each other in the cool of the evening, after they had eggs for breakfast in the morning, "Who's who? How much? And what's the matter?"

"It is too much to be too long anywhere," said the tough old man, Gimme the Ax.

And Please Gimme and Ax Me No Questions, the tough son and the tough daughter of Gimme the Ax, answered their father.

"It *is* too much to be too long anywhere."

So they sold everything they had, pigs, pastures, pepper pickers, pitchforks, everything except their ragbags and a few extras.

When the neighbors saw them selling everything they had, the different neighbors said, "They are going to Kansas, to Kokomo, to Canada, to Kankakee, to Kalamazoo, to Kamchatka, to the Chattahoochee."

One little sniffer with his eyes half shut and a mitten on his nose, laughed in his hat five ways and said, "They are going to the moon, and when they get there they will find everything is the same is it always was."

All the spot cash money he got for selling everything, pigs, pastures, pepper pickers, pitchforks, Gimme the Ax put in a ragbag and slung on his back like a rag picker going home.

Then he took Please Gimme, his oldest and youngest and only son, and Ax Me No Questions, his oldest and youngest and only daughter, and went to the railroad station.

The ticket agent was sitting at the window selling railroad tickets the same as always.

"Do you wish a ticket to go away and come back, or do you wish a ticket to go away and *never* come back?" the ticket agent asked wiping sleep out of his eyes.

"We wish a ticket to ride where the railroad tracks run off into the sky and never come back—send us far as the railroad rails go and then forty ways farther yet," was the reply of Gimme the Ax.

"So far? So early? So soon?" asked the ticket agent wiping more sleep out of his eyes. "Then I will give you a new ticket. It blew in. It is a long slick yellow leather slab ticket with a blue spanch across it."

Gimme the Ax thanked the ticket agent once, thanked the ticket agent twice, and then instead of thanking the ticket agent three times he opened the ragbag and took out all the spot cash money he got for selling everything, pigs, pastures, pepper pickers, pitchforks, and paid the spot cash money to the ticket agent.

Before he put in in his pocket he looked once, twice, three times at the long yellow leather slab ticket with a blue spanch across it.

Then with Please Gimme and Ax Me No Questions he got on the railroad train, showed the conductor his ticket and they started to ride where the railroad tracks run off into the blue sky and then forty ways farther yet.

The train ran on and on. It came to the place where the railroad tracks run off into the blue sky. And it ran on and on chick chick-a-chick chick-a-chick chick-a-chick.

Sometimes the engineer hooted and tooted the whistle. Sometimes the fireman rang the bell. Sometimes the open-and-shut of the steam hog's nose choked and spit pfisty-pfoost, pfisty-pfoost, pfisty-pfoost. But no matter what happened to the whistle and the bell and the steam hog, the train ran on and on to where the railroad tracks run off into the blue sky. And then it ran on and on more and more.

Sometimes Gimme the Ax looked in his pocket, put his fingers in and took out the long slick yellow leather slab ticket with a blue spanch across it.

"Not even the Kings of Egypt with all their climbing camels, and all their speedy, spotted, lucky lizards, ever had a ride like this," he said to his children.

Then something happened. They met another train running on the same track. One train was going one way. The other was going the other way. They met. They passed each other.

"What was it—what happened?" the children asked their father.

"One train went over, the other train went under," he answered. "This is the Over and Under country. Nobody gets out of the way of anybody else. They either go over or under."

Next they came to the country of the balloon pickers. Hanging down from the sky strung on strings so fine the eye could not see them at first, was the balloon crop of that summer. The sky was thick with balloons. Red, blue, yellow balloons, white, purple and orange balloons—peach, watermelon and potato balloons—rye loaf and wheat loaf balloons—link sausage and pork chop balloons—they floated and filled the sky.

The balloon pickers were walking on high stilts picking balloons. Each picker had his own stilts, long or short. For picking balloons near the ground he had short stilts. If he wanted to pick far and high he walked on a far and high pair of stilts.

Baby pickers on baby stilts were picking baby balloons. When they fell off the stilts, the handful of balloons they were holding kept them in the air till they got their feet into the stilts again.

"Who is that way up there in the sky climbing like a bird in the morning?" Ax Me No Questions asked her father.

"He was singing too happy," replied the father. "The songs came out of his neck and made him so light the balloons pulled him off his stilts."

"Will he ever come down again back to his own people?"

"Yes, his heart will get heavy when his songs are all gone. Then he will drop down to his stilts again."

The train was running on and on. The engineer hooted and tooted the whistle when he felt like it. The fireman rang the bell when he felt that way. And sometimes the open-and-shut of the steam hog had to go pfisty-pfoost, pfisty-pfoost.

"Next is the country where the circus clowns come from," said Gimme the Ax to his son and daughter. "Keep your eyes open."

They did keep their eyes open. They saw cities with ovens, long and short ovens, fat stubby ovens, lean lank ovens, all for baking either long or short clowns, or fat and stubby or lean and lank clowns.

After each clown was baked in the oven, it was taken out into the sunshine and put up to stand like a big white doll with a red mouth leaning against the fence.

Two men came along to each baked clown standing still like a doll. One man threw a bucket of white fire over it. The second man pumped a wind pump with a living red wind through the red mouth.

The clown rubbed his eyes, opened his mouth, twisted his neck, wiggled his ears, wriggled his toes, jumped away from the fence, and began turning handsprings, cartwheels, somersaults and flipflops in the sawdust ring near the fence.

"The next we come to is the Rootabaga Country, where the big city is the Village of Liver-and-Onions," said Gimme the Ax, looking again in his pocket to be sure he had the long slick yellow leather slab ticket with a blue spanch across it.

The train ran on and on till it stopped running straight and began running in zigzags like one letter Z put next to another Z and the next and the next.

The tracks and the rails and the ties and the spikes under the train all stopped being straight and changed to zigzags like one letter Z and another letter Z put next after the other.

"It seems like we go halfway and then back up," said Ax Me No Questions.

"Look out of the window and see if the pigs have bibs on," said Gimme the Ax. "If the pigs are wearing bibs then this is the Rootabaga Country."

And they looked out of the zigzagging windows of the zigzagging cars and the first pigs they saw had bibs on. And the next pigs and the next pigs they saw all had bibs on.

The checker pigs had checker bibs on, the striped pigs had striped bibs on. And the polka dot pigs had polka dot bibs on.

"Who fixes it for the pigs to have bibs on?" Please Gimme asked his father.

"The fathers and mothers fix it," answered Gimme the Ax. "The checker pigs have checker fathers and mothers. The striped pigs have striped fathers and mothers. And the polka dot pigs have polka dot fathers and mothers."

And the train went zigzagging on and on, running on the tracks and the rails and the spikes and the ties which were all zigzag like the letter Z and the letter Z.

And after a while the train zigzagged on into the Village of Liver-and-Onions, known as the biggest city in the big, big Rootabaga Country.

And so if you are going to the Rootabaga Country you will know when you get there, because the railroad tracks change from straight to zigzag, the pigs have bibs on and it is the fathers and mothers who fix it.

And if you start to go to that country remember first you must sell everything you have, pigs, pastures, pepper pickers, pitchforks, put the spot cash money in a ragbag, and go to the railroad station and ask the ticket agent for a long slick yellow leather slab ticket with a blue spanch across it.

And you mustn't be surprised if the ticket agent wipes sleep from his eyes and asks, "So far? So early? So soon?"

UNCLE REMUS

By JOEL CHANDLER HARRIS

Illustrations by A. B. FROST

UNCLE REMUS INITIATES THE LITTLE BOY

ONE evening recently, the lady whom Uncle Remus calls "Miss Sally" missed her little seven-year-old boy. Making search for him through the house and through the yard, she heard the sound of voices in the old man's cabin, and, looking through the window, saw the child sitting by Uncle Remus. His head rested against the old man's arm, and he was gazing with an expression of the most intense interest into the rough, weather-beaten face that beamed so kindly upon him. This is what "Miss Sally" heard:

"Bimeby, one day, arter Brer Fox bin doin' all dat he could fer ter ketch Brer Rabbit, en Brer Rabbit bin doin' all he could fer to keep 'im fum it, Brer Fox say to hisse'f dat he'd put up a game on Brer Rabbit, en he ain't mo'n got de wuds out'n his mouf twel Brer Rabbit come a lopin' up de big road, lookin' des ez plump, en ez fat,

en ez sassy ez a Moggin hoss in a barley-patch.

"'Hol' on dar, Brer Rabbit,' sez Brer Fox, sezee.

"'I ain't got time, Brer Fox,' sez Brer Rabbit, sezee, sorter mendin' his licks.

"'I wanter have some confab wid you, Brer Rabbit,' sez Brer Fox, sezee.

"'All right, Brer Fox, but you better holler fum whar you stan'. I'm monstus full er fleas dis mawnin',' sez Brer Rabbit, sezee.

"'I seed Brer B'ar yistiddy,'

60

sez Brer Fox, sezee, 'en he sorter rake me over de coals kaze you en me ain't make frens en live naberly, en I told 'im dat I'd see you.'

"Den Brer Rabbit scratch one year wid his off hinefoot sorter jub'usly, en den he ups en sez, sezee:

"'All a settin', Brer Fox. S'pose'n you drap roun' ter-morrer en take dinner wid me. We ain't got no great doin' at our house, but I speck de old 'oman en de chilluns kin sorter scramble roun' en git up sump'n fer ter stay yo' stummuck.'

"'I'm 'gree'ble, Brer Rabbit,' sez Brer Fox, sezee.

"'Den I'll 'pen on you,' sez Brer Rabbit, sezee.

"Nex'day, Mr. Rabbit an' Miss Rabbit got up soon, 'fo' day, en raided on a gyarden like Miss Sally's out dar, en got some cabbiges, en some roas'n years, en some sparrer-grass, en dey fix up a smashin' dinner. Bimeby one er de little Rabbits, playin' out in de backyard, come runnin' in hollerin', 'Oh, ma! oh, ma! I seed Mr. Fox a-comin'!' En den Brer Rabbit he tuck de chilluns by der years en make um set down, en den him and Miss Rabbit sorter dally roun' waitin' for Brer Fox. En dey keep on waitin', but no Brer Fox ain't come. Atter 'while Brer Rabbit goes to de do', easy like, en peep out, en dar, stickin' fum behime de cornder, wuz de tip-een' er Brer Fox tail. Den Brer Rabbit shot de do' en sot down, en put his paws behime his years en begin fer ter sing:

> "'De place wharbouts you spill de grease,
>   Right dar youer boun' ter slide,
> An' whar you fine a bunch er ha'r,
>   You'll sholy fine de hide.'

"Nex' day, Brer Fox sont word by Mr. Mink, en skuze hisse'f kaze he wuz too sick fer ter come, en he ax Brer Rabbit fer to come en take dinner wid him, en Brer Rabbit say he wuz 'gree'ble.

"Bimeby, w'en de shadders wuz at der shortes', Brer Rabbit he sorter brush up en santer down ter Brer Fox's house, en w'en he got dar, he hear somebody groanin', en he look in de do' and dar he see Brer Fox setin' up in a rockin' cheer all wrop up wid flannil, en he look mighty weak. Brer Rabbit look all 'roun', he did, but he ain't seen no dinner. De dish-pan wuz settin' on de table, en close by waz a kyarvin' knife.

"'Look like you gwineter have chicken fer dinner, Brer Fox,' sez Brer Rabbit, sezee.

"'Yes, Brer Rabbit, deyer nice, en fresh, en tender,' sez Brer Fox, sezee.

"Den Brer Rabbit sorter pull his mustarsh, en say: 'You ain't got no calamus root, is you, Brer Fox? I done got so now dat I can't eat no chicken 'ceppin she's seasoned up wid calamus root.' En wid dat Brer Rabbit lipt out er de do' and dodge 'mong de bushes, en sot dar watchin' fer Brer Fox; en he ain't watch long, nudder, kaze Brer Fox flung off de flannil en crope out er de house en got whar he could close in on Brer Rabbit, en bimeby Brer Rabbit holler out: 'Oh, Brer Fox! I'll des put yo' calamus root out yer on dish yer stump. Better come git it while hit's fresh,' and wid dat Brer Rabbit gallop off home. En Brer Fox ain't never kotch 'im yit, en w'at's mo', honey, he ain't gwineter."

HOW MR. RABBIT WAS TOO SHARP FOR MR. FOX

UNCLE REMUS," said the little boy one evening, when he had found the old man with little or nothing to do, "did the fox kill and eat the rabbit when he caught him with the Tar-Baby?"

"Law, honey, ain't I tell you 'bout dat?" replied the old darkey, chuckling slyly. "I 'clar ter grashus I ought er tole you dat, but old man Nod wuz ridin' on my eyelids 'twel a leetle mo'n I'd a dis-'member'd my own name, en den on to dat here come yo' mammy hollerin' atter you.

"W'at I tell you w'en I fus' begin? I tole you Brer Rabbit wuz a monstus soon creetur; leas'ways dat's w'at I laid out fer ter tell you. Well, den, honey, don't you go en make no udder calkalashuns, kaze in dem days Brer Rabbit en his fambly wuz at de head er de gang w'en enny racket wuz on han', en dar dey stayed. 'Fo' you begins fer ter wipe yo' eyes 'bout Brer Rabbit, you wait en see whar 'bouts Brer Rabbit gwineter fetch up at. But dat's needer yer ner dar.

"W'en Brer Fox fine Brer Rabbit mixt up wid de Tar-Baby, he

feel mighty good, en he roll on de groun' en laff. Bimeby he up'n say, sezee:

"'Well, I speck I got you dis time, Brer Rabbit,' sezee; 'maybe I ain't, but I speck I is. You been runnin' roun' here sassin' atter me a mighty long time, but I speck you done come ter de een' er de row. You bin cuttin' up yo' capers en bouncin' 'roun' in dis neighberhood ontwel you come ter b'leeve yo'se'f de boss er de whole gang. En den youer allers some'rs whar you got no bizness,' sez Brer Fox, sezee. 'Who ax you fer ter come en strike up a 'quaintance wid dish yer Tar-Baby? En who stuck you up dar whar you iz? Nobody in de roun' worril. You des tuck en jam yo'se'f on dat Tar-Baby widout waitin' fer enny invite,' sez Brer Fox, sezee, 'en dar you is, en dar you'll stay twel I fixes up a bresh-pile and fires her up, kaze I'm gwineter bobbycue you dis day, sho', sez Brer Fox, sezee.

"Den Brer Rabbit talk mighty 'umble.

"'I don't keer wa't you do wid me, Brer Fox,' sezee, 'so you don't fling me in dat brier-patch. Roas' me, Brer Fox,' sezee, 'but don't fling me in dat brier-patch,' sezee.

"'Hit's so much trouble fer ter kindle a fier,' sez Brer Fox, sezee, 'dat I speck I'll hatter hang you,' sezee.

"'Hang me des ez high as you please, Brer Fox,' sez Brer Rabbit, sezee, 'but do fer de Lord's sake don't fling me in dat brier-patch,' sezee.

"'I ain't got no string,' sez Brer Fox, sezee, 'en now I speck I'll hatter drown you,' sezee.

"'Drown me des ez deep ez you please, Brer Fox,' sez Brer Rabbit, sezee, 'but do don't fling me in dat brier-patch,' sezee.

"'Dey ain't no water nigh,' sez Brer Fox, sezee, 'en now I speck I'll hatter skin you,' sezee.

"'Skin me, Brer Fox,' sez Brer Rabbit, sezee, 'snatch out my eye-balls, t'ar out my years by de roots, en cut off my legs,' sezee, 'but do please, Brer Fox, don't fling me in dat brier-patch,' sezee.

"Co'se Brer Fox wanter hurt Brer Rabbit bad ez he kin, so he cotch 'im by de behime legs en slung 'im right in de middle er de brier-patch. Dar wuz a considerbul flutter whar Brer Rabbit struck de bushes, en Brer Fox sorter hang 'roun' fer ter see w'at wuz gwineter happen. Bimeby he hear somebody call 'im, en way up de hill he see Brer Rabbit settin' cross-legged on a chinkapin log koamin' de pitch outen his har wid a chip. Den Brer Fox know dat he bin swop off mighty bad. Brer Rabbit wuz bleedzed fer ter fling back some er his sass, en he holler out:

"'Bred en bawn in a brier-patch, Brer Fox—bred en bawn in a brier-patch!' en wid dat he skip out des ez lively ez a cricket in de embers."

OLD MR. RABBIT, HE'S A GOOD FISHERMAN

Brer RABBIT en Brer Fox wuz like some chilluns w'at I knows un," said Uncle Remus, regarding the little boy, who had come to hear another story, with an affectation of great solemnity. "Bofe un um wuz allers atter wunner nudder, a prankin' en a pester'n 'roun', but Brer Rabbit did have some peace, kaze Brer Fox done got skittish 'bout puttin' de clamps on Brer Rabbit.

"One day, w'en Brer Rabbit, en Brer Fox, en Brer Coon, en Brer B'ar, en a whole lot un um wuz clearin' up a new groun' fer ter plant a roas'n'year patch, de sun 'gun ter git sorter hot, en Brer Rabbit he got tired; but he didn't let on, kaze he 'fear'd de balance un um'd call 'im lazy, en he keep on totin' off trash en pilin' up bresh, twel bimeby he holler out dat he gotter brier in his han', en den he take 'n slip off, en hunt fer cool place fer ter res'. Atter w'ile he come 'crosst a well wid a bucket hangin' in it.

"'Dat look cool,' sez Brer Rabbit, sezee, 'en cool I speck she is. I'll des 'bout git in dar en take a nap,' en wid dat in he jump, he did, en he ain't no sooner fix hiss'f dan de bucket 'gun ter go down."

"Wasn't the Rabbit scared, Uncle Remus?" asked the little boy.

"Honey, dey ain't been no wusser skeer'd beas' sence de worril begin dan dish yer same Brer Rabbit. He fa'rly had a ager. He know whar he cum fum, but he dunner whar he gwine. Dreckly he feel de bucket hit de water, en dar she sot, but Brer Rabbit he keep mighty still, kaze he dunner w'at minit gwineter be de nex'. He des lay dar en shuck en shiver.

"Brer Fox allers got one eye on Brer Rabbit, en w'en he slip off fum de new groun' Brer Fox he sneak atter 'im. He know Brer Rabbit wuz atter some projick er nudder, en he tuck'n crope off, he did, en watch 'im. Brer Fox see Brer Rabbit come to de well en stop, en den he see 'im jump in de bucket, en den, lo en beholes, he see 'im go down outer sight. Brer Fox wuz de mos' 'stonish Fox dat you ever laid eyes on. He sot off dar in de bushes en study en study, but he don't make no head ner tails ter dis kinder bizness. Den he say ter hisse'f, sezee:

"'Well, ef dis don't bang my times,' sezee, 'den Joe's dead en Sal's a widder. Right down dar in dat well Brer Rabbit keep his money hid, en ef 'tain't dat den he done gone en 'skiver'd a gole-mine, en ef 'taint dat, den I'm gwineter see w'at's in dar,' sezee.

"Brer Fox crop up little nigher, he did, en lissen, but he don't year no fuss, en he keep on gittin' nigher, en yit he don't year nuthin'. Bimeby he git up close en peep down, but he don't see nuthin' en he don't year nuthin'. All dis time Brer Rabbit mighty nigh skeer'd outen his skin, en he fear'd fer ter move kaze de bucket might keel over en spill him out in de water. W'ile he sayin' his pra'rs over like a train er kyars runnin', ole Brer Fox holler out:

"'Heyo, Brer Rabbit! Who you wizzitin' down dar?" sezee.

"'Who? Me? Oh, I' des a fishin', Brer Fox,' sez Brer Rabbit, sezee. 'I des say ter myse'f dat I'd sorter sprize you all wid a mess er fishes fer dinner, en so here I is, en dar's de fishes. I'm a fishin' fer suckers, Brer Fox,' sez Brer Rabbit, sezee.

"'Is dey many un um down dar, Brer Rabbit?" sez Brer Fox, sezee.

"'Lots un um, Brer Fox; scoze

and scoze un um. De water is natally live wid um. Come down en he'p me haul um in, Brer Fox,' sez Brer Rabbit, sezee.

" 'How I gwinter git down, Brer Rabbit?'

" 'Jump inter de bucket, Brer Fox. Hit'll fetch you down all safe en soun'.'

"Brer Rabbit talk so happy en talk so sweet dat Brer Fox he jump in de bucket, he did, en, ez he went down, co'se his weight pull Brer Rabbit up. W'en dey pass one nudder on de half-way groun', Brer Rabbit he sing out:

> " 'Good-bye, Brer Fox, take keer yo' cloze,
> Fer dis-is de way de worril goes;
> Some goes up en some goes down,
> You'll git ter de bottom all safe en soun'.' "

"W'en Brer Rabbit got out, he galloped off en tole de fokes w'at de well b'long ter dat Brer Fox wuz down in dar muddyin' up de drinkin' water, en den he gallop back ter de well, en holler down ter Brer Fox:

> " 'Yer come a man wid a great big gun—
> W'en he haul you up, you jump en run.' "

"What then, Uncle Remus?" asked the little boy, as the old man paused.

"In des 'bout half n'our, honey, bofe un um wuz back in de new groun' wukkin des like dey never heer'd er no well, ceppin' dat eve'y now'n den Brer Rabbit'd bust out in er laff, en ole Brer Fox, he'd git a spell er de dry grins."

MR. RABBIT FINDS HIS MATCH AT LAST

Hit look like ter me dat I let on de udder night dat in dem days w'en de creeturs wuz santer'n 'roun' same like fokes, none un um wuz brash nuff fer ter ketch up wid Brer Rabbit," remarked Uncle Remus, reflectively.

"Yes," replied the little boy, "that's what you said."

"Well, den," continued the old man with unction, "dar's whar my 'membunce gin out, kaze Brer Rabbit did got kotched up wid, en hit cool 'im off like po'in' spring water on one er deze yer biggity fices."

"How was that, Uncle Remus?" asked the little boy.

"One day w'en Brer Rabbit wuz gwine lippity-clippitin' down de road, he meet up wid ole Brer Tarrypin, en atter dey pass de time er day wid wunner nudder, Brer Rabbit, he 'low dat he wuz much 'blije ter Brer Tarrypin fer de han' he tuck in de rumpus dat day down at Miss Meadows's."

"When he dropped off of the water-shelf on the Fox's head," suggested the little boy.

"Dat's de same time, honey. Den Brer Tarrypin 'low dat Brer Fox run mighty fas' dat day, but dat ef he'd er bin atter 'im stidder Brer Rabbit, he'd er kotch 'im. Brer Rabbit say he could er kotch 'im hisse'f but he didn't keer 'bout leavin' de ladies. Dey keep on talkin', dey did, twel bimeby dey gotter 'sputin' 'bout w'ich wuz de swif'es'. Brer Rabbit, he say he kin outrun Brer Tarrypin, en Brer Tarrypin, he des vow dat he kin outrun Brer Rabbit. Up en down dey had it, twel fus news you know Brer Tarrypin say he got a fifty-dollar bill in de chink er de chimbly at home, en dat bill done tole 'im dat he could beat Brer Rabbit in a fa'r race. Den Brer Rabbit say he got a fifty-dollar bill w'at say dat he kin leave Brer Tarrypin so fur behime, dat he could sow barley ez he went 'long en hit' ud be ripe nuff fer ter cut by de time Brer Tarrypin pass dat way.

"Enny how dey make de bet en put up de money, en ole Brer Tukky Buzzard, he wuz summoned fer ter be de jedge, en de stakeholder; en 'twan't long 'fo' all de 'rangements wuz made. De race wuz a five-mile heat, en de groun' wuz medjud off, en at de een'er ev'ey mile a pos' wuz stuck up. Brer Rabbit wuz ter run down de big road, en Brer Tarrypin, he say he'd gallup thoo de woods. Fokes tole 'im he could git long faster in de road, but ole Brer Tarrypin, he know w'at he doin'. Miss Meadows en de gals en mos' all de nabers got win' er de fun, en w'en de day wuz sot dey 'termin' fer ter be on han'. Brer Rabbit he train hisse'f ev'ey day, en he skip over de groun' des ez gayly ez a June cricket. Ole Brer Tarrypin, he lay low in de swamp. He had a wife en th'ee chilluns, ole Brer Tarrypin did, en dey wuz all de ve'y spit en image er de ole man. Ennybody w'at know one fum de udder gotter take a spy-glass, en den dey er li'ble fer ter git fooled.

"Dat's de way marters stan' twel de day er de race, en on dat day, ole Brer Tarrypin, en his ole 'oman, en his th'ee chilluns, dey got up 'fo' sun-up, en went ter de place. De ole 'oman, she tuck 'er stan' nigh de fus' mile-pos', she did, en de chilluns nigh de udders, up ter de las', en den old Brer Tarrypin, he tuck his stan'. Bimeby, here come de fokes: Jedge Buzzard, he come, en Miss Meadows en de gals, dey come, en den yer come Brer Rabbit wid ribbins tied 'roun his neck en streamin' fum his years. De fokes all went ter de udder een' er de track fer ter see how dey come out. W'en de time come Jedge Buzzard strut 'roun en pull out his watch, en holler out:

" 'Gents, is you ready?'

"Brer Rabbit, he say 'yes, en ole Miss Tarrypin holler 'go' fum de aidge er de woods. Brer Rabbit, he lit out on de race, en ole Miss Tarrypin, she put out for home. Jedge Buzzard, he riz en skimmed 'long fer ter see dat de race wuz runned fa'r. W'en Brer Rabbit got ter de fus' mile-pos' wunner de Tarrypin chilluns crawl out de woods, he did, en make fer de place. Brer Rabbit, he holler out:

" 'Whar is you, Brer Tarrypin?'

" 'Yer I come a bulgin','' sez de Tarrypin, sezee.

"Brer Rabbit so glad he's ahead dat he put out harder dan ever, en de Tarrypin, he make fer home. W'en he come ter de nex' pos', nudder Tarrypin crowl out er de woods.

" 'Whar is you, Brer Tarrypin?' sez Brer Rabbit, sezee.

" 'Yer I come a bilin','' sez de Tarrypin, sezee.

"Brer Rabbit, he lit out, he did, en come ter nex' pos', en dar wuz de Tarrypin. Den he come ter nex', en dar wuz de Tarrypin. Den he had one mo' mile fer ter run, en he feel like he gittin' bellust. Bimeby, ole Brer Tarrypin look way off down de road en he see Jedge Buzzard sailin' 'long en he know hit's time fer 'im fer ter be up. So he scramble outen de woods, en roll 'cross de ditch, en shuffle thoo de crowd er folks en git ter de mile-pos' en crawl behime it. Bimeby, fus' news you know, yer come Brer Rabbit. He look 'roun' en he don't see Brer Tarrypin, en den he squall out:

"'Gimme de money, Brer Buzzard! Gimme de money!'"

"Den Miss Meadows en de gals, dey holler and laff fit ter kill deyse'f, en ole Brer Tarrypin, he raise up fum behime de pos' en sez, sezee:

"'Ef you'll gimme time fer ter ketch my breff, gents en ladies, one en all, I speck I'll finger dat money myse'f,' sezee, en sho nuff, Brer Tarrypin tie de pu's 'roun' his neck and skaddle off home."

"But, Uncle Remus," said the little boy, dolefully, "that was cheating."

"Co'se, honey. De creeturs 'gun ter cheat, en de fokes tuck it up, en hit keep on spreadin'. Hit mighty ketchin', en you mine yo' eye, honey, dat somebody don't cheat you 'fo' yo' ha'r git gray ez de old nigger's."

From Old Story Books

THE OUPHE OF THE WOOD

By JEAN INGELOW

A N Ouphe!" perhaps you exclaim. "And pray what might that be?"

An Ouphe,[1] fair questioner—though you may never have heard of him—was a creature well known (by hearsay at least) to your great-great-grandmother. It was currently reported that every forest had one within its precincts, who ruled over the woodmen, and exacted tribute from them in the shape of little blocks of wood ready hewn for the fire of his underground palace—such blocks as are bought at shops in these degenerate days, and called in London "kindling."

It was said that he had a silver ax, with which he marked those trees that he did not object to have cut down; moreover, he was supposed to possess great riches, and to appear but seldom above ground, and when he did, to look like an old man, in all respects but one, which was that he always carried some green ash-keys with him which he could not conceal, and by which he might be known.

Did I hear you say that you don't believe he ever existed? It matters not at all to my story whether you do or not. He certainly does not exist now. The Commissioners of Woods and Forests have much to answer for, if it was they who put an end to his reign; but I do not think they did; it is more likely that the spelling-book used in woodland districts disagreed with his constitution.

After this short preface, please to listen while I tell you that once in a little black-timbered cottage at the skirts of a wood a young woman sat before the fire rocking her baby, and, as she did so, building a castle in the air: "What a good thing it would be," she thought to herself, "if we were rich!"

It had been a bright day, but the evening was chilly; and, as she

---

[1] *Ouphe,* pronounced "oof," is an old-fashioned word for goblin or elf.

watched the glowing logs that were blazing on her hearth, she wished that all the lighted part of them would turn to gold.

She was very much in the habit—this little wife—of building castles in the air, particularly when she had nothing else to do, or her husband was late coming home to supper. Just as she was thinking how late he was, there was a tap at the door, and an old man walked in, who said: "Mistress, will you give a poor man a warm at your fire?"

"And welcome," said the young woman, setting him a chair.

So he sat down as close to the fire as he could, and spread out his hands to the flames. He had a little knapsack on his back, and the young woman did not doubt that he was an old soldier.

"Maybe you are used to the hot countries," she said.

"All countries are much the same to me," replied the stranger. "I see nothing to find fault with in this one. You have fine hawthorn trees hereabouts; just now they are as white as snow; and then you have a noble wood behind you."

"Ah, you may well say that," said the young woman. "It is a noble wood to us; it gets us bread. My husband works in it."

"And a fine sheet of water there is in it," continued the old man. "As I sat by it today, it was pretty to see those cranes, with red legs, stepping from leaf to leaf of the water-lilies so lightly."

As he spoke he looked rather wistfully at a little saucepan which stood upon the hearth.

"Why, I shouldn't wonder if you were hungry," said the young woman, laying her baby in the cradle, and spreading a cloth on the round table. "My husband will be home soon, and if you like to stay and sup with him and me, you will be kindly welcome."

The old man's eyes sparkled when she said this, and he looked so very old and seemed so weak that she pitied him. He turned a little aside from the fire, and watched her while she set a brown loaf on the table, and fried a few slices of bacon; but all was ready, and the kettle had been boiling some time before there were any signs of the husband's return.

"I never knew Will to be so late before," said the stranger. "Perhaps he is carrying his logs to the saw-pits."

"Will!" exclaimed the wife. "What, you know my husband, then? I thought you were a stranger in these parts."

"Oh, I have been past this place several times," said the old man, looking rather confused; "and so, of course, I have heard of your husband. Nobody's stroke in the wood is so regular and strong as his."

"And I can tell you he is the handiest man at home," began his wife.

"Ah, ha," said the old man, smiling at her eagerness; "and here he comes, if I am not mistaken."

At that moment the woodman entered.

"Will," said his wife, as she took his bill-book from him and hung up his hat, "here's an old soldier came to sup with us, my dear." And as she spoke, she gave her husband a gentle push toward the old man, and made a sign that he should speak to him.

"Kindly welcome, master," said the woodman. "Wife, I'm hungry; let's to supper."

The wife turned some potatoes out of the little saucepan, set a jug of beer on the table, and they all began to sup. The best of everything was offered by the wife to the stranger. The husband, after looking earnestly at him for a few minutes, kept silence.

"And where might you be going to lodge tonight, good man, if I'm not too bold?" asked she.

The old man heaved a deep sigh, and said he supposed he must lie out in the forest.

"Well, that would be a great pity," remarked his kind hostess. "no wonder your bones ache if you have no better shelter." As she said this, she looked appealingly at her husband.

"My wife, I'm thinking, would like to offer you a bed," said the woodman; "at least, if you don't mind sleeping in this clean kitchen, I think that we could toss you up something of that sort that you need not disdain."

"Disdain, indeed!" said the wife. "Why, Will, when there's not a tighter cottage than ours in all the wood, and with a curtain, as we have, and a brick floor, and everything so good about us—"

The husband laughed; the old man looked on with a twinkle in his eye.

"I'm sure I shall be humbly grateful," said he.

Accordingly, when supper was over, they made him up a bed on the floor, and spread clean sheets upon it of the young wife's own spinning, and heaped several fresh logs on the fire. Then they wished the stranger good night, and crept up the ladder to their own snug little chamber.

"Disdain, indeed!" laughed the wife, as soon as they shut the door. "Why, Will, how could you say it? I should like to see him disdain me and mine. It isn't often, I'll engage to say, that he sleeps in such a well-furnished kitchen."

The husband said nothing, but laughed secretly to himself.

"What are you laughing at, Will?" said his wife, as she put out the candle.

"Why, you soft little thing," answered the woodman, "didn't you see that bunch of green ash-keys in his cap; and don't you know that nobody would dare to wear them but the Ouphe of the Wood? I saw him cutting those very keys for himself as I passed to the saw-mill this morning, and I knew him again directly, though he has disguised himself as an old man."

"Bless us!" exclaimed the little wife; "is the Wood Ouphe in our cottage? How frightened I am! I wish I hadn't put the candle out."

The husband laughed more and more.

"Will," said his wife, in a solemn voice, "I wonder how you dare laugh, and that powerful creature under the very bed where you lie!"

"And she to be so pitiful over him," said the woodman, laughing till the floor shook under him, "and to talk and boast of our house, and insist on helping him to more potatoes, when he has a palace of his own, and heaps of riches! Oh, dear! oh, dear!"

"Don't laugh, Will," said the wife, "and I'll make you the most beautiful firmity[1] you ever tasted tomorrow. Don't let him hear you laughing."

"Why, he comes for no harm," said the woodman. "I've never cut down any trees that he had not marked, and I've always laid his toll

[1] *Firmity*: generally written frumenty; wheat boiled in milk with sugar and fruit.

of the wood, neatly cut up, beside his foot-path, so I am not afraid. Besides, don't you know that he always pays where he lodges, and very handsomely, too?"

"Pays, does he?" said the wife. "Well, but he is an awful creature to have so near one. I would much rather he had really been an old soldier. I hope he is not looking after my baby; he shall not have him, let him offer ever so much."

The more the wife talked, the more the husband laughed at her fears, till at length he fell asleep, whilst she lay awake, thinking and thinking, till by degree she forgot her fears, and began to wonder what they might expect by way of reward. Hours appeared to pass away during these thoughts. At length, to her great surprise, while it was still quite dark, her husband called to her from below:

"Come down, Kitty; only come down and see what the Ouphe has left us."

As quickly as possible Kitty started up and dressed herself, and ran down the ladder, and then she saw her husband kneeling on the floor over the knapsack, which the Ouphe had left behind him. Kitty rushed to the spot, and saw the knapsack bursting open with gold coins, which were rolling out over the brick floor. Here was good fortune! She began to pick them up, and count them into her apron.

The more she gathered, the faster they rolled, till she left off counting, out of breath with joy and surprise.

"What shall we do with all this money?" said the delighted woodman.

They consulted for some time. At last they decided to bury it in the garden, all but twenty pieces, which they would spend directly. Accordingly, they dug a hole and carefully hid the rest of the money, and then the woodman went to the town, and soon returned laden with the things they had agreed upon as desirable possessions: namely, a leg of mutton, two bottles of wine, a necklace for Kitty, some tea and sugar, a grand velvet waistcoat, a silver watch, a large clock, a red silk cloak, and a hat and a feather for the baby, a quilted petticoat, a great many muffins and crumpets, a rattle, and two new pairs of shoes.

How enchanted they both were! Kitty cooked the nice things,

and they dressed themselves in the finery, and sat down to a very good dinner. But, alas! the woodman drank so much of the wine that he soon got quite tipsy, and began to dance and sing. Kitty was very much shocked; but when he proposed to dig up some more of the gold, and go to market for some more wine and some more blue velvet waistcoats, she remonstrated very strongly. Such was the change that had come over this loving couple, that they presently began to quarrel, and from words the woodman soon got to blows, and, after beating his little wife, lay down on the floor and fell fast asleep, while she sat crying in a corner.

The next day they both felt very miserable, and the woodman had such a terrible headache, that he could neither eat nor work; but the day after, being pretty well again, he dug up some more gold and went to town, where he bought such quantities of fine clothes and furniture and so many good things to eat, that in the end he was obliged to buy a wagon to bring them home in, and great was the delight of his wife when she saw him coming home on the top of it, driving the four gray horses himself.

They soon began to unpack the goods and lay them out on the grass, for the cottage was far too small to hold them.

"There are some red silk curtains with gold rods," said the woodman.

"And grand indeed they are!" exclaimed his wife, spreading them over the onion bed.

"And here's a great looking-glass," continued the woodman, setting one up against the outside of the cottage, for it would not go in the door.

So they went on handing down the things, and it took nearly the whole afternoon to empty the wagon. No wonder, when it contained, among other things, a coral and bells for the baby, and five very large tea-trays adorned with handsome pictures of impossible scenery, two large sofas covered with green damask, three bonnets trimmed with feathers and flowers, two glass tumblers for them to drink out of—for Kitty had decided that mugs were very vulgar things—six books bound in handsome red morocco, a mahogany table, a large tin sauce-pan, a spit, and silver waiter, a blue coat with gilt buttons, a yellow waistcoat, some pictures, a dozen bottles of wine, a quarter of lamb, cakes, tarts, pies, ale, porter, gin, silk stockings, blue and red and white shoes, lace, ham, mirrors, three clocks, a four-post bedstead, and a bag of sugar candy.

These articles filled the cottage and garden; the wagon stood outside the paling. Though the little kitchen was very much encumbered with furniture they contrived to make a fire in it; and, having eaten a sumptuous dinner, they drank each other's health, using the new tumblers to their great satisfaction.

"All these things remind me that we must have another house built," said Kitty.

"You may do just as you please about that, my dear," replied her husband, with a bottle of wine in his hand.

"My dear," said Kitty, "how vulgar you are! Why don't you drink out of one of our new tumblers, like a gentleman?"

The woodman refused, and said it was much more handy to drink it out of the bottle. "Handy, indeed!" retorted Kitty; "yes, and by that means none will be left for me."

Thereupon another quarrel ensued, and the woodman, being by this time quite tipsy, beat his wife again.

The next day they went and got numbers of workmen to build them a new house in their garden. It was quite astonishing even to Kitty, who did not know much about building, to see how quick these workmen were; in one week the house was ready. But in the meantime, the woodman, who had very often been tipsy, felt so unwell that he could not look after them; therefore it is not surprising that they stole a great many of his fine things while he lay smoking on the green damask sofa which stood on the carrot bed. Those articles which the workmen did not steal the rain and dust spoilt; but that they thought did not much matter, for still more than half the gold was left; so they soon furnished the new house. And now Kitty had a servant, and used to sit every morning on a couch dressed in silks and jewels till dinner time, when the most delicious hot beefsteaks, and sausage pudding, or roast goose were served up, with more sweet pies, fritters, tarts, and cheese-cakes than they could possibly eat.

As for the baby, he had three elegant cots, in which he was put to sleep by turns; he was allowed to tear his picture books as often as he pleased, and to eat so many sugar-plums and macaroons that they often made him quite ill.

The woodman looked very pale and miserable, though he often said what a fine thing it was to be rich. He never thought of going to his work, and used generally to sit in the kitchen till dinner was ready, watching the spit. Kitty wished she could see him looking as well and cheerful as in old days, though she felt naturally proud that her husband should always be dressed like a gentleman, namely, in a blue coat, red waistcoat, and top boots.

He and Kitty could never agree as to what should be done with the rest of the money; in fact, no one would have known them for the same people; they quarreled almost every day, and lost nearly all their love for one another. Kitty often cried herself to sleep—a thing she had never done when they were poor; she thought it was very strange that she should be a lady, and yet not be happy. Every morning, when the woodman was sober, they invented new plans for making themselves happy, yet strange to say, none of them succeeded, and matters grew worse and worse. At last Kitty thought she should be happy if she had a coach; so she went to the place where the knapsack was buried, and began to dig; but the garden was so trodden down that she could not dig deep enough, and soon got tired of trying. At last she called the servant, and told her the secret as to where the money was, promising her a gold piece if she could dig it up. The servant dug with all her strength, and with a great deal of trouble they got the knapsack up, and Kitty found that not many gold pieces were left.

However, she resolved to have the coach, so she took them and went to the town, where she bought a yellow chariot, with a most beautiful coat of arms upon it, and two cream-colored horses to draw it.

In the meantime the maid ran to the magistrates, and told them she had discovered something very dreadful, which was, that her mistress had nothing to do but dig in the ground and that she could make money come—coined money: "Which," said the maid, "is a very terrible thing, and it proves that she must be a witch."

The mayor and aldermen were very much shocked, for witches were commonly believed in in those days; and when they heard that Kitty had dug up money that very morning, and bought a yellow coach with it, they decided that the matter must be investigated.

When Kitty drove up to her own door, she saw the mayor and aldermen standing in the kitchen waiting for her. She demanded what they wanted, and they said they were come in the king's name to search the house.

Kitty immediately ran upstairs and took the baby out of his cradle, lest any of them should steal him, which, of course, seemed a very probable thing for them to do. Then she went to look for her husband, who, shocking to relate, was quite tipsy, quarreling and arguing with the mayor, and she actually saw him box an alderman's ears.

"The thing is proved," said the indignant mayor; "this woman is certainly a witch."

Kitty was very much bewildered at this; but how much more when she saw her husband seize the mayor—yes, the very mayor himself—and shake him so hard that he actually shook his head off, and it rolled under the dresser! "If I had not seen this with my own eyes," said Kitty, "I could not have believed it—even now it does not seem at all real."

All the aldermen wrung their hands.

"Murder! murder!" cried the maid.

"Yes," said the aldermen, "this woman and her husband must immediately be put to death, and the baby must be taken from them and made a slave."

In vain Kitty fell on her knees; the proofs of their guilt were so plain that there was no hope of mercy; and they were just going to be led out to execution when—why, then she opened her eyes, and saw that she was lying in bed in her own little chamber where she had lived and been so happy; her baby beside her in his wicker cradle was crowing and sucking his fingers.

"So, then, I have never been rich, after all," said Kitty; "and it was all only a dream! I thought it was very strange at the time that a man's head should roll off."

And she heaved a deep sigh, and put her hand to her face, which was wet with the tears she had shed when she thought that she and her husband were going to be executed.

"I am very glad, then, my husband is not a drunken man; and he does *not* beat me; but he goes to work every day, and I am as happy as a queen.

Just then she heard her husband's good-tempered voice whistling as he went down the ladder.

"Kitty, Kitty," said he, "come, get up, my little woman; it's later than usual, and our good visitor will want his breakfast."

"Oh, Will, Will, do come here," answered the wife; and presently her husband came up again, dressed in his fustian jacket, and looking quite healthy and good-tempered—not at all like the pale man in the blue coat, who sat watching the meat while it roasted.

"Oh, Will, I have had such a frightful dream," said Kitty, and she began to cry; "we are not going to quarrel and hate each other, are we?"

"Why, what a silly little thing thou art to cry about a dream," said the woodman, smiling. "No, we are not going to quarrel as I know of. Come, Kitty, remember the Ouphe."

"Oh, yes, yes, I remember," said Kitty, and she made haste to dress herself and come down.

"Good morning, mistress; how have you slept?" said the Ouphe, in a gentle voice, to her.

"Not so well as I could have wished, sir," said Kitty.

The Ouphe smiled. "*I* slept very well," he said. "The supper was good, and kindly given, without any thought of reward."

"And that is the certain truth," interrupted Kitty: "I never had the least thought what you were till my husband told me."

The woodman had gone out to cut some fresh cresses for his guest's breakfast.

"I am sorry, mistress," said the Ouphe, "that you slept uneasily— my race are said sometimes by their presence to affect the dreams of you mortals. Where is my knapsack? Shall I leave it behind me in payment of bed and board?"

"Oh, no, no, I pray you don't," said the little wife, blushing and stepping back; "you are kindly welcome to all you have had, I'm sure: don't repay us so, sir."

"What, mistress, and why not?" asked the Ouphe, smiling. "It is as full of gold pieces as it can hold, and I shall never miss them."

"No, I entreat you, do not," said Kitty, "and do not offer it to my husband, for maybe he has not been warned as I have."

Just then the woodman came in.

"I have been thanking your wife for my good entertainment," said the Ouphe, "and if there is anything in reason that I can give either of you—"

"Will, we do very well as we are," said his wife, going up to him and looking anxiously in his face.

"I don't deny," said the woodman, thoughtfully, "that there are one or two things I should like my wife to have, but somehow I've not been able to get them for her yet."

"What are they?" asked the Ouphe.

"One is a spinning-wheel," answered the woodman; "she used to spin a good deal when she was at home with her mother."

"She shall have a spinning-wheel," replied the Ouphe; "and is there nothing else, my good host?"

"Well," said the woodman, frankly, "since you are so obliging, we should like a hive of bees."

"The bees you shall have also; and now, good morning both, and a thousand thanks to you."

So saying, he took his leave, and no pressing could make him stay to breakfast.

"Well," thought Kitty, when she had had a little time for reflection, "a spinning-wheel is just what I wanted; but if people had told me this time yesterday morning that I should be offered a knapsack full of money, and should refuse it, I could not possibly have believed them!"

BROWNIE AND THE COOK

By *DINAH MARIA MULOCK CRAIK*

Illustration by J. PATTERSON

THERE was once a little Brownie, who lived—where do you
think he lived?—In a coal cellar.

Now a coal cellar may seem a most curious place to choose to live
in; but then a Brownie is a curious creature—a fairy and yet not one
of that sort of fairies who fly about on gossamer wings, and dance in
the moonlight, and so on. He never dances; and as to wings, what
use would they be to him in a coal cellar? He is a sober, stay-at-
home, household elf—nothing much to look at, even if you did see
him, which you are not likely to do—only a little old man, about a
foot high, all dressed in brown, with a brown face and hands, and a
brown peaked cap, just the color of a brown mouse. And, like a
mouse, he hides in corners—especially kitchen corners, and only
comes out after dark when nobody is about, and so sometimes people
call him Mr. Nobody.

I said you were not likely to see him. I never did, certainly, and
never knew anybody that did; but still, if you were to go into Devonshire, you would hear many funny stories about Brownies in general.
So I may as well tell you the adventures of one particular Brownie,
who belonged to a family there; which family he had followed from
house to house most faithfully, for years and years.

A good many people had heard him—or supposed they had—
when there were extraordinary noises about the house; noises which
must have come from a mouse or a rat—or a Brownie. But nobody
had ever seen him except the children—the three little boys and three
little girls—who declared he often came to play with them when
they were alone, and was the nicest companion in the world, though
he was such an old man—hundreds of years old! He was full of fun
and mischief, and up to all sorts of tricks; but he never did anybody
any harm—unless they deserved it.

Brownie was supposed to live under one particular coal, in the darkest corner of the cellar, which was never allowed to be disturbed. Why he had chosen it nobody knew, and how he lived there nobody knew either; nor what he lived upon. Except that, ever since the family could remember, there had always been a bowl of milk put behind the coal-cellar door for the Brownie's supper. Perhaps he drank it—perhaps he didn't; anyhow, the bowl was always found empty next morning. The old Cook, who had lived all her life in the family, had never once forgotten to give Brownie his supper; but at last she died, and a young Cook came in her stead, who was very apt to forget everything. She was also both careless and lazy, and disliked taking the trouble to put a bowl of milk in the same place every night for Mr. Nobody. "She didn't believe in Brownies," she said; "she had never seen one, and seein's believing." So she laughed at the other servants, who looked very grave, and put the bowl of milk in its place as often as they could, without saying much about it.

But once, when Brownie woke up, at his usual hour for rising— ten o'clock at night, and looked round in search of his supper— which was, in fact, his breakfast—he found nothing there. At first he could not imagine such neglect, and went smelling and smelling about for his bowl of milk—it was not always placed in the same corner now—but in vain.

"This will never do," said he; and being extremely hungry, began running about the coal cellar to see what he could find. His eyes were as useful in the dark as in the light—like a pussy-cat's; but there was nothing to be seen—not even a potato paring, or a dry crust, or a well-gnawed bone, such as Tiny, the terrier, sometimes brought into the coal cellar and left on the floor. Nothing, in short, but heaps of coals and coal-dust; which even a Brownie cannot eat, you know.

"Can stand this; quite impossible!" said the Brownie, tightening his belt to make his poor little inside feel less empty. He had been asleep so long—about a week I believe, as was his habit when there was nothing to do—that he seemed ready to eat his own head, or his boots, or anything. "What's to be done? Since nobody brings my supper, I must go and fetch it."

He spoke quickly, for he always thought quickly, and made up his mind in a minute. To be sure, it was a very little mind, like his little body; but he did the best he could with it, and was not a bad sort of old fellow, after all. In the house he had never done any harm—and often some good, for he frightened away all the rats, mice, and black beetles. Not the crickets—he liked them, as the old Cook had done: she said they were such cheerful creatures, and always brought luck to the house. But the young Cook could not bear them, and used to pour boiling water down their holes, and set basins of beer for them with little wooden bridges up to the rim, that they might walk up, tumble in, and be drowned.

So there was not even a cricket singing in the silent house when Brownie put his head out of his coal-cellar door, which, to his surprise, he found open. Old Cook used to lock it every night; but the young Cook had left that key, and the kitchen and pantry keys, too, all dangling in the lock, so that any thief might have got in, and wandered all over the house without being found out.

"Hurrah, here's luck!" cried Brownie, tossing his cap up in the air, and bounding right through the scullery into the kitchen. It was quite empty, but there was a good fire burning itself out, just for its own amusement, and the remains of a capital supper were spread on the table—enough for half-a-dozen people.

Would you like to know what there was? Devonshire cream, of course; and part of a large dish of junket, which is something like curds and whey. Lots of bread and butter and cheese, and half an apple-pudding. Also a great jug of cider and another of milk, and several half-full glasses, and no end of dirty plates, knives, and forks. All were scattered about the table in most untidy fashion, just as the servants had risen from their supper, without putting anything away.

Brownie screwed up his little old face and turned up his button of a nose, and gave a long whistle. You might not believe it, seeing he lived in a coal cellar, but really he liked tidiness, and always played his pranks upon disorderly or slovenly folk.

"Whew!" said he; "here's a chance. What a supper I'll get now!"

And he jumped on to a chair and thence to a table, but so quietly that the large black cat with four white paws (called Muff, because she was so fat and soft and her fur so long), who sat dozing in front of the fire, just opened one eye and went to sleep again. She had tried to get her nose into the milk jug, but it was too small; and the junket dish was too deep for her to reach, except with one paw. She didn't care much for bread and cheese and apple-pudding, and was very well fed besides; so, after wandering round the table she had jumped down from it again, and settled herself to sleep on the hearth.

But Brownie had no notion of going to sleep. He wanted his supper, and oh! what a supper he did eat! first one thing and then another, and then trying everything all over again. And oh! what a lot he drank!—first milk and then cider, and then mixed the two together in a way that would have disagreed with anybody except a Brownie. As it was, he was obliged to slacken his belt several times, and at last he took it off altogether. But he must have had a most extraordinary capacity for eating and drinking—since, after he had cleared off all the food, he was just as lively as ever, and began jumping about on the table as if he had had no supper at all.

His jumping was a little unfortunate, for there happened to be a clean white table-cloth: as this was only Monday, it had had no time to get dirty—untidy as the Cook was. And you know Brownie lived in a coal cellar, and his feet were black with running about in coal dust. So, wherever he trod, he left the impression behind; until at last the whole table-cloth was covered with black marks.

Not that he minded this; in fact, he took great pains to make the cloth as dirty as possible; and then laughing loudly, "Ho, ho, ho!" leaped on to the hearth, and began teasing the cat; squeaking like a mouse, or chirping like a cricket, or buzzing like a fly; and altogether disturbing poor Pussy's mind so much that she went and hid herself in the farthest corner and left him the hearth all to himself, where he lay at ease till daybreak.

Then, hearing a slight noise overhead, which might be the servants getting up, he jumped on to the table again—gobbled up the few remaining crumbs for his breakfast, and scampered off to his coal cellar; where he hid himself under his big coal, and fell asleep for the day.

Well, the Cook came downstairs rather earlier than usual, for she remembered she had to clear off the remains of supper; but lo and behold! there was nothing left to clear! Every bit of food was eaten up—the cheese looked as if a dozen mice had been nibbling at it, and nibbled it down to the very rind; the milk and cider were all drunk

He began teasing the cat.

—and mice don't care for milk and cider, you know. As for the apple-pudding, it had vanished altogether; and the dish was licked as clear as if Boxer, the yard dog, had been at it in his hungriest mood.

"And my white table-cloth—oh, my clean white table-cloth! What

can have been done to it?" cried she in amazement. For it was all over little black footmarks, just the size of a baby's foot—only babies don't wear shoes with nails in them, and don't run about and climb on kitchen tables after all the family have gone to bed.

Cook was a little frightened; but her fright changed to anger when she saw the large black cat stretched comfortably on the hearth. Poor Muff had crept there for a little snooze after Brownie went away.

"You nasty cat! I see it all now; it's you that have eaten up all the supper; it's you that have been on my clean table-cloth with your dirty paws."

They were white paws, and as clean as possible; but Cook never thought of that, any more than she did of the fact that cats don't usually drink cider or eat apple-pudding.

"I'll teach you to come stealing food in this way; take that—and that—and that!"

Cook got hold of a broom and beat poor Pussy till the creature ran mewing away. She couldn't speak, you know—unfortunate cat! and tell people that it was Brownie who had done it all.

Next night Cook thought she would make all safe and sure; so, instead of letting the cat sleep by the fire, she shut her up in the chilly coal cellar—locked the door, put the key in her pocket, and went off to bed; leaving the supper as before.

When Brownie woke up and looked out of his hole, there was as usual no supper for him, and the cellar was close shut. He peered about, to try and find some cranny under the door to creep out at, but there was none. And he felt so hungry that he could almost have eaten the cat, who kept walking to and fro in a melancholy manner —only she was alive, and he couldn't well eat her alive—besides, he knew she was old, and had an idea she might be too tough; so he merely said politely, "How do you do, Mrs. Pussy?" to which she answered nothing—of course.

Something must be done, and luckily Brownies can do things which nobody else can do. So he thought he would change himself into a mouse, and gnaw a hole through the door. But then he suddenly remembered the cat, who, though he had decided not to eat her, might take this opportunity of eating him. So he thought it advisable to wait till she was fast asleep, which did not happen for a good while. At length, quite tired with walking about, Pussy turned round on her tail six times, curled down in a corner, and fell fast asleep.

Immediately Brownie changed himself into the smallest mouse possible; and, taking care not to make the least noise, gnawed a hole in the door, and squeezed himself through—immediately turning into his proper shape again, for fear of accidents.

The kitchen fire was at its last glimmer; but it showed a better supper than even last night, for the Cook had had friends with her, a brother and two cousins, and they had been exceedingly merry. The food they had left behind was enough for three Brownies at least, but this one managed to eat it all up. Only once, in trying to cut a great slice of beef, he let the carving-knife and fork fall with such a clatter that Tiny the terrier, who was tied up at the foot of the stairs, began to bark furiously. However, he brought her her puppy, which had been left in a basket in a corner of the kitchen, and so succeeded in quieting her.

After that he enjoyed himself amazingly, and made more marks than ever on the white table-cloth—for he began jumping about like a pea on a trencher, in order to make his particularly large supper agree with him.

Then, in the absence of the cat, he teased the puppy for an hour or two, till, hearing the clock strike five, he thought it as well to turn into a mouse again, and creep back cautiously into his cellar. He was only just in time, for Muff opened one eye, and was just going to pounce upon him, when he changed himself back into a Brownie. She was so startled that she bounded away, her tail growing into twice its natural size, and her eyes gleaming like round green globes. But Brownie only said, "Ha, ha, ho!" and walked deliberately into his hole.

When Cook came downstairs and saw that the same thing had happened again—that the supper was all eaten, and the table-cloth blacker than ever with the extraordinary footmarks, she was greatly puzzled. Who could have done it all? Not the cat, who came mewing out of the coal cellar the minute she unlocked the door. Possibly a rat—but then would a rat have come within reach of Tiny?

"It must have been Tiny herself, or her puppy," which just came rolling out of its basket over Cook's feet. "You little wretch! You and your mother are the greatest nuisance imaginable. I'll punish you!"

And, quite forgetting that Tiny had been safely tied up all night, and that her poor little puppy was so fat and helpless it could scarcely stand on its legs—and so was unlikely to jump on chairs and tables, she gave them both such a thrashing that they ran howling together out of the kitchen door, where the kind little kitchen-maid took them up in her arms.

"You ought to have beaten the Brownie, if you could catch him," said she, indignantly. "He'll do it again and again, you'll see, for he can't bear an untidy kitchen. You'd better do as poor old Cook did, and clear the supper things away, and put the odds and ends safe in the larder; also," she added mysteriously, "if I were you, I'd put a bowl of milk behind the coal-cellar door."

"Nonsense!" answered the young Cook, and flounced away. But afterwards she thought better of it, and did as she was advised, grumbling all the time, but doing it.

Next morning the milk was gone! Perhaps Brownie had drunk it up; anyhow nobody could say that he hadn't. As for the supper, Cook having safely laid it on the shelves of the larder, nobody touched it. And the table-cloth, which was wrapped up tidily and put in the dresser drawer, came out as clean as ever, with not a single black footmark upon it. No mischief being done, the cat and the dog both escaped beating, and Brownie played no more tricks with anybody—till the next time.

THE GREEDY SHEPHERD

By FRANCES BROWNE

Illustrations by KATHARINE PYLE

ONCE upon a time there lived in the south country two brothers, whose business it was to keep sheep on a great grassy plain, which was bounded on the one side by a forest and on the other by a chain of high hills. No one lived on that plain but shepherds, who dwelt in low cottages thatched with heath, and watched their sheep so carefully that no lamb was ever lost, nor had one of the shepherds ever traveled beyond the foot of the hills and the skirts of the forest.

There were none among them more careful than these two brothers, one of whom was called Clutch, and the other Kind. Though brethren born, two men of distant countries could not be more unlike in disposition. Clutch thought of nothing in this world but how to catch and keep some profit for himself, while Kind would have shared his last morsel with a hungry dog. This covetous mind made Clutch keep all his father's sheep when the old man was dead and gone, because he was the eldest brother, allowing Kind nothing but the place of a servant to help him in looking after them. Kind wouldn't quarrel with his brother for the sake of the sheep, so he helped him to keep them and Clutch had all his own way. This made him agreeable. For some time the brothers lived peaceably in their father's cottage, which stood low and lonely under the shadow of a great sycamore tree, and kept their flock with pipe and crook on the grassy plain, till new troubles arose through Clutch's covetousness.

On that plain there was neither town, nor city, nor market place, where people might sell or buy, but the shepherds cared little for trade. The wool of their flocks made them clothes; their milk gave them butter and cheese; at feast times every family killed a lamb or so. Their fields yielded them wheat for bread; the forest supplied them with firewood for winter; and every midsummer, which is the sheep-shearing time, traders from a certain far-off city came through it by an ancient way to purchase all the wool the shepherds could spare, and give them in exchange either goods or money.

One midsummer it so happened that these traders praised the wool of Clutch's flock above all they found on the plain, and gave him the highest price for it. That was an unlucky happening for the sheep: from thenceforth Clutch thought he could never get enough wool off them. At the shearing time nobody clipped so close, and, in spite of all Kind could do or say, he left the poor sheep as bare as if they had been shaven; and as soon as the wool grew long enough to keep them warm, he was ready with the shears again—no matter how chilly might be the days, or how near the winter. Kind didn't like these doings, and many a debate they caused between him and his brother. Clutch always tried to persuade him that close clipping was good for the sheep, and Kind always strove to make him think he had got all the wool—so they were never done with disputes. Still Clutch sold the wool and stored up his profits, and one midsummer after another passed. The shepherds began to think him a rich man, and close clipping might have become the fashion, but for a strange thing which happened to his flock.

The wool had grown well that summer. He had taken two crops off them, and was thinking of a third—though the misty mornings of autumn were come, and the cold evenings made the shepherds put on their winter cloaks—when first the lambs, and then the ewes, began to stray away; and search as the brothers would, none of them was ever found again. Clutch blamed Kind with being careless, and watched with all his might. Kind knew it was not his fault, but he looked sharper than ever. Still the straying went on. The flocks grew smaller every day, and all the brothers could find out was that the closest clipped were the first to go, and, count the flock when they might, some were sure to be missed at the folding.

Kind grew tired of watching and Clutch lost his sleep with vexation. The other shepherds, over whom he had boasted of his wool and his profits, were not sorry to see pride having a fall. Most of them pitied Kind, but all of them agreed that they had marvelous ill luck, and kept as far from them as they could for fear of sharing it. Still the flock melted away as the months wore on. Storms and cold weather never stopped them from straying, and when the spring came back nothing remained with Clutch and Kind but three old ewes, the quietest and lamest of their whole flock. They were watching these ewes one evening in the primrose time, when Clutch, who had never kept his eyes off them that day, said:

"Brother, there is wool to be had on their backs."

"It is too little to keep them warm," said Kind. "The east wind still blows sometimes"; but Clutch was off to the cottage for the bag and shears.

Kind was grieved to see his brother so covetous and to divert his mind he looked up at the great hills; it was a sort of comfort to him, ever since their losses began, to look at them evening and morning. Now their far-off heights were growing crimson with the setting sun, but as he looked, three creatures like sheep scoured up a cleft in one of them as fleet as any deer; and when Kind turned, he saw his brother coming with the bag and shears, but not a single ewe was to be seen. Clutch's first question was, what had become of them; and when Kind told him what he saw, the eldest brother scolded him with might and main for ever lifting his eyes off them:

"Much good the hills and the sunset do us," said he, "now that we have not a single sheep. The other shepherds will hardly give us room among them at shearing time or harvest; but for my part, I'll not stay on this plain to be despised for poverty. If you like to come with me and be guided by my advice, we shall get service somewhere. I have heard my father say that there were great shepherds living in old times beyond the hills; let us go and see if they will take us for sheep-boys."

Kind would rather have stayed and tilled his father's wheat-field, hard by the cottage; but since his elder brother would go, he resolved to bear him company. Accordingly, next morning Clutch took his bag and shears, Kind took his crook and pipe, and away they went over the plain and up the hills. All who saw them thought that they had lost their senses, for no shepherd had gone there for a hundred years, and nothing was to be seen but wide moorlands full of rugged rocks, and sloping up, it seemed, to the very sky. Kind persuaded his brother to take the direction the sheep had taken, but the ground was so rough and steep that after two hours' climbing they would gladly have turned back, if it had not been that their sheep were gone and the shepherds would laugh at them.

By noon they came to the stony cleft, up which the three old ewes had scoured like deer; but both were tired and sat down to rest. Their feet were sore and their hearts were heavy; but as they sat there, there came a sound of music down the hills, as if a thousand shepherds had been playing on their tops. Clutch and Kind had never heard such music before. As they listened, the soreness passed from their feet and the heaviness from their hearts; and getting up, they followed the sound up the cleft, and over a wide heath covered with purple bloom; till, at sunset, they came to the hilltop, and saw a broad pasture where violets grew thick among the grass, and thousands of snow-white sheep were feeding, while an old man sat in the midst of them playing on his pipe. He wore a long coat, the color of the holly leaves; his hair hung to his waist and his beard to his knees; but both were as white as snow, and he had the countenance of one who had led a quiet life and known no cares nor losses.

"Good father," said Kind, for his elder brother hung back and was afraid, "tell us what land is this, and where can we find service; for my brother and I are shepherds, and can well keep flocks from straying, though we have lost our own."

"These are the hill pastures," said the old man, "and I am the ancient shepherd. My flocks never stray, but I have employment for you. Which of you can shear best?"

"Good father," said Clutch, taking courage, "I am the closest shearer in all the plain country; you would not find as much wool as would make a thread on a sheep when I have done with it."

"You are the man for my business," replied the old shepherd. "When the moon rises, I will call the flock you have to shear. Till then sit down and rest, and take your supper out of my wallet."

Clutch and Kind gladly sat down by him among the violets, and opening a leathern bag which hung by his side, the old man gave them cakes and cheese, and a horn cup to drink from a stream hard by. The brothers felt fit for any work after that meal; and Clutch rejoiced in his own mind at the chance he had got for showing his skill with the shears. "Kind will see how useful it is to cut close," he thought to himself; but they sat with the old man, telling him the news of the plain, till the sun went down and the moon rose, and all the snow-white sheep gathered and laid themselves down behind him. Then he took his pipe and played a merry tune, when immediately there was heard a great howling, and up the hills came a troop of shaggy wolves, with hair so long that their eyes could scarcely be seen. Clutch would have fled for fear, but the wolves stopped, and the old man said to him:

"Rise and shear—this flock of mine have too much wool on them."

Clutch had never shorn wolves before, yet he couldn't think of losing the good service and went forward with a stout heart; but the first of the wolves showed his teeth, and all the rest raised such a howl the moment he came near them that Clutch was glad to throw down his shears, and run behind the old man for safety.

"Good father," cried he, "I will shear sheep, but not wolves."

"They must be shorn," said the old man, "or you go back to the

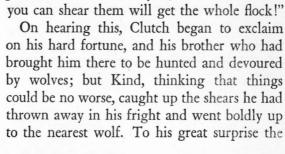

plains, and them after you; but whichever of you can shear them will get the whole flock!"

On hearing this, Clutch began to exclaim on his hard fortune, and his brother who had brought him there to be hunted and devoured by wolves; but Kind, thinking that things could be no worse, caught up the shears he had thrown away in his fright and went boldly up to the nearest wolf. To his great surprise the

wild creature seemed to know him and stood quietly to be shorn, while the rest of the flock gathered round as if waiting their turn. Kind clipped neatly, but not too close, as he had wished his brother to do with the sheep, and heaped up the hair on one side. When he had done with one, another came forward, and Kind went on shearing by the bright moonlight till the whole flock were shorn. Then the old man said:

"Ye have done well; take the wool and the flock for your wages, return with them to the plain, and if you please, take this little-worth brother of yours for a boy to keep them."

Kind did not much like keeping wolves, but before he could make answer they had all changed into the very sheep which had strayed away so strangely. All of them had grown fatter and thicker of fleece, and the hair he had cut off lay by his side, a heap of wool so fine and soft that its like had never been seen on the plain.

Clutch gathered it up in his empty bag, and glad was he to go back to the plain with his brother; for the old man sent them away with their flock, saying no man must see the dawn of day on that pasture but himself, for it was the ground of the fairies. So Clutch and Kind went home with great gladness. All the shepherds came to hear their wonderful story, and ever after liked to keep near them because they had such good luck. They keep the sheep together till this day, but Clutch has grown less greedy, and Kind alone uses the shears.

THE LIGHT PRINCESS

By GEORGE MAC DONALD

Illustrations by DOROTHY LATHROP

I

WHAT! NO CHILDREN?

ONCE upon a time, so long ago that I have quite forgotten the date, there lived a king and queen who had no children. And the king said to himself, "All the queens of my acquaintance have children, some three, some seven, and some as many as twelve; and my queen has not one. I feel ill-used." So he made up his mind to be cross with his wife about it. But she bore it all like a good, patient queen as she was. Then the king grew very cross indeed. But the queen pretended to take it all as a joke and a very good one, too.

"Why don't you have any daughters, at least?" said he. "I don't say *sons;* that might be too much to expect."

"I am sure, dear king, I am very sorry," said the queen.

"So you ought to be," retorted the king; "you are not going to make a virtue of *that,* surely."

But he was not an ill-tempered king, and in any matter of less moment would have let the queen have her own way with all his heart. This, however, was an affair of state.

The queen smiled.

"You must have patience with a lady, you know, dear king," said she.

She was, indeed, a very nice queen, and heartily sorry that she could not oblige the king immediately.

The king tried to have patience, but he succeeded very badly. It was more than he deserved, therefore, when at last, the queen gave him a daughter—as lovely a little princess as ever cried.

II

WON'T I, JUST?

THE day grew near when the infant must be christened. The king wrote all the invitations with his own hand. Of course somebody was forgotten.

Now it does not generally matter if somebody *is* forgotten, only you must mind who. Unfortunately, the king forgot without intending to forget; and so the chance fell upon the Princess Makemnoit, which was awkward. For the princess was the king's own sister; and he ought not to have forgotten her. But she had made herself so disagreeable to the old king, their father, that he had forgotten her in making his will; and so it was no wonder that her brother forgot her in writing his invitations. But poor relations don't do anything to keep you in mind of them. Why don't they? The king could not see into the garret she lived in, could he?

She was a sour, spiteful creature. The wrinkles of contempt crossed the wrinkles of peevishness and made her face as full of wrinkles as a pat of butter. If ever a king could be justified in forgetting anybody, this king was justified in forgetting his sister, even at a christening. She looked very odd, too. Her forehead was as large as all the rest of her face and projected over it like a precipice. When she was angry, her little eyes flashed blue. When she hated anybody, they shone yellow and green. What they looked like when she loved anybody, I do not know; for I never heard of her loving anybody but herself, and I do not think she could have managed that if she had not somehow got used to herself. But what made it highly imprudent in the king to forget her was—that she was awfully clever. In fact, she was a witch; and when she bewitched anybody, he very soon had enough of it; for she beat all the wicked fairies in wickedness, and all the clever ones in cleverness. She despised all the modes we read of in history in which offended fairies and witches have taken their revenges; and therefore, after waiting and waiting in vain for an invitation, she made up her mind at last to go without one and make the whole family miserable, like a princess as she was.

So she put on her best gown, went to the palace, was kindly received by the happy monarch, who forgot that he had forgotten her, and took her place in the procession to the royal chapel. When they were all gathered about the font, she contrived to get next to it, and throw something into the water; after which she maintained a very respectful demeanor till the water was applied to the child's face. But at that moment she turned round in her place three times, and muttered the following words, loud enough for those beside her to hear:

> "Light of spirit, by my charms,
>   Light of body, every part,
> Never weary human arms—
>   Only crush thy parents' heart!"

They all thought she had lost her wits and was repeating some foolish nursery rhyme; but a shudder went through the whole of them notwithstanding. The baby, on the contrary, began to laugh and crow; while the nurse gave a start and a smothered cry, for she thought she was struck with paralysis: she could not feel the baby in her arms. But she clasped it tight and said nothing.

The mischief was done.

III

SHE CAN'T BE OURS

HER atrocious aunt had deprived the child of all her gravity. If you ask me how this was effected, I answer, "In the easiest way in the world. She had only to destroy gravitation." For the princess was a philosopher, and knew all the *ins* and *outs* of the laws of gravitation as well as the *ins* and *outs* of her boot-lace. And being a witch as well, she could abrogate those laws in a moment; or at least so clog their wheels and rust their bearings that they would not work at all. But we have more to do with what followed than with how it was done.

The first awkwardness that resulted from this unhappy privation was, that the moment the nurse began to float the baby up and down, she flew from her arms toward the ceiling. Happily the resistance of the air brought her ascending career to a close within a foot of it. There she remained, horizontal as when she left her nurse's arms, kicking and laughing amazingly. The nurse in terror flew to the bell and begged the footman who answered it to bring up the house-steps directly. Trembling in every limb, she climbed up on the steps and had to stand upon the very top and reach up before she could catch the floating tail of the baby's long clothes.

When the strange fact came to be known, there was a terrible commotion in the palace. The occasion of its discovery by the king was naturally a repetition of the nurse's experience. Astonished that he felt no weight when the child was laid in his arms, he began to wave her up and—not down; for she slowly ascended to the ceiling as before, and there remained floating in perfect comfort and satis-faction, as was testified by her peals of tiny laughter. The king stood staring up in speechless amazement and trembled so that his beard shook like grass in the wind. At last, turning to the queen, who was just as horror-struck as himself, he said, gasping, staring, and stammering:

"She *can't* be ours, queen!"

Now the queen was much cleverer than the king and had begun already to suspect that "this effect defective came by cause."

"I am sure she is ours," answered she. "But we ought to have taken better care of her at the christening. People who were never invited ought not to have been present."

"Oh, ho!" said the king, tapping his forehead with his forefinger, "I have it all. I've found her out. Don't you see it, queen? Princess Makemnoit has bewitched her."

"That's just what I say," answered the queen.

"I beg your pardon, my love; I did not hear you. John, bring the steps I get on my throne with."

For he was a little king with a great throne, like many other kings.

The throne-steps were brought, and set upon the dining table, and John got up on the top of them. But he could not reach the little princess, who lay like a baby-laughter-cloud in the air, exploding continuously.

"Take the tongs, John," said his Majesty; and getting up on the table, he handed them to him.

John could reach the baby now, and the little princess was handed down by the tongs.

IV

WHERE IS SHE?

ONE fine summer day, a month after these, her first adventures, during which time she had been very carefully watched, the princess was lying on the bed in the queen's own chamber, fast asleep. One of the windows was open, for it was noon, and the day was so sultry that the little girl was wrapped in nothing less ethereal than slumber itself. The queen came into the room, and not observing that the baby was on the bed, opened another window. A frolicsome fairy wind, which had been watching for a chance of mischief, rushed in at the one window, and taking its way over the bed where the child was lying, caught her up, and rolling and floating her along like a piece of flue or a dandelion seed, carried her with it through the opposite window, and away. The queen went downstairs, quite ignorant of the loss she had herself occasioned.

When the nurse returned, she supposed that her Majesty had carried her off, and, dreading a scolding, delayed making inquiry about her. But hearing nothing, she grew uneasy, and went at length to the queen's boudoir, where she found her Majesty.

"Please, your Majesty, shall I take the baby?" said she.

"Where is she?" asked the queen.

"Please forgive me. I know it was wrong."

"What do you mean?" said the queen, looking grave.

"Oh, don't frighten me, your Majesty?" exclaimed the nurse, clasping her hands.

The queen saw that something was amiss, and fell down in a faint. The nurse rushed about the palace, screaming, "My baby, my baby!"

The princess was the ball.

Everyone ran to the queen's room.
But the queen could give no orders.
They soon found out, however, that
the princess was missing, and in a
moment the palace was like a beehive
in a garden; and in one minute more
the queen was brought to herself by
a great shout and a clapping of
hands. They had found the princess
fast asleep under a rosebush, to which
the elvish little wind-puff had carried
her, finishing its mischief by shaking
a shower of red rose-leaves all over
the little white sleeper. Startled by
the noise the servants made, she woke,
and furious with glee, scattered the
rose-leaves in all directions, like a
shower of spray in the sunset.

She was watched more carefully after this, no doubt; yet it would
be endless to relate all the odd incidents resulting from this peculiarity of the young princess. But there never was a baby in a house,
not to say a palace, that kept the household in such constant good
humor, at least below-stairs. If it was not easy for her nurses to hold
her, at least she made neither their arms nor their hearts ache. And
she was so nice to play at ball with! There was positively no danger
of letting her fall. They might throw her down, or knock her down,
or push her down, but they couldn't *let* her down. It is true, they
might let her fly into the fire or the coal-hole or through the window; but none of these accidents had happened as yet. If you heard
peals of laughter resounding from some unknown region, you might
be sure enough of the cause. Going down into the kitchen or *the
room,* you would find Jane and Thomas, and Robert and Susan, all
and sum, playing at ball with the little princess. She was the ball
herself and did not enjoy it the less for that. Away she went, flying
from one to another, screeching with laughter. And the servants
loved the ball itself better even than the game. But they had to take

some care how they threw her, for if she received an upward direction she would never come down again without being fetched.

V

WHAT IS TO BE DONE?

BUT above-stairs it was different. One day, for instance, after breakfast, the king went into his counting-house and counted out his money. The operation gave him no pleasure.

"To think," said he to himself, "that every one of these gold sovereigns weighs a quarter of an ounce, and my real, live, flesh-and-blood princess weighs nothing at all!"

And he hated his gold sovereigns as they lay with a broad smile of self-satisfaction all over their yellow faces.

The queen was in the parlor, eating bread and honey. But at the second mouthful she burst out crying and could not swallow it. The king heard her sobbing. Glad of anybody, but especially of his queen, to quarrel with, he clashed his gold sovereigns into his money-box, clapped his crown on his head, and rushed into the parlor.

"What is all this about?" exclaimed he. "What are you crying for, queen?"

"I can't eat it," said the queen, looking ruefully at the honey-pot.

"No wonder!" retorted the king. "You've just eaten your breakfast—two turkey eggs and three anchovies."

"Oh, that's not it!" sobbed her Majesty. "It's my child, my child!"

"Well, what's the matter with your child? She's neither up the chimney nor down the draw-well. Just hear her laughing."

Yet the king could not help a sigh, which he tried to turn into a cough, saying:

"It is a good thing to be light-hearted, I am sure, whether she be ours or not."

"It is a bad thing to be light-headed," answered the queen, looking with prophetic soul far into the future.

" 'Tis a good thing to be light-handed," said the king.

" 'Tis a bad thing to be light-fingered," answered the queen.

" 'Tis a good thing to be light-footed," said the king.

" 'Tis a bad thing—" began the queen; but the king interrupted her.

"In fact," said he, with the tone of one who concludes an argument in which he has had only imaginary opponents, and in which, therefore, he has come off triumphant—"in fact, it is a good thing altogether to be light-bodied."

"But it is a bad thing altogether to be light-minded," retorted the queen, who was beginning to lose her temper.

This last answer quite discomfited his Majesty, who turned on his heel, and betook himself to his counting-house again. But he was not halfway toward it, when the voice of his queen overtook him.

"And it's a bad thing to be light-haired," screamed she, determined to have more last words, now that her spirit was roused.

The queen's hair was black as night; and the king's had been, and his daughter's was, golden as morning. But it was not this reflection on his hair that arrested him; it was the double use of the word *light*. For the king hated all witticisms, and punning especially. And besides, he could not tell whether the queen meant light-*haired* or light-*heired;* for why might she not aspirate her vowels when she was exasperated herself?

He turned upon his other heel and rejoined her. She looked angry still, because she knew that she was guilty, or, what was much the same, knew that he thought so.

"My dear queen," said he, "duplicity of any sort is exceedingly objectionable between married people of any rank, not to say kings and queens; and the most objectionable form duplicity can assume is that of punning."

"There!" said the queen. "I never made a jest but I broke it in the making. I am the most unfortunate woman in the world!"

She looked so rueful that the king took her in his arms, and they sat down to consult.

"Can you bear this?" said the king.

"No, I can't," said the queen.

"Well, what's to be done?" said the king.

"I'm sure I don't know," said the queen. "But might you not try an apology?"

"To my old sister, I suppose you mean?" said the king.

"Yes," said the queen.

"Well, I don't mind," said the king.

So he went the next morning to the house of the princess, and, making a very humble apology, begged her to undo the spell. But the princess declared, with a grave face, that she knew nothing at all about it. Her eyes, however, shone pink, which was a sign that she was happy. She advised the king and queen to have patience and to mend their ways. The king returned disconsolate. The queen tried to comfort him.

"We will wait till she is older. She may then be able to suggest something herself. She will know at least how she feels, and explain things to us."

"But what if she should marry?" exclaimed the king, in sudden consternation at the idea.

"Well, what of that?" rejoined the queen.

"Just think! If she were to have children! In the course of a hundred years the air might be as full of floating children as of gossamers in autumn."

"That is no business of ours," replied the queen. "Besides by that time they will have learned to take care of themselves."

A sigh was the king's only answer.

He would have consulted the court physicians; but he was afraid they would try experiments upon her.

VI

SHE LAUGHS TOO MUCH

MEANTIME, notwithstanding awkward occurrences, and griefs that she brought upon her parents, the little princess laughed and grew— not fat, but plump and tall. She reached the age of seventeen without having fallen into any worse scrape than a chimney; by rescuing her from which, a little bird-nesting urchin got fame and a black face. Nor, thoughtless as she was, had she committed anything worse than laughter at everybody and everything that came in her way.

When she was told, for the sake of experiment, that General Clan-runfort was cut to pieces with all his troops, she laughed; when she heard that the enemy was on his way to besiege her papa's capital, she laughed hugely; but when she was told that the city would certainly be abandoned to the mercy of the enemy's soldiery—why, then she laughed immoderately. She never could be brought to see the serious side of anything. When her mother cried, she said:

"What queer faces mamma makes! And she squeezes water out of her cheeks! Funny mamma!"

And when her papa stormed at her, she laughed, and danced round and round him, clapping her hands and crying: "Do it again, papa. Do it again! It's such fun! Dear, funny papa!"

And if he tried to catch her she glided from him in an instant, not in the least afraid of him but thinking it part of the game not to be caught. With one push of her foot she would be floating in the air above his head; or she would go dancing backward and forward and sideways like a great butterfly. It happened several times, when her father and mother were holding a consultation about her in private, that they were interrupted by vainly repressed outbursts of laughter over their heads; and looking up with indignation, saw her floating at full length in the air above them, whence she regarded them with the most comical appreciation of the position.

One day an awkward accident happened. The princess had come out upon the lawn with one of her attendants, who held her by the hand. Spying her father at the other side of the lawn, she snatched her hand from the maid's and sped across to him. Now when she wanted to run alone, her custom was to catch up a stone in each hand so that she might come down again after a bound. Whatever she wore as a part of her attire had no effect in this way; even gold, when it thus became as it were a part of herself, lost all its weight for the time. But whatever she only held in her hands retained its downward tendency. On this occasion she could see nothing to catch up but a huge toad that was walking across the lawn as if he had a hundred years to do it in. Not knowing what disgust meant, for this was one of her peculiarities, she snatched up the toad and bounded away. She had almost reached her father, and he was holding out his arm to receive her and take from her lips the kiss which hovered on them like a butterfly on a rosebud, when a puff of wind blew her aside into the arms of a young page who had just been receiving a message from his Majesty. Now it was no great peculiarity in the princess that, once she was set a-going, it always cost her time and trouble to check herself. On this occasion there was no time. She *must* kiss—and she kissed the page. She did not mind it much; for she had no shyness in her composition; and she knew, besides, that she could not help it. So she only laughed, like a musical box. The poor page fared the worst. For the princess, trying to correct the unfortunate tendency of the kiss, put out her hands to keep her off the page; so that along with the kiss, he received, on the other cheek, a slap with the huge black toad which she poked right into his eye. He tried to laugh, too, but the attempt resulted in such an odd contortion of countenance as showed that there was no danger of his pluming himself on the kiss. As for the king, his dignity was greatly hurt and he did not speak to the page for a whole month.

I may here remark that it was very amusing to see her run, if her mode of progression could properly be called running. For first she would make a bound; then, having alighted, she would run a few steps and make another bound. Sometimes she would fancy she had reached the ground before she actually had and her feet would go backward and forward, running upon nothing at all, like those of a chicken on its back. Then she would laugh like the very spirit of fun; only in her laugh there was something missing. What it was I find myself unable to describe. I think it was a certain tone, depending upon the possibility of sorrow—*morbidezza,* perhaps. She never smiled.

VII

TRY METAPHYSICS

AFTER a long avoidance of the painful subject, the king and queen resolved to hold a council of three upon it; and so they sent for the princess. In she came, sliding and flitting and gliding from one piece of furniture to another, and put herself at last in an armchair, in a sitting posture. Whether she could be said *to sit,* seeing she received no support from the seat of the chair, I do not pretend to determine.

"My dear child," said the king, "you must be aware by this time that you are not exactly like other people."

"Oh, you dear funny papa! I have got a nose, and two eyes, and all the rest. So have you. So has mamma."

"Now be serious, my dear, for once," said the queen.

"No, thank you, mamma; I had rather not."

"Would you not like to be able to walk like other people?" said the king.

"No, indeed, I should think not. You only crawl. You are such slow coaches!"

"How do you feel, my child?" he resumed, after a pause of discomfiture.

"Quite well, thank you."

"I mean, what do you feel like?"

"Like nothing at all, that I know of."

"You must feel like something."

"I feel like a princess with such a funny papa and such a dear pet of a queen-mamma!"

"Now really!" began the queen; but the princess interrupted her.

"Oh, yes," she added, "I remember. I have a curious feeling, sometimes, as if I were the only person that had any sense in the whole world."

She had been trying to behave herself with dignity; but now she burst into a violent fit of laughter, threw herself backward over the chair and went rolling about the floor in an ecstasy of enjoyment. The king picked her up more easily than one does a down quilt, and replaced her in her former relation to the chair. The exact preposition expressing this relation I do not happen to know.

"Is there nothing you wish for?" resumed the king, who had learned by this time that it was useless to be angry with her.

"Oh, you dear papa!—yes," answered she.

"What is it, my darling?"

"I have been longing for it—oh, such a time!—ever since last night."

"Tell me what it is."

"Will you promise to let me have it?"

The king was on the point of saying yes, but the wiser queen checked him with a single motion of her head.

"Tell me what it is first," said he.

"No, no. Promise first."

"I dare not. What is it?"

"Mind, I hold you to your promise. It is—to be tied to the end of a string—a very long string indeed, and be flown like a kite. Oh, such fun! I would rain rose-water, and hail sugar-plums, and snow whipped cream, and—and—and—"

A fit of laughing checked her; and she would have been off again over the floor, had not the king started up and caught her just in time. Seeing that nothing but talk could be got out of her, he rang the bell and sent her away with two of her ladies-in-waiting.

"Now, queen," he said, turning to her Majesty, "what *is* to be done?"

"There is but one thing left," answered she. "Let us consult the college of Metaphysicians."

"Bravo!" cried the king; "we will."

Now at the head of this college were two very wise Chinese philosophers—by name Hum-Drum and Kopy-Keck. For them the king sent; and straightway they came. In a long speech he communicated to them what they knew very well already—as who did not?—namely, the peculiar condition of his daughter in relation to the globe on which she dwelt; and requested them to consult together as to what might be the cause and probable cure of her *infirmity*. The king laid stress upon the word but failed to discover his own pun. The queen laughed; but Hum-Drum and Kopy-Keck heard with humility and retired in silence.

Their consultation consisted chiefly in propounding and supporting for the thousandth time each his favorite theories. For the condition of the princess afforded delightful scope for the discussion of every question arising from this division of thought—in fact, for a consideration of all the Metaphysics of the Chinese Empire. But it is only justice to say that they did not altogether neglect the discussion of the practical question, *what was to be done*.

Hum-Drum was a Materialist, and Kopy-Keck was a Spiritualist. The former was slow and sententious; the latter was quick and flighty: the latter had generally the first word; the former the last.

"I reassert my former assertion," began Kopy-Keck, with a plunge. "There is not a fault in the princess, body or soul; only they are wrongly put together. Listen to me now, Hum-Drum, and I will tell you in brief what I think. Don't speak. Don't answer me. I *won't* hear you till I have done. At that decisive moment when souls seek their appointed habitations, two eager souls met, struck, rebounded, lost their way, and arrived each at the wrong place. The soul of the princess was one of those, and she went far astray. She does not belong by rights to this world at all, but to some other planet, probably Mercury. Her proclivity to her true sphere destroys all the natural influence which this orb would otherwise possess over her corporeal frame. She cares for nothing here. There is no relation between her and this world.

"She must therefore be taught, by the sternest compulsion, to take an interest in the earth as the earth. She must study every department of its history—its animal history; its vegetable history; its mineral history; its social history; its moral history; its political history; its scientific history; its literary history; its musical history; its artistical history; above all, its metaphysical history. She must begin with the Chinese dynasty and end with Japan. But first of all she must study geology, and especially the history of the extinct races of animals—their natures, their habits, their loves, their hates, their revenges. She must—"

"Hold, h-o-o-old!" roared Hum-Drum. "It is certainly my turn now. My rooted and insubvertible conviction is, that the causes of the anomalies evident in the princess's condition are strictly and solely physical. But that is only tantamount to acknowledging that they exist. Hear my opinion. From some cause or other, of no importance to our inquiry, the motion of her heart has been reversed. That remarkable combination of the suction and the force pump works the wrong way—I mean in the case of the unfortunate princess, it draws in where it should force out and forces out where it should draw in. The offices of the auricles and the ventricles are subverted. The blood is sent forth by the veins, and returns by the arteries. Consequently it is running the wrong way through all her corporeal organism—lungs and all. Is it then at all mysterious, seeing that such is the case, that on the other particular of gravitation as well, she should differ from normal humanity? My proposal for the cure is this:

"Phlebotomize until she is reduced to the last point of safety. Let it be effected, if necessary, in a warm bath. When she is reduced to a state of perfect asphyxy, apply a ligature to the left ankle, drawing it as tight as the bone will bear. Apply at the same moment another of equal tension around the right wrist. By means of plates constructed for the purpose, place the other foot and hand under the receivers of two air-pumps. Exhaust the receivers. Exhibit a pint of French brandy, and await the result."

"Which would presently arrive in the form of grim Death," said Kopy-Keck.

"If it should, she would yet die in doing our duty," retorted Hum-Drum.

But their Majesties had too much tenderness for their volatile offspring to subject her to either of the schemes of the equally unscrupulous philosophers. Indeed, the most complete knowledge of the laws of nature would have been unserviceable in her case; for it was impossible to classify her. She was a fifth imponderable body, sharing all the other properties of the ponderable.

VIII

TRY A DROP OF WATER

PERHAPS the best thing for the princess would have been to fall in love. But how a princess who had no gravity could fall into anything is a difficulty—perhaps *the* difficulty. As for her own feelings on the subject, she did not even know that there was such a beehive of honey and stings to be fallen into. But now I come to mention another curious fact about her.

The palace was built on the shores of the loveliest lake in the world; and the princess loved this lake more than father or mother. The root of this preference, no doubt, although the princess did not recognize it as such, was, that the moment she got into it, she recovered the natural right of which she had been so wickedly deprived—namely gravity. Whether this was owing to the fact that water had been employed as the means of conveying the injury, I do not know. But it is certain that she could swim and dive like the duck that her old nurse said she was. The manner in which this alleviation of her misfortune was discovered was as follows:

One summer evening, during the carnival of the country, she had been taken upon the lake by the king and queen, in the royal barge. They were accompanied by many of the courtiers in a fleet of little boats. In the middle of the lake she wanted to get into the lord chancellor's barge, for his daughter, who was a great favorite with her, was in it with her father. Now though the old king rarely condescended to make light of his misfortune, yet, happening on this occasion to be in a particularly good humor, as the barges approached each other he caught up the princess to throw her into the chancellor's barge. He lost his balance, however, and dropping into the bottom of the barge lost his hold of his daughter; not, however, before imparting to her the downward tendency of his own person though in a somewhat different direction; for, as the king fell into the boat, she fell into the water. With a burst of delighted laughter she disappeared into the lake. A cry of horror ascended from the boats. They had never seen the princess go down before. Half the men were under water in a moment; but they had all, one after another, come up to the surface again for breath, when —tinkle, tinkle, babble, and gush! came the princess's laugh over the water from far away. There she was, swimming like a swan. Nor would she come out for king or queen, chancellor or daughter. She was perfectly obstinate.

But at the same time she seemed more sedate than usual. Perhaps that was because a great pleasure spoils laughing. At all events, after this, the passion of her life was to get into the water, and she was always the better behaved and the more beautiful the more she had of it. Summer and winter it was quite the same; only she could not stay so long in the water when they had to break the ice to let her in. Any day, from morning to evening in summer, she might be descried—a streak of white in the blue water—lying as still as the shadow of a cloud, or shooting along like a dolphin, disappearing, and coming up again far off just where one did not expect her. She would have been in the lake of a night too, if she could have had her way, for the balcony of her window overhung a deep pool in it; and through a shallow reedy passage she could have swum out into the wide wet water and no one would have been any the wiser. Indeed, when she happened to wake in the moonlight she could hardly resist the temptation. But there was the sad difficulty of getting into it. She had as great a dread of the air as some children have of the water. For the slightest gust of wind would blow her away; and a gust might arise in the stillest moment. And if she gave herself a push toward the water and just failed of reaching it, her situation would be dreadfully awkward, irrespective of the wind; for at best there she would have to remain, suspended in her nightgown, till she was seen and angled for by somebody from the window.

"Oh! if I had my gravity," thought she, contemplating the water, "I would flash off this balcony like a long white seabird, headlong into the darling wetness. Heigh-ho!"

This was the only consideration that made her wish to be like other people.

Another reason for her being fond of the water was that in it alone she enjoyed any freedom. For she could not walk out without a *cortège,* consisting in part of a troop of light-horse, for fear of the liberties which the wind might take with her. And the king grew more apprehensive with increasing years, till at last he would not allow her to walk abroad at all without some twenty silken cords fastened to as many parts of her dress, and held by twenty noblemen. Of course horseback was out of the question. But she bade good-bye to all this ceremony when she got into the water.

And so remarkable were its effects upon her, especially in restoring her for the time to the ordinary human gravity, that Hum-Drum and Kopy-Keck agreed in recommending the king to bury her alive for three years; in the hope that, as the water did her so much good, the earth would do her yet more. But the king had some vulgar prejudices against the experiment and would not give his consent. Foiled in this, they yet agreed to another recommendation, which, seeing that one imported his opinions from China and the other from Thibet, was very remarkable indeed. They argued that, if water of external origin and application could be so efficacious, water from a deeper source might work a perfect cure; in short, that if the poor afflicted princess could by any means be made to cry, she might recover her lost gravity.

But how was this to be brought about? Therein lay all the difficulty—to meet which the philosophers were not wise enough. To make the princess cry was as impossible as to make her weigh. They sent for a professional beggar; commanded him to prepare his most touching oracle of woe; helped him out of the court charade box to whatever he wanted for dressing up, and promised great rewards in the event of his success. But it was all in vain. She listened to the mendicant artist's story, and gazed at his marvelous make-up, till she could contain herself no longer and went into the most undignified contortions for relief, shrieking, positively screeching with laughter.

When she had a little recovered herself, she ordered her attendants to drive him away and not give him a single copper; whereupon his look of mortified discomfiture wrought her punishment and his revenge, for it sent her into violent hysterics, from which she was with difficulty restored.

But so anxious was the king that the suggestion should have a fair trial, that he put himself in a rage one day, and, rushing up to her room, gave her an awful whipping. Yet not a tear would flow. She looked grave and her laughing sounded uncommonly like screaming—that was all. The good old tyrant, though he put on his best gold spectacles to look, could not discover the smallest cloud in the serene blue of her eyes.

IX

PUT ME IN AGAIN

It must have been about this time that the son of a king, who lived a thousand miles from Lagobel, set out to look for the daughter of a queen. He traveled far and wide, but as surely as he found a princess, he found some fault in her. Of course he could not marry a mere woman, however beautiful; and there was no princess to be found worthy of him. Whether the prince was so near perfection that he had a right to demand perfection itself, I cannot pretend to say. All I know is, that he was a fine, handsome, brave, generous, well-bred and well-behaved youth, as all princes are.

In his wanderings he had come across some reports about our princess; but as everybody said she was bewitched, he never dreamed that she could bewitch him. For what indeed could a prince do with a princess that had lost her gravity! Who could tell what she might not lose next? She might lose her visibility, or her tangibility; or, in short, the power of making impressions upon the radical sensorium; so that he should never be able to tell whether she was dead or alive. Of course he made no further inquiries about her.

One day he lost sight of his retinue in a great forest. These forests are very useful in delivering princes from their courtiers, like a sieve that keeps back the bran. Then the princes get away to follow their fortune. In this they have the advantage of the princesses who are forced to marry before they have had a bit of fun. I wish our princesses got lost in a forest sometimes.

One lovely evening, after wandering about for many days, he found that he was approaching the outskirts of this forest; for the trees had got so thin that he could see the sunset through them; and he soon came upon a kind of heath. Next he came upon signs of human neighborhood; but by this time it was getting late and there was nobody in the fields to direct him.

After traveling for another hour, his horse, quite worn out with long labor and lack of food, fell, and was unable to rise again. So he continued his journey on foot. At length he entered another wood—not a wild forest, but a civilized wood, through which a foot-path led him to the side of a lake. Along this path the prince pursued his way through the gathering darkness. Suddenly he paused, and listened. Strange sounds came across the water. It was, in fact, the princess laughing. Now there was something odd in her laugh, as I have already hinted; for the hatching of a really hearty laugh requires the incubation of gravity; and perhaps this was how the prince mistook the laughing for screaming. Looking over the lake he saw something white in the water; and, in an instant, he had torn off his tunic, kicked off his sandals, and plunged in. He soon reached the white object and found that it was a woman. There was not light enough to show that she was a princess but quite enough to show that she was a lady, for it does not want much light to see that.

Now I cannot tell how it came about—whether she pretended to be drowning, or whether he frightened her, or caught her so as to embarrass her—but certainly he brought her to shore in a fashion ignominious to a swimmer, and more nearly drowned than she had ever expected to be; for the water had got into her throat as often as she had tried to speak.

At the place to which he bore her, the bank was only a foot or two above the lake; so he gave her a strong lift out of the water, to lay her on the bank. But, her gravitation ceasing the moment she left the water, away she went up into the air, scolding and screaming.

"You naughty, *naughty*, NAUGHTY, NAUGHTY man!" she cried.

No one had ever succeeded in putting her into a passion before. When the prince saw her ascend, he thought he must have been bewitched and have mistaken a great swan for a lady. But the princess caught hold of the topmost cone upon a lofty fir. This came off; but she caught at another; and, in fact, stopped herself by gathering cones, dropping them as the stalks gave way. The prince, meantime, stood in the water, staring and forgetting to get out. But the princess disappearing, he scrambled on shore and went in the direction of the tree. There he found her climbing down one of the branches toward the stem. But in the darkness of the wood, the prince continued in some bewilderment as to what the phenomenon

Dorothy Lathrop

The son of a king set out to look for the daughter of a queen.

[See page 113]

ould be; until, reaching the ground, and seeing him standing there, he caught hold of him and said: "I'll tell papa."

"Oh, no, you won't!" returned the prince.

"Yes, I will," she persisted. "What business had you to pull me down out of the water and throw me to the bottom of the air? I never did you any harm."

"Pardon me. I did not mean to hurt you."

"I don't believe you have any brains; and that is a worse loss than our wretched gravity. I pity you."

The prince now saw that he had come upon the bewitched princess and had already offended her. But before he could think what to say next, she burst out angrily, giving a stamp with her foot that would have sent her aloft again but for the hold she had of his arm:

"Put me up directly."

"Put you up where, you beauty?" asked the prince.

He had fallen in love with her almost, already; for her anger made her more charming than anyone else had ever beheld her; and, as far as he could see, which certainly was not far, she had not a single fault about her, except, of course, that she had not any gravity. No prince, however, would judge of a princess by weight. The loveliness of her foot he would hardly estimate by the depth of the impression it could make in mud.

"Put you up where, you beauty?" asked the prince.

"In the water, you stupid!" answered the princess.

"Come, then," said the prince.

The condition of her dress, increasing her usual difficulty in walking, compelled her to cling to him; and he could hardly persuade himself that he was not in a delightful dream, notwithstanding the torrent of musical abuse with which she overwhelmed him. The prince being therefore in no hurry, they came upon the lake at quite another part where the bank was twenty-five feet high at least; and when they had reached the edge, he turned toward the princess, and said: "How am I to put you in?"

"That is your business," she answered, quite snappishly. "You took me out—put me in again."

"Very well," said the prince; and catching her up in his arms he sprang with her from the rock. The princess had just time to give one delighted shriek of laughter before the water closed over them. When they came to the surface, she found that, for a moment or two, she could not even laugh, for she had gone down with such a rush that it was with difficulty she recovered her breath. The instant they reached the surface—

"How do you like falling in?" said the prince.

After some effort the princess panted out:

"Is that what you call *falling in?*"

"Yes," answered the prince, "I should think it a very tolerable specimen."

"It seemed to me like going up," rejoined she.

"My feeling was certainly one of elevation, too," the prince conceded.

The princess did not appear to understand him, for she retorted with his question: "How do *you* like falling in?"

"Beyond everything," answered he, "for I have fallen in with the only perfect creature I ever saw."

"No more of that; I am tired of it," said the princess.

Perhaps she shared her father's aversion to punning.

"Don't you like falling in, then?" said the prince.

"It is the most delightful fun I ever had in my life," answered she. "I never fell before. I wish I could learn. To think I am the only person in my father's kingdom that can't fall!"

Here the poor princess looked almost sad.

"I shall be most happy to fall in with you any time you like," said the prince devotedly.

"Thank you. I don't know. Perhaps it would not be proper. But I don't care. At all events, as we have fallen in, let us have a swim together."

"With all my heart," responded the prince.

And away they went, swimming and diving and floating, until at last they heard cries along the shore, and saw lights glancing in all directions. It was now quite late and there was no moon.

"I must go home," said the princess. "I am very sorry, for this is delightful."

"So am I," returned the prince. "But I am glad I haven't a home to go to—at least, I don't exactly know where it is."

"I wish I hadn't one either," rejoined the princess; "it is so stupid! I have a great mind," she continued, "to play them all a trick. Why couldn't they leave me alone? They won't trust me in the lake for a single night! You see where that green light is burning? That is the window of my room. Now if you would just swim there with me very quietly, and when we are all but under the balcony give me such a push—*up* you call it—as you did a little while ago, I should be able to catch hold of the balcony and get in at the window; and then they may look for me till tomorrow morning!"

"With more obedience than pleasure," said the prince gallantly; and away they swam, very gently.

"Will you be in the lake tomorrow night?" the prince ventured to ask.

"To be sure I will. I don't think so. Perhaps," was the princess's somewhat strange answer.

But the prince was intelligent enough not to press her further; and merely whispered as he gave her the parting lift, "Don't tell." The only answer the princess returned was a roguish look. She was already a yard above his head. The look seemed to say, "Never fear. It is too good fun to spoil that way."

So perfectly like other people had she been in the water that even yet the prince could scarcely believe his eyes when he saw her ascend slowly, grasp the balcony, and disappear through the window. He turned, almost expecting to see her still by his side. But he was alone in the water. So he swam away quietly and watched the lights moving about the shore for hours after the princess was safe in her chamber. As soon as they disappeared he landed in search of his tunic and sword, and after some trouble found them again. Then he made the best of his way round the lake to the other side. There the wood was wilder and the shore steeper—rising more immediately toward the mountains which surrounded the lake on all sides, and kept sending it messages of silvery streams from morning to night, and all night long. He soon found a spot where he could see the green light in the princess's room, and where even in the broad day-

light he would be in no danger of being discovered from the oppo
site shore. It was a sort of cave in the rock, where he provided him
self a bed of withered leaves and lay down too tired for hunger t
keep him awake. All night long he dreamed that he was swimming
with the princess.

X

LOOK AT THE MOON

EARLY the next morning the prince set out to look for something
to eat which he soon found at a forester's hut, where for many day
following he was supplied with all that a brave prince could conside
necessary. And having plenty to keep him alive for the present, h
would not think of wants not yet in existence.

Whenever Care intruded, this prince always bowed him out i
the most princely manner.

When he returned from his breakfast to his watch-cave, he saw
the princess already floating about in the lake, attended by the kin
and queen—whom he knew by their crowns—and a great compan
in lovely little boats with canopies of all the colors of the rainbow
and flags and streamers of a great many more. It was a very brigh
day, and soon the prince, burned up with the heat, began to lon
for the cold water and the cool princess. But he had to endure ti
twilight; for the boats had provisions on board, and it was not ti
the sun went down that the gay party began to vanish. Boat afte
boat drew away to the shore, following that of the king and quee
till only one, apparently the princess's own boat, remained. But sh
did not want to go home even yet, and the prince thought he saw
her order the boat to the shore without her. At all events, it rowe
away; and now, of all the radiant company, only one white spec
remained. Then the prince began to sing.

And this is what he sang:

"Lady fair,
Swan-white,
Lift thine eyes,

Banish night
By the might
Of thine eyes.

"Snowy arms,
Oars of snow,
Oar her hither,
Plashing low.
Soft and slow,
Oar her hither.

"Stream behind her
O'er the lake,
Radiant whiteness!
In her wake
Following, following for her sake,
Radiant whiteness!

"Cling about her,
Waters blue;
Part not from her,
But renew
Cold and true
Kisses round her.

"Lap me round,
Waters sad
That have left her
Make me glad,
For ye had
Kissed her ere ye left her."

Before he had finished his song, the princess was just under the place where he sat, and looking up to find him. Her ears had led her truly.

"Would you like a fall, princess?" said the prince, looking down.

"Ah, there you are! Yes, if you please, prince," said the princess, looking up.

"How do you know I am a prince, princess?" said the prince.

"Because you are a very nice young man, prince," said the princess.

"Come up then, princess."

"Fetch me, prince."

The prince took off his scarf, then his swordbelt, then his tunic, and tied them all together, and let them down. But the line was far too short. He unwound his turban and added it to the rest, when it was all but long enough; and his purse completed it. The princess just managed to lay hold of the knot of money and was beside him in a moment. This rock was much higher than the other, and the splash and the dive were tremendous. The princess was in ecstasies of delight, and their swim was delicious.

Night after night they met and swam about in the dark clear lake; where, such was the prince's gladness that (whether the princess's way of looking at things infected him, or he was actually getting light-headed) he often fancied that he was swimming in the sky instead of the lake. But when he talked about being in heaven the princess laughed at him dreadfully.

When the moon came, she brought them fresh pleasure. Everything looked strange and new in her light, with an old, withered, yet unfading newness. When the moon was nearly full, one of their great delights was to dive deep in the water, and then, turning round, look up through it at the great blot of light close above them, shimmering and trembling and wavering, spreading and contracting, seeming to melt away, and again grow solid. Then they would shoot up through the blot; and lo! there was the moon, far off, clear and steady and cold, and very lovely, at the bottom of a deeper and bluer lake than theirs, as the princess said.

The prince soon found out that while in the water the princess was very like other people. And besides this, she was not so forward in her questions or pert in her replies at sea as on shore. Neither did she laugh so much; and when she did laugh, it was more gently. She seemed altogether more modest and maidenly in the water than out of it. But when the prince, who had really fallen in love when he fell in the lake, began to talk to her about love, she always turned her head toward him and laughed. After a while she began to look puzzled, as if she were trying to understand what he meant but could not—revealing a notion that he meant something. But as soon as ever she left the lake she was so altered that the prince said to himself, "If I marry her, I see no help for it: we must turn merman and mermaid and go to sea at once."

XI

HISS!

THE princess's pleasure in the lake had grown to a passion and she could scarcely bear to be out of it for an hour. Imagine, then, her consternation, when, diving with the prince one night, a sudden suspicion seized her that the lake was not so deep as it used to be. The prince could not imagine what had happened. She shot to the surface and, without a word, swam at full speed toward the higher side of the lake. He followed, begging to know if she was ill or what was the matter. She never turned her head, or took the smallest notice of his question. Arrived at the shore, she coasted the rocks with minute inspection. But she was not able to come to a conclusion, for the moon was very small and so she could not see well. She turned therefore and swam home without saying a word to explain her conduct to the prince, of whose presence she seemed no longer conscious. He withdrew to his cave in great perplexity and distress.

Next day she made many observations, which, alas! strengthened her fears. She saw that the banks were too dry; and that the grass on the shore and the trailing plants on the rocks were withering away. She caused marks to be made along the borders and examined them, day after day, in all directions of the wind; till at last the horrible idea became a certain fact—the surface of the lake was slowly sinking.

The poor princess nearly went out of the little mind which she had. It was awful to her to see the lake, which she loved more than any living thing, lie dying before her eyes. It sank away, slowly vanishing. The tops of rocks that had never been seen till now began to appear, far down in the clear water. Before long they were dry in the sun. It was fearful to think of the mud that would soon lie there baking and festering, full of lovely creatures dying and ugly creatures coming to life, like the unmaking of a world. And how hot the sun would be without any lake. She could not bear to swim in it any more and began to pine away. Her life seemed bound up with it; and ever as the lake sank, she pined. People said she would not live an hour after the lake was gone. But she never cried.

Proclamation was made to all the kingdom that whosoever should discover the cause of the lake's decrease would be rewarded after a princely fashion. Hum-Drum and Kopy-Keck applied themselves to their physics and metaphysics; but in vain. Not even they could suggest a cause.

Now the fact was that the old princess was at the root of the mischief. When she heard that her niece found more pleasure in the water than anyone else had out of it, she went into a rage and cursed herself for her want of foresight.

"But," said she, "I will soon set all right. The King and the people shall die of thirst; their brains shall boil and frizzle in their skulls before I will lose my revenge."

And she laughed a ferocious laugh that made the hairs on the back of her black cat stand erect with terror.

Then she went to an old chest in the room, and opening it, took out what looked like a piece of dried seaweed. This she threw into a tub of water. Then she threw some powder into the water and stirred it with her bare arm, muttering over it words of hideous sound, and yet more hideous import. Next she set the tub aside and took from the chest a huge bunch of a hundred rusty keys that clattered in her shaking hands. Then she sat down and proceeded to oil them all. Before she had finished, out from the tub, the water of which had kept on in a slow motion ever since she had ceased stirring it, came the head and half the body of a huge gray snake. But the witch did not look round. It grew out of the tub, waving itself backwards and forwards with a slow horizontal motion till it reached the old princess, when it laid its head upon her shoulder, and gave a low hiss in her ear. She started—but with joy; and seeing the head resting on her shoulder, drew it toward her and kissed it. Then she drew it all out of the tub and wound it round her body. It was one of those dreadful creatures which few have ever beheld— The White Snakes of Darkness.

Then she took the keys and went down to her cellar; and as she unlocked the door she said to herself:

"This *is* worth living for!"

Locking the door behind her, she descended a few steps into the cellar, and, crossing it, unlocked another door into a dark, narrow passage. She locked this also behind her and descended a few more steps. If anyone had followed the witch-princess, he would have heard her unlock exactly one hundred doors and descend a few steps after unlocking each. When she had unlocked the last, she entered a vast cave, the roof of which was supported by huge natural pillars of rock. Now this roof was the under side of the bottom of the lake.

She then untwined the snake from her body and held it by the tail high above her. The hideous creature stretched up its head toward the roof of the cavern which it was just able to reach. It then began to move its head backwards and forwards with a slow oscillating motion as if looking for something. At the same moment the witch began to walk round and round the cavern, coming nearer to the center every circuit, while the head of the snake described the same path over the roof that she did on the floor, for she kept holding it up. And still it kept slowly oscillating. Round and round the cavern they went, ever lessening the circuit, till at last the snake made a sudden dart, and clung to the roof with its mouth. That's right, my beauty!" cried the princess; "drain it dry."

She let it go, left it hanging, and sat down on a great stone, with her black cat, which had followed her all round the cave, by her side. Then she began to knit and mutter awful words. The snake hung like a huge leech, sucking at the stone; the cat stood with his back arched and his tail like a piece of cable, looking up at the snake; and the old woman sat and knitted and muttered. Seven days and seven nights they remained thus; when suddenly the serpent dropped from the roof as if exhausted, and shriveled up till it was again like a piece of dried seaweed. The witch started to her feet, picked it up, put it in her pocket, and looked up at the roof. One drop of water was trembling on the spot where the snake had been sucking. As soon as she saw that, she turned and fled, followed by her cat. Shutting the door in a terrible hurry, she locked it, and having muttered some frightful words, sped to the next, which she also locked and muttered over; and so with all the hundred doors, till she arrived in her own cellar. Then she sat down on the floor ready to faint, but listening with malicious delight to the rushing of the water which she could hear distinctly through all the hundred doors.

But this was not enough. Now that she had tasted revenge, she lost her patience. Without further measures, the lake would be too long in disappearing. So the next night, with the last shred of the dying old moon rising, she took some of the water in which she had revived the snake, put it in a bottle and set out, accompanied by her cat. Before morning she had made the entire circuit of the lake, muttering fearful words as she crossed every stream and casting into it some of the water out of her bottle. When she had finished the circuit she muttered yet again, and flung a handful of water toward the moon. Thereupon every spring in the country ceased to throb and bubble, dying away like the pulse of a dying man. The next day there was no sound of falling water to be heard along the borders of the lake. The very courses were dry; and the mountains showed no silvery streaks down their dark sides. And not alone had the fountains of Mother Earth ceased to flow; for all the babies throughout the country were crying dreadfully—only without tears.

XII

WHERE IS THE PRINCE?

NEVER since the night when the princess left him so abruptly had the prince had a single interview with her. He had seen her once or twice in the lake; but, as far as he could discover, she had not been in it any more at night. He had sat and sung and looked in vain for his Nereid; while she, like a true Nereid, was wasting away with her lake, sinking as it sank, withering as it dried. When at length he discovered the change that was taking place in the level of the water, he was in great alarm and perplexity. He could not tell whether the lake was dying because the lady had forsaken it; or whether the lady would not come because the lake had begun to sink. But he resolved to know this much at least.

He disguised himself, and, going to the palace, requested to see the lord chamberlain. His appearance at once gained his request; and the lord chamberlain, being a man of some insight, perceived that there was more in the prince's solicitation than met the ear. He felt likewise that no one could tell whence a solution of the present difficulties might arise. So he granted the prince's prayer to be made shoeblack to the princess. It was rather cunning in the prince to request such an easy post, for the princess could not possibly soil as many shoes as other princesses.

He soon learned all that could be told about the princess. He went nearly distracted; but after roaming about the lake for days and diving in every depth that remained, all that he could do was to put an extra polish on the dainty pair of boots that was never called for.

For the princess kept to her room, with the curtains drawn to shut out the dying lake. But she could not shut it out of her mind for a moment. It haunted her imagination so that she felt as if the lake were her soul, drying up within her, first to mud, then to madness and death. She thus brooded over the change with all its dreadful accompaniments, till she was nearly distracted. As for the prince, she had forgotten him. However much she had enjoyed his company in the water, she did not care for him without it. And she seemed to have forgotten her father and mother, too.

The lake went on sinking. Small slimy spots began to appear, which glittered steadily amidst the changeful shine of the water. These grew to broad patches of mud which widened and spread, with rocks here and there, and floundering fishes and crawling eels swarming. The people went everywhere catching these, and looking for anything that might have dropped from the royal boats.

At length the lake was all but gone, only a few of the deepest pools remained unexhausted.

It happened one day that a party of youngsters found themselves on the brink of one of these pools in the very center of the lake. It was a rocky basin of considerable depth. Looking in, they saw at the bottom something that shone yellow in the sun. A little boy jumped in and dived for it. It was a plate of gold covered with writing. They carried it to the king.

On one side of it stood these words:

> "Death alone from death can save.
> Love is death, and so is brave.
> Love can fill the deepest grave.
> Love loves on beneath the wave."

Now this was enigmatical enough to the king and courtiers. But the reverse of the plate explained it a little. Its writing amounted to this:

"If the lake should disappear, they must find the hole through which the water ran. But it would be useless to try to stop it by any ordinary means. There was but one effectual mode. The body of a living man could alone stanch the flow. The man must give himself of his own will; and the lake must take his life as it filled. Otherwise the offering would be of no avail. If the nation could not provide one hero, it was time it should perish."

XIII

HERE I AM

THIS was a very disheartening revelation to the king—not that he was unwilling to sacrifice a subject, but that he was hopeless of finding a man willing to sacrifice himself. No time was to be lost, however, for the princess was lying motionless on her bed, and taking no nourishment but lake water, which was now none of the best. Therefore the king caused the contents of the wonderful plate of gold to be published throughout the country.

No one, however, came forward.

The prince, having gone several days' journey into the forest to consult a hermit whom he had met there on his way to Lagobel, knew nothing of the oracle till his return.

When he had acquainted himself with all the particulars he sat down and thought:

"She will die if I don't do it, and life would be nothing to me without her; so I shall lose nothing by doing it. And life will be as pleasant to her as ever, for she will soon forget me. And there will be so much more beauty and happiness in the world!—To be sure, I shall not see it." (Here the poor prince gave a sigh.) "How lovely the lake will be in the moonlight, with that glorious creature sporting in it like a wild goddess!—It is rather hard to be drowned by inches, though. Let me see—that will be seventy inches of me to drown." (Here he tried to laugh, but could not.) "The longer the better, however," he resumed; "for can I not bargain that the princess shall be beside me all the time? So I shall see her once more, kiss her perhaps—who knows?—and die looking in her eyes. It will be no death. At least, I shall not feel it. And to see the lake filling for the beauty again!—All right! I am ready."

He kissed the princess's boot, laid it down, and hurried to the king's apartment. But feeling, as he went, that anything sentimental would be disagreeable, he resolved to carry off the whole affair with nonchalance. So he knocked at the door of the king's counting-house, where it was all but a capital crime to disturb him.

When the king heard the knock he started up and opened the door in a rage. Seeing only the shoeblack, he drew his sword. This, I am sorry to say, was his usual mode of asserting his regality when he thought his dignity was in danger. But the prince was not in the least alarmed.

"Please, your Majesty, I'm your butler," said he.

"My butler, you lying rascal! What do you mean?"

"I mean, I will cork your big bottle."

"Is the fellow mad?" bawled the king, raising the point of his sword.

"I will put the stopper—plug—what you call it, in your leaky lake, grand monarch," said the prince.

The king drew his sword.

The king was in such a rage that before he could speak he had time to cool and to reflect that it would be a great waste to kill the only man who was willing to be useful in the present emergency, seeing that in the end the insolent fellow would be as dead as if he had died by his Majesty's own hand.

"Oh!" he said at last, putting up his sword with difficulty, it was so long; "I am obliged to you, you young fool! Take a glass of wine?"

"No, thank you," replied the prince.

"Very well," said the king. "Would you like to run and see your parents before you make your experiment?"

"No, thank you," said the prince.

"Then we will go and look for the hole at once," said his Majesty, and proceeded to call some attendants.

"Stop, please your Majesty; I have a condition to make," interposed the prince.

"What!" exclaimed the king, "A condition, and with me! How dare you?"

"As you please," returned the prince coyly. "I wish your Majesty a good morning."

"You wretch! I will have you put in a sack, and stuck in the hole."

"Very well, your Majesty," replied the prince, becoming a little more respectful, lest the wrath of the king should deprive him of the pleasure of dying for the princess. "But what good will that do your Majesty? Please to remember that the oracle says the victim must offer himself."

"Well, you *have* offered yourself," retorted the king.

"Yes, upon one condition."

"Condition again!" roared the king, once more drawing his sword. "Begone! Somebody else will be glad to take the honor off your shoulders."

"Your Majesty knows it will not be easy to get another to take my place."

"Well, what is your condition?" growled the king, feeling that the prince was right.

"Only this," replied the prince; "that as I must on no account die before I am fairly drowned and the waiting will be rather wearisome, the princess, your daughter, shall go with me, feed me with her own hands, and look at me now and then to comfort me; for you must confess it *is* rather hard. As soon as the water is up to my eyes, she may go and be happy, and forget her poor shoeblack."

Here the prince's voice faltered, and he very nearly grew sentimental, in spite of his resolution.

"Why didn't you tell me before what your condition was? Such a fuss about nothing!" exclaimed the king.

"Do you grant it?" persisted the prince.

"Of course I do," replied the king.

"Very well. I am ready."

"Go and have some dinner, then, while I set my people to find the place."

The king ordered out his guards and gave directions to the officers to find the hole in the lake at once. So the bed of the lake was marked out in divisions and thoroughly examined, and in an hour or so the hole was discovered. It was in the middle of a stone, near the center of the lake, in the very pool where the golden plate had been found. It was a three-cornered hole of no great size. There was water all round the stone but very little was flowing through the hole.

XIV

THIS IS VERY KIND OF YOU

The prince went to dress for the occasion, for he was resolved to die like a prince.

When the princess heard that a man had offered to die for her, she was so transported that she jumped off the bed, feeble as she was, and danced about the room for joy. She did not care who the man was; that was nothing to her. The hole wanted stopping; and if only a man would do, why, take one. In an hour or two more everything was ready. Her maid dressed her in haste and they carried her to the side of the lake. When she saw it she shrieked and covered her face with her hands. They bore her across to the stone where they had already placed a little boat for her. The water was not deep enough to float it, but they hoped it would be before long.

They laid her on cushions, placed in the boat wines and fruits and other nice things, and stretched a canopy over all.

In a few minutes the prince appeared. The princess recognized him at once but did not think it worth while to acknowledge him.

"Here I am," said the prince. "Put me in."

"They told me it was a shoeblack," said the princess.

"So I am," said the prince. "I blacked your little boots three times a day, because they were all I could get of you. Put me in."

The courtiers did not resent his bluntness except by saying to each other that he was taking it out in impudence.

But how was he to be put in? The golden plate contained no instructions on this point. The prince looked at the hole and saw but one way. He put both his legs into it, sitting on the stone, and, stooping forward, covered the corner that remained open with his two hands. In this uncomfortable position he resolved to abide his fate, and turning to the people, said:

"Now you can go."

The king had already gone home to dinner.

"Now you can go," repeated the princess after him, like a parrot. The people obeyed her and went.

Presently a little wave flowed over the stone, and wetted one of the prince's knees. But he did not mind it much. He began to sing, and the song he sang was this:

> "As a world that has no well,
> Darkly bright in forest dell;
> As a world without the gleam
> Of the downward-going stream;
> As a world without the glance
> Of the ocean's fair expanse;
> As a world where never rain
> Glittered on the sunny plain;—
> Such, my heart, thy world would be,
> If no love did flow in thee.
>
> "As a world without the sound
> Of the rivulets underground;
> Or the bubbling of the spring
> Out of darkness wandering;

Or the mighty rush and flowing
Of the river's downward going;
Or the music-showers that drop
On the outspread beech's top;
Or the ocean's mighty voice,
When his lifted waves rejoice;—
Such, my soul, thy world would be,
If no love did sing in thee.

"Lady, keep thy world's delight;
Keep the waters in thy sight.
Love hath made me strong to go,
For thy sake, to realms below,
Where the water's shine and hum
Through the darkness never come.
Let, I pray, one thought of me
Spring, a little well, in thee;
Lest thy loveless soul be found
Like a dry and thirsty ground."

"Sing again, prince. It makes it less tedious," said the princess.

But the prince was too much overcome to sing any more, and a long pause followed.

"This is very kind of you, prince," said the princess at last, quite coolly, as she lay in the boat with her eyes shut.

"I am sorry I can't return the compliment," thought the prince; "but you are worth dying for, after all."

Again a wavelet, and another, and another flowed over the stone and wetted both the prince's knees; but he did not speak or move. Two—three—four hours passed in this way, the princess apparently asleep and the prince very patient. But he was much disappointed in his position, for he had none of the consolation he had hoped for.

At last he could bear it no longer. "Princess!" said he.

But at that moment up started the princess, crying:

"I'm afloat! I'm afloat!"

And the little boat bumped against the stone.

"Princess!" repeated the prince, encouraged at seeing her wide awake and looking eagerly at the water.

"Well?" said she, without looking round.

"Your papa promised that you should look at me, and you haven't looked at me once."

"Did he? Then I suppose I must. But I am sleepy!"

"Sleep then, darling, and don't mind me," said the poor prince.

"Really, you are very good," replied the princess. "I think I will go to sleep again."

"Just give me a glass of wine and a biscuit first," said the prince, very humbly.

"With all my heart," said the princess, and gaped as she said it. She got the wine and the biscuit, however, and, leaning over the side of the boat toward him, was compelled to look at him.

"Why, prince," she said, "you don't look well! Are you sure you don't mind it?"

"Not a bit," answered he, feeling very faint indeed. "Only I shall die before it is of any use to you, unless I have something to eat."

"There, then," said she, holding out the wine to him.

"Ah! you must feed me. I dare not move my hands. The water would run away directly."

"Good gracious!" said the princess; and she began at once to feed him with bits of biscuit and sips of wine.

As she fed him, he contrived to kiss the tips of her fingers now and then. She did not seem to mind it, one way or the other. But the prince felt better.

"Now, for your own sake, princess," said he, "I cannot let you go to sleep. You must sit and look at me, else I shall not be able to keep up."

"Well, I will do anything to oblige you," answered she, with condescension; and, sitting down, she did look at him and kept looking at him with wonderful steadiness, considering all things.

The sun went down and the moon rose, and gush after gush the waters were rising up the prince's body. They were up to his waist now.

"Why can't we go and have a swim?" said the princess. "There seems to be water enough just about here."

"I shall never swim more," said the prince.

"Oh, I forgot," said the princess, and was silent.

So the water grew and grew, and rose up and up on the prince.
And the princess sat and looked at him. She fed him now and then.
The night wore on. The waters rose and rose. The moon rose likewise higher and higher and shone full on the face of the dying
prince. The water was up to his neck.

"Will you kiss me, princess?" said he feebly.

The nonchalance was all gone now.

"Yes, I will," answered the princess, and kissed him with a long,
sweet, cold kiss.

"Now," said he, with a sight of content, "I die happy."

He did not speak again. The princess gave him some wine for the last
time: he was past eating. Then she
sat down again and looked at him.
The water rose and rose. It touched
his chin. It touched his lower lip.
It touched between his lips. He shut
them hard to keep it out. The princess began to feel strange. It touched
his upper lip. He breathed through
his nostrils. The princess looked
wild. It covered his nostrils. Her

"Will you kiss me, princess?"

eyes looked scared, and shone strange in the moonlight. His head fell
back; the water closed over it and the bubbles of his last breath bub-
bled up through the water. The princess gave a shriek, and sprang
into the lake.

She laid hold first of one leg, and then of the other, and pulled and
tugged but she could not move either. She stopped to take breath,
and that made her think that he could not get any breath. She was
frantic. She got hold of him and held his head above the water,
which was possible now his hands were no longer on the hole. But
it was of no use, for he was past breathing.

Love and water brought back all her strength. She got under the
water, and pulled and pulled with her whole might, till at last she

got one leg out. The other easily followed. How she got him into the boat she never could tell; but when she did she fainted away. Coming to herself, she seized the oars, kept herself steady as best she could, and rowed and rowed, though she had never rowed before. Round rocks, and over shallows, and through mud she rowed, till she got to the landing-stairs of the palace. By this time her people were on the shore, for they had heard her shriek. She made them carry the prince to her own room, and lay him on her bed, and light a fire, and send for the doctors.

"But the lake, your highness!" said the chamberlain, who, roused by the noise, came in, in his nightcap.

"Go and drown yourself in it!" she said.

This was the last rudeness of which the princess was ever guilty; and one must allow that she had good cause to feel provoked with the lord chamberlain.

Had it been the king himself, he would have fared no better. But both he and the queen were fast asleep. And the chamberlain went back to his bed. Somehow, the doctors never came. So the princess and her old nurse were left with the prince. But the old nurse was a wise woman and knew what to do.

They tried everything for a long time without success. The princess was nearly distracted between hope and fear, but she tried on and on, one thing after another, and everything over and over again.

At last, when they had all but given it up, just as the sun rose, the prince opened his eyes.

XV

LOOK AT THE RAIN!

THE princess burst into a passion of tears and *fell* on the floor. There she lay for an hour, and her tears never ceased. All the pent-up crying of her life was spent now. And a rain came on, such as had never been seen in that country. The sun shone all the time, and the great drops, which fell straight to the earth, shone likewise. The palace was in the heart of a rainbow. It was a rain of rubies, and sapphires, and emeralds, and topazes. The torrents poured from the

mountains like molten gold; and if it had not been for its subterranean outlet, the lake would have overflowed and inundated the country. It was full from shore to shore.

But the princess did not heed the lake. She lay on the floor and
wept. And this rain within doors was far more wonderful than the
rain out of doors. For when it abated a little, and she proceeded to
rise, she found to her astonishment that she could not. At length after
many efforts she succeeded in getting upon her feet; but she tumbled
down again directly. Hearing her fall, her old nurse uttered a yell
of delight and ran to her, screaming:

"My darling child, she's found her gravity!"

"Oh, that's it, is it?" said the princess, rubbing her shoulder and
her knee alternately. "I consider it very unpleasant. I feel as if I
should be crushed to pieces."

"Hurrah!" cried the prince from the bed. "If you've come round,
princess, so have I. How's the lake?"

"Brimful," answered the nurse.

"Then we're all happy."

"That we are indeed!" answered the princess, sobbing.

And there was rejoicing all over the country that rainy day. Even
the babies forgot their past troubles, and danced and crowed amazingly. And the king told stories, and the queen listened to them.
And he divided the money in his box, and she the honey in her pot,
among all the children. And there was such jubilation as was never
heard of before.

Of course the prince and princess were betrothed at once. But the
princess had to learn to walk before they could be married with any
propriety. And this was not so easy at her time of life, for she could
walk no more than a baby. She was always falling down and hurt-
ing herself.

"Is this the gravity you used to make so much of?" said she one
day to the prince, as he raised her from the floor. "For my part, I
was a great deal more comfortable without it."

"No, no, that's not it. This is it," replied the prince, as he took
her up and carried her about like a baby, kissing her all the time.
"This is gravity."

"That's better," said she. "I don't mind that so much."

And she smiled the sweetest, loveliest smile in the prince's face. And she gave him one kiss in return for all his; and he thought them overpaid, for he was beside himself with delight. I fear she complained of her gravity more than once after this, notwithstanding.

It was a long time before she got reconciled to walking. But the pain of learning it was quite counterbalanced by two things, either of which would have been sufficient consolation. The first was, that the prince himself was her teacher; and the second, that she could tumble into the lake as often as she pleased. Still, she preferred to have the prince jump in with her; and the splash they made before was nothing to the splash they made now.

The lake never sank again. In process of time, it wore the roof of the cavern quite through, and was twice as deep as before.

The only revenge the princess took upon her aunt was to tread pretty hard on her gouty toe the next time she saw her. But she was sorry for it the very next day, when she heard that the water had undermined her house, and that it had fallen in the night, burying her in its ruins; whence no one ever ventured to dig up her body. There she lies to this day.

So the prince and the princess lived and were happy; and had crowns of gold, and clothes of gold, and shoes of leather, and children of boys and girls, not one of whom was ever known, on the most critical occasion, to lose the smallest atom of his or her due proportion of gravity.

Dreams and Enchantments

THE SELLER OF DREAMS

By *HENRY BESTON*

Illustration by WARREN CHAPPELL

ONCE upon a time a mother called her only son into the kitchen, gave him a basket of fine, fresh eggs, and bade him carry them to his Aunt Jane, who lived a few miles down the valley. The son, a lively lad about twelve years of age, obeyed his mother with joy, and clapping his little green hat on his head, stepped forth into the road. It was a beautiful clear morning in the spring, and the earth, released from the icy chains of winter, was rejoicing in her freedom and the return of the sun. A few birds, just back from the southland, rocked on twigs swollen with bursting buds, a thousand rills flowing from everywhere and in every direction sparkled and sang, and the air was sweet with the odor of plowed fields.

The boy, whose name was Peter, walked along whistling. Suddenly he saw a spot on the road shining as dazzlingly as if a bit of the sun itself had fallen to the earth. "A bit of glass," thought Peter. But it was not a bit of glass after all, but a fine golden florin which must have dropped from somebody's purse.

Peter stooped, picked up the gold piece, put it in his pocket, and walked off whistling louder than ever. In a little while he came to a place where the road wound down a little hill, and Peter saw, trudging up this hill, a very strange-looking old man. He was a very old man; his face was puckered up into a thousand wrinkles, like the skin of a shrunken apple, and he had long, snow-white hair and a white beard which reached almost to his waist. Moreover, he was strangely dressed in a robe of cherry scarlet, and wore golden shoes. From a kind of belt hung two horns on silver chains, one an ordinary cow's horn, the other a beautiful horn carved of the whitest ivory, and decorated with little figures of men and animals.

"I'll have one please," said Peter.

"Dreams to sell! Dreams to sell!" called out the old man as he caught sight of Peter. "Don't you want to buy a dream, young man?"

"What kind of dreams have you?" asked Peter.

"Good, bad, true, false—all kinds," replied the seller of dreams. "I have even thrilling nightmares. Dreams to sell! Dreams to sell!"

"How much does a dream cost?" asked Peter.

"A golden florin," answered the merchant.

"I'll have one, please," said Peter; and he handed over the florin.

The old man took a kind of wonderful sugar-plum out of the ivory horn, and gave it to Peter to eat. "You will have the dream next time you sleep," said he, and trudged on.

So Peter continued his journey, stopping every once in a while to look back at the strange old man, who was slowly climbing the hill. At length Peter came to a little quiet grove of pines, and there he sat down on a big stone and ate the luncheon which his mother had prepared for him. The sun was high in the heavens; it was close on to high noon. Now, as Peter was contentedly munching his bread and cheese, he heard, at first far away, then quite near at hand, the clear notes of a coachman's horn. The notes of the second call died away in a great pattering of hoofs and tinkling of little bells, and suddenly, arriving in a great swirl of yellow dust, came a magnificent coach drawn by twelve white horses. A lady, very richly dressed and wearing many sparkling diamonds, sat within the coach. To Peter's astonishment, the lady was his Aunt Jane.

The coach stopped with a great jingling of the twelve harnesses, and Aunt Jane leaned out of the window, and said to Peter, "What are you doing here, child?"

"I was on my way to your cottage with a basket of fresh eggs."

"Well, it's fortunate I found you," said Aunt Jane, "for I have given up living in the cottage, and have now got a castle of my own. Jump in, Peter, and don't forget your basket."

So Peter climbed into the coach, closed the door behind him, and was driven away. The coach went over hill and down dale; it went through strange forests from whose branches green parrots whooped and shrieked; it rolled through valleys in strange shining mountains. Peter stole a look at Aunt Jane and saw that she was wearing a crown.

"Are you a queen, Aunt Jane," he asked.

"Indeed, I am," replied his aunt. "You see, Peter, two days ago, while I was looking for my white cow which had strayed away, I came upon the magnificent castle to which we are now going. It has four beautiful towers, and a door set with diamonds. 'Whose castle is this?' I said to the lodge-keeper. 'It's nobody's, marm,' said he. 'What,' said I, 'do you mean to say nobody owns this fine castle?' 'That's just what I mean to say, marm,' answered he; 'the castle belongs to anyone who wants it.' So into the castle I walked, and I didn't go out, you may be sure, till I had been into every room that I could find. Then I put on these clothes and these diamonds, which I found in a cupboard, and went down and told the servants I intended to be queen. You see, Peter, dear, there's nothing that a woman of determination and energy can't accomplish."

The coach rolled on, and soon Peter caught sight of Aunt Jane's castle. It was rather large, and had an enormous round tower at each corner—a thing which brought to Peter's mind the picture of an elephant lying on its back. Peter and Aunt Jane, accompanied by a train of servants dressed in blue-and-buff livery, walked into the castle through the diamond-studded door.

"Do you think you could eat a little more of something?" said Aunt Jane, taking off her white kid gloves. "Because if you can I'll have a place set for you at the luncheon table."

And Peter, who like all boys, could eat a little more anywhere and at any time, readily answered, "Yes." So Peter and Aunt Jane sat down to a wonderful little table covered with a snow-white cloth.

"Draw your chair nearer, Peter dear," said Aunt Jane.

"I can't," said Peter, "it's stuck to the floor."

And so it was; the chair was stuck to the floor, and no amount of pushing or pulling could budge it.

"That's odd," said Aunt Jane; "but never mind, I'll push the table over to the chair."

But like the chair, the table refused to budge. Peter then tried to slide his plate of soup closer to him, but the plate, which the servant had placed on the cloth an instant before, had evidently frozen to the table in some extraordinary manner and could not be moved an inch. The soup in the plate, however, was not fastened to the dish, nor were the wonderful strawberry-cakes and the delicious ices with which the dinner closed.

"You don't suppose this castle is enchanted, do you, Aunt Jane?"

"Not a bit of it," replied Aunt Jane. "And even if it were," she continued recklessly, "I shouldn't mind, for there's nothing that a woman of determination and energy can't accomplish." There was a pause, and then Aunt Jane added, "I am going to have some guests to dinner this evening, so run round and amuse yourself as well as you can. There's ever so much to see in the castle, and in the garden there's a pond with swans in it."

Attended by her servants, Aunt Jane majestically walked away.

Peter spent the afternoon exploring the castle. He went through room after room; he scurried through the attics like a mouse, and was even lost for a while in the cellars. And everywhere he went, he found everything immovable. The beds, tables, and chairs could neither be moved about nor lifted up, and even the clocks and vases were mysteriously fastened to their places on the shelves.

The night came on. Coach after coach rolled up to the diamond door, which sparkled in the moonlight. When the guests had all arrived, a silver trumpet sounded, and Aunt Jane, dressed in a wonderful gown of flowering brocade edged with pearls, came solemnly down the great stairway of the castle hall. Two little black boys, dressed in oriental costume and wearing turbans, held up her gorgeous train, and she looked very grand indeed. Peter, to his great surprise, found himself dressed in a wonderful suit of plum-colored velvet.

"Welcome, my friends," said Queen Jane, who had opened a wonderful ostrich-feather fan. "Are we not fortunate in having so beautiful a night for our dinner?"

And the Queen, giving her arm to a splendid officer in the uniform of the King's dragoons, led the way to the banquet-hall.

The wonderful party, all silks and satins, and gleaming with jewels, swept like a peacock's tail behind her. Soon dinner was over, and the guests began to stray by twos and threes to the ballroom. Aunt Jane and the soldier led off the grand march; then came wonderful, stately minuets, quadrilles, and sweet old-fashioned waltzes. The merriment was at its height when somebody ran heavily up the great stairs leading to the ballroom; and the guests, turning round to see whence came the clatter, saw standing in the doorway a strange old man dressed in a robe of cherry scarlet and wearing golden shoes. It was the seller of dreams. His white hair was disheveled, his robe was awry, and there was dust on his golden shoes.

"Foolish people!" screamed the old seller of dreams, his voice rising to a shriek. "Run for your lives! This castle lies under a terrible enchantment; in a few minutes it will turn upside down. Have you not seen that everything is fastened to the floor? Run for your lives!"

Immediately there was a great babble of voices, some shrieks, and more confusion, and the guests ran pell-mell down the great stairs and out the castle door. To Peter's dismay, Aunt Jane was not among them. So into the castle he rushed again, calling at the top of his voice, "Aunt Jane! Aunt Jane!" He ran through the brilliantly lit and deserted ballroom; he saw himself running in the great mirrors of the gallery. "Aunt Jane!" he cried; but no Aunt Jane replied.

Peter rushed up the stairs leading to the castle tower, and emerged upon the balcony. He saw the black shadow of the castle thrown upon the grass far below by the full moon; he saw the great forest, so bright above and so dark and mysterious below, and the long snow-clad range of the Adamant Mountains. Suddenly a voice, louder than the voice of any human being, a voice deep, ringing, and solemn as the sound of a great bell, cried: "'Tis time!"

Immediately everything became as black as ink, people shrieked, the enchanted castle rolled like a ship at sea, and leaning far to one side, *began to turn upside down.* Peter felt the floor of the balcony tip beneath him; he tried to catch hold of something, but could find nothing; suddenly, with a scream, he fell. He was falling, falling, falling, falling, falling.

When Peter came to himself, instead of its being night, it was still noonday, and he was sitting on the same stone in the same quiet roadside grove from which he had caught sight of his Aunt Jane in her wonderful coach. A blue jay screamed at him from overhead. For Aunt Jane, the coach, and the enchanted castle had been only a dream. Peter, you see, had fallen asleep under the pines, and while he slept, he had dreamed the dream he purchased from the seller of dreams.

Very glad to be still alive, Peter rubbed his eyes, took up his basket of eggs, and went down the road whistling.

THE LOST HALF-HOUR

By HENRY BESTON

Illustrations by WARREN CHAPPELL

ONCE upon a time there was an old widow woman who had three sons: the first two were clever enough, but the third, Bobo by name, was little better than a silly simpleton. All his mother's scoldings and beatings—and she smacked the poor lad soundly a dozen times a day—did him no good whatever.

Now it came to pass that one morning Princess Zenza, the ruler of the land, happened to pass by the cottage and heard Bobo being given a terrible tongue-lashing. Curious as to the cause of all the noise, the Princess drew rein, and summoned Bobo's mother to come near. On hearing her story, it occurred to the Princess that so silly a lad might amuse her; so she gave the mother a golden florin, and took poor silly Bobo with her to be her page.

You may be sure that it did not take the wise folk at the castle long to discover how great a simpleton had arrived. Courtiers, footmen, lackeys, turnspits even, were forever sending him off on ridiculous errands. Now he would be sent to find a white crow's feather, or a spray of yellow bluebells; now he was ordered to look for a square wheel, or a glass of dry water. Everybody laughed at him and made fun of him—that is, everybody except little Tilda, the kitchen-maid. When poor Bobo used to return from some wild-goose chase, tired out, mud-stained, and often enough wet to the skin, instead of laughing, little Tilda would find him a glass of warm milk, hang his coat by the fire to dry, and tell him not to be such a simpleton again. Thus, after a while, Bobo learned to ask Tilda's advice before going on a wild-goose chase, and was in this way saved from many a jest.

Tilda, the kitchen-maid, was as sweet and pretty as she was kind and good. She was said to be the daughter of an old crone who had come to the castle one day, asking for help.

One pleasant mid-summer morning, when Bobo had been nearly

a year at the castle, Princess Zenza overslept half an hour and did not come down to breakfast at the usual time. When she did get up, she found her court waiting for her in the castle gardens. As she came down the steps of the garden terrace, the Princess looked up at the castle clock to see how late she was, and said to her lady-in-waiting: "Dear me—why, I've lost half an hour this morning!"

At these words, Bobo, who was in attendance, pricked up his ears and said: "Please, Your Highness, perhaps I can find it."

At this idea of finding a lost half-hour, the Princess laughed, and found herself echoed by the company.

"Shall we send Bobo in search of the lost half-hour?" said the Princess to the courtiers.

"Yes! Yes!" cried the courtiers. "Bobo shall look for the lost half-hour."

"I'll give him a horse," said one. "I'll give him my old hat," said another. "He can have an old sword I broke last week," said still another.

And so, in less time than it takes to tell about it, poor simpleton Bobo was made ready for his journey.

Before he left the castle, Bobo went down to the kitchen to say good-bye to Tilda.

"What, off again?" said the little kitchen-maid. "Where are you going now?"

"The Princess has lost a half-hour and I am going in search of it," said Bobo, proudly. And he told how the Princess herself had commanded him to seek the half-hour through the world, and promised to bring Tilda a splendid present when he returned.

The good kitchen-maid said little, for she feared lest some misadventure overtake the poor simpleton; but when the chief cook was not looking, she tucked a fresh currant-bun into Bobo's pocket, and wished him the best of good fortune.

So Bobo went to the castle gate, and mounted his horse, which stumbled and was blind in one eye.

"Good-bye, Bobo," cried the assembled courtiers, who were almost beside themselves with laughter at the simpleton and his errand. "Don't fail to bring back the lost half-hour!"

So Bobo rode over the hills and far away. Every now and then he would stop a passer-by and ask him if he had seen a lost half-hour.

The first person whom he thus questioned was an old man who was wandering down the high road that leads from the Kingdom of the East to the Kingdom of the West.

"A lost half-hour?" said the old man. "I've lost something much more serious, I've lost my reputation. You haven't seen a lost reputation lying about here, have you? It was very dignified and wore tortoise-shell glasses."

But Bobo had to answer "No," and the old man wandered on again.

Another day the simpleton encountered a tall, dark, fierce kind of fellow, who answered his polite question with a scream of rage.

"A half-hour," he roared. "No, I haven't seen your half-hour; I wouldn't tell you if I had; what's more, I don't want to see it. I'm looking for something I've lost myself. I've lost my temper. I lost it two years ago at home, and haven't been able to find it anywhere since. Answer me, you silly, have you seen a lost temper anywhere? It's about the size of a large melon and has sharp little points."

On Bobo's answering "No," this dreadful person uttered so perfectly awful a screech of rage, that Bobo's horse took fright and ran away with him, and it was all that Bobo could do to rein him in, three miles farther down the road.

Still farther along, Bobo came to Zizz, the capital city of the Kingdom of the Seven Brooks, and was taken before the King himself.

"A lost half-hour?" said the King. "No, I am quite sure it has not been seen in my dominions. Would you mind asking, as you go through the world, for news of my little daughter?" (Here the poor old King took out a great green handkerchief and wiped his eyes.) "She was stolen by the fairies one midsummer eve fifteen years ago. Find her, worthy Bobo, and an immense reward will be yours."

So Bobo left the proud city of Zizz, and once again rode over the hills and far away. But never a sign of the lost half-hour did he find, although he asked thousands of people. His faithful white horse died, and he continued his way on foot.

Three long years passed, and Bobo grew into a handsome lad, but remained a simpleton still. Finally, after he had wandered all about Fairyland, he came to the edge of the sea. Finding a ship moored in a little harbor, Bobo asked the sailors if they had seen a lost half-hour.

"No," said the sailors, "but we are going to the Isles of Iron; suppose you go with us. The lost half-hour may be there."

So Bobo went aboard the ship, and sailed out upon the dark sea.

For two days the weather was warm and clear, but on the third day, there came a dreadful storm, and on the third night the vessel was driven far off her course into the unknown ocean, and was wrecked upon a mysterious island of rocks that shone in the night like wet matches. A great wave swept the decks, and Bobo was borne away from his companions and carried toward the shining land. Though pounded and battered by the foaming waves, the simpleton at length managed to reach the beach, and took refuge in a crevice of the cliff during the stormy night.

When the dawn broke, all sign of the ship had disappeared. Looking about, Bobo found himself on a lovely island whose heart was a high mountain mass hidden in the fog still sweeping in from the sea. There was not a house, a road, or a path to be seen. Suddenly Bobo noticed a strange little door in the bark of a great lonely tree, and, opening this door, he discovered a little cupboard in which were a pair of wooden shoes. Above the shoes was a card, saying simply:

PUT US ON.

So Bobo sat down on a stone by the foot of the tree, and put on the wooden shoes, which fitted him very nicely. Now these shoes were magic shoes, and Bobo had hardly stepped into them before they turned his feet inland. So Bobo obediently let the shoes guide him. At corners the shoes always turned in the right direction, and if Bobo forgot and blundered on the wrong way, the shoes swiftly began to pinch his toes.

For two days Bobo walked inland toward the great mountain. A warm wind blew the clouds and rain away, the sun shone sweet and clear. On the morning of the third day, the simpleton entered a wood of tall silent trees, and as that day was drawing to a close, turrets of a magnificent castle rose far away over the leaves of the forest.

Bobo arrived at twilight.

He found himself in a beautiful garden, lying between the castle walls and the rising slopes of a great mountain. Strange to say, not a living creature was to be seen, and though there were lights in the

PUT · US · ON

castle, there was not even a warder at the gate. Suddenly a great booming bell struck seven o'clock; Bobo began to hear voices and sounds; and then, before the humming of the bell had died away, a youth mounted on a splendid black horse dashed at lightning speed out of the castle and disappeared in the wood. An old man with a white beard, accompanied by eleven young men—whom Bobo judged, from their expressions, to be brothers—stood by the gate to see the horseman ride away.

Plucking up courage, Bobo came forward, fell on his knee before the old man, and told his story.

"Truly, you should thank the storm fairies," said the old man; "for had you not been wrecked upon this island, never would you have discovered the lost half-hour. I am Father Time himself, and these are my twelve sons, the Hours. Every day, one after the other, they ride for an hour round the whole wide world. Seven O'Clock has just ridden forth. Yes, you shall have the lost half-hour, but you must look after my sons' horses for the space of a whole year."

To this Bobo willingly agreed. So Twelve O'Clock, who was the youngest of the Hours, took him to the stables and showed him the little room in the turret that he was to have. And thus for a year Bobo served Father Time and his sons. He took such good care of the great black horses of the Hours of the Night, and the white horses of the Hours of the Day, that they were never more proud and strong, nor their coats smoother and more gleaming.

When the year was up, Bobo again sought out Father Time.

"You have served faithfully and well," said Father Time. "Here is your reward." And with these words, he placed in Bobo's hands a small square casket made of ebony. "The half-hour lies inside. Don't try to peek at it or open the box until the right time has come. If you do, the half-hour will fly away and disappear forever."

"Farewell, Bobo," said kind young Twelve O'Clock, who had been the simpleton's good friend. "I, too, have a gift for thee. Drink this cup of water to the last drop." And the youth handed the simpleton a silver cup full to the brim of clear shining water.

Now this water was the water of wisdom, and when Bobo had drunk it, he was no longer a simpleton. And being no longer a simpleton, he remembered the man who had lost his reputation, the man who had lost his temper, and the king whose daughter had been stolen by the fairies. So Bobo made so bold as to ask Father Time about them, for Father Time knows everything that has happened in the whole wide world.

"Tell the first," said Father Time, "that his reputation has been broken into a thousand pieces, which have been picked up by his neighbors and carried home. If he can persuade his neighbors to give them up, he should be able to piece together a pretty good reputation again. As for the man who lost his temper, tell him that it is to be found in the grass by the roadside, close by the spot where you first met him. As for the missing daughter, she is the kitchen-maid in Princess Zenza's palace, who is known as Tilda."

So Bobo thanked Father Time, and at noon Twelve O'Clock placed him behind him on the white charger, and hurried away. So fast they flew that Bobo, who was holding the ebony casket close against his heart, was in great danger of falling off. When they got to the seashore, the white horse hesitated not an instant, but set foot upon the water, which bore him up as if it had been, not water, but earth itself. Once arrived at the shore of Fairyland, Twelve O'Clock stopped, wished Bobo good-speed, and, rising in the air, disappeared into the glare of the sun. Bobo, with the precious ebony casket in his hand, continued on in the direction of Princess Zenza's palace.

On the second morning of his journey, he happened to see far ahead of him on the highway the unfortunate aged man who had lost his reputation. To him, therefore, Bobo repeated the counsel of Father Time, and sent him hurrying home to his neighbors' houses. Of the man who had lost his temper, Bobo found no sign. In the grass by the roadside, however, he did find the lost temper—a queer sort of affair like a melon of fiery red glass all stuck over with uneven spines and brittle thorns. Bobo, with great goodness of heart, took along this extraordinary object, in the hope of finding its angry possessor.

Farther on, the lad encountered Tilda's father, the unhappy King, and delivered his message. The joy of the monarch knew no bounds, and Bobo, the one-time simpleton, became on the spot Lord Bobo of the Sapphire Hills, Marquis of the Mountains of the Moon, Prince of the Valley of Golden Apples, and Lord Seneschal of the proud City of Zizz—in a word, the greatest nobleman in all Fairyland. Then, having got together a magnificent cohort of dukes, earls, and counts, all in splendid silks, and soldiers in shining armor, the delighted King rode off to claim his missing daughter from Princess Zenza.

So on they rode, the harnesses jingling, the bridle-bells ringing, and the breastplates of the armed men shining in the sun. After a week of almost constant progress (for the King was so anxious to see his beloved daughter that he would hardly give the cavalcade time to rest), they came to the frontiers of Princess Zenza's kingdom. Strange to say, black mourning banners hung from the trees, and

every door in the first village which the travelers saw was likewis
hung with black streamers. On the steps of one of the cottages sat a
old woman, all alone and weeping with all her might.

"What *is* the matter, my good woman?" said the King.

"O sir," said the peasant woman, "evil days have fallen upon ou
unhappy kingdom. Three days ago a terrible dragon alighted in th
gardens of the palace and sent word to Princess Zenza that if withir
three days she did not provide him with someone brave enough t
go home with him and cook his meals and keep his cavern tidy, h
would burn our fields with his fiery breath. Yet who, I ask you
would be housekeeper for a dragon? Suppose he didn't like th
puddings you made for him—why, he might eat you up! All woulc
have been lost had not a brave little kitchen-maid named Tild:
volunteered to go. It is for her that we are mourning. At two o'clocl
she is to be carried off by the dragon. It is almost two now. Alas
Alas!"

Hardly were the words out of her mouth, when the town bel
struck twice, solemnly and sadly.

"Quick! quick!" cried the King and Bobo in the same breath
"Let us hurry to the castle. We may save her yet."

But they knew in their hearts that they were too late, and tha
poor Tilda had given herself to the dragon. And so it proved. I
spite of his mad dash, Bobo, who had spurred on ahead, arrivec
exactly half an hour late. The monstrous dragon with Tilda in hi
claws was just a little smoky speck far down the southern sky
Princess Zenza and her court stood by, wringing their jeweled hand:

Suddenly Bobo thought of the half-hour. He had arrived hal
an hour late, *but he could have that half-hour back again!* Thing
should be exactly as they were half an hour before.

He opened the cover of the ebony box. Something like a winge
white flame escaped from it, and flew hissing through the air to th
sun. As for the sun itself, turning round like a cart-wheel and hissin,
like ten thousand rockets, it rolled back along the sky to the eas
The hands of the clocks, which marked half-past two, whirred bacl
to two o'clock in a twinkling. And, sure enough, there was brav
little Tilda standing alone in a great field waiting for the dragon t

ome and take her away. Lumbering heavily along like a monstrous
urtle, and snorting blue smoke, the dragon was advancing toward
er.

Bobo ran down into the field and stood beside Tilda, ready to
efend her to the end.

The dragon came nearer and nearer. Suddenly, angered by the
ight of Bobo and his drawn sword, he roared angrily, but continued
) approach. Bobo struck at him with his sword. The blade broke
pon his steely scales. The dragon roared again. Now just as the
ragon's mouth was its widest, Bobo who had been searching his
ockets desperately, hurled into it *the lost temper.*

There was a perfectly terrific Bang! As if a million balloons had
lown up all at once. For the dragon had blown up. The lost temper
ad finished him. Only one fragment of him, a tiny bit of a claw,
vas ever found.

Everybody, you may be sure, began to cry "Hurrah" and "Hooray,"
nd soon they were firing off cannon and ringing all the bells. Then
'ilda's father took her in his arms, and told her that she was a real
rincess. The Grand Cross of the Order of the Black Cat was con-
erred upon Bobo by Princess Zenza, who also asked his pardon for
aving treated him so shabbily. This Bobo gave readily. A won-
erful fête was held. When the rejoicings were over, Bobo and Tilda
vere married, and lived happily together all their days.

THE DUTCH CHEESE

By WALTER DE LA MARE

ONCE upon a time there lived, with his sister Griselda, in cottage near the Forest of Oghh, a young farmer whos name was John. Brother and sister, they lived alone, except for thei sheep-dog, Sly, their flock of sheep, the numberless birds of the forest and the fairies. John loved his sister beyond telling; he loved Sly and he delighted to listen to the birds singing at twilight round th darkening margin of the forest. But he feared and hated the fairies And, having a very stubborn heart, the more he feared, the more h hated them; and the more he hated them, the more they pestered him.

Now this was a tribe of fairies sly, small, tricksy-hearted and mis chievous, and not of the race of fairies noble, silent, and remote fron man. They were a sort of gypsy fairies, very nimble, and of aer and prankish company, and, partly for mischief and partly for lov of her, were always striving to charm John's dear sister Griseld away with their music and fruits and dancing. He more than hal believed it was they who years ago had decoyed into the forest hi poor old father, who had gone out fagot-cutting in his sheepskin hat with his ass; and his mother, too, soon after, who had gone out look ing for him.

But fairies, even of this small tribe, hate no man. They mocked him and mischiefed him: they spilt his milk, rode astraddle on hi rams, garlanded his old ewes with sow-thistle and briony, sprinkled water on his kindling wood, loosed his bucket into the well, and hid his great leather shoes. But all this they did, not for hate—for the came and went soft as evening moths about Griselda—but because in his fear and fury he shut up his sister from them, and because he wa sullen and stupid. Yet he did nothing but fret himself. He set trap for them, and caught starlings; he fired his blunderbuss at then under the moon, and scared his sheep; he put dishes of sour milk in their way, and sticky leaves and brambles where their rings were green in the meadows; but all to no purpose. When at dusk, too, he heard their faint, far, elfin music, he would sit in the door blowing into his father's great bassoon till the black forest re-echoed with its sad, solemn, wooden voice. But that was of no avail either. At last he grew so sour that he made Griselda utterly miserable. Her cheeks lost their scarlet and her eyes their sparkling. Then the fairies began to plague John in earnest, lest their lovely, loved child of man, Griselda, should die.

Now one summer's evening—and most nights are cold in that great forest—John, having put away his mournful bassoon and bolted the door, was squatting, moody and gloomy, with Griselda on his hearth beside the fire. And he leaned back his great hairy head and stared straight up the chimney to where in the black sky the Seven Sisters sat aglitter. And suddenly, while he lolled there on his stool watching that tiny seven, there appeared against the dark sky a mischievous, elvish head secretly peeping down at him; and busy hands sprinkling dew on his wide upturned face. He heard the laughter too of the fairies miching and gamboling on his thatch, and in a rage he started up, seized a great round cheese that lay on a platter, and with all his force threw it clean and straight up the sooty chimney at the faces of mockery clustered above. And after that, though Griselda sighed at her spinning wheel, he heard no more. Even the cricket that had been whistling all through the evening fell silent, and John supped on his black bread and onions alone.

Next day Griselda woke at dawn and put her head out of the little window beneath the thatch, and the day was white with mist.

"'Twill be another hot day," she said to herself, combing her beautiful hair.

But when John went down, so white and dense with mist were the fields that even the green borders of the forest were invisible, and the whiteness went to the sky. Swathing and wreathing itself, opal and white as milk, all morning the mist grew thicker and thicker about the little house. When John went out about nine o'clock to peer about him, nothing was to be seen at all. He could hear his sheep bleating, the kettle singing, Griselda sweeping, but straight up above him hung only, like a small round fruit, a little cheese-red beamless sun; straight up above him, though the hands of the clock were not yet got to ten. And he clenched his fists and stamped in his rage. But no one answered him, no voice mocked him but his own. For when these idle, mischievous fairies have played a trick on an enemy they soon weary of it.

All day long that little sullen lantern burned above the mist, sometimes red, so that the white mist was dyed to amber, and sometimes milky pale. The trees dropped water from every leaf. Every flower asleep in the garden was neckleted with beads; and nothing but a drenched old forest crow visited the lonely cottage that afternoon to cry: "Kah, Kah, Kah!" and fly away. But Griselda knew her brother's mood too well to speak of it, or to complain. And she sang on gayly in the house, though she was more sorrowful than ever.

The next day John went out to tend his flocks. And wherever he went the red sun seemed to follow. When at last he found his sheep, they were drenched with the clinging mist and were huddled together in dismay. And when they saw him it seemed that they cried out with a unanimous bleating voice:

"O ma-a-a-ster!"

And he stood counting them. And a little apart from the rest stood his old ram Soll, with a face as black as soot; and there, perched on his back, impish and sharp and scarlet, rode and tossed and sang just such another fairy as had mocked John from the chimney-top. A fire seemed to break out in his body, and, picking up a handful of stones, he rushed at Soll through the flock. They scattered, bleating, out into the mist. And the fairy, all a-cock-a-hoop on the old ram's back, took its small ears between finger and thumb, and as fast as John ran, so fast jogged Soll, till all the young farmer's stones were thrown, and he found himself alone in a quagmire so sticky and befogged that it took him till afternoon to grope his way out. And only Griselda's singing over her broth-pot guided him at last home.

Next day he sought his sheep far and wide, but not one could he find. To and fro he wandered, shouting and calling and whistling to Sly, till, heartsick and thirsty, they were both wearied out. Yet bleatings seemed to fill the air, and a faint, beautiful bell tolled on out of the mist; and John knew the fairies had hidden his sheep, and he hated them more than ever.

After that he went no more into the fields, brightly green beneath the enchanted mist. He sat and sulked, staring out of the door at the dim forests far away, glimmering faintly red beneath the small red sun. Griselda could not sing any more, she was too tired and hungry. And just before twilight she went out and gathered the last few pods of peas from the garden for their supper.

And while she was shelling them, John within doors in the cottage heard again the tiny timbrels and the distant horns, and the odd, clear, grasshopper voices calling and calling her, and he knew in his heart that, unless he relented and made friends with the fairies, Griselda would surely one day run away to them and leave him forlorn. He scratched his great head, and gnawed his broad thumb. They had taken his father, they had taken his mother, they might take his sister—but he *wouldn't* give in.

So he shouted, and Griselda in fear and trembling came in out of the garden with her basket and basin and sat down in the gloaming to finish shelling her peas.

And as the shadows thickened and the stars began to shine, the malevolent singing came nearer, and presently there was a groping and stirring in the thatch, a tapping at the window, and John knew the fairies had come—not alone, not one or two or three, but in their company and bands—to plague him, and entice away Griselda. He shut his mouth and stopped up his ears with his fingers, but when, with great staring eyes, he saw them capering like bubbles in a glass, like flames along straw, on his very doorstep, he could contain himself no longer. He caught up Griselda's bowl and flung it—peas, water, and all—full in the snickering faces of the Little Folk! There came a shrill, faint twitter of laughter, a scampering of feet, and then all was utterly still.

Griselda tried in vain to keep back her tears. She put her arms round John's neck and hid her face in his sleeve.

"Let me go!" she said, "let me go, John, just a day and a night, and I'll come back to you. They are angry with us. But they love me; and if I sit on the hillside under the boughs of the trees beside the pool and listen to their music just a little while, they will make the sun shine again and drive back the flocks, and we shall be happy as ever. Look at poor Sly, John dear, he is hungrier even than I am." John heard only the mocking laughter and the tap-tapping and the rustling and crying of the fairies, and he wouldn't let his sister go.

And it began to be marvelously dark and still in the cottage. No stars moved across the casement, no water-drops glittered in the candleshine. John could hear only one low, faint, unceasing stir and rustling all around him. So utterly dark and still it was, that even Sly woke from his hungry dreams and gazed up into his mistress's face and whined.

They went to bed; but still, all night long, while John lay tossing on his mattress, the rustling never ceased. The old kitchen clock ticked on and on, but there came no hint of dawn. All was pitch-black and now all was utterly silent. There wasn't a whisper, not a creak, not a sigh of air, not a footfall of mouse, not a flutter of moth, not a settling of dust to be heard at all. Only desolate silence. And John at last could endure his fears and suspicions no longer. He got out of bed and stared from his square casement. He could see nothing. He tried to thrust it open; it would not move. He went downstairs and unbarred the door and looked out. He saw, as it were, a deep, clear, green shade, from behind which the songs of the birds rose faint as in a dream.

And then he sighed like a grampus and sat down, and knew that the fairies had beaten him. Like Jack's beanstalk, in one night had grown up a dense wall of peas. He pushed and pulled and hacked with his ax, and kicked with his shoes, and buffeted with his blunderbuss. But it was all in vain. He sat down once more in his chair beside the hearth and covered his face with his hands. And at last Griselda, too, awoke, and came down with her candle. And she comforted her brother, and told him if he would do what she bade she would soon make all right again. And he promised her.

So with a scarf she bound tight his hands behind him; and with a rope she bound his feet together, so that he could neither run nor throw stones, peas, or cheeses. She bound his eyes and ears and mouth with a napkin, so that he could neither see, hear, smell, nor cry out. And, that done, she pushed and pulled him like a great bundle, and at last rolled him out of sight into the chimney-corner against the wall. Then she took a small sharp pair of needlework scissors that her godmother had given her, and snipped and snipped, till at last there came a little hole in the thick green hedge of peas. And putting her mouth there she called softly through the little hole. And the fairies drew near the doorstep, and nodded and nodded and listened.

And then and there Griselda made a bargain with them for the forgiveness of John—a lock of golden hair; a dish of ewes' milk; three and thirty bunches of currants, red, white, and black; a bag of thistle-down, three handkerchiefs full of lambs' wool; a jar of honey; a peppercorn of spice; and she to sit one full hour each evening of summer on the hillside, in the shadow and still greenness that slope down from that great Forest toward the meadows, where the fairy mounds are, and their brindled cattle graze.

Her brother lay blind and deaf and dumb as a fagot. She promised all.

And then, instead of a rustling and a creeping, there came a rending and clattering and crashing. Instead of green shade, light of amber; then white. And as the thick hedge withered and shrank, and the merry and furious dancing sun scorched and scorched and scorched, there came, above the singing of the birds, the bleatings of sheep—and behold sooty Soll and hungry Sly met square upon the doorstep; and all John's sheep shone white as hoarfrost on his pastures; and every lamb was garlanded with pimpernel and eyebright; and the old fat ewes stood still, with saddles of moss; and their laughing riders sat and saw Griselda standing in the doorway in her bounteous yellow hair.

As for John, tied up like a sack in the chimney-corner, down came his cheese again *crash!* upon his head, and, not being able to say anything, he said nothing.

A TALE OF THREE TAILS

By *CHARLES J. FINGER*

DOWN in Honduras there is a town called Pueblo de Chamelecón which is not much of a town after all. There is only one street in it, and the houses are like big beehives that have been squared up, and the roofs are of straw. There is no sidewalk, no roadway, and the houses are unfenced, so that you step from the room into the sandy street and, because of the heat, when you are inside you wish that you were out, and when you are outside you wish that you were in. So the children of the place spend much time down at the little river. At least they did when I was there.

I rode there on a donkey and, the day being hot, let the animal graze, or sleep, or think, or dream, or work out problems—or whatever it is that a donkey does with his spare time—and I watched the children in the water. There was one, a little baby just able to toddle around, who crawled down to the water's edge, rolled in and swam about like a little dog, much as the babies of Tierra del Fuego will swim in the icy waters of the Far South. He came out on my side of the water, as lively as a grig, smiling every bit as friendly as any other little chap of his age, white, brown, or yellow.

I stayed there that night because the day did not get cool, and in the evening the people sat outside of their houses and played their guitars and sang. Now I had with me a little musical instrument like a tiny organ, which I bought in France, and it was so compact and handy that I could carry it everywhere as easily as I could a blanket. In fact, I used to ride with it behind my saddle, wrapped in my bedding. Well, as the people seemed to like their music, I brought out mine, so we had a very jolly concert, in spite of my poor voice, which they politely pretended not to notice. Then later, from curiosity, the children came about me and, to amuse them as well as myself, having done so badly at the singing, I did a few tricks with wads of rolled paper and a couple of tin cups, and the little boy who had swum across the pond laughed as loudly as anyone there. That

leased his father mightily, so much indeed that he brought me a cup
f goat's milk and some cassava bread and told me that I was a fine
:llow. To please me further, he sang a very, very, long song. It was
ll about the parrot and the wonderful things it did, a parrot that
ad lived long among people and learned their songs, and when the
ird flew back to the forest, it still sang, and so well that all the other
arrots in the forest learned to sing the song from beginning to end.
ut what was curious was that, at the end of every other verse, there
vas this line:

"When the rat had a tail like a horse."

So, when he had done, I asked him about that, for all the rats
had seen had tails which were far from beautiful, according to my
otion. The man listened gravely, then said: "But certainly, once
he rat had a tail like a horse."

"When was that?" I asked.

"When the rabbit had a tail like a cat," he said.

"But I am still puzzled," I told him. "Was it long ago?"

"It was when the deer's tail was plumed like the tail of a dog,"
e told me.

As we talked, a kind of polite silence was upon all the people
athered about us; then a very, very, old woman who was smoking
cigar nodded her head and said: "But Tio Ravenna is right. It was
n the days of Hunbatz, who lived on beetles and spiders, and I
eard it from my mother's mother, and she from the mother of her
nother." Then the old woman went on smoking with her eyes
losed, and all who were there nodded at one another, thinking, I
uppose, that the old grandmother would presently tell the story.
3ut of course, they who knew her well were wiser than to ask her to
ell the Tale of Three Tails, so everyone waited.

Presently, a little girl gave the old grandmother a piece of sugar
nd asked: "Was it two brothers, or three, who had to clear the great
orest? I am not sure."

At that the little old lady's eyes were bright, and she threw away
ier cigar and said:

"Two brothers. That I have told you before." After a little sigh,

which was only pretending that she was weary of telling the tal
she said: "You know that I have told it to you before, and it
wrong that I should have to tell it so often. But you see this."

So saying, she took from her bosom, where she had it fastene
to a silk thread, a little piece of jade and let us see it. It was broke
from a larger piece, but we could make out on it a carving which
saw to be a deer with a tail like a sheep dog's. We passed it abou
and everyone looked at it carefully, although certainly all of the
must have seen it time and time again, and when it came to the ol
grandmother again she replaced it and told us the Tale of Thro
Tails, just as I have written it here.

Once, long ago, the rat had a beautiful tail like a horse, with lon
sweeping hairs, though it was before my time of life. It was in th
days of old Hunbatz, and he was a wizard who lived in the dark o
the great forest that used to be on the other side of the big river. I
those days things were not as now and animals were different; som
larger, some smaller. The deer, as you have seen on the stone
showed you, had a tail like a dog, and the rabbit's tail was long an
furry like the tail of a cat.

Now, in that land there was a hunter with whom neither lasso no
arrow ever failed, and he had two sons, beautiful to look at an
brave of heart, stout and quick of foot. Not only did the brothe
work better than any men had ever worked, but they could pla
ball and sing, throwing the ball higher than birds could fly, an
singing in a way that brought the wild things to hear them. Nor wa
there living creature able to run as swiftly as the two brothers. Th
birds alone could outrace them.

The brothers being grown, their father thought that it was tim
for them to make a home for themselves, so he chose a place on th
farther side of the forest, and told them to clear it, which, he sai
could be done in seven days. It was no little forest, you must remem
ber, but a vast place, where sunlight never pierced, and the roots o
trees were like great ropes; a jungle that stretched for miles an
miles, and the tangle in it was so thick that a monkey could barel
get through without squeezing. Deep in the forest there was a black

ness like the blackness of night. The trunks of the trees were so large that three men holding hands could not circle them, and where there were no trees, there were vines and snakelike lianas and thorn bushes and flowers so great that a man could lie down to sleep in the shade of them.

The first day, the brothers took a great space, piling the trees at one corner, clearing the tangle and leaving all as smooth as the water of a lake. They sang as they worked, and they sang as they rested in the heat of the day, and the organ bird and the flute bird answered them from the gold-green shade. So pleasant was their music that the old iguana, though he was as big as a man, came from his resting place in the trees to listen.

Seeing how things were going, old Hunbatz in the dark of the forest grew very angry, fearing that his hiding place would soon dwindle and vanish. So he went to the great gray owl, his friend, and they talked the matter over between them. The owl told Hunbatz that he must set the father's heart against the brothers, telling him that the boys were lazy and instead of working spent their time in playing with the ball and in singing.

"Go," said the owl, "to their father, and when he asks how the lads fare with their work, say to him:

> " 'They sing and they play
> For half of the day.'

It may fall out that he will grow angry and cut off their heads, and thus the forest will be safe for us."

That seemed to the wizard to be good advice, and before the close of the day's work, old Hunbatz, who could fly by flapping his hands in a certain way like a swimmer, cast himself into the air and flew with great swiftness to the place where the father lived. But he took care to dress himself like a woodman.

"Well met," said the father, seeing Hunbatz, but thinking him no wizard of course. "From where do you come?"

"From the other side of the forest," was the reply.

"Then perchance you saw my two sons who are clearing the forest," said the father.

"I did," said Hunbatz.

"And how are the boys doing?" asked the father.

At that old Hunbatz shook his head sadly and answered, as the owl had told him:

> "They sing and they play
> For half of the day."

That, you know, was quite untrue, for while they sang, there was no stopping of work, and as for the play, it is true that they threw the ball from one to the other, but so clever were they that one would throw the ball so high that it would take hours and hours before it came down again, and of course, while it was in the air, the brothers went on working.

"I would cut off their heads to teach them a lesson," said Hunbatz, "if they were sons of mine." Then he turned on his heel and went away, not flying until he was out of the father's sight, for he did not wish any man to know that he was a wizard.

To be sure, the good man was grieved and his face clouded, when he heard the tale of Hunbatz, but he said nothing, and, a short time after, the brothers came home. He was much surprised when, asking the lads how much work they had done that day, they told him that they had cleared off the space of forest he had bidden them to. After much thought, he told them that the next day they would have to do twice as much as before. The brothers thought the new task hard, but they went to work with a good will and on the second day the trees fell like corn before a man with a machete, and before night they had finished that which they had been given to do.

Again old Hunbatz flew through the air to the father and tried to set him against the boys, and again that night, when the boys were home, their task was set for the next day twice as much as the day before. It was the same the third day, and the fourth, until at last the boys came to a point where by the mightiest working they could not move a stick or a blade of grass more. And yet, because of old Hunbatz, the father set them a task still greater.

On the fifth day, things looked very hopeless for the boys, and their hearts were sad as they looked at the forest and saw the task

that their father had set them to do. They went to work feeling for
the first time it would be impossible for the sun to go down on their
finished task, and the heart of old Hunbatz was glad. But the birds
in the forest were silent that morning, for they too knew that there
were sad hearts in the brothers. Even the grasshoppers and the mos-
quitoes and the bees were still, and as for the boys, not a note of joy
could they raise.

Then to them came the iguana, wise old lizard who knew everything that went on in the forest, and as soon as he had heard what
the brothers had to say he smiled and called on them to listen, after
making sure that there was no living creature to hear except the
birds, for of them he had no fear, knowing the birds tell no secrets.

"Be cheerful," said the iguana, "and I will tell you a charm. It is
this: mark about the handles of your working tools rings of black,
white, red, and green, and before you start to work, sing:

> " 'I must do what I can,
>   Is the thought of a man.'

And if your hearts are brave, you will see what happens."

Having said this and smiled on the brothers, the old iguana
climbed into a tree and stretched himself along the branch of it
where he could best see, and the birds gathered in a great circle, a
matchless melody going up to the sky.

So the brothers took their axes, their spades, their hoes, and their
machetes, and painted about the handles of them rings of black and
of white and of red and of green, and their voices rang sweet and
clear as they sang, as the iguana had told them:

> "I must do what I can,
>   Is the thought of a man."

No sooner had the last words passed than the whole company of
birds broke out into a chorus, singing, chattering, chirping, whistling,
screaming, each according to its manner and, without hands touching them, axes went to work cutting down trees, machetes chopped
at lianas and vines, spades cleared and dug; and trees, bushes, and
weeds piled themselves in great heaps at the edge of the clearing, so

that in less than an hour the whole task was done. Then it was that all things in the forest were glad and the good iguana smiled broadly. The very monkeys joined in and, catching the ball the brothers threw, tossed it from tree to tree till it passed through the whole jungle and back.

But old Hunbatz was angry beyond measure, so angry that he whirled about on his heels three hundred times, turning so rapidly that he looked like a storm cloud, and his long whiskers were tangled about him like a mantle. But the faster he whirled, the more his anger boiled, and, flapping his hands, he shot into the air, going so swiftly that his very clothes were scorched.

"How are the boys?" asked the father, when Hunbatz stood before him.

For answer, Hunbatz screamed: "Your boys are idle fellows!

"They sing and they play
For half of the day.

Had I such sons, I would cut their heads off to teach them a lesson."

Said the father: "Tomorrow I shall go to the forest, and if you have not spoken truth, then this arrow which has never yet missed a mark shall find one in your heart. But if it is as you say, then my sons shall feel my anger."

Old Hunbatz did not like that at all, for well he knew that the hunter's arrows were never wasted. So back he flew to the owl and the two of them whispered together. That night there was a great gathering of the animals: the hare, the deer, the rat, the jaguar, the puma, the opossum, and may others. The rat, the deer, and the rabbit led them, and in a wonderfully short time, not only were all things restored and the work of the day undone, but the trees and the bushes and the vines and the lianas that had been moved on the other days were put back in their old places, growing and blooming, as though the brothers had never been at the forest at all.

Sad was the hour the next morning when the hunter came with his two sons and saw the forest as though hand had never touched it. The brothers could not believe their eyes. Grinning from the thick of a rubber tree was the face of Hunbatz, and on his shoulder was the owl. For a moment the father thought to cut off the heads of the lads to teach them a lesson, but on second thought he told them that he would give them another chance.

"What should have been done is not done," he said. "I will grant you a day and a night to clear all the forest as you told me it was cleared. Tomorrow morning I will come again, and see whether all is well done." At that he left them and went his way.

No sooner had he gone than the two brothers went to see the iguana, who told them of the witchery of the owl and Hunbatz and bade them to act as before. So they made the ring about the handles of their working tools once more and sang:

> "I must do what I can,
> Is the thought of a man."

And, as on the day before, axes, machetes, and spades went to work and in a short time all was clear again. Then the iguana told the brothers of the evil that Hunbatz had done and bade them set traps and keep watch that night. So three traps were made and set, and when night fell, from all parts of the forest there came animals led by the rat, the deer, and the rabbit, and old Hunbatz and the owl watched from the dark caves of the leaves.

No sooner had the first three animals stepped into the clearing than they were caught fast in the traps, whereupon the rest of the animals turned and fled. Then the brothers rushed to the traps. The rabbit gave a great jump when he felt the jaws close upon his beautiful catlike tail, but it was chopped off close to the body. The deer, with his tail like a plume, fared no better. So both deer and rabbit fled to the woods ashamed, and, as you see for yourself, have had no tails ever since. As for the rat, he was far too wise to jump as the rabbit and deer had done. But seeing the brothers coming, he pulled and pulled and pulled so that all the beautiful hair was stripped, leaving him with but a bare and ugly thing of a tail as you see today.

The next morning when the hunter-father came, there was the forest cleared and all in good order as the boys had said. So he sought out old Hunbatz, who flapped his hands and flew for very fear. But so fast he went that his clothes were burnt off, and his skin was baked into a hard crust by the great heat, and he fell to the earth and so became what we call an armadillo. As for the two brothers, they lived very happily for many, many years, and things went well and the land they lived in was a land of good harvest and fruit trees.

So now you know the Tale of Three Tails and if you do not believe it, look at the rat, the deer, the rabbit and the armadillo.

THE SEVENTH PRINCESS

By ELEANOR FARJEON

DID you ever hear the tale of the Six Princesses who lived for the sake of their hair alone? This is it.

There was once a King who married a Gypsy, and was as careful of her as if she had been made of glass. For fear she would run away, he put her in a palace in a park with a railing all around it, and never let her go outside. The Queen was too loving to tell him how much she longed to go beyond the railing, but she sat for hours on the palace roof, looking toward the meadows to the east, the river to the south, the hills to the west, and the markets to the north.

In time the Queen bore the King twin daughters as bright as the sunrise, and on the day they were christened the King in his joy asked her what she would have for a gift. The Queen looked from her roof to the east, saw May on the meadows, and said:

"Give me the Spring!"

The King called fifty thousand gardeners, and bade each one bring in a root of wild flowers or a tender birch tree from outside, and plant it within the railing. When it was done he walked with the Queen in the flowery park, and showed her everything, saying:

"Dear wife, the Spring is yours."

But the Queen only sighed.

The following year two more Princesses, as fair as the morning, were born, and once again, on their christening-day, the King told the Queen to choose a gift. This time she looked from the roof to the south, and, seeing the water shining in the valley, said:

"Give me the river!"

The King summoned fifty thousand workmen and told them so to conduct the river into the park that it should supply a most beautiful fountain in the Queen's pleasure-grounds.

Then he led his wife to the spot where the fountain rose and fell in a marble basin, and said:

"You now have the river."

167

But the Queen only gazed at the captive water rising and falling in its basin, and hung her head.

Next year two more Princesses, as golden as the day, were born, and the Queen, given her choice of a gift, looked north from the roof into the busy town, and said: "Give me the people!"

So the King sent fifty thousand trumpeters down to the market place, and before long they returned, bringing six honest market women with them.

"Here, dear Queen, are the people," said the King.

The Queen secretly wiped her eyes, and then gave her six beautiful babies into the charge of the six buxom women, so that the Princesses had a nurse apiece.

Now in the fourth year the Queen bore only one daughter, a little one, and dark like herself, whereas the King was big and fair.

"What gift will you choose?" said the King, as they stood on the roof on the day of the christening.

The Queen turned her eyes to the west, and saw a wood-pigeon and six swans flying over the hills.

"Oh!" cried she, "give me the birds!"

The King instantly sent fifty thousand fowlers forth to snare the birds. While they were absent the Queen said:

"Dear King, my children are in their cots and I am on my throne, but presently the cots will be empty and I shall sit on my throne no more. When that day comes, which of our seven daughters will be Queen in my stead?"

Before the King could answer, the fowlers returned with the birds. The King looked from the humble pigeon, with its little round head sunk in the soft breast-feathers, to the royal swans with their long white necks, and said:

"The Princess with the longest hair shall be Queen."

Then the Queen sent for the six Nurses and told them what the King had said. "So remember," she added, "to wash and brush and comb my daughters' hair without neglect, for on you will depend the future Queen."

"And who will wash and brush and comb the hair of the Seventh Princess?" they asked.

"I will do that myself," said the Queen.

Each Nurse was exceedingly anxious that her own Princess should be Queen, and every fine day they took the children out into the flowery meadow and washed their hair in the water of the fountain, and spread it in the sun to dry. Then they brushed it and combed it till it shone like yellow silk, and plaited it with ribbons, and decked it with flowers. You never saw such lovely hair as the Princesses had, or so much trouble as the Nurses took with it. And wherever the six fair girls went, the six swans went with them.

But the Seventh Princess, the little dark one, never had her hair washed in the fountain. It was kept covered with a red handkerchief, and tended in secret by the Queen as they sat together on the roof and played with the pigeon.

At last the Queen knew that her time had come. So she sent for her daughters, blessed them one by one, and bade the King carry her up to the roof. There she looked from the meadows to the river, from the markets to the hills and closed her eyes.

Now hardly had the King done drying his own, when a trumpet sounded at his gate, and a page came running in to say that the Prince of the World had come. So the King threw open his doors, and the Prince of the World came in, followed by his servant. The Prince was all in cloth of gold, and his mantle was so long that when he stood before the King it spread the whole length of the room, and the plume in his cap was so tall that the tip touched the ceiling. In front of the Prince walked his servant, a young man all in rags.

The King said:

"Welcome, Prince of the World!" and held out his hand.

The Prince of the World did not answer; he stood there with his mouth shut and his eyes cast down. But his Ragged Servant said, "Thank you, King of the Country!" And he took the King's hand and shook it heartily.

This surprised the King greatly.

"Cannot the Prince speak for himself?" he asked.

"If he can," said the Ragged Servant, "nobody has ever heard him do so. As you know, it takes all sorts to make the world: those who shriek and those who are silent, those who are rich and those who are poor, those who think and those who do, those who look up and those who look down. Now, my master has chosen me for his servant, because between us we make up the world of which he is Prince. For he is rich and I am poor, and he thinks things and I do them, and he looks down and I look up, and he is silent, so I do the talking."

"Why has he come?" asked the King.

"To marry your daughter," said the Ragged Servant, "for it takes all sorts to make a world and there must be a woman as well as a man."

"No doubt," said the King. "But I have seven daughters. He cannot marry them all."

"He will marry the one that is to be Queen," said the Ragged Servant.

"Let my daughters be sent for," said the King, "for the time is now come to measure the length of their hair."

So the Seven Princesses were summoned before the King. The six fair ones came in with their Nurses, and the little dark one came in by herself. The Ragged Servant looked quickly from one to another, but the Prince of the World kept his eyes down and did not look at any of them.

Then the King sent for the Court Tailor with his tape-measure; and when he came, the six fair Princesses shook down their hair till it trailed on the ground behind them.

One by one they had it measured, while the six Nurses looked on with pride—for had they not taken just as much care as they could of their darlings' hair? But, alas! as neither more care nor less had been spent upon any of them, it was now discovered that each of the six Princesses had hair exactly as long as the others.

The Court held up its hands in amazement, the Nurses wrung theirs in despair, the King rubbed his crown, the Prince of the World kept his eyes on the ground, and the Ragged Servant looked at the Seventh Princess.

"What shall we do," said the King, "if my youngest daughter's hair is the same length as the rest?"

"I don't think it is, sir," said the Seventh Princess, and her sisters looked anxious as she untied the red handkerchief from her head. And indeed her hair was not the same length as theirs, for it was cropped close to her head, like a boy's.

"Who cut your hair, child?" asked the King.

"My Mother, if you please, sir," said the Seventh Princess. "Every day as we sat on the roof she snipped it with her scissors."

"Well! well!" cried the King. "Whichever is meant to be Queen, it isn't you!"

That is the story of the Six Princesses who lived for the sake of their hair alone. They spent the rest of their lives having it washed, brushed, and combed by the Nurses, till their locks were as white as their six pet swans.

And the Prince of the World spent the rest of *his* life waiting with his eyes cast down until one of the Princesses should grow the longest hair, and become his Queen. As this never happened, for all I know he is waiting still.

But the Seventh Princess tied on her red handkerchief again, and ran out of the palace to the hills and the river and the meadows and the markets; and the pigeon and the Ragged Servant went with her.

"But," said she, "what will the Prince of the World do without you in the palace?"

"He will have to do as best he can," said the Ragged Servant, "for it takes all sorts to make the world, those that are in and those that are out."

THE TWO YOUTHS WHOSE FATHER WAS UNDER THE SEA

A Story Told under the Big Tree of Bunlahy

By PADRAIC COLUM

ONCE upon a time, and if it wasn't upon my time nor upon your time, it was upon a good time, anyway, when jackdaws built their nests in old men's beards, and turkeys went up and down the laneways smoking pipes of tobacco, and the roofs of the houses of Bunlahy were thatched with pancakes, and ponies, saddled and all, went along the roadways, saying, "Who's for a ride, who's for a ride?" Well, in those times there were two brothers whose names were Jack Sea and John Sea, and they were named Jack and John because there was no difference between them—one had the same appearance as the other.

One day one of them was swimming with other boys and he swam farther than any of them. Then the other brother who was standing with the lookers-on heard a boy say, "So far can Jack Sea swim, and yet he doesn't know who his father is, or where he lives, or if he lives at all." When John Sea heard this said, he made up his mind that he would not rest until he knew who his father was, and where he lived, or if he lived at all. So he went back to the house and told his grandfather what was in his mind to do. His grandfather filled a basket with provisions for him and told him he had his leave to go seek his father. "But whether you should go east or west, or north or south, I don't know, for your father was never seen on our land." If his mother had been there (but she was no longer alive) she would have told him that her father had sent her to fish on a certain day, telling her to land only what came heavy upon her line. She had gone out on the sea in a boat; she had felt a very heavy pull, and she had let the boat drift until she had come to an island. There she had landed what was on her line, and, behold! it was a young man, and a very princely-looking young man. She and he had lived on the island as man and wife, until a night came when he had said, "I am drawn back to the sea by the power of the Hag of the Waves. Beware of her sister, the Hag of the Hollows." The Fisherman's daughter never saw him again. He went under the waves, and she took her boat and went back to her father's. A while afterwards she had children, twins, and they were Jack Sea and John Sea.

So John Sea started out with his basket of provisions, and before he left the house his grandfather said to him, "Leave the knife that was your father's, and if the blade gets rusty we'll know that something has befallen you, and your brother will go in search of you." He went straight on from the door of his grandfather's house. He had been going from the full of daylight to the fall of dark when he sat down under a big tree and began to eat provisions out of his basket. As he did a red Fox came across the hill, and, stepping to where he sat, looked at him as if he wanted something from him. So John Sea took provision out of his basket, and gave it to him, and the red Fox ate standing beside him. Then the Fox said, "The hungry season is upon us, John Sea, and if you give me provision for my wife and my young ones, I'll not forget it to you." John Sea put his hand into the basket and gave him bread and meat and plenty of it. "My thanks to you, John Sea, and if ever you are in danger, call on the red Fox of the Three Rocks and he'll come to your help." And saying this the red Fox went across the hill.

Where he was when the sun sank, there he rested, and the next day he went on again. And so he was resting and traveling and traveling and resting until he came to a Giant's castle that was between a deep wood and a wide sea. There he asked for work and work was given him. It was to tend the pigs. He took out the drove to the wood in the morning, and in the evening he brought them back to the cave where their lairs were. And for his first month's work he was given a hawk, and for his second month's work he was given a hound, and for his third month's work he was given a horse. So John Sea fared, and in that time not a speck of rust came on the blade of the knife that hung against the wall of his grandfather's house.

One night, when he was lying in the moonlight outside the cave where the Giant's pigs were grunting and turning and turning and grunting, he heard a purring, and when he looked up he saw a running hare. She ran round him once, and ran round him twice, and ran round him for the third time, and as she did the hare said:

> "John Sea, John Sea,
> Follow you me;
> Follow me, John,
> And your quest is won."

John Sea rose from where he was resting, mounted his horse, took his hawk upon his shoulder, and rode where the hare ran.

She ran into the deep of the wood, and John Sea on his horse, with his hawk and his hound, followed her. But when he was under the oak branches of the mid-wood he lost sight of the hare. He stopped there and he made a shelter of branches and moss; he placed himself within it, with his horse and his hawk and his hound; they were closed from the creatures of the night and the dark wood.

His hound had taken a bird from the ground and his hawk had taken a bird from the air, and John Sea struck fire to cook the birds for his supper. As the light of the fire went through the branches of the shelter, he heard purring again, and then he heard a hand upon a door, and then a crying voice saying, "Let me to your fire and your shelter! Let me in, let me in!"

"Who are you that are out with the things of the night and the things of the dark wood?"

"An old woman I am, weary, weary."

"Not of good kind can you be who are with the things of the night and the things of the dark wood."

"I am an old woman, and if you won't let me to your fire and your shelter, I die, I die."

"Old woman, I will let you in."

"But your horse, your hound, and your hawk will attack me, I know."

"What shall I do, then, with my horse, my hound, and my hawk?"

"Tether them, tether them, tether them with this. When they are tethered I'll come into your shelter."

She handed him a hair of her head, a long hair. With that hair he tied his hawk, his hound, and his horse. Then he opened the door.

She came to the fire, a bent old woman with a pointed chin, and a beak of a nose, and a brown, rusty cloak upon her. "Where are you, hawk?" she said.

"Oh, I'm tied tightly, tightly, tied by my master."

"Where are you, hound?" she said.

"Oh, I'm tied tightly, tightly, tied by my master."

"Where are you horse," she said.

"Oh, I'm tied tightly, tightly, tied by my master."

She took up the birds and pulled them to pieces and ate them, feathers and all. "And since the horse, the hound, and the hawk are tethered, I can do what I came to do," she said. "I am the hare that led you far, John Sea, and I am the Hag of the Hollows, and this is where the quest for your father ends."

She took a rod that was under her rusty cloak and struck him with it, and John Sea fell on the ground, changed into a stone that was blue like the sea. She went her way then; and when daylight came, the horse, the hound, and the hawk broke the tether that held them and went back to the Giant's castle.

The blade that was hanging against the wall in the Fisherman's house became rusty all over, and Jack Sea went to search for his brother, his grandfather filling a basket with provisions for him. From the door of his grandfather's house he went straight on. He had been going from the full of daylight to the fall of dark when he sat down under a big tree and began to eat provisions out of his basket. And as he did an Eagle flew down and crouched before him. Jack Sea took provision out of the basket and gave it to the Eagle, and the Eagle ate it heartily. Then she said, "The hungry season is upon us, Jack Sea, and if you give me provision for my young ones, I'll not forget you." Jack Sea put his hand into the basket and gave her bread and meat and plenty of it, and the Eagle, taking it in her claws and rising up, said, "My thanks to you, Jack Sea, and if ever you are in danger, call on the Eagle of the One Rock, and she'll come to your help." And saying this the Eagle flew away.

Where the sun sank, there he rested, and the next day he went on again. And he was resting and traveling, traveling and resting, till he came to the Giant's castle that was between the deep wood and the wide sea. There he asked for work and work was given him. It was to tend the Giant's cattle. He took out the herd to the pasture in the morning, and in the evening he brought them back to the cave where their byre was. And for the first month's work he was given a hawk, and for the second month's work he was given a hound, and for the third month's work he was given a horse. But no one knew how he fared, for the knife that had been hanging against the wall of the Fisherman's house he had brought with him.

One night, when he was lying in the moonlight outside the cave where the Giant's cattle were lowing and bellowing, he heard a purring, and when he looked up he saw a running hare. She ran round him once, and she ran round him twice, and she ran round him for the third time, and as she did the hare said:

> "Jack Sea, Jack Sea,
> Follow you me;
> Jack, follow aright,
> And your quest end this night."

Jack Sea rose from where he was resting, mounted his horse, took his hawk upon his shoulder, and rode where the hare ran.

He followed her into the deep of the wood. Under the oak branches of the mid-wood he lost sight of her. He stopped there and he made a shelter of branches and moss; he placed himself within it with his horse, his hawk, and his hound.

His hound had taken a bird from the ground and his hawk had taken a bird from the air, and Jack Sea struck fire to cook the birds for his supper. He heard the purring again. He heard a hand upon the door. He heard a crying voice saying, "Let me to your fire and your shelter! Let me in, let me in!"

"Who are you that are out with the things of the night and the things of the dark wood?"

"An old woman I am, weary, weary."

"Not of good kind can you be to be out with the things of the night and the things of the dark wood."

"I am an old woman, and if you don't let me in to your fire and your shelter, I die, I die."

"Old woman, I will let you in."

"But your horse, your hound, and your hawk will attack me, I know."

"What shall I do, then, with my horse, my hound, and my hawk?"

"Tether them, tether them, tether them with this. When they are tethered, I'll come into your shelter."

She handed him a long hair, a hair of her head. He threw the hair into the fire. There was a crackling then.

"What is that that is crackling? How can I come in until I know what is crackling?"

"The pitch that is in the wood is crackling, for a fire is burning. And now I open the door for you, and that's all I'll do."

So she came in with her brown, rusty cloak about her. "Where are you hawk?" she said. "Where are you, hound? Where are you, horse?" And when hawk and hound and horse answered her, she took up the birds that were on the ground and pulled them to pieces and ate them, feathers and all. "I am the hare that led you so far, and I am the Hag of the Hollows, and this is where your quest ends, Jack Sea," she said.

As she did, the hawk flew at her, the hound sprang at her, the horse struck her with a hoof. Down she went upon the ground, and she had Jack Sea standing above her, his father's knife in his hand. And when she saw the blade she said, "Do not use it on me and I'll bring your brother back to you."

"What else will you do for me if I spare you, Hag of the Hollows?"

"I will show you how to come to your father."

"Your life is spared you."

At her bidding he struck with her rod the blue stone that was in the wood, and his brother, John Sea, stood before him. She told them how they might come to their father: "The Hag of the Waves keeps him in the caves of the sea. Until she is dead and gone he cannot come up from where he is. Her life depends upon an Egg. That Egg is in a Duck, and that Duck is in the Stag that is on the Brow of the Bare Mountain. When you get the Egg, go to the High Cliff and break it with the blade of the knife you have. The Hag of the Waves will be no more after that is done, and then you will see your father."

They let the Hag of the Hollows go from them and Jack Sea and John Sea went back to the Giant's Castle.

They spent their days searching for the Stag of the Bare Mountain. Once, when they were not ready for hunting him, the Stag came down from the top of the Mountain. Bending his head that had big antlers upon it he ran at them. All the weapons they had was the knife that Jack Sea carried.

"Fox of the Three Rocks, help us, for we're in danger," John Sea cried out. Then, as the Stag ran at them, the Fox crossed him, and going between his legs, threw him down. On the ground lay the Stag of the Bare Mountain. Jack Sea struck between his antlers, and where the knife pierced a blue Duck flew up.

She would have gone away only Jack Sea cried out, "Eagle of the One Rock, we're danger; come and help us." Then the Eagle appeared in the sky and circled round the Duck. Down came the Duck; she settled on the ground, and under the wings of the Eagle she laid the Egg. "Thanks to you, Fox of the Three Rocks; thanks to you, Eagle of the One Rock," the brothers cried as they took up the Egg. They went then to the High Cliff that looked over the sea.

And there, running up and down like the bird that is called the Gobadaun, was a figure like the Hag of the Hollows. She cried out to them when she saw Jack Sea and John Sea on the cliff above her. One held the Egg in his hand, the other struck it with the blade of his knife. As the Egg broke, the figure below turned to foam, the brown foam on the waves that in a while was blown away.

Then the brothers saw a man rise up from the sea, and they both ran down to where he stood. And he, seeing the knife in the hands of one of the brothers, put his arms around both. Princely looking was he. But when Jack Sea and John Sea looked upon him, they knew that he was not one whom they could ever walk with, nor one they could ever speak about. They stood silent as he was silent; in a while he went from them and back into the sea, putting into his belt the knife that Jack sea held to him.

But if he took the knife he gave them other things; on the arm of each he put a great ring of gold. And when they went back to where their grandfather lived, the young men there looked at the arm-rings and said, "John Sea and Jack Sea know who their father is, and we know that he is no common man." But the brothers did not stay to hear what was said about them. Bidding their grandfather a kind farewell, they went back to the Giant's castle. I believe they married the Giant's two daughters, and came to own castle and pasture and wood.

> "So stretch the rope
> With twists of hay,
> And if they didn't live happy,
> That we may!"

THE STONE LION

By CONSTANCE SMEDLEY

HERE is the Tibetan farmer, with his shaggy hair and lamb
skin cap, as he sits at ease discussing the light refreshment
the Prince's servants have been handing round.

You perceive he is carefully peeling a banana; and the Prince
noticed how respectfully his thick fingers touched the fruit, and how
slowly and earnestly they stripped the golden rind from the luscious
contents. His eating bowl held nothing else, in contrast to the heap
of fruit and sweetmeats which the other guests had willingly accepted, and the Prince noticed his blunt features and simple, honest
looks with favor. He could not remember having encountered him
in the market, although he was so striking a figure in his thick
mountain garments, and he directed the Market King to bid the
Tibetan tell his story.

"First letting us know to what felicitous circumstance we owe the
pleasure of his company," added the Prince.

"The truth is, your Highness, that the original circumstance
which led to my coming to Timbuktu was far from felicitous," said
he. "I grieve to confess that inadvertently I shot and brought to
earth a wild goose as it winged its way across the Celestial Lake. My
remorse was great, and resulted in my making a pilgrimage around
the Holy Mountain. During those hours of solitude and prayer, the
message came that I must atone by greater kindness to the goats and
yak I tended. On my return, therefore, I lavished love and care upon
them, and they repaid me by growing the finest fleeces that ever
trader marketed. So beautiful were my cherished goats that their
fame spread to Kashmir, and one day the most famous weaver of
that country set out for my hut on the borders of the lake. He was a
long time on his journey to the far north, but when he found me
and beheld the fleeces he cried that his journey had been abundantly
rewarded.

"Then he told me he desired to weave the finest shawl that had

180

ever been woven in Kashmir. He stayed some time with me, for he was full of admiration for my goats. He had never seen the like of their long horns, flattened and wavy, and as he watched them bounding and grazing on the high tablelands, he beheld new patterns of curves and spirals for his shawl. He was also interested in a neighbor who dyed the velvet for which Tibet is celebrated. The fresh and glossy tints appealed to him, and my neighbor was glad to tell him how they were produced.

"At the end of the summer we had become as brothers, and this shawl that he was to weave from the fleeces of my goats was as much a part of my existence as his own. It seemed indeed as if my pilgrimage had been blessed, and when he departed I accompanied him at his request, and spent the year with him in Kashmir. Very different was Kashmir from the stern and desolate mountains of Tibet. The lake by which he lived was small, and adorned by floating gardens made of reeds and sedge and lilies, coated with mud and covered with a multitude of flowers. I cultivated his crops of cucumber and melons that also grew upon the floating gardens, while he devoted all his time to the weaving of the shawl. When it was finished, we agreed that we must take it together to the mart of Timbuktu; our coming coincided with your visit, and thus the fleeces of the goats I tended have the honor of being touched by the hands of the Prince who owns the greatest treasures on this earth.

"*Om mani padme hum.*

"The jewel in the lotus leaf has been revealed.

"Thus have I experienced fulfillment.

"Your coming has crowned my repentance and my pilgrimage, and I thank thee, O Prince, for being the instrument of my destiny."

"Have you a story?" said the Prince.

"Indeed yes," said the Tibetan, "though it has something of the grimness of the north therein. My story is called: 'THE STONE LION: or, THE GUARDIAN OF THE MOUNTAIN.' "

Once upon a time two brothers lived in a big house with their mother. The elder brother was a shrewd business man, but the younger brother, though willing, was kind and simple, and had no talent for sharp dealing. As a goldsmith, the elder brother had continued opportunities for getting the better of his customers, and as he was a skillful workman they admired the cunning of his art and never thought to question his assurances as to the purity of his gold.

But the younger brother had neither the skill in devising of ornaments nor in mixing the gold with alloy, and moreover always answered the customers truthfully; so that one day the elder brother summoned him and told him to pack up and leave the house and seek his fortune elsewhere.

"You will do better as a farmer," said he. "I recommend you to grow nuts and peaches; or perhaps you could breed white eagles, or tend buffaloes. I am not going to share my patrimony with you any longer, for while you are with me I shall never become rich."

Thus the younger brother was turned out of his home, with his few clothes as his sole start in life, while his brother remained in possession of their home and patrimony. But the younger brother was destined to take with him the greatest treasure of all, for their mother was so grieved at the elder brother's behavior, she packed up, too, and accompanied her younger son.

She had a little money and some household tools, and they traveled comfortably enough. Presently they came to a great mountain at the foot of which stood an empty hut which belonged to no one. It was not far from a town, and the boy took their ax and chopped some wood. This they bound into neat fagots which the boy carried into town and sold. He returned with a store of black barley, apples, and figs; and some argol, as that was cheaper than wood for fuel.

Soon he had cut down the dead trees and bushes near their hut, and had to go increasingly farther in search of more. The mountain was very desolate and grand, and in his expeditions he never encountered a soul. In the town they had many tales to tell of the perils of the mountain, but because no one cared to climb the heights they were willing to pay good prices for his wood, and the boy was able to support his mother.

One day he ventured farther than he had yet climbed, and on the hillside came upon a life-sized lion carved out of stone.

"This must be the Guardian of the Mountain," thought the simple lad. There was an abundance of dry wood near, and when he went down to the town he bought two large candles, and when he next went up the mountain sought out the lion, placed the candles on each side, and, kneeling before him, thanked him for the hut in which they lived and the protection of the mountain.

When the lion opened his mouth and spoke, the boy was neither afraid nor surprised, so exceedingly lifelike was the carving.

"What are you doing so far up the mountain?" asked the lion.

"Chopping wood," said the boy. "But I do not cut down the young trees, nor do I harm the older ones. I clear the thickets of the under-growth and lop off the dead branches of the trees. My mother tells me I must first be a good forester, and second, a trader; for all the wealth in the world is not so valuable as a well-timbered mountain. She says the trees protect from drought and keep the streams full, and their roots hold the soil together. I beg for your patronage and assistance, and will readily observe any instructions you give me."

"Come again tomorrow without an ax, but with a bucket," said the Stone Lion, "and don't bring any more candles as I don't want the mountain set on fire." Then he snapped his jaws together and looked as if he had never opened them.

The boy thanked the lion and remained until the candles were burned out; then he went down to the town, sold his wood, and bought a new bucket to do the lion honor; for his mother had only one and needed hers. But she brought out the only thing of value she possessed. This was a ceremonial scarf; she told the boy to put it on when he knelt before the lion.

The lion opened his mouth directly the boy knelt down, and said: "Hold the bucket under my mouth, but when it is nearly full, you must tell me, for on no account must anything that I am going to give you fall to the ground."

The boy obeyed, and out of the lion's jaws poured a stream of gold. He told the lion directly the bucket was three-parts full, and the jaws promptly closed. But the boy carried his treasure down the mountain to his mother, who was thus enabled to purchase a large farmhouse. She also bought a good stock of oxen and buffalo and sheep, and they were able to live in comfortable prosperity, al-though they kept to fair dealing and never got the better of anyone.

They became both respected and popular, and presently news of their prosperity came to the elder brother. He could scarcely believe his ears when he heard of the big house and pasture lands, of the velvets the mother went dressed in, of the turquoise brooch the younger brother wore on market days, and the good table they kept and to which they welcomed every traveler.

They were living in better style than the elder brother himself, and he was so curious that he decided to pay them a visit. He set off, therefore, accompanied by his wife and carrying a very small piece of cloth as a present. He pretended to be very surprised at finding them in such affluence, and told them he had been worrying as to how they were getting on and had come to offer them assistance.

But his mother and younger brother assured him they had no need of anything, and instead they pressed all kinds of good things on him, and at last, as the younger brother took no notice of his hints, the elder came out with a plain question.

The younger brother was ready enough to tell him where the wealth had come from; ready, too, to describe the Stone Lion and to tell exactly what the lion had commanded.

When the elder brother and his wife retired for the night, they talked everything over and decided there was no need to go up the mountain to chop wood, nor to burn candles before the lion.

"You had better take him a couple of candles," said the wife, "and if he does not wish them to burn on account of the mountain being set on fire, you can just light them and immediately blow them out and bring them down again. But you had better take them. It will look rather crude if you only go up with a bucket."

"I was thinking of borrowing one of my brother's oxen," said the elder brother, "then I could take up a vat in the oxcart. It seems a pity to confine oneself to a bucket."

"But, as he is evidently a tyrant, he will expect you to do exactly what he says," replied his wife. "Besides, it looks as if you were ready to take trouble in the matter if you lug a great heavy bucket all the way up the mountain. I will help you, of course."

So the elder brother borrowed the largest bucket his brother possessed, the one into which they milked the buffaloes. When the lion

w him stagger up and set the huge receptacle under his chin, he
ened his mouth with a terrible expression and said, "What do
u want?"

"To do you honor, sire," said the elder brother, feeling in his
uch for the candles. They were so small, it was not easy to find
em. He set the candles on either side of the Stone Lion, and took
t his tinder-box. And then he hesitated. It had just occurred to
m that if he did not light them he could take them back to the
der and exchange them for something more useful, or get the
oney back.

"I am thinking of all this dry grass," said the brother, after he had
etended great difficulty in getting a spark so that the lion had
enty of time to stop him. But the lion's jaws were closed tightly,
ith the grimmest expression.

"It would be a great pity if the mountain took fire," said the elder
other.

Still the lion did not answer. The elder brother waited awhile,
en very unwillingly lit his candles.

At this the lion opened his mouth. How terrible he looked!
reat storm-clouds were hanging low upon the mountain's crest, and
e lion seemed to crouch with awful majesty. Again he roared, so
at the rocks echoed with dull thunder and the mountain shivered.
cold blast came from his jaws, and circled on and on amongst
e jagged peaks, wafting the storm-clouds into wreaths and whirls.

"What is this under my chin?" said the lion.

"A bucket, your Highness," faltered the elder brother. "My
other told me you commanded him to bring one."

"Tell me when the bucket is nearly full, as nothing that I give
u must fall to the ground," said the lion, and thereupon a stream
gold issued from its jaws.

The elder brother took no heed of the lowering clouds, the snow
at was beginning to eddy in the icy air, or the growing darkness.
he stream of gold usurped his vision; he pressed the gold pieces
wn so that they might lie well together, but though the bucket
as brimming he could not bring himself to tell the lion to stop.
stead he gave the bucket a shake, hoping to shake down the gold.

But the glittering pieces slid over the side and scattered on the ground. Immediately the storm ceased. But the lion's mouth remained open.

Then in a hoarse voice it said, "The largest piece has stuck in my throat; put your hand in my mouth and pull it out."

The elder brother was only too delighted to obey; but directly his hand and arm were inside, the cavernous jaws snapped together and there was the elder brother held fast in the insensible stone.

Then the storm broke in its full fury.

When his wife came out of the shelter of the thicket where he had left her, she found him half hanging to the lion's mouth with a bucketful of stones and earth beside him.

"Say no word to my mother and brother," he whimpered, "or they will come out and slay me, because I have been so unhappy to annoy His Majesty the lion through a most unfortunate accident, a pure oversight on my part, I assure His Majesty."

But the lion remained stonily silent; and the man commanded his wife to return to their own home and bring him food and rugs, the nights were bitterly cold so high up in the mountain.

She did as she was bid, and through her faithful service the man was able to remain alive, uncomfortable as his condition was. But after many months she came weeping.

"I have sold the last of our household goods," said she, "and the last of your goldsmith's stock is gone: we have no home, no shop, and no possessions. Would that you had never sought the lion in order to become rich!"

At this the lion's jaws opened wide, and a mighty roar of laughter resounded through the mountain.

"Quick!" cried his wife; but the man's arm was already out of the lion's jaws and he was running down the mountain as fast as he could.

He went straight to his younger brother to plead for help for his wife and child, and received money to buy a small farm, at his request, a long way from the mountain. There they spent the rest of their days in humble circumstances, and never did they come near the mountain again.

ALADDIN

From the ARABIAN NIGHTS

Illustrations by ERIC PAPE and JOHN D. BATTEN

THERE once lived, in one of the large and rich cities of China, a tailor, named Mustapha. He was very poor. He could hardly, by his daily labor, maintain himself and his family, which consisted only of his wife and a son.

His son, who was called Aladdin, was a very careless and idle fellow. He was disobedient to his father and mother, and would go out early in the morning and stay out all day, playing in the streets and public places with idle children of his own age.

When he was old enough to learn a trade, his father took him into his own shop, and taught him how to use his needle; but all his father's endeavors to keep him at his work were vain, for no sooner was his back turned than he was gone for that day. Mustapha chastised him; but Aladdin was incorrigible, and his father, to his great grief, was forced to abandon him to his idleness, and was so much troubled about him that he fell sick and died in a few months.

Aladdin, who was now no longer restrained by the fear of a father, gave himself entirely over to his idle habits, and was never out of the streets from his companions. This course he followed till he was fifteen years old, without giving his mind to any useful pursuit or the least reflection on what would become of him. As he was one day playing, according to custom, in the street with his evil associates, a stranger passing by stood to observe him.

This stranger was a sorcerer known as the African magician, as he had been but two days arrived from Africa, his native country.

The African magician, observing in Aladdin's countenance something which assured him that he was a fit boy for his purpose, inquired his name and history from some of his companions; and when he had learned all he desired to know, went up to him, and taking him aside from his comrades, said, "Child, was not your

father called Mustapha the tailor?" "Yes, sir," answered the boy;
"but he has been dead a long time."

At these words the African magician threw his arms about Aladdin's neck, and kissed him several times, with tears in his eyes, and
said, "I am your uncle. Your worthy father was my own brother.
I knew you at first sight; you are so like him." Then he gave Aladdin a handful of small money, saying, "Go, my son, to your mother,
give my love to her, and tell here that I will visit her tomorrow,
that I may see where my brother lived so long, and ended his days."

Aladdin ran to his mother, overjoyed at the money his uncle had
given him. "Mother," said he, "have I an uncle?" "No, child," replied his mother, "you have no uncle by your father's side or mine."
"I am just now come," said Aladdin, "from a man who says he is
my uncle and my father's brother. He cried and kissed me when I
told him my father was dead, and gave me money, sending his love
to you, and promising to come and pay you a visit that he may see
the house my father lived in and died in." "Indeed, child," replied
the mother, "your father had no brother, nor have you an uncle."

The next day the magician found Aladdin playing in another part
of the town, and embracing him as before, put two pieces of gold
into his hand and said to him, "Carry this, child, to your mother.
Tell her that I will come and see her tonight, and bid her get us
something for supper; but first show me the house where you live."

Aladdin showed the African magician the house, and carried the
two pieces of gold to his mother, who went out and bought provisions; and, considering she wanted various utensils, borrowed them
of her neighbors. She spent the whole day in preparing the supper;
and at night, when it was ready, said to her son, "Perhaps the
stranger knows not how to find our house; go and bring him, if you
meet with him."

Aladdin was just ready to go when the magician knocked at the
door, and came in loaded with wine and all sorts of fruits which he
brought for a dessert. After he had given what he brought into
Aladdin's hands, he saluted his mother, and desired her to show him
the place where his brother Mustapha used to sit on the sofa; and
when she had done so, he fell down and kissed it several times;

crying out, with tears in his eyes, "My poor brother, how unhappy am I, not to have come soon enough to give you one last embrace!" Aladdin's mother desired him to sit down in the same place.

"No," he said, "I shall not do that; but give me leave to sit opposite to it, that, although I see not the master of a family so dear to me, I may at least behold the place where he used to sit."

When the magician had made choice of a place and sat down, he began to enter into discourse with Aladdin's mother. "My good sister," said he, "do not be surprised at your never having seen me all the time you have been married to my brother Mustapha of happy memory. I have been forty years absent from this country, which is my native place as well as my late brother's; and during that time have traveled into the Indies, Persia, Arabia, Syria, and Egypt, and afterward crossed over into Africa, where I took up my abode. At last, as it is natural for a man, I was desirous to see my native country again and to embrace my dear brother; and finding I had strength enough to undertake so long a journey, I made the necessary preparations, and set out. Nothing ever afflicted me so much as hearing of my brother's death. But God be praised for all things! It is a comfort for me to find, as it were, my brother in a son who has his most remarkable features."

The African magician, perceiving that the widow wept at the remembrance of her husband, changed the conversation, and turning toward her son, asked him, "What business do you follow? Are you of any trade?"

At this question the youth hung down his head, and was not a little abashed when his mother answered, "Aladdin is an idle fellow. His father, when alive, strove all he could to teach him his trade but could not succeed; and since his death, notwithstanding all I can say to him, he does nothing but idle away his time in the streets as you saw him, without considering he is no longer a child; and if you do not make him ashamed of it, I despair of his ever coming to any good. For my part, I am resolved one of these days to turn him out of doors, and let him provide for himself."

After these words Aladdin's mother burst into tears; and the magician said, "This is not well, nephew; you must think of helping yourself, and getting your livelihood. There are many sorts of trades. Perhaps you do not like your father's and would prefer another; I will endeavor to help you. If you have no mind to learn any handicraft, I will take a shop for you, furnish it with all sorts of fine stuffs and linen, and then with the money you make from them you can lay in fresh goods, and live in an honorable way. Tell me freely what you thing of my proposal; you shall always find me ready to keep my word."

This plan just suited Aladdin, who hated work. He told the magician he had a greater inclination to that business than to any other, and that he should be much obliged to him for his kindness. "Well, then," said the African magician, "I will carry you with me tomorrow, clothe you as handsomely as the best merchants in the city, and afterward we will open a shop as I mentioned."

The widow, after his promises of kindness to her son, no longer doubted that the magician was her husband's brother. She thanked him for his good intentions; and after having exhorted Aladdin to render himself worthy of his uncle's favor, served up supper, at which they talked of several indifferent matters; and then the magician took his leave and retired.

He came again the next day as he had promised, and took Aladdin with him to a merchant who sold all sorts of clothes for different ages and ranks ready made, and a variety of fine stuffs, and bade Aladdin choose those he preferred, which he paid for.

When Aladdin found himself so handsomely equipped, he returned his uncle thanks, who thus addressed him: "As you are soon to be a merchant, it is proper you should frequent these shops, and be acquainted with them." He then showed him the largest and finest mosques, carried him to the khans or inns where the merchants and travelers lodged, and afterwards to the sultan's palace, where he had free access; and at last brought him to his own khan, where, meeting with some merchants he had become acquainted with since his arrival, he gave them a treat, to make them and his pretended nephew acquainted.

This entertainment lasted till night, when Aladdin would have taken leave of his uncle to go home; the magician would not let him go by himself, but conducted him to his mother, who, as soon as she saw him so well dressed, was transported with joy and bestowed a thousand blessings upon the magician.

Early the next morning, the magician called again for Aladdin, and said he would take him to spend the day in the country, and on the next he would purchase the shop. He then led him out at one of the gates of the city to some magnificent palaces, to each of which belonged beautiful gardens into which anybody might enter. At every building he came to, he asked Aladdin if he did not think it fine; and the youth was ready to answer, when any one presented itself, crying out, "Here is a finer house, uncle, than any we have yet seen." By this artifice the cunning magician led Aladdin some way into the country; and as he meant to carry him further to execute his design, he took an opportunity to sit down in one of the gardens, on the brink of a fountain of clear water which discharged itself by a lion's mouth of bronze into a basin, pretending to be tired. "Come, nephew," said he, "you must be weary, as well as I; let us rest ourselves and we shall be better able to pursue our walk."

The magician next pulled from his girdle a handkerchief with cakes and fruit and during this short repast he exhorted his nephew to leave off bad company and to seek that of wise and prudent men to improve by their conversation; "For," said he, "you will soon be at mans' estate, and you cannot too early begin to imitate their example." When they had eaten as much as they liked, they got up and pursued their walk through gardens separated from one another only by small ditches, which marked out the limits without interrupting the communication, so great was the confidence the inhabitants reposed in each other. By this means the African magician drew Aladdin insensibly beyond the gardens, and crossed the country till they nearly reached the mountains.

At last they arrived between two mountains of moderate height and equal size, divided by a narrow valley, which was the place where the magician intended to execute the design that had brought him from Africa to China. "We will go no farther now," said he to Aladdin; "I will show you here some extraordinary things, which, when you have seen, you will thank me for; but while I strike a

light, gather up all the loose dry sticks you can see to kindle a fir
with."

Aladdin found so many dried sticks that he soon collected a grea
heap. The magician presently set them on fire; and when they wer
in a blaze, threw in some incense, pronouncing several magical word
which Aladdin did not understand.

He had scarcely done so when the earth opened just before th
magician, and disclosed a stone with a brass ring fixed in it. Alac
din was so frightened that he would have run away, but the magicia
caught hold of him and gave him such a box on the ear that h
knocked him down. Aladdin got up trembling, and, with tears i
his eyes, said to the magician: "What have I done, uncle, to b
treated in this severe manner?" "I am your uncle," answered th
magician; "I supply the place of your father, and you ought to mak
no reply. But, child," added he, softening, "do not be afraid; for
shall not ask anything of you but that you obey me punctually, i
you would reap the advantages which I intend you. Know, ther
that under this stone there is hidden a treasure, destined to be your
and which will make you richer than the greatest monarch in th
world. No person but yourself is permitted to lift this stone, or ente
the cave; so you must punctually execute what I may command, fo
it is a matter of great consequence both to you and me."

Aladdin, amazed at all he saw and heard, forgot what was pas
and, rising, said: "Well, uncle, what is to be done? Command me,
am ready to obey." "I am overjoyed, child," said the African magi
cian, embracing him. "Take hold of the ring, and lift up that stone.
"Indeed, uncle," replied Aladdin, "I am not strong enough; yo
must help me." "You have no occasion for my assistance," answere
the magician; "if I help you, we shall be able to do nothing. Tak
hold of the ring and lift it up; you will find it will come easily.
Aladdin did as the magician bade him, raised the stone with eas
and laid it on one side.

When the stone was pulled up, there appeared a staircase abou
three or four feet deep leading to a door. "Descend, my son," sai
the African magician, "those steps, and open that door. It will lea
you into a palace divided into three great halls. In each of these yo

will see four large brass cisterns placed on each side, full of gold and silver; but take care you do not meddle with them. Before you enter the first hall, be sure to tuck up your robe, wrap it about you, and then pass through the second into the third without stopping. Above all things, have a care that you do not touch the walls so much as with your clothes; for if you do, you will die instantly. At the end of the third hall, and you will find a door which opens into a garden planted with fine trees loaded with fruit. Walk directly across the garden to a terrace, where you will see a niche before you, and in that niche a lighted lamp. Take the lamp down and put it out. When you have thrown away the wick and poured out the liquor, put it in your waistband and bring it to me. Do not be afraid that the liquor will spoil your clothes, for it is not oil and the lamp will be dry as soon as it is thrown out."

After these words the magician drew a ring off his finger, and put it on one of Aladdin's, saying: "It is a talisman against all evil, so long as you obey me. Go, therefore, boldly, and we shall both be rich all our lives."

Aladdin descended the steps, and, opening the door, found the three halls just as the African magician had described. He went through them with all the precaution the fear of death could inspire, crossed the garden without stopping, took down the lamp from the niche, threw out the wick and the liquor, and, as the magician had desired, put it in his waistband. But as he came down from the terrace, seeing it was perfectly dry, he stopped in the garden to observe the trees, which were loaded with extraordinary fruit of different colors on each tree. Some bore fruit entirely white, and some clear and transparent as crystal; some pale red, and others deeper; some green, blue, and purple, and others yellow; in short, there was fruit of all colors. The white were pearls; the clear and transparent, diamonds; the deep red, rubies; the paler, balas rubies; the green, emeralds; the blue, turquoises; the purple, amethysts; and the yellow, topazes. Aladdin, ignorant of their value, would have preferred figs, or grapes, or pomegranates; but as he had his uncle's permission, he resolved to gather some of every sort. Having filled the two new purses his uncle had bought for him with his clothes, he wrapped some up in the skirts of his vest, and crammed his bosom as full as it could hold.

Aladdin, having thus loaded himself with riches of which he knew not the value, returned through the three halls with the utmost precaution, and soon arrived at the mouth of the cave where the African magician awaited him with the utmost impatience. As soon as Aladdin saw him, he cried out, "Pray, uncle, lend me your hand, to help me out." "Give me the lamp first," replied the magician; "it will be troublesome to you." "Indeed, uncle," answered Aladdin, "I cannot now, but I will as soon as I am up." The African magician was determined that he would have the lamp before he would help him up; and Aladdin, who had encumbered himself so much with his fruit that he could not well get at it, refused to give it him till he was out of the cave. The African magician, provoked at this obstinate refusal, flew into a passion, threw a little of his incense into the fire, and pronounced two magical words, when the stone which had closed the mouth of the staircase moved into its place, with the earth over it, as it lay at the arrival of the magician and Aladdin.

This action of the magician plainly revealed to Aladdin that he was no uncle of his, but one who designed him evil. The truth was that he had learned from his magic books the secret and the value of this wonderful lamp, the owner of which would be made richer than any earthly ruler, and hence his journey to China. His art had also told him that he was not permitted to take it himself, but must receive it as a voluntary gift from the hands of another person. Hence he employed young Aladdin, and hoped by a mixture of kindness and authority to make him obedient to his word and will. When he found that his attempt had failed, he set out to return to Africa, but avoided the town lest any person who had seen him leave in company with Aladdin should make inquiries after the youth. Aladdin being suddenly enveloped in darkness, cried, and called out to his uncle to tell him he was ready to give him the lamp; but in vain, since his cries could not be heard. He descended to the bottom of the steps with a design to get into the palace, but the door, which was opened before by enchantment, was now shut by the same means. He then redoubled his cries and tears, sat down on the steps without any hopes of ever seeing light again, and in an expectation of passing from the present darkness to a speedy death. In this great emergency he said, "There is no strength or power but in the great and high God"; and in joining his hands to pray he rubbed the ring which the magician had put on his finger. Immediately a genie of frightful aspect appeared, and said, "What wouldst thou have? I am ready to obey thee. I serve him who possesses the ring on thy finger; I and the other slaves of that ring."

At another time Aladdin would have been frightened at the sight of such a figure, but the danger he was in made him answer without hesitation, "Whoever thou art, deliver me from this place."

He had no sooner spoken these words than he found himself on the very spot where the magician had last left him, and no sign of cave or opening, nor disturbance of the earth. Returning God thanks to find himself once more in the world, he made the best of his way home. When he got within his mother's door, the joy of seeing her and his weakness for want of sustenance made him so faint that he remained for a long time as dead. As soon as he recovered he related to his mother all that had happened to him, and they were both very vehement in their complaints of the cruel magician. Aladdin slept very soundly till late the next morning, when the first thing he said to his mother was that he wanted something to eat, and wished she would give him his breakfast.

"Alas! child," said she, "I have not a bit of bread to give you: you ate up all the provisions I had in the house yesterday; but I have a little cotton, which I have spun; I will go and sell it, and buy bread and something for our dinner."

"Mother," replied Aladdin, "keep your cotton for another time, and give me the lamp I brought home with me yesterday! I will go and sell it, and the money I shall get for it will serve both for breakfast and dinner, and perhaps supper, too."

Aladdin's mother took the lamp, and said to her son, "Here it is, but it is very dirty; if it was a little cleaner I believe it would bring something more." She took some fine sand and water to clean it; but had no sooner began to rub it than in an instant a hideous genie of gigantic size appeared before her, and said to her in a voice of thunder, "What wouldst thou have? I am ready to obey thee as thy slave, and the slave of all those who have the lamp in their hands, I and the other slaves of the lamp."

Aladdin's mother, terrified at the sight of the genie, fainted; when Aladdin, who had seen such a phantom in the cavern, snatched the lamp out of his mother's hand, and said to the genie boldly, "I am hungry; bring me something to eat." The genie disappeared immediately, and in an instant returned with a large silver tray holding twelve covered dishes of the same metal, which contained the most delicious viands; six large white bread cakes on two plates, two flagons of wine, and two silver cups. All these he placed upon a carpet and disappeared; this was done before Aladdin's mother recovered from her swoon.

Aladdin had fetched some water, and sprinkled it in her face to recover her. Whether that or the smell of the meat effected her cure, it was not long before she came to herself. "Mother," said Aladdin, "be not afraid; get up and eat; here is what will put you in heart, and at the same time satisfy my extreme hunger."

His mother was much surprised to see the great tray, twelve dishes, six loaves, the two flagons and cups, and to smell the savory odor which exhaled from the dishes. "Child," said she, "to whom are we obliged for this great plenty and liberality? Has the sultan been made acquainted with our poverty, and had compassion on us?" It is no matter, mother," said Aladdin, "let us sit down and eat; for you have almost as much need of a good breakfast as myself; when we have done, I will tell you."

Accordingly, both mother and son sat down, and ate with the better relish as the table was so well furnished. But all the time Aladdin's mother could not forbear looking at and admiring the tray and dishes, though she could not judge whether they were silver or any other metal, and the novelty more than the value attracted her attention.

The mother and son sat at breakfast till it was dinner time, and then they thought it would be best to put the two meals together; yet after this they found they should have enough left for supper, and two meals for the next day.

When Aladdin's mother had taken away and set by what was left, she went and sat down by her son on the sofa, saying, "I expect now that you should satisfy my impatience, and tell me exactly what passed between the genie and you while I was in a swoon"; which he readily complied with.

She was in as great amazement at what her son told her as at the appearance of the genie; and said to him, "But, son, what have we to do with genies? I never heard that any of my acquaintance had ever seen one. How came that vile genie to address himself to me, and not to you, to whom he had appeared before in the cave?" Mother," answered Aladdin, "the genie you saw is not the one who appeared to me. If you remember, he that I first saw called himself the slave of the ring on my finger; and this you saw called himself the slave of the lamp you had in your hand; but I believe you did not hear him, for I think you fainted as soon as he began to speak."

"What!" cried the mother. "Was your lamp, then, the occasion of that cursed genie's addressing himself rather to me than to you? Ah, my son, take it out of my sight, and put it where you please. I had rather you would sell it than run the hazard of being frightened to death again by touching it; and if you would take my advice you would part also with the ring, and not have anything to do with genies, who, as our prophet has told us, are only devils."

"With your leave, mother," replied Aladdin, "I shall now take care how I sell a lamp which may be so serviceable both to you and me. That false and wicked magician would not have undertaken so long a journey to secure this wonderful lamp if he had not known its value to exceed that of gold and silver. And since we have honestly come by it, let us make profitable use of it, without making any great show, and exciting the envy and jealousy of our neighbors. However, since the genies frighten you so much I will take it out of your sight, and put it where I may find it when I want it. The ring I cannot resolve to part with; for without that you had never seen me again; and though I am alive now, perhaps, if it were gone, I might not be some moments hence; therefore, I hope you will give me leave to keep it, and to wear it always on my finger."

Aladdin's mother replied that he might do what he pleased; for her part she would have nothing to do with genies, and never say anything more about them.

But the next night they had eaten all the provisions the genie had brought; and the next day Aladdin, who could not bear the thought of hunger, putting one of the silver dishes under his vest went out early to sell it, and addressing himself to a Jew whom he met in the streets, took him aside, and pulling out the plate, asked him if he would buy it. The cunning Jew took the dish, examined it, and as soon as he found it was good silver asked Aladdin how much he valued it. Aladdin, who had never been used to such traffic, told him he would trust to his judgment and honor. The Jew was somewhat confounded at this plain dealing; and doubting whether Aladdin understood the material or the full value of what he offered to sell, took a piece of gold out of his purse and gave it him, though it was but the sixtieth part of the worth of the plate. Aladdin, taking the money very eagerly, retired in so much haste that the Jew, not content with the exorbitancy of his profit, was vexed he had not penetrated into his ignorance, and was going to run after him to endeavor to get some change out of the piece of gold; but he ran so fast and had got so far that it would have been impossible for him to overtake him.

Before Aladdin went home he called at a baker's, bought some cakes of bread, changed his money, and on his return gave the rest to his mother, who went and purchased provisions enough to last them some time. After this manner they lived, till Aladdin had sold the twelve dishes singly, as necessity pressed, to the Jew, for the same money; who, after the first time, durst not offer him less for fear of losing so good a bargain. When he had sold the last dish, he had recourse to the tray, which weighed ten times as much as the dishes, and would have carried it to his old purchaser but that it was too large and cumbersome; therefore he was obliged to bring him home with him to his mother's, where, after the Jew had examined the weight of the tray, he laid down ten pieces of gold, with which Aladdin was very well satisfied.

When all the money was spent, Aladdin had recourse again to the lamp. He took it in his hand, looked for that part where his mother had rubbed it with the sand, rubbed it also, when the genie immediately appeared and said, "What wouldst thou have? I am ready to obey thee as thy slave, and the slave of all those who have that lamp in their hands; I and the other slaves of the lamp." "I am hungry," said Aladdin; "bring me something to eat." The genie disappeared, and presently returned with a tray, the same number of covered dishes as before, set them down, and vanished.

As soon as Aladdin found that their provisions were again exhausted, he took one of the dishes, and went to look for his Jew chapman; but passing by a goldsmith's shop, the goldsmith perceiving him called to him and said, "My lad, I imagine that you have something to sell to the Jew, whom I often see you visit; but perhaps you do not know that he is the greatest rogue among the Jews. I will give you the full worth of what you have to sell, or I will direct you to other merchants who will not cheat you."

This offer induced Aladdin to pull his plate from under his vest and show it to the goldsmith, who at first sight saw that it was made of the finest silver and asked him if he had sold such as that to the Jew; when Aladdin told him he had sold him twelve such, for a piece of gold each. "What a villain!" cried the goldsmith. "But," added he, "my son, what is past cannot be recalled. By showing you the value of this plate, which is of the finest silver we use in our shops, I will let you see how much the Jew has cheated you."

The goldsmith took a pair of scales, weighed the dish, and assured him that his plate would fetch by weight sixty pieces of gold, which he offered to pay down immediately.

Alladin thanked him for his fair dealing and never after went to any other person.

Though Aladdin and his mother had an inexhaustible treasure in their lamp, and might have had whatever they wished for, yet they lived with the same frugality as before, and it may easily be supposed that the money for which Aladdin had sold the dishes and tray was sufficient to maintain them some time.

During this interval, Aladdin frequented the shops of the principal merchants, where they sold cloths of gold and silver, linens, silk stuffs, and jewelry, and oftentimes joining in their conversation, acquired a knowledge of the world and a desire to improve himself. By his acquaintance among the jewelers he came to know that the fruits which he had gathered when he took the lamp were, instead of colored glass, stones of inestimable value; but he had the prudence not to mention this to anyone, not even to his mother.

One day as Aladdin was walking about the town, he heard an order proclaimed commanding the people to shut up their shops and houses, and keep within doors while the Princess Badroulboudour, the sultan's daughter, went to the bath and returned.

This proclamation inspired Aladdin with an eager desire to see the princess's face, which he determined to gratify by placing himself behind the door of the bath, so that he could not fail to see her face.

Aladdin had not long concealed himself before the princess came. She was attended by a great crowd of ladies, slaves and mutes, who walked on each side and behind her. When she came within three or four paces of the door of the bath, she took off her veil, and gave Aladdin an opportunity of a full view of her face.

The princess was a noted beauty; her eyes were large, lively, and sparkling; her smile bewitching; her nose faultless; her mouth small; her lips vermilion. It is not therefore surprising that Aladdin, who had never before seen such a blaze of charms, was dazzled and enchanted.

After the princess had passed by and entered the bath, Aladdin quitted his hiding place and went home. His mother perceived him to be more thoughtful and melancholy than usual, and asked what had happened to make him so, or if he was ill. He then told his mother all his adventure, and concluded by declaring, "I love the princess more than I can express, and am resolved that I will ask her in marriage of the sultan."

Aladdin's mother listened with surprise to what her son told her; but when he talked of asking the princess in marriage, she laughed aloud. "Alas! child," said she, "what are you thinking of? You must be mad to talk thus."

"I assure you, mother," replied Aladdin, "that I am not mad, but in my right senses. I foresaw that you would reproach me with folly and extravagance; but I must tell you once more that I am resolved to demand the princess of the sultan in marriage, nor do I despair of success. I have the slaves of the Lamp and of the Ring to help me, and you know how powerful their aid is. And I have another secret to tell you: those pieces of glass, which I got from the trees in the garden of the subterranean palace, are jewels of inestimable value and fit for the greatest monarchs. All the precious stones the jewelers have in Bagdad are not to be compared to mine for size and beauty; and I am sure that the offer of them will secure the favor of the sultan. You have a large porcelain dish fit to hold them; fetch it, and let us see how they will look when we have arranged them according to their different colors."

Aladdin's mother brought the china dish, when he took the jewels out of the two purses in which he had kept them, and placed them in order according to his fancy. But the brightness and luster they emitted in the daytime, and the variety of the colors, so dazzled the eyes both of mother and son that they were astonished beyond measure. Aladdin's mother, emboldened by the sight of these rich jewels, and fearful lest her son should be guilty of greater extravagance, complied with his request, and promised to go early the next morning to the palace of the sultan. Aladdin rose before daybreak, awakened his mother, pressing her to go to the sultan's palace and to get admittance if possible before the grand vizier, the other viziers, and the great officers of state went in to take their seats in the divan, where the sultan always attended in person.

Aladdin's mother took the china dish in which they had put the jewels the day before, wrapped it in two fine napkins, and set forward for the sultan's palace. When she came to the gates, the grand vizier, the other viziers, and most distinguished lords of the court were just gone in; but notwithstanding the crowd of people was great, she got into the divan, a spacious hall, the entrance into which was very magnificent. She placed herself just before the sultan, grand vizier, and the great lords, who sat in council on his right and left hand. Several causes were called according to their order, pleaded and adjudged, until the time the divan generally broke up, when the sultan, rising, returned to his apartment attended by the grand vizier; the other viziers and ministers of state then retired, as also did all those whose business had called them thither.

Aladdin's mother, seeing the sultan retire, and all the people depart, judged rightly that he would not sit again that day and resolved to go home; and on her arrival said with much simplicity, "Son, I have seen the sultan, and am very well persuaded he has seen me too, for I placed myself just before him; but he was so much taken up with those who attended on all sides of him that I pitied him and wondered at his patience. At last I believe he was heartily tired, for he rose up suddenly and would not hear a great many who were ready prepared to speak to him, but went away, at which I was well pleased, for indeed I began to lose all patience and was extremely fatigued with staying so long. But there is no harm done: I will go again tomorrow; perhaps the sultan may not be so busy."

The next morning she repaired to the sultan's palace with the present as early as the day before; but when she came there she found the gates of the divan shut. She went six times afterwards on the days appointed, placed herself always directly before the sultan, but with as little success as the first morning.

On the sixth day, however, after the divan was broken up, when the sultan returned to his own apartment he said to his grand vizier, "I have for some time observed a certain woman who attends constantly every day that I give audience, with something wrapped up in a napkin; she always stands up from the beginning to the breaking up of the audience, and affects to place herself just before me. If this woman comes to our next audience, do not fail to call her that I may hear what she has to say." The grand vizier made answer by lowering his hand, and then lifting it up above his head, signifying his willingness to lose it if he failed.

On the next audience day, when Aladdin's mother went to the divan and placed herself in front of the sultan as usual, the grand vizier immediately called the chief of the mace-bearers, and, pointing to her, bade him bring her before the sultan. The old woman at once followed the mace-bearer, and when she reached the sultan, bowed her head down to the carpet which covered the platform of the throne and remained in that posture till he bade her rise, which she had no sooner done than he said to her, "Good woman, I have observed you to stand many days, from the beginning to the rising of the divan; what business brings you here?"

After these words, Aladdin's mother prostrated herself a second time, and, when she arose, said, "Monarch of monarchs, I beg of you to pardon the boldness of my petition and to assure me of your pardon and forgiveness." "Well," replied the sultan, "I will forgive you, be it what it may, and no hurt shall come to you. Speak boldly."

When Aladdin's mother had taken all these precautions for fear of the sultan's anger, she told him faithfully the errand on which her son had sent her, and the event which led to his making so bold a request in spite of all her remonstrances.

The sultan hearkened to this discourse without showing the least anger; but, before he gave her any answer, asked her what she had brought tied up in the napkin. She took the china dish, which she had set down at the foot of the throne, untied it, and presented it to the sultan.

The sultan's amazement and surprise were inexpressible when he saw so many large, beautiful, and valuable jewels collected in the dish. He remained for some time lost in admiration. At last, when he had recovered himself, he received the present from Aladdin's mother's hand, saying, "How rich! how beautiful!" After he had admired and handled all the jewels one after another, he turned to his grand vizier and showing him the dish, said, "Behold! Admire! Wonder! And confess that your eyes never beheld jewels so rich and beautiful before!" The vizier was charmed. "Well," continued the sultan, "what sayest thou to such a present? Is it not worthy of the princess my daughter? And ought I not to bestow her on one who values her at so great a price?" "I cannot but own," replied the grand vizier, "that the present is worthy of the princess; but I beg of your Majesty to grant me three months before you come to a final resolution. I hope before that time my son, whom you have regarded with your favor, will be able to make a nobler present than this Aladdin, who is an entire stranger to your Majesty."

The sultan granted his request, and he said to the old woman, "Good woman, go home and tell your son that I agree to the proposal you have made me; but I cannot marry the princess my daughter for three months. At the expiration of that time come again."

Aladdin's mother returned home much more gratified than she had expected, and told her son with much joy the condescending answer she had received from the sultan's own mouth; and that she was to come to the divan again that day three months.

Aladdin thought himself the most happy of all men at hearing this news, and thanked his mother for the pains she had taken in the affair, the good success of which was of so great importance to his peace that he counted every day, week, and even hour as it passed. When two of the three months were passed, his mother one evening, having no oil in the house, went out to buy some, and found a general rejoicing—the houses dressed with foliage, silks, and carpeting, and everyone striving to show their joy according to their ability. The streets were crowded with officers in habits of ceremony, mounted on horses richly caparisoned, each attended by a great many footmen. Aladdin's mother asked the oil merchant what was the meaning of all this preparation of public festivity. "Whence came you, good woman," said he, "that you don't know that the grand vizier's son is to marry the Princess Badroulboudour, the sultan's daughter, tonight? She will return presently from the bath; and these officers whom you see are to assist at the cavalcade to the palace, where the ceremony is to be solemnized."

Aladdin's mother on hearing this news ran home very quickly. "Child," cried she, "you are undone; the sultan's fine promise will come to naught! This night the grand vizier's son is to marry the Princess Badroulboudour."

At this account Aladdin was thunderstruck, and he bethought himself of the lamp and of the genie who had promised to obey him; and without indulging in idle words against the sultan, the vizier, or his son, he determined, if possible, to prevent the marriage.

When Aladdin had got into his chamber, he took the lamp, rubbed it in the same place as before, when immediately the genie appeared and said to him, "What wouldst thou have? I am ready to obey thee as thy slave; I and the other slaves of the lamp." "Hear me," said Aladdin. "Thou hast hitherto obeyed me; but now I am about to impose on thee a harder task. The sultan's daughter, who was promised me as my bride, is this night married to the son of the grand vizier. Bring them both hither to me immediately they retire to their bedchamber."

"Master," replied the genie, "I obey you."

Aladdin supped with his mother as was their wont, and then went to his own apartment and sat up to await the return of the genie according to his commands.

In the meantime the festivities in honor of the princess's marriage were conducted in the sultan's apartment with great magnificence. The ceremonies were at last brought to a conclusion, and the princess and the son of the vizier retired to the bedchamber prepared for them. No sooner had they entered it and dismissed their attendants, than the genie, the faithful slave of the lamp, to the great amazement and alarm of the bride and bridegroom, took up the bed, and, by an agency invisible to them, transported it in an instant into Aladdin's chamber, where he set it down. "Remove the bridegroom," said Aladdin to the genie, "and keep him prisoner till tomorrow dawn, and then return with him here." On Aladdin being left alone with the princess, he endeavored to assuage her fears, and explained to her the treachery practised upon him by the sultan her father. At break of day the genie appeared at the appointed hour, bringing back the bridegroom, whom, by breathing upon, he had left motionless and entranced at the door of Aladdin's chamber during the night; and, at Aladdin's command, transported the couch with the bride and bridegroom on it, by the same invisible agency, into the palace of the sultan.

At the instant that the genie had set down the couch with the bride and groom in their own chamber, the sultan came to the door to offer his good wishes to his daughter.

The grand vizier's son, who was almost perished with cold by standing in his thin under-garment all night, no sooner heard the knocking at the door than he ran into the robing chamber.

The sultan, having opened the door, went to the bedside, kissed the princess on the forehead, but was extremely surprised to see her look so melancholy. She only cast at him a sorrowful look, expressive of great affliction. He suspected there was something extraordinary in this silence, and thereupon went immediately to the sultana's apartment, told her in what a state he had found the princess, and how she had received him. "Sire," said the sultana, "I will go and see her; she will not receive me in the same manner."

The princess received her mother with sighs and tears, and signs of deep dejection. At last, upon her pressing on her the duty of telling her all her thoughts, she gave to the sultana a precise description of all that happened to her during the night; on which the sultana enjoined on her the necessity of silence and discretion, as no one would give credence to so strange a tale. The grand vizier's son, elated with the honor of being the sultan's son-in-law, kept silence on his part, and the events of the night were not allowed to cast the least gloom on the festivities on the following day in continued celebration of the royal marriage.

When night came the bride and bridegroom were again attended to their chamber with the same ceremonies as on the preceding evening. Aladdin, knowing that this would be so, had already given his commands to the genie of the lamp; and no sooner were they alone than their bed was removed in the same mysterious manner as on the preceding evening; and having passed the night in the same unpleasant way, they were in the morning conveyed to the palace of the sultan. Scarcely had they been replaced in their apartment than the sultan came to make his compliments to his daughter, when the princess could no longer conceal from him the unhappy treatment she had been subjected to, and told him all that had happened, as she had already related it to her mother. The sultan, on hearing these strange tidings, consulted with the grand vizier; and finding from him that his son had been subjected to even worse treatment by a invisible agency, he determined to declare the marriage to be cancelled, and all the festivities, which were yet to last for several days, to be countermanded and terminated.

This sudden change in the mind of the sultan gave rise to various speculations and reports. Nobody but Aladdin knew the secret, and he kept it with the most scrupulous silence; and neither the sultan nor the grand vizier, who had forgotten Aladdin and his request, had the least thought that he had any hand in the strange adventures that befell the bride and bridegroom.

On the very day that the three months contained in the sultan's promise expired, the mother of Aladdin again went to the palace, and stood in the same place in the divan. The sultan knew her again, and directed his vizier to have her brought before him.

After having prostrated herself, she made answer in reply to the sultan. "Sire, I come at the end of three months to ask of you the fulfillment of the promise you made to my son." The sultan little thought the request of Aladdin's mother was made to him in earnest, or that he would hear any more of the matter. He therefore took counsel with his vizier, who suggested that the sultan should attach such conditions to the marriage that no one in the humble condition of Aladdin could possibly fulfill. In accordance with the suggestion of the vizier, the sultan replied to the mother of Aladdin: "Good woman, it is true sultans ought to abide by their word, and I am ready to keep mine, by making your son happy in marriage with the princess my daughter. But as I cannot marry her without some, further proof of your son being able to support her in royal state, you may tell him I will fulfill my promise as soon as he shall send me forty trays of massy gold, full of the same sort of jewels you have already made me a present of, and carried by the like number of black slaves, who shall be led by as many young and handsome white slaves, all dressed magnificently. On these conditions I am ready to bestow the princess my daughter upon him; therefore, good woman, go and tell him so, and I will wait till you bring me his answer."

Aladdin's mother prostrated herself a second time before the sultan's throne, and retired. On her way home she laughed within herself at her son's foolish imagination. "Where," said she, "can he get so many large gold trays, and such precious stones to fill them? It is altogether out of his power, and I believe he will not be much pleased with my embassy this time." When she came home full of these thoughts, she told Aladdin all the circumstances of her interview with the sultan and the conditions on which he consented to the marriage. "The sultan expects your answer immediately!" said she; and then added, laughing, "I believe he may wait long enough!"

"Not so long, mother, as you imagine," replied Aladdin. "This demand is a mere trifle, and will prove no bar to my marriage with the princess. I will prepare at once to satisfy his request."

Aladdin retired to his own apartment and summoned the genie of the lamp, and required him immediately to prepare and present the gift before the sultan closed his morning audience, according to the terms in which it had been prescribed. The genie professed his obedience to the owner of the lamp and disappeared. Within a very short time, a train of forty black slaves, led by the same number of white slaves, appeared opposite the house in which Aladdin lived. Each black slave carried on his head a basin of massy gold, full of pearls, diamonds, rubies, and emeralds. Aladdin then addressed his mother: "Madam, pray lose no time; before the sultan and the divan rise, I would have you return to the palace with this present as the dowry demanded for the princess, that he may judge by my diligence and exactness of the ardent and sincere desire I have to procure myself the honor of this alliance."

As soon as this magnificent procession, with Aladdin's mother at its head, had begun to march from Aladdin's house, the whole city was filled with the crowds of people desirous to see so grand a sight. The graceful bearing, elegant form, and wonderful likeness of each slave; their grave walk at an equal distance from each other; the luster of their jeweled girdles and the brilliancy of the aigrettes of precious stones in their turbans excited the greatest admiration in the spectators. As they had to pass through several streets to the palace, the whole length of the way was lined with files of spectators. Nothing, indeed, was ever seen so beautiful and brilliant in the sultan's palace, and the richest robes of the emirs of his court were not to be compared to the costly dresses of these slaves, whom they supposed to be kings.

As the sultan, who had been informed of their approach, had given orders for them to be admitted, they met with no obstacle but went into the divan in regular order; one part turning to the right, and the other to the left. After they were all entered, and had formed a semicircle before the sultan's throne, the black slaves laid the

Eric Pape

Aladdin and the princess.

[See page 214]

golden trays on the carpet, prostrated themselves, touching the carpet with their foreheads, and at the same time the white slaves did the same. When they rose, the black slaves uncovered the trays, and then all stood with their arms crossed over their breasts.

In the meantime, Aladdin's mother advanced to the foot of the throne and having prostrated herself, said to the sultan, "Sire, my son knows this present is much below the notice of Princess Badroulboudour; but hopes, nevertheless, that your Majesty will accept of it and make it agreeable to the princess, and with the greater confidence since he has endeavored to conform to the conditions you were pleased to impose."

The sultan, overpowered at the sight of such more than royal magnificence, replied without hesitation to the words of Aladdin's mother: "Go and tell your son that I wait with open arms to embrace him; and the more haste he makes to come and receive the princess my daughter from my hands, the greater pleasure he will do me." As soon as Aladdin's mother had retired the sultan put an end to the audience; and rising from his throne, ordered that the princess's attendants should come and carry the trays into their mistress's apartment, whither he went himself to examine them with her at his leisure. The fourscore slaves were conducted into the palace; and the sultan, telling the princess of their magnificent apparel, ordered them to be brought before her apartment that she might see through the lattices he had not exaggerated in his account of them.

In the meantime Aladdin's mother reached home, and showed in her air and countenance the good news she brought her son. "My son," said she, "you may rejoice you are arrived at the height of your desires. The sultan has declared that you shall marry the Princess Badroulboudour. He waits for you with impatience."

Aladdin, enraptured with this news, made his mother very little reply, but retired to his chamber. There he rubbed his lamp, and the obedient genie appeared. "Genie," said Aladdin, "convey me at once to a bath, and supply me with the richest and most magnificent robe ever worn by a monarch."

No sooner were the words out of his mouth than the genie rendered him, as well as himself, invisible, and transported him into a

hummum of the finest marble of all sorts of colors, where he wa
undressed, without seeing by whom, in a magnificent and spac
ous hall. He was then well rubbed and washed with various scente
waters. After he had passed through several degrees of heat, he cam
out quite a different man from what he was before. His skin wa
clear as that of a child, his body lightsome and free; and when h
returned into the hall, he found, instead of his own poor raiment,
robe the magnificence of which astonished him. The genie helpe
him to dress and when he had done, transported him back to hi
own chamber where he asked him if he had any other command:

"Yes," answered Aladdin; "bring me a charger that surpasses i
beauty and goodness the best in the sultan's stables, with a saddl
bridle, and other caparisons to correspond with his value. Furnis
also twenty slaves as richly clothed as those who carried the presen
to the sultan, to walk by my side and follow me, and twenty more t
go before me in two ranks. Besides these, bring my mother si
women slaves to attend her, as richly dressed at least as any of th
Princess Badroulboudour's, each carrying a complete dress fit for an
sultana. I want also ten thousand pieces of gold in ten purses. Mak
haste."

As soon as Aladdin had given these orders, the genie disappeared
but presently returned with the horse, the forty slaves, ten of whom
carried each a purse containing ten thousand pieces of gold, and si
women slaves, each carrying on her head a different dress for Alad
din's mother wrapped up in a piece of silver tissue, and presente
them all to Aladdin.

He presented the six women slaves to his mother, telling her they
were her slaves and that the dresses they had brought were for he
use. Of the ten purses Aladdin took four, which he gave to hi
mother telling her those were to supply her with necessaries; th
other six he left in the hands of the slaves who brought them, with
an order to throw them by handfuls among the people as they wen
to the sultan's palace. The six slaves who carried the purses he or
dered likewise to go before him, three on the right and three on
the left.

When Aladdin had thus prepared himself for his first interview with the sultan, he dismissed the genie, and immediately mounting his charger, began his march, and though he never was on horseback before, appeared with a grace the most experienced horseman might envy. The innumerable concourse of people through whom he passed made the air echo with their acclamations, especially every time the six slaves who carried the purses threw handfuls of gold among the populace.

On Aladdin's arrival at the palace, the sultan was surprised to find him more richly and magnificently robed than he had ever been himself, and was impressed with his good looks and dignity of manner, which were so different from what he expected in the son of one so humble as Aladdin's mother. He embraced him with all the demonstrations of joy, and when he would have fallen at his feet, held him by the hand, and made him sit near his throne. He shortly after led him, amid the sounds of trumpets, hautboys, and all kinds of music, to a magnificent entertainment, at which the sultan and Aladdin ate by themselves and the great lords of the court, according to their rank and dignity, sat at different tables. After the feast the sultan sent for the chief cadi, and commanded him to draw up a contract of marriage between the Princess Badroulboudour and Aladdin. When the contract had been drawn, the sultan asked Aladdin if he would stay in the palace and complete the ceremonies of the marriage that day.

"Sire," said Aladdin, "though great is my impatience to enter on the honor granted me by your Majesty, yet I beg you to permit me first to build a palace worthy to receive the princess your daughter. I pray you to grant me sufficient ground near your palace, and I will have it completed with the utmost expedition."

The sultan granted Aladdin his request, and again embraced him. After which Aladdin took his leave with as much politeness as if he had been bred up and had always lived at court.

Aladdin returned home in the order he had come, amid the acclamations of the people, who wished him all happiness and prosperity. As soon as he dismounted, he retired to his own chamber, took the lamp, and summoned the genie as usual, who professed his allegiance.

"Genie," said Aladdin, "build me a palace fit to receive the Princess Badroulboudour. Let its materials be made of nothing less than porphyry, jasper, agate, lapis-lazuli, and the finest marble. Let its walls be massive gold and silver bricks laid alternately. Let each front contain six windows, and let the lattices of these (except one, which must be left unfinished) be enriched with diamonds, rubies, and emeralds, so that they shall exceed everything of the kind ever seen in the world. Let there be an inner and outer court in front of the palace, and a spacious garden; but above all things, provide a safe treasure-house, and fill it with gold and silver. Let there be also kitchens and store-houses, stables full of the finest horses, with their equerries and grooms and hunting equipage, officers, attendants, and slaves, both men and women, to form a retinue for the princess and myself. Go and execute my wishes."

When Aladdin gave these commands to the genie the sun was set. The next morning at daybreak the genie presented hmself, and having obtained Aladdin's consent, transported him in a moment to a palace he had made. The genie led him through all the apartments, where he found officers and slaves, habited according to their rank and the services to which they were appointed. The genie then showed him the treasury, which was opened by a treasurer, where Aladdin saw large vases of different sizes piled up to the top with money, ranged all round the chamber. The genie thence led him to the stables, where were some of the finest horses in the world, and the grooms busy in dressing them; from thence they went to the storehouses, which were filled with all things necessary both for food and ornament.

When Aladdin had examined every portion of the palace, and particularly the hall with the four-and-twenty windows, and found it to far exceed his fondest expectations, he said, "Genie, there is one thing wanting—a fine carpet for the princess to walk upon from the sultan's palace to mine. Lay one down immediately."

The genie disappeared, and Aladdin saw what he desired executed in an instant. The genie then returned and carried him to his own home.

When the sultan's porters came to open the gates they were

mazed to find what had been an unoccupied garden filled up with a magnificent palace, and a splendid carpet extending to it all the way from the sultan's palace. They told the strange tidings to the grand vizier, who informed the sultan, who exclaimed, "It must be Aladdin's palace, which I gave him leave to build for my daughter. He has wished to surprise us, and let us see what wonders can be done in only one night."

Aladdin, on his being conveyed by the genie to his own home, requested his mother to go to the Princess Badroulboudour and tell her that the palace would be ready for her reception in the evening. She went, attended by her women slaves, in the same order as on the preceding day. Shortly after her arrival at the princess's apartment, the sultan himself came in, and was surprised to find her, whom he knew as his suppliant at his divan in such humble guise, to be now more richly and sumptuously attired than his own daughter. This gave him a higher opinion of Aladdin, who took such care of his mother and made her share his wealth and honors. Shortly after her departure Aladdin, mounting his horse and attended by his retinue of magnificent attendants, left his paternal home forever, and went to the palace in the same pomp as on the day before. Nor did he forget to take with him the wonderful lamp to which he owed all his good fortune, nor to wear the ring which was given him as a talisman. The sultan entertained Aladdin with the utmost magnificence, and at night, on the conclusion of the marriage ceremonies, the princess took leave of the sultan her father. Bands of music led the procession followed by a hundred state ushers, and the like number of black mutes, in two files, with their officers at their head. Four hundred of the sultan's young pages carried flambeaux on each side, which, together with the illuminations of the sultan's and Aladdin's palaces, made it as light as day. In this order the princess, conveyed in her litter, and accompanied also by Aladdin's mother carried in a superb litter and attended by her women slaves, proceeded on the carpet which was spread from the sultan's palace to that of Aladdin. On her arrival Aladdin was ready to receive her at the entrance, and led her into a large hall, illuminated with an infinite number of wax candles, where a noble feast was served up. The dishes were of massy gold and contained the most delicate viands. The vases, basins, and goblets were gold also, and of exquisite workmanship, and all the other ornaments and embellishments of the hall were answerable to this display. The princess, dazzled to see so much riches collected in one place, said to Aladdin: "I thought, prince, that nothing in the world was so beautiful as the sultan my father's palace, but the sight of this hall alone is sufficient to show I was deceived."

When the supper was ended, there entered a company of female dancers who performed according to the custom of the country, singing at the same time verses in praise of the bride and bridegroom. About midnight Aladdin's mother conducted the bride to the nuptial apartment, and he soon after retired.

The next morning the attendants of Aladdin presented themselves to dress him, and brought him another habit as rich and magnificent as that worn the day before. He then ordered one of the horses to be got ready, mounted him, and went in the midst of a large troop of slaves to the sultan's palace, to entreat him to take a repast in the princess's palace, attended by his grand vizier and all the lords of his court. The sultan consented with pleasure, rose up immediately, and preceded by the principal officers of his palace, and followed by all the great lords of his court, accompanied Aladdin.

The nearer the sultan approached Aladdin's palace the more he was struck with its beauty; but when he entered it, came into the hall, and saw the windows enriched with diamonds, rubies, emeralds, all large perfect stones, he was completely surprised, and said to his son-in-law: "This palace is one of the wonders of the world; for where in all the world besides shall we find walls built of massy gold and silver, and diamonds, rubies, and emeralds composing the windows? But what most surprises me is that a hall of this magnificence should be left with one of its windows incomplete and unfinished." "Sire," answered Aladdin, "the omission was by design, since I wished that you should have the glory of finishing this hall," "I take your intention kindly," said the sultan, "and will give order about it immediately."

After the sultan had finished this magnificent entertainment provided for him and for his court by Aladdin, he was informed that the jewelers and goldsmiths attended; upon which he returned to the hall, and showed them the window which was unfinished. "I sent for you," said he "to fit up this window in as great perfection as the rest. Examine them well, and make all the despatch you can."

The jewelers and goldsmiths examined the three-and-twenty windows with great attention, and after they had consulted together to know what each could furnish, they returned and presented themselves before the sultan, whose principal jeweler, undertaking to speak for the rest, said: "Sire, we are all willing to exert our utmost care and industry to obey you; but among us all we cannot furnish jewels enough for so great a work." "I have more than are necessary," said the sultan; "come to my palace, and you shall choose what may answer your purpose."

When the sultan returned to his palace, he ordered his jewels to be brought out, and the jewelers took a great quantity, particularly those Aladdin had made him a present of, which they soon used without making any great advance in their work. They came again several times for more, and in a month's time had not finished half their work. In short, they used all the jewels the sultan had, and borrowed of the vizier, but yet the work was not half done.

Aladdin, who knew that all the sultan's endeavors to make this window like the rest were in vain, sent for the jewelers and goldsmiths, and not only commanded them to desist from their work, but ordered them to undo what they had begun and to carry all their jewels back to the sultan and to the vizier. They undid in a few hours what they had been six weeks about, and retired, leaving Aladdin alone in the hall. He took the lamp which he carried about him, rubbed it, and presently the genie appeared. "Genie," said Aladdin, "I ordered thee to leave one of the four-and-twenty windows of this hall imperfect, and thou hast executed my commands punctually; now I would have thee make it like the rest." The genie immediately disappeared. Aladdin went out of the hall, and returning soon after, found the window as he wished it to be, like the others.

In the meantime, the jewelers and goldsmiths repaired to the palace, and were introduced into the sultan's presence, where the chief jeweler presented the precious stones which he had brought back. The sultan asked them if Aladdin had given them any reason for so doing, and they answering that he had given them none, he ordered a horse to be brought, which he mounted, and rode to his son-in-law's palace, with some few attendants on foot, to inquire why he had ordered the completion of the window to be stopped. Aladdin met him at the gate, and without giving any reply to his inquiries, conducted him to the grand saloon, where the sultan, to his great surprise, found the window which was left imperfect to correspond exactly with the others. He fancied at first that he was mistaken, and examined the two windows on each side, and afterwards all the four-and-twenty; but when he was convinced that the window which several workmen had been so long about was finished in so short a time, he embraced Aladdin and kissed him between his eyes.

"My son," said he, "what a man you are to do such surprising things always in the twinkling of an eye! There is not your fellow in the world; the more I know, the more I admire you."

The sultan returned to the palace, and after this went frequently to the window to contemplate and admire the wonderful palace of his son-in-law.

Aladdin did not confine himself in his palace, but went with much state, sometimes to one mosque, and sometimes to another, to prayers, or to visit the grand vizier or the principal lords of the court. Every time he went out, he caused two slaves who walked by the side of his horse, to throw handfuls of money among the people as he passed through the streets and squares. This generosity gained him the love and blessings of the people, and it was common for them to swear by his head. Thus Aladdin, while he paid all respect to the sultan, won by his affable behavior and liberality the affections of the people.

Aladdin had conducted himself in this manner several years, when the African magician, who had for some years dismissed him from his recollection, determined to inform himself with certainty whether he perished, as he supposed, in the subterranean cave or not. After he had resorted to a long course of magic ceremonies, and had formed a horoscope by which to ascertain Aladdin's fate, what was his surprise to find the appearances to declare that Aladdin, instead

John D. Batten

"Who will change old lamps for new ones?"

[See page 218]

of dying in the cave, had made his escape, and was living in royal splendor by the aid of the genie of the wonderful lamp!

On the very next day, the magician set out and traveled with the utmost haste to the capital of China, where, on his arrival, he took up his lodging in a khan.

He then quickly learned about the wealth, charities, happiness, and splendid palace of Prince Aladdin. Directly he saw the wonderful fabric, he knew that none but the genies, the slaves of the lamp, could have performed such wonders; and piqued to the quick at Aladdin's high estate, he returned to the khan.

On his return he had recourse to an operation of geomancy to find out where the lamp was—whether Aladdin carried it about with him, or where he left it. The result of his consultation informed him, to his great joy, that the lamp was in the palace. "Well," said he, rubbing his hands in glee, "I shall have the lamp, and I shall make Aladdin return to his original mean condition."

The next day the magician learned, from the chief superintendent of the khan where he lodged, that Aladdin had gone on a hunting expedition which was to last for eight days, of which only three had expired. The magician wanted to know no more. He resolved at once on his plans. He went to a coppersmith and asked for a dozen copper lamps: the master of the shop told him he had not so many by him, but if he would have patience till the next day he would have them ready. The magician appointed his time, and desired him to take care that they should be handsome and well polished.

The next day the magician called for the twelve lamps, paid the man his full price, put them into a basket hanging on his arm, and went directly to Aladdin's palace. As he approached, he began crying, "Who will change old lamps for new ones?" As he went along, a crowd of children collected, who hooted, and thought him, as did all who chanced to be passing by, a madman or a fool to offer to change new lamps for old ones.

The African magician regarded not their scoffs, hootings or all they could say to him, but still continued crying, "Who will change old lamps for new ones?" He repeated this so often, walking backward and forward in front of the palace, that the princess, who was then in the hall with the four-and-twenty windows, hearing a man cry something, and seeing a great mob crowding about him, sent one of her women slaves to know what he cried.

The slave returned laughing so heartily that the princess rebuked her. "Madam," answered the slave, laughing still, "who can forbear laughing, to see an old man with a basket on his arm full of fine new lamps, asking to change them for old ones? The children and mob crowding about him so that he can hardly stir, make all the noise they can in derision of him."

Another female slave, hearing this, said: "Now you speak of lamps, I know not whether the princess may have observed it, but there is an old one upon a shelf of the Prince Aladdin's robing-room, and whoever owns it will not be sorry to find a new one in its stead. If the princess chooses, she may have the pleasure of trying if this old man is so silly as to give a new lamp for an old one, without taking anything for the exchange."

The princess, who knew not the value of this lamp and the interest that Aladdin had to keep it safe, entered into the pleasantry, and commanded a slave to take it and make the exchange. The slave obeyed, went out of the hall, and no sooner got to the palace gates than he saw the African magician, called to him, and, showing him the old lamp said, "Give me a new lamp for this."

The magician never doubted but this was the lamp he wanted. There could be no other such in this palace, where every utensil was gold or silver. He snatched it eagerly out of the slave's hand, and, thrusting it as far as he could into his breast, offered him his basket and bade him choose which he liked best. The slave picked out one, and carried it to the princess; but the change was no sooner made than the place rung with the shouts of the children, deriding the magician's folly. The African magician stayed no longer near the palace, nor cried any more, "New lamps for old ones!" but made the best of his way to his khan. His end was answered; and by his silence he got rid of the children and the mob.

As soon as he was out of sight of the two palaces, he hastened down the least frequented streets; and, having no more occasion for his lamps or basket, set all down in a spot where nobody saw him.

Then going down another street or two, he walked till he came to one of the city gates, and pursuing his way through the suburbs which were very extensive, at length reached a lonely spot, where he stopped till the darkness of the night as the most suitable time for the design he had in contemplation. When it became quite dark, he pulled the lamp out of his breast and rubbed it. At that summons the genie appeared, and said, "What wouldst thou have? I am ready to obey thee as thy slave, and the slave of all those who have that lamp in their hands; both I and the other slaves of the lamp." "I command thee," replied the magician, "to transport me immediately, and the palace which thou and the other slaves of the lamp have built in this city, with all the people in it, to Africa." The genie made no reply, but, with the assistance of the other genies, the slaves of the lamp, immediately transported him and the palace entire to the spot whither he had been desired to convey it.

Early the next morning when the sultan, according to custom, went to contemplate and admire Aladdin's palace, his amazement was unbounded to find that it could nowhere be seen. He could not comprehend how so large a palace, which he had seen plainly every day for some years, should vanish so soon and not leave the least remains behind. In his perplexity he ordered the grand vizier to be sent for with expedition.

The grand vizier, who in secret bore no good will to Aladdin, intimated his suspicion that the palace was built by magic, and that Aladdin had made his hunting excursion an excuse for the removal of his palace with the same suddenness with which it had been erected. He induced the sultan to send a detachment of his guards and to have Aladdin seized as a prisoner of state. On his son-in-law being brought before him, he would not hear a word from him but ordered him to be put to death. The decree caused so much discontent among the people, whose affection Aladdin had secured by his largesses and charities, that the sultan, fearful of an insurrection, was obliged to grant him his life. When Aladdin found himself at liberty, he again addressed the sultan: "Sire, I pray you to let me know the crime by which I have thus lost the favor of thy countenance." "Your crime," answered the sultan, "wretched man! do you not

know it? Follow me, and I will show you." The sultan then took
Aladdin into the apartment from whence he was wont to look and
admire his palace, and said, "You ought to know where your palace
stood. Look! and tell me what has become of it." Aladdin did so,
and, being utterly amazed at the loss of his palace, was speechless.
At last, recovering himself, he said: "It is true, I do not see the palace.
It is vanished; but I had no concern in its removal. I beg you to give
me forty days, and if in that time I cannot restore it I will offer my
head to be disposed of at your pleasure." "I give you the time you
ask, but at the end of the forty days forget not to present yourself
before me."

Aladdin went out of the sultan's palace in a condition of exceeding
humiliation. The lords who had courted him in the days of his
splendor now declined to have any communication with him. For
three days he wandered about the city, exciting the wonder and compassion of the multitude by asking everybody he met if they had seen
his palace or could tell him anything of it. On the third day he wandered into the country, and, as he was approaching a river, he fell
down the bank with so much violence that he rubbed the ring which
the magician had given him so hard, by holding on the rock to save
himself, that immediately the same genie appeared whom he had
seen in the cave where the magician had left him. "What wouldst
thou have?" said the genie. "I am ready to obey thee as thy slave,
and the slave of all those that have that ring on their finger; both I
and the other slaves of the ring."

Aladdin, agreeably surprised at an offer of help so little expected,
replied, "Genie, show me where the palace I caused to be built now
stands, or transport it back where it first stood." "Your command,"
answered the genie, 'is not wholly in my power; I am only the slave
of the ring, and not of the lamp." "I command thee, then," replied
Aladdin, "by the power of the ring, to transport me to the spot where
my palace stands, in what part of the world soever it may be." These
words were no sooner out of his mouth than the genie transported
him into Africa, to the midst of a large plain, where his palace stood
at no great distance from a city, and placing him exactly under the
window of the princess's apartment, left him.

Now it so happened that shortly after Aladdin had been transported by the slave of the ring to the neighborhood of his palace, one
of the attendants of the Princess Badroulboudour, looking through
the window, perceived him, and instantly told her mistress. The
princess, who could not believe the joyful tidings, hastened herself
to the window, and, seeing Aladdin, immediately opened it. The
noise of opening the window made Aladdin turn his head that way,
and perceiving the princess, he saluted her with an air that expressed
his joy.

"To lose no time," said she to him, "I have sent to have the private
door opened for you. Enter, and come up."

The private door, which was just under the princess's apartment,
was soon opened, and Aladdin conducted up into the chamber. It is
impossible to express the joy of both at seeing each other after so
cruel a separation. After embracing, and shedding tears of joy, they
sat down, and Aladdin said, "I beg of you, princess, to tell me what
is become of an old lamp which stood upon a shelf in my robing
chamber?"

"Alas!" answered the princess, "I was afraid our misfortune might
be owing to that lamp; and what grieves me most is that I have
been the cause of it. I was foolish enough to change the old lamp
for a new one, and the next morning I found myself in this unknown
country, which I am told is Africa."

"Princess," said Aladdin, interrupting her, "you have explained all
by telling me we are in Africa. I desire you only to tell me if you
know where the old lamp now is." "The African magician carries it
carefully wrapt up in his bosom," said the princess; "and this I can
assure you, because he pulled it out before me and showed it to me
in triumph."

"Princess," said Aladdin, "I think I have found the means to
deliver you and to regain possession of the lamp, on which all my
prosperity depends. To execute this design it is necessary for me to
go to the town. I shall return by noon, and will then tell you what
must be done by you to insure success. In the meantime I shall disguise myself; and I beg that the private door may be opened at the
first knock."

When Aladdin was out of the palace, he looked around him on all sides, and perceiving a peasant going to the country, hastened after him; and when he had overtaken him, made a proposal to him to change clothes, which the man agreed to. When they had made the exchange, the countryman went about his business and Aladdin entered the neighboring city. After traversing several streets, he came to that part of the town where the merchants and artisans had their particular streets according to their trades. He went into that of the druggists, and entering one of the largest and best furnished shops, asked the druggist if he had a certain powder which he named.

The druggist, judging Aladdin by his habit to be very poor, told him he had it but that it was very dear. Upon which Aladdin, penetrating his thoughts, pulled out his purse, and, showing him some gold, asked for half a dram of the powder, which the druggist weighed and gave him, telling him the price was a piece of gold. Aladdin put the money into his hand and hastened to the palace, which he entered at once by the private door. When he came into the princess's apartment, he said to her, "Princess, you must take your part in the scheme which I propose for our deliverance. You must overcome your aversion to the magician and assume a most friendly manner toward him, and ask him to oblige you by partaking of an entertainment in your apartments. Before he leaves ask him to exchange cups with you, which he, gratified at the honor you do him, will gladly do, when you must give him the cup containing the powder. On drinking it he will instantly fall asleep, and we will obtain the lamp, whose slaves will do all our bidding and restore us and the palace to the capital of China."

The princess obeyed to the utmost her husband's instructions. She assumed a look of pleasure on the next visit of the magician, and asked him to an entertainment, which he most willingly accepted. At the close of the evening, during which the princess had tried all she could to please him, she asked him to exchange cups with her, and, giving the signal, had the drugged cup brought to her which she gave to the magician. He drank it out of compliment to the princess to the very last drop, when he fell backward lifeless on the sofa.

The princess, in anticipation of the success of her scheme, had so placed her women from the great hall to the foot of the staircase, that the word was no sooner given that the African magician was fallen backward than the door was opened and Aladdin admitted to the hall. The princess rose from her seat, and ran overjoyed to embrace him; but he stopped her, and said, "Princess, retire to your apartment, and let me be left alone while I endeavor to transport you back to China as speedily as you were brought from thence."

When the princess, her women, and slaves were gone out of the hall, Aladdin shut the door, and going directly to the dead body of the magician, opened his vest, took out the lamp which was carefully wrapped up, and rubbing it, the genie immediately appeared. "Genie," said Aladdin, "I command thee to transport this palace instantly to the place from whence it was brought hither." The genie bowed his head in token of obedience and disappeared. Immediately the palace was transported into China, and its removal was only felt by two little shocks, the one when it was lifted up, the other when it was set down, and both in a very short interval of time.

On the morning after the restoration of Aladdin's palace, the sultan was looking out of his window and mourning over the fate of his daughter, when he thought that he saw the vacancy created by the disappearance of the palace to be again filled up. On looking more attentively he was convinced beyond the power of doubt that it was his son-in-law's palace. Joy and gladness succeeded to sorrow and grief. He at once ordered a horse to be saddled, which he mounted that instant, thinking he could not make haste enough to the palace.

Aladdin rose that morning by daybreak, put on one of the most magnificent habits his wardrobe afforded, and went up into the hall of twenty-four windows, from whence he perceived the sultan approaching, and received him at the foot of the great staircase, helping him to dismount.

He led the sultan into the princess's apartment. The happy father embraced her with tears of joy; and the princess on her side afforded similar testimonies of her extreme pleasure. After a short interval devoted to mutual explanations of all that had happened, the sultan restored Aladdin to his favor and expressed his regret for the apparent harshness with which he had treated him. "My son," said he, "be not displeased at my proceedings against you; they arose from my paternal love, and therefore you ought to forgive the excesses to which it hurried me." "Sire," replied Aladdin, "I have not the least reason to complain of your conduct, since you did nothing but what your duty required. This infamous magician, the basest of men, was the sole cause of my misfortune."

The African magician, who was thus twice foiled in his endeavor to ruin Aladdin, had a younger brother who was as skillful a magician as himself and exceeded him in wickedness and hatred of mankind. By mutual agreement they communicated with each other once a year, however widely separate might be their place of residence from each other. The younger brother, not having received as usual his annual communication, prepared to take a horoscope and ascertain his brother's proceedings. He, as well as his brother, always carried a geomantic square instrument about him; he prepared the sand, cast the points, and drew the figures. On examining the planetary crystal, he found that his brother was no longer living, but had been poisoned; and by another observation, that he was in the capital of the kingdom of China; also that the person who had poisoned him was of mean birth, though married to a princess, a sultan's daughter.

When the magician had informed himself of his brother's fate, he resolved immediately to avenge his death, and at once departed for China; where, after crossing plains, rivers, mountains, deserts, and a long tract of country without delay, he arrived after incredible fatigues. When he came to the capital of China, he took a lodging at a khan. His magic art soon revealed to him that Aladdin was the person who had been the cause of the death of his brother. He had heard, too, all the persons of repute in the city talking of a woman called Fatima, who was retired from the world, and of the miracles she wrought. As he fancied that this woman might be serviceable to him in the project he had conceived, he made more minute inquiries, and requested to be informed more particularly who that holy woman was and what sort of miracles she performed.

"What!" said the person whom he addressed, "Have you never seen nor heard of her? She is the admiration of the whole town, for her fasting, her austerities, and her exemplary life. Except Mondays and Fridays, she never stirs out of her little cell; and on those days on which she comes into the town she does an infinite deal of good; for there is not a person who is diseased but she puts her hand on them and cures them."

Having ascertained the place where the hermitage of the holy woman was, the magician went at night, and, plunging a poniard into her heart—killed this good woman. In the morning he dyed his face of the same hue as hers, and arraying himself in her garb, taking her veil, the large necklace she wore round her waist, and her stick, went straight to the palace of Aladdin.

As soon as the people saw the holy woman, as they imagined him to be, they presently gathered about him in a great crowd. Some begged his blessing, some kissed his hand, and others, more reserved, only the hem of his garment; while others, suffering from disease, stooped for him to lay his hands upon them, which he did, muttering some words in form of prayer, and, in short, counterfeiting so well that everybody took him for the holy woman. He came at last to the square before Aladdin's palace. The crowd and the noise was so great that the princess, who was in the hall of four-and-twenty windows, heard it, and asked what was the matter. One of the women told her it was a great crowd of people collected about the holy woman to be cured of diseases by the imposition of her hands.

The princess, who had long heard of this holy woman but had never seen her, was very desirous to have some conversation with her; which the chief officer perceiving, told her it was an easy matter to bring her to her if she desired and commanded it; and the princess, expressing her wishes, he immediately sent four slaves for the pretended holy woman.

As soon as the crowd saw the attendants from the palace, they made way; and the magician, perceiving also that they were coming for him, advanced to meet them, overjoyed to find his plot succeed so well. "Holy woman," said one of the slaves, "the princess wants to see you, and has sent us for you." "The princess does me too great an honor," replied the false Fatima; "I am ready to obey her command," and at the same time followed the slaves to the palace.

When the pretended Fatima had made her obeisance, the princess said, "My good mother, I have one thing to request, which you must not refuse me; it is, to stay with me, that you may edify me with your way of living and that I may learn from your good example." "Princess," said the counterfeit Fatima, "I beg of you not to ask what I cannot consent to without neglecting my prayers and devotion." "That shall be no hindrance to you," answered the princess; "I have a great many apartments unoccupied; you shall choose which you like best, and have as much liberty to perform your devotions as if you were in your own cell."

The magician, who really desired nothing more than to introduce himself into the palace, where it would be a much easier matter for him to execute his designs, did not long excuse himself from accepting the obliging offer which the princess made him. "Princess," said he, "whatever resolution a poor wretched woman as I am may have made to renounce the pomp and grandeur of this world, I dare not presume to oppose the commands of so pious and charitable a princess."

Upon this the princess, rising up, said, "Come with me; I will show you what vacant apartments I have, that you may make choice of that you like best." The magician followed the princess, and of all the apartments she showed him made choice of that which was the worst, saying that he only accepted it to please her.

Afterward, the princess would have brought him back again into the great hall to make him dine with her; but he, considering that he should then be obliged to show his face, which he had always taken care to conceal with Fatima's veil, and fearing that the princess should find out that he was not Fatima, begged of her earnestly to excuse him, telling her that he never ate anything but bread and dried fruits, and desiring to eat that slight repast in his own apartment. The princess granted his request, saying, "You may be as free here, good mother, as if you were in your own cell: I will order you a dinner, but remember I expect you as soon as you have finished your repast."

After the princess had dined and the false Fatima had been sent for by one of the attendants, he again waited upon her.

"My good mother," said the princess, "I am overjoyed to see so holy a woman as yourself, who will confer a blessing upon this palace. But now I am speaking of the palace, pray how do you like it? And before I show it all to you, tell me first what you think of this hall."

Upon this question the counterfeit Fatima surveyed the hall from one end to the other. When he had examined it well, he said to the princess, "As far as such a solitary being as I am, who am unacquainted with what the world calls beautiful, can judge, this hall is truly admirable; there wants but one thing." "What is that, good mother?" demanded the princess; "tell me, I conjure you. For my part, I always believed, and have heard say, it wanted nothing; but if it does, it shall be supplied."

"Princess," said the false Fatima, with great dissimulation, "forgive me the liberty I have taken; but my opinion is, if it can be of any importance, that if a roc's egg were hung up in the middle of the dome, this hall would have no parallel in the four quarters of the world and your palace would be the wonder of the universe."

"My good mother," said the princess, "what is a roc, and where may one get an egg?" "Princess," replied the pretended Fatima, "it is a bird of prodigious size which inhabits the summit of Mount Caucasus; the architect who built your palace can get you one."

After the princess had thanked the false Fatima for what she believed her good advice, she conversed with her upon other matters; but could not forget the roc's egg, which she resolved to request of Aladdin when next he should visit her apartments. He did so in the course of that evening, and shortly after he entered the princess thus addressed him: "I always believed that our palace was the most superb, magnificent, and complete in the world: but I will tell you now what it wants, and that is a roc's egg hung up in the midst of the dome." "Princess," replied Aladdin, "it is enough that you think it wants such an ornament; you shall see by the diligence which I use in obtaining it, that there is nothing which I would not do for your sake."

Aladdin left the Princess Badroulboudour that moment, and went up into the hall of four-and-twenty windows, where, pulling out of his bosom the lamp, which after the danger he had been exposed to he always carried about him, he rubbed it; upon which the genie immediately appeared. "Genie," said Aladdin, "I command thee in the name of this lamp, bring a roc's egg to be hung up in the middle of the dome of the hall of the palace."

Aladdin had no sooner pronounced these words than the hall shook as if ready to fall; and the genie said in a loud and terrible voice, "Is it not enough that I and the other slaves of the lamp have done everything for you, but you, by an unheard-of-ingratitude, must command me to bring my master, and hang him up in the midst of this dome? This attempt deserves that you, the princess, and the palace, should be immediately reduced to ashes; but you are spared because this request does not come from yourself. Its true author is the brother of the African magician, your enemy, whom you have destroyed. He is now in your palace, disguised in the habit of the holy woman Fatima whom he has murdered; at his suggestion your wife makes this pernicious demand. His design is to kill you, therefore take care of yourself." After these words the genie disappeared.

Aladdin resolved at once what to do. He returned to the princess's apartment, and, without mentioning a word of what had happened, sat down, and complained of a great pain which had suddenly seized his head. On hearing this the princess told him how she had invited the holy Fatima to stay with her, and that she was now in the palace; and at the request of the prince, ordered her to be summoned to her at once.

When the pretended Fatima came, Aladdin said, "Come hither, good mother; I am glad to see you here at so fortunate a time. I am tormented with a violent pain in my head, and request your assistance, and hope you will not refuse me that cure which you impart to afflicted persons."

So saying, he rose, but held down his head. The counterfeit Fatima advanced toward him, with his hand all the time on a dagger concealed in his girdle under his gown; which Aladdin observing, he snatched the weapon from his hand, pierced him to the heart with his own dagger, and then pushed him down on the floor.

"My dear prince, what have you done?" cried the princess in surprise. "You have killed the holy woman!" "No, my princess," answered Aladdin with emotion, "I have not killed Fatima, but a villain, who would have assassinated me if I had not prevented him. This wicked man," added he, uncovering his face, "is the brother of the magician who attempted our ruin. He has strangled the true Fatima, and disguised himself in her clothes with intent to murder me."

Aladdin then informed her how the genie had told him these facts, and how narrowly she and the palace escaped destruction through his treacherous suggestion which had led to her request.

Thus was Aladdin delivered from the persecution of the two brothers, who were magicians. Within a few years afterwards the sultan died in a good old age, and as he left no male children, the Princess Badroulboudour succeeded him, and she and Aladdin reigned together many years, and left a numerous and illustrious posterity.

ALI BABA

From the ARABIAN NIGHTS

Illustration by JOHN D. BATTEN

THERE once lived in a town of Persia two brothers, one named Cassim, and the other Ali Baba. Their father divided a small inheritance equally between them. Cassim married a very rich wife and became a wealthy merchant. Ali Baba married a woman as poor as himself, and lived by cutting wood, and bringing it upon three asses into the town to sell.

One day, when Ali Baba was in the forest, and had just cut wood enough to load his asses, he saw at a distance a great cloud of dust which seemed to approach him. He observed it with attention, and distinguished soon after a body of horsemen whom he suspected might be robbers. He determined to leave his asses to save himself. He climbed up a large tree planted on a high rock, whose branches were thick enough to conceal him and yet enabled him to see all that passed without being discovered.

The troop, who were to the number of forty, all well mounted and armed, came to the foot of the rock on which the tree stood and there dismounted. Every man unbridled his horse, tied him to some shrub, and hung about his neck a bag of corn which they brought behind them. Then each of them took off his saddle-bag, which seemed to Ali Baba to be full of gold and silver from its weight. One, whom he took to be their captain, came under the tree in which Ali Baba was concealed; and, making his way through some shrubs, pronounced these words—"Open, Sesame!" As soon as the captain of the robbers had thus spoken, a door opened in the rock; and after he had made all his troop enter before him, he followed them, when the door shut again of itself.

The robbers stayed within the rock some time, during which Ali Baba, fearful of being caught, remained in the tree.

At last the door opened again, and as the captain went in last so he came out first, and stood to see them all pass by him; when Ali Baba heard him make the door close by pronouncing these words, "Shut, Sesame!" Every man at once went and bridled his horse, fastened his wallet, and mounted again. When the captain saw them all ready, he put himself at their head, and they returned the way they had come.

Ali Baba followed them with his eyes as far as he could see them, and afterwards stayed a considerable time before he descended. Remembering the words the captain of the robbers used to cause the door to open and shut, he had the curiosity to try if his pronouncing them would have the same effect. Accordingly, he went among the shrubs, and perceiving the door concealed behind them, stood before it and said, "Open, Sesame!" The door instantly flew wide open.

Ali Baba, who expected a dark, dismal cavern, was surprised to see a well-lighted and spacious chamber, which received the light from an opening at the top of the rock, and in which were all sorts of provisions, rich bales of silk, stuff, brocade, and valuable carpeting, piled upon one another, gold and silver ingots in great heaps, and money in bags. The sight of all these riches made him suppose that this cave must have been occupied for ages by robbers, who had succeeded one another.

Ali Baba went boldly into the cave, and collected as much of the gold coin, which was in bags, as he thought his three asses could carry. When he had loaded them with the bags, he laid wood over them in such a manner that they could not be seen. When he had passed in and out as often as he wished, he stood before the door, and pronouncing the words, "Shut, Sesame!" the door closed of itself. He then made the best of his way to town.

When Ali Baba got home, he drove his asses into a little yard, shut the gates very carefully, threw off the wood that covered the panniers, carried the bags into the house, and ranged them in order before his wife. He then emptied the bags, which raised such a great heap of gold as dazzled his wife's eyes, and then he told her the whole adventure from beginning to end, and above all recommended her to keep it secret.

The wife rejoiced greatly at their good fortune, and would count all the gold piece by piece. "Wife," replied Ali Baba, "you do not know what you undertake, when you pretend to count the money; you will never have done. I will dig a hole and bury it. There is no time to be lost." "You are in the right, husband," replied she; "but let us know, as nigh as possible, how much we have. I will borrow a small measure, and measure it while you dig the hole."

Away the wife ran to her brother-in-law Cassim, who lived just by, and, addressing herself to his wife, desired her to lend her a measure for a little while. Her sister-in-law asked whether she would have a great or a small one. The other asked for a small one. She bade her stay a little and she would readily fetch one.

The sister-in-law did so, but as she knew Ali Baba's poverty she was curious to know what sort of grain his wife wanted to measure, and, artfully putting some suet at the bottom of the measure, brought it to her, with the excuse that she was sorry that she had made her stay so long, but that she could not find it sooner.

Ali Baba's wife went home, set the measure upon the heap of gold, filled it, and emptied it often upon the sofa till she had done, when she was very well satisfied to find the number of measures amounted to so many as they did, and went to tell her husband, who had almost finished digging the hole. While Ali Baba was burying the gold, his wife, to show her exactness and diligence to her sister-in-law, carried the measure back again, but without taking notice that a piece of gold had stuck to the bottom. "Sister," said she, giving it to her again, "you see that I have not kept your measure long. I am obliged to you for it, and return it with thanks."

As soon as Ali Baba's wife was gone, Cassim's wife looked at the bottom of the measure, and was in inexpressible surprise to find a piece of gold sticking to it. Envy immediately possessed her breast. "What!" said she, "has Ali Baba gold so plentiful as to measure it? Whence has he all this wealth?"

Cassim, her husband, was at his counting-house. When he came home his wife said to him, "Cassim, I know you think yourself rich, but Ali Baba is infinitely richer than you. He does not count his money, but measures it." Cassim desired her to explain the riddle, which she did by telling him the stratagem she had used to make the discovery, and showed him the piece of money, which was so old that they could not tell in what prince's reign it was coined.

Cassim, after he had married the rich widow, had never treated Ali Baba as a brother, but neglected him; and now, instead of being pleased, he conceived a base envy at his brother's prosperity. He could not sleep all that night, and went to him in the morning before sunrise. "Ali Baba," said he, "I am surprised at you! You pretend to be miserably poor, and yet you measure gold. My wife found this at the bottom of the measure you borrowed yesterday."

By this discourse, Ali Baba perceived that Cassim and his wife, through his own wife's folly, knew what they had so much reason to conceal; but what was done could not be undone. Therefore, without showing the least surprise or trouble, he confessed all, and offered his brother part of his treasure to keep the secret.

"I expect as much," replied Cassim haughtily; "but I must know exactly where this treasure is, and how I may visit it myself when I choose; otherwise, I will go and inform against you, and then you will not only get no more, but will lose all you have, and I shall have a share for my information."

Ali Baba told him all he desired, even to the very words he was to use to gain admission into the cave.

Cassim rose the next morning long before the sun, and set out for the forest with ten mules bearing great chests which he designed to fill, and followed the road which Ali Baba had pointed out to him. It was not long before he reached the rock, and found out the place by the tree and other marks which his brother had given him. When he reached the entrance of the cavern, he pronounced the words, "Open Sesame!" The door immediately opened, and when he was in, closed upon him, On examining the cave, he was in great admiration to find much more riches than he had expected from Ali Baba's narration. He quickly laid as many bags of gold as he could carry at the door of the cavern; but his thoughts were so full of the great riches he should possess, that he could not think of the necessary word to make it open, and instead of "Open Sesame" said, "Open, Barley!" and was amazed to find that the door remained fast shut. He named other grains, but still the door would not open.

Cassim had never expected such an incident, and was so alarmed at the danger he was in, that the more he endeavored to remember the word "Sesame," the more his memory was confounded, and he had as much forgotten it as if he had never heard it mentioned. He threw down the bags he had loaded himself with, and walked distractedly up and down the cave, without having the least regard to the riches that were round him.

About noon the robbers visited their cave. At some distance they saw Cassim's mules straggling about the rock, with great chests on their backs. Alarmed at this, they galloped full speed to the cave. They drove away the mules, who strayed through the forest so far that they were soon out of sight, and went directly, with their naked sabers in their hands, to the door, which, on their captain pronouncing the proper words, immediately opened.

Cassim, who heard the noise of the horses' feet, at once guessed the arrival of the robbers, and resolved to make one effort for his life. He rushed to the door, and no sooner saw it open, than he ran out and threw the leader down, but could not escape the other robbers, who with their scimitars soon deprived him of life.

The first care of the robbers after this was to examine the cave. They found all the bags which Cassim had brought to the door to be ready to load his mules, and carried them again to their places, but they did not miss what Ali Baba had taken away before. Then holding a council, and deliberating upon this occurrence, they guessed that Cassim, when he was in could not get out again, but could not imagine how he had learned the secret words by which he alone could enter. They could not deny the fact of his being there; and to terrify any person or accomplice who should attempt the same thing, they agreed to cut Cassim's body into four quarters— to hang two on one side, and two on the other, within the door of the cave. They had no sooner taken this resolution than they put it in execution; and when they had nothing to detain them, left the place of their hoards well closed. They mounted their horses, went to beat the roads again, and to attack the caravans they might meet.

In the meantime, Cassim's wife was very uneasy when night came, and her husband was not returned. She ran to Ali Baba in great alarm, and said: "I believe, brother-in-law, that you know Cassim is gone to the forest, and upon what account; it is now night, and he has not returned; I am afraid some misfortune has happened to him." Ali Baba told her that she need not frighten herself, for that certainly Cassim would not think it proper to come into the town till the night should be pretty far advanced.

Cassim's wife, considering how much it concerned her husband to keep the business secret, was the more easily persuaded to believe her brother-in-law. She went home again, and waited patiently till midnight. Then her fear redoubled, and her grief was the more sensible because she was forced to keep it to herself. She repented of her foolish curiosity, and cursed her desire of prying into the affairs of her brother and sister-in-law. She spent all the night in weeping; and, as soon as it was day, went to them, telling them by her tears the cause of her coming.

Ali Baba did not wait for his sister-in-law to desire him to go to see what was become of Cassim, but departed immediately with his three asses, begging of her first to moderate her affliction. He went to the forest, and when he came near the rock, having seen neither his brother nor the mules in his way, was seriously alarmed at finding some blood spilled near the door, which he took for an ill omen; but when he had pronounced the word, and the door had opened, he was struck with horror at the dismal sight of his brother's body. He was not long in determining how he should pay the last dues to his brother; but without adverting to the little fraternal affection he had shown for him, went into the cave to find something to enshroud his remains; and having loaded one of his asses with them, covered them over with wood. The other two asses he loaded with bags of gold, covering them with wood also as before; and then bidding the door shut, came away; but he was so cautious as to stop some time at the end of the forest, that he might not go into the town before night. When he came home, he drove the two asses loaded with gold into his little yard, and left the care of unloading them to his wife, while he led the other to his sister-in-law's house.

Ali Baba knocked at the door, which was opened by Morgiana, a clever, intelligent slave, who was fruitful in inventions to meet the most difficult circumstances. When he came into the court, he un-loaded the ass, and taking Morgiana aside, said to her: "You must observe an inviolable secrecy. Your master's body is contained in these two panniers. We must bury him as if he had died a natural death. Go now and tell your mistress. I leave the matter to your wit and skillful devices."

Ali Baba helped to place the body in Cassim's house, again recom-mended to Morgiana to act her part well, and then returned with his ass.

Morgiana went out early the next morning to a druggist, and asked for a sort of lozenge which was considered efficacious in the most dangerous disorders. The apothecary inquired who was ill. She replied, with a sigh, that it was her good master, Cassim himself, and that he could neither eat nor speak. In the evening Morgiana went to the same druggist's again, and with tears in her eyes, asked for an essence which they used to give to sick people only when at the last extremity. "Alas!" said she, taking it from the apothecary, "I am afraid that this remedy will have no better effect than the lozenges; and that I shall lose my good master."

On the other hand, as Ali Baba and his wife were often seen to go between Cassim's and their own house all that day, and to seem melancholy, nobody was surprised in the evening to hear the lament-able shrieks and cries of Cassim's wife and Morgiana, who gave out everywhere that her master was dead. The next morning at day-break, Morgiana went to an old cobbler whom she knew to be always early at his stall, and bidding him good morrow, put a piece of gold into his hand, saying, "Baba Mustapha, you must bring with you your sewing tackle, and come with me; but I must tell you, I shall blindfold you when you come to such a place."

Baba Mustapha seemed to hesitate a little at these words. "Oh! oh!" replied he, "you must have me do something against my con-science, or against my honor?" "God forbid," said Morgiana, putting another piece of gold into his hand, "that I should ask anything that is contrary to your honor! Only come with me and fear nothing."

Baba Mustapha went with Morgiana, who, after she had bound his eyes with a handkerchief at the place she had mentioned, conveyed him to her deceased master's house, and never unloosed his eyes till he had entered the room where she had put the corpse together.

"Baba Mustapha," said she, "you must make haste and sew the parts of this body together; and when you have done, I will give you another piece of gold."

After Baba Mustapha had finished his task, she blindfolded him again, gave him the third piece of gold as she had promised, and recommending secrecy to him, carried him back to the place where she first bound his eyes, pulled off the bandage, and let him go home, but watched him that he returned toward his stall, till he was quite out of sight, for fear he should have the curiosity to return and dodge her; she then went home. Morgiana, on her return, warmed some water to wash the body, and at the same time Ali Baba perfumed it with incense, and wrapped it in the burying clothes with the accustomed ceremonies. Not long after, the proper officer brought the bier, and when the attendants of the mosque, whose business it was to wash the dead, offered to perform their duty, she told them that it was done already. Shortly after this the imam and the other ministers of the mosque arrived. Four neighbors carried the corpse to the burying ground, following the imam, who recited some prayers. Ali Baba came after with some neighbors, who often relieved the others in carrying the bier to the burying ground. Morgiana, a slave to the deceased, followed in the procession, weeping, beating her breast, and tearing her hair. Cassim's wife stayed at home mourning, uttering lamentable cries with the women of the neighborhood, who came according to custom during the funeral, and, joining their lamentations with hers, filled the quarter far and near with sounds of sorrow.

In this manner Cassim's melancholy death was concealed, and hushed up between Ali Baba, his widow, and Morgiana, his slave, with so much contrivance that nobody in the city had the least knowledge or suspicion of the cause of it. Three or four days after the funeral, Ali Baba removed his few goods openly to his sister-in-law's house, in which it was agreed that he should in future live; but the money he had taken from the robbers he conveyed thither by night. As for Cassim's warehouse, he intrusted it entirely to the management of his eldest son.

While these things were being done, the forty robbers again visited their retreat in the forest. Great, then, was their surprise to find Cassim's body taken away with some of their bags of gold. "We are certainly discovered," said the captain. "The removal of the body and the loss of some of our money plainly show that the man whom we killed had an accomplice; and for our own lives' sake we must try and find him. What say you, my lads?"

All the robbers unanimously approved of the captain's proposal.

"Well," said the captain, "one of you, the boldest and most skillful among you, must go into the town, disguised as a traveler and a stranger, to try if he can hear any talk of the man whom we have killed, and endeavor to find out who he was and where he lived. This is a matter of the first importance, and for fear of any treachery, I propose that whoever undertakes this business without success, even though the failure arises only from an error of judgment, shall suffer death."

Without waiting for the sentiments of his companions, one of the robbers started up, and said, "I submit to this condition, and think it an honor to expose my life to serve the troop."

After this robber had received great commendations from the captain and his comrades, he disguised himself so that nobody would take him for what he was; and taking his leave of the troop that night, went into the town just at daybreak, and walked up and down, till accidentally he came to Baba Mustapha's stall, which was always open before any of the shops. Baba Mustapha was seated with an awl in his hand, just going to work.

The robber saluted him, bidding him good morrow; and, perceiving that he was old, said, "Honest man, you begin to work very early: is it possible that one of your age can see so well? I question, even if it were somewhat lighter, whether you could see to stitch."

"You do not know me," replied Baba Mustapha; "for old as I am, I have extraordinary good eyes; and you will not doubt it when I tell you that I sewed the body of a dead man together in a place where I had not so much light as I have now."

"A dead body!" exclaimed the robber, with affected amazement. "Yes, yes," answered Baba Mustapha; "I see you want to have me speak out, but you shall know no more."

The robber felt sure that he had discovered what he sought. He pulled out a piece of gold, and putting it into Baba Mustapha's hand, said to him, "I do not want to learn your secret, though I can assure you you might safely trust me with it. The only thing I desire of you is to show me the house where you stitched up the dead body."

"If I were disposed to do you that favor," replied Baba Mustapha, "I assure you I cannot. I was taken to a certain place, whence I was

"It was here," said Baba Mustapha, "I was blind-folded; and I turned this way."

led blindfold to the house, and afterwards brought back again in the same manner; you see, therefore, the impossibility of my doing what you desire."

"Well," replied the robber, "you may, however, remember a little of the way that you were led blindfold. Come, let me blind your eyes at the same place. We will walk together; perhaps you may recognize some part; and as everybody ought to be paid for their trouble, there is another piece of gold for you; gratify me in what I ask you." So saying, he put another piece of gold into his hand.

The two pieces of gold were great temptations to Baba Mustapha. He looked at them a long time in his hand without saying a word, but at last he pulled out his purse and put them in. "I cannot promise," said he to the robber, "that I can remember the way exactly; but since you desire, I will try what I can do." At these words Baba Mustapha rose up, to the great joy of the robber, and led him to the place where Morgiana had bound his eyes. "It was here," said Baba Mustapha, "I was blindfolded; and I turned this way." The robber tied his handkerchief over his eyes, and walked by him till they stopped directly at Cassim's house, where Ali Baba then lived. The thief, before he pulled off the band, marked the door with a piece of chalk, which he had ready in his hand, and then asked him if he knew whose house that was; to which Baba Mustapha replied, that as he did not live in that neighborhood he could not tell.

The robber, finding he could discover no more from Baba Mustapha, thanked him for the trouble he had taken, and left him to go back to his stall, while he returned to the forest, persuaded that he should be very well received.

A little after the robber and Baba Mustapha had parted, Morgiana went out of Ali Baba's house upon some errand, and upon her return, seeing the mark the robber had made, stopped to observe it. "What can be the meaning of this mark?" said she to herself; "somebody intends my master no good: however, with whatever intention it was done, it is advisable to guard against the worst." Accordingly, she fetched a piece of chalk, and marked two or three doors on each side in the same manner, without saying a word to her master or mistress.

In the meantime, the robber rejoined his troop in the forest, and recounted to them his success, expatiating upon his good fortune in meeting so soon with the only person who could inform him of what he wanted to know. All the robbers listened to him with the utmost satisfaction; when the captain, after commending his diligence, addressing himself to them all, said, "Comrades, we have no time to lose: let us set off well armed, without its appearing who we are; but that we may not excite any suspicion, let only one or two go into he town together, and join at our rendezvous, which shall be the great square. In the meantime, our comrade who brought us the good news and I will go and find out the house, that we may consult what had best be done."

This speech and plan were approved of by all, and they were soon ready. They filed off in parties of two each, after some interval of time, and got into the town without being in the least suspected. The captain, and he who had visited the town in the morning as spy, came in the last. He led the captain into the street where he had marked Ali Baba's residence; and when they came to the first of the houses which Morgiana had marked, he pointed it out. But the captain observed that the next door was chalked in the same manner, and in the same place; and showing it to his guide, asked him which house it was, that or the first. The guide was so confounded that he knew not what answer to make, but still more puzzled when he and the captain saw five or six houses similarly marked. He assured the captain, with an oath, that he had marked but one, and could not tell who had chalked the rest, so that he could not distinguish the house which the cobbler had stopped at.

The captain, finding that their design had failed, went directly to the place of rendezvous, and told his troop that they had lost their labor, and must return to their cave. He himself set them the example, and they all returned as they had come.

When the troop was all got together, the captain told them the reason of their returning; and presently the conductor was declared by all worthy of death. He condemned himself, acknowledging that he ought to have taken better precaution, and prepared to receive the stroke from him who was appointed to cut off his head. But as the safety of the troop required the discovery of the second intruder into the cave, another of the gang, who promised himself that he should succeed better, presented himself, and his offer being accepted, he went and corrupted Baba Mustapha, as the other had done; and, being shown the house, marked it in a place more remote from sight with red chalk.

Not long after, Morgiana whose eyes nothing could escape, went out, and seeing the red chalk, and arguing with herself as she had

done before, marked the other neighbors houses in the same plac
and manner.

The robber, at his return to his company, valued himself mucl
on the precaution he had taken, which he looked upon as an infal
lible way of distinguishing Ali Baba's house from the others; and th
captain and all of them thought it must succeed. They conveye
themselves into the town with the same precaution as before; bu
when the robber and his captain came to the street they found th
same difficulty, at which the captain was enraged, and the robber i
as great confusion as his predecessor.

Thus the captain and his troop were forced to retire a second time
and much more dissatisfied; while the robber, who had been th
author of the mistake, underwent the same punishment, which h
willingly submitted to.

The captain, having lost two brave fellows of his troop, wa
afraid of diminishing it too much by pursuing this plan to get infor
mation of the residence of their plunderer. He found by their ex
ample that their heads were not so good as their hands on such occa
sions, and therefore resolved to take upon himself the importan
commission.

Accordingly, he went and addressed himself to Baba Mustapha
who did him the same service he had done to the other robbers. H
did not set any particular mark on the house, but examined and ob
served it so carefully, by passing often by it, that it was impossibl
for him to mistake it.

The captain, well satisfied with his attempt, and informed of wha
he wanted to know, returned to the forest; and when he came int
the cave, where the troop waited for him, said, "Now, comrades
nothing can prevent our full revenge, as I am certain of the house
and in my way hither I have thought how to put it into execution
but if anyone can form a better expedient, let him communicate it.
He then told him his contrivance; and as they approved of it, or
dered them to go into the villages about, and buy nineteen mules
with thirty-eight large leather jars, one full of oil, and the other
empty.

In two or three days' time the robbers had purchased the mule and jars, and as the mouths of the jars were rather too narrow for his purpose, the captain caused them to be widened; and after having put one of his men into each, with the weapons which he thought fit, leaving open the seam which had been undone to leave them room to breathe, he rubbed the jars on the outside with oil from the full vessel.

Things being thus prepared, when the nineteen mules were loaded with thirty-seven robbers in jars, and the jar of oil, the captain, as their driver, set out with them, and reached the town by the dusk of the evening, as he had intended. He led them through the streets till he came to Ali Baba's, at whose door he designed to have knocked; but was prevented by his sitting there after supper to take a little fresh air. He stopped his mules, addressed himself to him, and said, "I have brought some oil a great way to sell at tomorrow's market; and it is now so late that I do not know where to lodge: If I should not be troublesome to you, do me the favor to let me pass the night with you, and I shall be very much obliged by your hospitality."

Though Ali Baba had seen the captain of the robbers in the forest, and had heard him speak, it was impossible to know him in the disguise of an oil merchant. He told him he should be welcome, and immediately opened the gates for the mules to go into the yard. At the same time he called to a slave, and ordered him, when the mules were unloaded, to put them into the stable and to feed them; and then went to Morgiana to bid her to get a good supper for his guest. After they had finished supper, Ali Baba, charging Morgiana afresh to take care of his guest, said to her, "Tomorrow morning I design to go to the bath before day; take care my bathing linen be ready, give them to Abdalla [which was the slave's name] and make me some good broth against I return." After this he went to bed.

In the meantime the captain of the robbers went into the yard, took off the lid of each jar, and gave his people orders what to do. Beginning at the first jar, and so on to the last, he said to each man: "As soon as I throw some stones out of the chamber window where I lie, do not fail to come out, and I will immediately join you." After this he returned into the house, when Morgiana, taking up a light, conducted him to his chamber, where she left him; and he, to avoid any suspicion, put the light out soon after, and laid himself down in his clothes that he might be the more ready to rise.

Morgiana, remembering Ali Baba's orders, got his bathing linen ready, and ordered Abdalla to set on the pot for the broth; but while she was preparing it the lamp went out, and there was no more oil in the house, nor any candles. What to do she did not know, for the broth must be made. Abdalla, seeing her very uneasy, said, "Do not fret and tease yourself, but go into the yard and take some oil out of one of the jars."

Morgiana thanked Abdalla for his advice, took the oil-pot and went into the yard; when, as she came nigh the first jar, the robber within said softly, "Is it time?"

Though naturally much surprised at finding a man in the jar instead of the oil she wanted, she immediately felt the importance of keeping silence, as Ali Baba, his family, and herself were in great danger; and, collecting herself, without showing the least emotion she answered, "Not yet, but presently." She went quietly in this manner to all the jars, giving the same answer, till she came to the jar of oil.

By this means Morgiana found that her master Ali Baba had admitted thirty-eight robbers into his house, and that this pretended oil merchant was their captain. She made what haste she could to fill her oil-pot, and returned to the kitchen, where, as soon as she had lighted her lamp, she took a great kettle, went again to the oil-jar, filled the kettle, set it on a large wood fire, and as soon as it boiled, went and poured enough into every jar to stifle and destroy the robber within.

When this action, worthy of the courage of Morgiana, was executed without any noise as she had projected, she returned into the kitchen with the empty kettle; and having put out the great fire she had made to boil the oil, and leaving just enough to make the broth, put out the lamp also, and remained silent, resolving not to go to rest till she had observed what might follow through a window of the kitchen which opened into the yard.

She had not waited long before the captain of the robbers got up, opened the window, and finding no light and hearing no noise, or any one stirring in the house, gave the appointed signal by throwing little stones, several of which hit the jars, as he doubted not by the sound they gave. He then listened, but not hearing or perceiving anything whereby he could judge that his companions stirrred, he began to grow very uneasy, threw stones a second time and also a third time, and could not comprehend the reason that none of them should answer his signal. Much alarmed, he went softly down into the yard, and going to the first jar, while asking the robber whom he thought alive if he was in readiness, smelled the hot boiled oil, which sent forth a steam out of the jar. Hence he suspected that his plot to murder Ali Baba and plunder his house was discovered. Examining all the jars one after another, he found that all his gang were dead; and, enraged to despair at having failed in his design, he forced the lock of a door that led from the yard to the garden, and climbing over the walls, made his escape.

When Morgiana saw him depart, she went to bed satisfied and pleased to have succeeded so well in saving her master and family.

Ali Baba rose before day, and, followed by his slave, went to the baths entirely ignorant of the event which had happened at home.

When he returned from the baths, he was very much surprised to see the oil jars, and that the merchant was not gone with the mules. He asked Morgiana, who opened the door, the reason of it. "My good master," answered she, "God preserve you and all your family! You will be better informed of what you wish to know when you have seen what I have to show you, if you will follow me."

As soon as Morgiana had shut the door, Ali Baba followed her, when she requested him to look into the first jar, and see if there was any oil. Ali Baba did so, and seeing a man, started back in alarm, and cried out. "Do not be afraid," said Morgiana, "the man you see there can neither do you nor anybody else any harm. He is dead." "Ah, Morgiana," said Ali Baba, "what is it you show me? Explain yourself." "I will," replied Morgiana. "Moderate your astonishment, and do not excite the curiosity of your neighbors; for it is of great importance to keep this affair secret. Look into all the other jars."

Ali Baba examined all the other jars, one after another; and when he came to that which had the oil in, found it prodigiously sunk, and stood for some time motionless, sometimes looking at the jars, and sometimes at Morgiana, without saying a word, so great was his surprise.

At last, when he had recovered himself, he said, "And what is become of the merchant?"

"Merchant!" answered she; "he is as much one as I am. I will tell you who he is and what is become of him; but you had better hear the story in your own chamber; for it is time for your health that you had your broth after your bathing."

Morgiana then told him all she had done, from the first observing the mark upon the house, to the destruction of the robbers and the flight of their captain.

On hearing of these brave deeds from the lips of Morgiana, Ali Baba said to her, "God, by your means, has delivered me from the snares these robbers laid for my destruction. I owe, therefore, my life to you; and, for the first token of my acknowledgment, give you your liberty from this moment, till I can complete your recompense as I intend."

Ali Baba's garden was very long, and shaded at the further end by a great number of large trees. Near these he and the slave Abdalla dug a trench, long and wide enough to hold the bodies of the robbers; and as the earth was light, they were not long in doing it. When this was done, Ali Baba hid the jars and weapons; and as he had no occasion for the mules, he sent them at different times to be sold in the market by his slave.

While Ali Baba took these measures, the captain of the forty robbers returned to the forest with inconceivable mortification. He did not stay long: the loneliness of the gloomy cavern became frightful to him. He determined, however, to avenge the fate of his companions, and to accomplish the death of Ali Baba. For this purpose he returned to the town and took a lodging in a khan, and disguised himself as a merchant in silks. Under this assumed character, he gradually conveyed a great many sorts of rich stuffs and fine linen to his lodging from the cavern, but with all the necessary precautions to conceal the place whence he brought them. In order to dispose of the merchandise, when he had thus amassed them together, he took a warehouse which happened to be opposite to Cassim's, which Ali Baba's son had occupied since the death of his uncle.

He took the name of Cogia Houssain, and, as a newcomer, was, according to custom, extremely civil and complaisant to all the merchants his neighbors. Ali Baba's son was, from his vicinity, one of the first to converse with Cogia Houssain, who strove to cultivate his friendship more particularly. Two or three days after he was settled, Ali Baba came to see his son, and the captain of the robbers recognized him at once, and soon learned from his son who he was. After this he increased his assiduities, caressed him in the most engaging manner, made him some small presents, and often asked him to dine and sup with him, when he treated him very handsomely.

Ali Baba's son did not choose to lie under such obligation to Cogia Houssain; but was so much straitened for want of room in his house that he could not entertain him. He therefore acquainted his father, Ali Baba, with his wish to invite him in return.

Ali Baba with great pleasure took the treat upon himself. "Son," said he, "tomorrow being Friday, which is a day that the shops of such great merchants as Cogia Houssain and yourself are shut, get him to accompany you, and as you pass by my door, call in. I will go and order Morgiana to provide a supper."

The next day Ali Baba's son and Cogia Houssain met by appointment, took their walk, and as they returned, Ali Baba's son led Cogia Houssain through the street where his father lived, and when they came to the house, stopped and knocked at the door. "This, sir," said he, "is my father's house, who, from the account I have given him of your friendship, charged me to procure him the honor of your acquaintance; and I desire you to add this pleasure to those for which I am already indebted to you."

Though it was the sole aim of Cogia Houssain to introduce himself into Ali Baba's house that he might kill him without hazarding his own life or making any noise, yet he excused himself and offered to take his leave; but a slave having opened the door, Ali Baba's son took him obligingly by the hand, and, in a manner forced him in.

Ali Baba received Cogia Houssain with a smiling countenance

and in the most obliging manner he could wish. He thanked him for all the favors he had done his son; adding withal, the obligation was the greater as he was a young man not much acquainted with the world, and that he might contribute to his information.

Cogia Houssain returned the compliment by assuring Ali Baba that though his son might not have acquired the experience of older men, he had good sense equal to the experience of many others. After a little more conversation on different subjects, he offered again to take his leave, when Ali Baba, stopping him, said, "Where are you going, sir, in so much haste? I beg you would do me the honor to sup with me, though my entertainment may not be worthy of your acceptance; such as it is, I heartily offer it." "Sir," replied Cogia Houssain, "I am thoroughly persuaded of your good will; but the truth is, I can eat no victuals that have any salt in them; therefore judge how I should feel at your table." "If that is the only reason," said Ali Baba, "it ought not to deprive me of the honor of your company; for, in the first place, there is no salt ever put into my bread, and as to the meat we shall have tonight, I promise you there shall be none in that. Therefore you must do me the favor to stay. I will return immediately."

Ali Baba went into the kitchen, and ordered Morgiana to put no salt in the meat that was to be dressed that night; and to make quickly two or three ragouts besides what he had ordered, but be sure to put no salt in them.

Morgiana, who was always ready to obey her master, could not help being surprised at his strange order. "Who is this strange man," said she, "who eats no salt with his meat? Your supper will be spoiled if I keep it back so long." "Do not be angry, Morgiana," replied Ali Baba; "he is an honest man, therefore do as I bid you."

Morgiana obeyed, though with no little reluctance, and had a curiosity to see this man who ate no salt. To this end, when she had finished what she had to do in the kitchen, she helped Abdalla to carry up the dishes; and looking at Cogia Houssain, knew him at first sight, notwithstanding his disguise, to be captain of the robbers, and examining him very carefully, perceived that he had a dagger under his garment. "I am not in the least amazed," said she to herself, "that this wicked man, who is my master's greatest enemy, would eat no salt with him, since he intends to assassinate him; but I will prevent him."

Morgiana, while they were at supper, determined in her own mind to execute one of the boldest acts ever meditated.

When Abdalla came for the dessert or fruit, and had put it with the wine and glasses before Ali Baba, Morgiana retired, dressed herself neatly, and with a suitable head-dress like a dancer, girded her waist with a silver-gilt girdle to which there hung a poniard with a hilt and guard of the same metal, and put a handsome mask on her face.

When she had thus disguised herself, she said to Abdalla, "Take your tabor, and let us go and divert our master and his son's friend, as we do sometimes when he is alone."

Abdalla took his tabor and played all the way into the hall before Morgiana, who, when she came to the door, made a low obeisance by way of asking leave to exhibit her skill, while Abdalla left off playing. "Come in, Morgiana," said Ali Baba, "and let Cogia Houssain see what you can do, that he may tell us what he thinks of your performance."

Cogia Houssain, who did not expect this diversion after supper, began to fear he should not be able to take advantage of the opportunity he thought he had found; but hoped if he now missed his aim to secure it another time, by keeping up a friendly correspondence with the father and son; therefore, though he could have wished Ali Baba would have declined the dance, he pretended to be obliged to him for it, and had the complaisance to express his satisfaction at what he saw, which pleased his host.

As soon as Abdalla saw that Ali Baba and Cogia Houssain had done talking, he began to play on the tabor and accompanied it with an air to which Morgiana, who was an excellent performer, danced in such a manner as would have created admiration in any company.

After she had danced several dances with much grace, she drew the poniard, and holding it in her hand, began a dance in which she outdid herself by the many different figures, light movements, and the surprising leaps and wonderful exertions with which she accompanied it. Sometimes she presented the poniard to one breast, sometimes to another, and oftentimes seemed to strike her own. At last she snatched the tabor from Abdalla with her left hand, and holding the dagger in her right, presented the other side of the tabor, after the manner of those who get a livelihood by dancing and solicit the liberality of the spectators.

Ali Baba put a piece of gold into the tabor, as did also the son; and Cogia Houssain, seeing that she was coming to him, had pulled his purse out of his bosom to make her a present; but while he was putting his hand into it, Morgiana, with a courage and resolution worthy of herself, plunged the poniard into his breast.

Ali Baba and his son, shocked at this action, cried out aloud. "Unhappy woman!" exclaimed Ali Baba, "what have you done, to ruin me and my family?" "It was to preserve, not to ruin you," answered Morgiana; "for see here," continued she, opening the pretended Cogia Houssain's garment, and showing the dagger, "what an enemy you had entertained! Look well at him, and you will find him to be both the fictitious oil merchant, and the captain of the gang of forty robbers. Remember, too, that he would eat no salt with you; and what would you have more to persuade you of his wicked design? Before I saw him, I suspected him as soon as you told me you had such a guest. I knew him, and you now find that my suspicion was not groundless."

Ali Baba, who immediately felt the new obligation he had to Morgiana for saving his life a second time, embraced her: "Morgiana," said he, "I gave you your liberty, and then promised you that my gratitude should not stop there, but that I would soon give you higher proofs of its sincerity, which I now do by making you my daughter-in-law." Then addressing himself to his son, he said: "I believe you, son, to be so dutiful a child that you will not refuse Morgiana for your wife. You see that Cogia Houssain sought your friendship with a treacherous design to take away my life; and if he had succeeded, there is no doubt but he would have sacrificed you also to his revenge. Consider, that by marrying Morgiana you marry the preserver of my family and your own."

The son, far from showing any dislike, readily consented to the marriage; not only because he would not disobey his father but also because it was agreeable to his inclination. After this they thought of burying the captain of the robbers with his comrades, and did it so privately that nobody discovered their bones till many years later, when no one had any concern in the publication of this remarkable history. A few days afterwards Ali Baba celebrated the nuptials of his son and Morgiana with great solemnity, a sumptuous feast, and the usual dancing and spectacles; and had the satisfaction to see that his friends and neighbors, whom he invited, had no knowledge of the true motives of the marriage; but that those who were not unacquainted with Morgiana's good qualities commended his generosity and goodness of heart. Ali Baba did not visit the robber's cave for a whole year, as he supposed the other two might be alive.

At the year's end, when he found they had not made any attempt to disturb him, he had the curiosity to make another journey. He mounted his horse, and when he came to the cave he alighted, tied his horse to a tree, then approaching the entrance, and pronouncing the words, "Open, Sesame!" the door opened. He entered the cavern and by the condition he found things in, judged that nobody had been there since the captain had fetched the goods for his shop. From this time he believed he was the only person in the world who had the secret of opening the cave, and that all the treasure was at his sole disposal. He put as much gold into his saddle-bag as his horse could carry, and returned to town. Some years later he carried his son to the cave and taught him the secret, which descended to his posterity, who, using their good fortune with moderation, lived in honor and splendor.

A CHINESE FAIRY TALE

By LAURENCE HOUSMAN

TIKI-PU was a small grub of a thing; but he had a true love of Art deep down in his soul. There it hung mewing and and complaining, struggling to work its way out through the raw exterior that bound it.

Tiki-pu's master professed to be an artist: he had apprentices and students, who came daily to work under him; and a large studio littered about with the performance of himself and his pupils. On the walls hung also a few real works by the older men, all long dead.

This studio Tiki-pu swept; for those who worked in it he ground colors, washed brushes, and ran errands, bringing them their dog chops and bird's nest soup from the nearest eating-house whenever they were too busy to go out to it themselves. He himself had to feed mainly on the bread crumbs which the students screwed into pellets for their drawings and then threw about upon the floor. It was on the floor, also, that he had to sleep at night.

Tiki-pu looked after the blinds, and mended the paper window-panes, which were often broken when the apprentices threw their brushes and mahl-sticks at him. Also he strained rice paper over the linen-stretchers, ready for the painters to work on; and for a treat, now and then, a lazy one would allow him to mix a color for him. Then it was that Tiki-pu's soul came down into his fingertips, and his heart beat so that he gasped for joy. Oh, the yellows and the greens, and the lakes and the cobalts, and the purples which sprang from the blending of them! Sometimes it was all he could do to keep himself from crying out.

Tiki-pu, while he squatted and ground at the color-powders, would listen to his master lecturing to the students. He knew by heart the names of all the painters and their schools; and the name of the great leader of them all, who had lived and passed from their midst more than three hundred years ago, he knew that, too, a name like the sound of the wind, Wio-wani: the big picture at the end of the studio was by him.

That picture! To Tiki-pu it seemed worth all the rest of the world put together. He knew, too, the story which was told of it, making it as holy to his eyes as the tombs of his own ancestors. The apprentices joked over it, calling it "Wio-wani's back door," "Wio-wani's nightcap," and many other nicknames; but Tiki-pu was quite sure, since the picture was so beautiful, that the story must be true.

Wio-wani, at the end of a long life, had painted it: a garden full of trees and sunlight, with high-standing flowers and green paths, and in their midst a palace. "The place where I would like to rest," said Wio-wani, when it was finished.

So beautiful was it then, that the Emperor himself had come to see it; and gazing enviously at those peaceful walks, and the palace nestling among the trees, had sighed and owned that he, too, would be glad of such a resting place. Then Wio-wani stepped into the picture, and walked away along a path till he came, looking quite small and far-off, to a low door in the palace wall. Opening it, he turned and beckoned to the Emperor; but the Emperor did not follow; so Wio-wani went in by himself, and shut the door between himself and the world forever.

That happened three hundred years ago; but for Tiki-pu the story was as fresh and true as if it had happened yesterday. When he was left to himself in the studio, all alone and locked up for the night, Tiki-pu used to go and stare at the picture till it was too dark to see, and at the little palace with the door in its wall by which Wio-wani had disappeared out of life. Then his soul would go down into his finger tips, and he would knock softly and fearfully at the beautifully painted door, saying, "Wio-wani, are you there?"

Little by little in the long-thinking nights, and the slow early mornings when light began to creep back through the papered windows of the studio, Tiki-pu's soul became too much for him. He who could strain paper, and grind colors, and wash brushes, had everything within reach for becoming an artist, if it was the will of Fate that he should be one.

He began timidly at first, but in a little while he grew bold. With

the first wash of light he was up from his couch on the hard floor
and was daubing his soul out on scraps, and odds-and-ends, and
stolen pieces of rice paper.

Before long, the short spell of daylight which lay between dawn
and the arrival of the apprentices to their work did not suffice him.
It took him so long to hide all traces of his doings, to wash out the
brushes, and rinse clean the paint-pots he had used, and on the top
of that to get the studio swept and dusted, that there was hardly time
left him in which to indulge the itching of his fingers.

Driven by necessity, he became a pilferer of candle ends, picking
them from their sockets in the lanterns which the students carried
on dark nights. Now and then one of these would remember that,
when last used, his lantern had had a candle in it, and would accuse
Tiki-pu of having stolen it. "It is true," he would confess; "I was
hungry—I have eaten it." The lie was so probable, he was believed
easily, and was well beaten accordingly. Down in the ragged linings
of his coat Tiki-pu could hear the candle ends rattling as the buffet-
ing and chastisement fell upon him, and often he trembled lest his
hoard should be discovered. But the truth of the matter never leaked
out; and at night, as soon as he guessed that all the world outside
was in bed, Tiki-pu would mount one of his candles on a wooden
stand and paint by the light of it, blinding himself over his task,
till the dawn came and gave him a better and cheaper light to
work by.

Tiki-pu quite hugged himself over the results; he believed he was
doing very well. "If only Wio-wani were here to teach me," thought
he, "I would be in the way of becoming a great painter!"

The resolution came to him one night that Wio-wani *should* teach
him. So he took a large piece of rice paper and strained it, and sitting
down opposite "Wio-wani's back door," began painting. He had
never set himself so big a task as this; by the dim stumbling light of
his candle he strained his eyes nearly blind over the difficulties of it;
and at last was almost driven to despair. How the trees stood row
behind row, with air and sunlight between, and how the path went
in and out, winding its way up to the little door in the palace-wall,
were mysteries he could not fathom. He peered and peered and

dropped tears into his paint-pots; but the secret of the mystery of such painting was far beyond him.

The door in the palace-wall opened; out came a little old man and began walking down the pathway toward him.

The soul of Tiki-pu gave a sharp leap in his grubby little body. "That must be Wio-wani himself and no other!" cried his soul.

Tiki-pu pulled off his cap and threw himself down on the floor with reverent grovelings. When he dared to look up again, Wio-wani stood over him big and fine; just within the edge of his canvas he stood and reached out a hand.

"Come along with me, Tiki-pu!" said the great one. "If you want to know how to paint I will teach you."

"Oh, Wio-wani, were you there all the while?" cried Tiki-pu ecstatically, leaping up and clutching with his smeary little puds the hand which the old man extended to him.

"I was there," said Wio-wani, "looking at you out of my little window. Come along in!"

Tiki-pu took a heave and swung himself into the picture, and fairly capered when he found his feet among the flowers of Wio-wani's beautiful garden. Wio-wani had turned, and was ambling gently back to the door of his palace, beckoning to the small one to follow him; and there stood Tiki-pu, opening his mouth like a fish to all the wonders that surrounded him. "Celestiality, may I speak?" he said suddenly.

"Speak," replied Wio-wani; "what is it?"

"The Emperor, was not he the very flower of fools not to follow when you told him?"

"I cannot say," answered Wio-wani, "but he certainly was no artist."

Then he opened the door, that door which he had so beautifully painted, and led Tiki-pu in. And outside the little candle end sat and guttered by itself, till the wick fell overboard, and the flame kicked itself out, leaving the studio in darkness and solitude to wait for the growings of another dawn.

It was a full day before Tiki-pu reappeared; he came running down the green path in great haste, jumped out of the frame on to the studio floor, and began tidying up his own messes of the night, and the apprentices' of the previous day. Only just in time did he have things ready by the hour his master and the others returned to work.

All that day they kept scratching their left ears, and could not think why; but Tiki-pu knew, for he was saying over to himself all the things that Wio-wani, the great painter, had been saying about them and their precious productions. As he ground their colors for them and washed their brushes, and filled his famished little body with the bread crumbs they threw away, little they guessed from what an immeasurable distance he looked down upon them all, and had Wio-wani's word for it tickling his right ear all the day long.

Now before long, Tiki-pu's master noticed a change in him; and though he bullied him, and thrashed him, and did all that a careful master should do, he could not get the change out of him. So in a short while he grew suspicious. "What is the boy up to?" he wondered. "I have my eye on him all day: it must be at night that he gets into mischief."

It did not take Tiki-pu's master a night's watching to find out that some thing surreptitious was certainly going on. When it was dark he took up his post outside the studio, to see whether by any chance Tiki-pu had some way of getting out; and before long he saw a faint light showing through the window. So he came and thrust his finger softly through one of the panes, and put his eye to the hole.

There inside was a candle burning on a stand, and Tiki-pu squatting with paint-pots and brush in front of Wio-wani's last masterpiece.

"What fine piece of burglary is this?" thought he. "What serpent have I been harboring in my bosom? Is this beast of a grub of a boy thinking to make himself a painter and cut me out of my reputation and prosperity?" For even at that distance he could perceive plainly that the work of this boy went head and shoulders beyond his, or that of any painter then living.

Presently Wio-wani opened his door and came down the path, as was his habit now each night, to call Tiki-pu to his lesson. He advanced to the front of his picture and beckoned for Tiki-pu to come in with him; and Tiki-pu's master grew clammy at the knees as he beheld Tiki-pu catch hold of Wio-wani's hand and jump into the picture, and skip up the green path by Wio-wani's side, and in through the little door that Wio-wani had painted so beautifully on the end wall of his palace!

For a time Tiki-pu's master stood glued to the spot with grief and horror. "Oh, you deadly little underling! Oh, you poisonous little caretaker, you parasite, you vampire, you fly in amber!" cried he, "Is that where you get your training? Is it there that you dare to go trespassing; into a picture that I purchased for my own pleasure and profit, and not for yours? Soon we will see whom it really belongs to!"

He ripped out the paper of the largest window-pane and pushed his way through into the studio. Then in great haste he took up paint-pot and brush, and sacrilegiously set himself to work upon Wio-wani's last masterpiece. In the place of the doorway by which Tiki-pu had entered he painted a solid brick wall; twice over he painted it, and mortared every brick to its place. And when he had quite finished he laughed, and called "Good night, Tiki-pu!" and went home to be quite happy.

The next day all the apprentices were wondering what had become of Tiki-pu; but as the master himself said nothing, and as another boy came to act as color-grinder and brush-washer to the establishment, the apprentices very soon forgot all about him.

In the studio the master used to sit at work with his students all about him, and a mind full of ease and contentment. Now and then he would throw a glance across to the bricked-up doorway of Wio-wani's palace, and laugh to himself, thinking how well he had served out Tiki-pu for his treachery and presumption.

One day—it was five years after the disappearance of Tiki-pu—he was giving his apprentices a lecture on the glories and the beauties and the wonders of Wio-wani's painting—how nothing for color could excel, or for mystery could equal it. To add point to his eloquence, he stood waving his hands before Wio-wani's last masterpiece, and all his students and apprentices sat round him and looked.

Suddenly he stopped at mid-word and broke off in the full flight of his eloquence, as he saw something like a hand come and take down the top brick from the face of paint which he had laid over the little door in the palace-wall which Wio-wani had so beautifully painted. In another moment there was no doubt about it; brick by brick the wall was being pulled down, in spite of its double thickness.

The lecturer was altogether too dumfounded and terrified to utter a word. He and all his apprentices stood round and stared while the demolition of the wall proceeded. Before long he recognized Wio-wani with his flowing white beard; it was his handiwork, this pulling down of the wall! He still had a brick in his hand when he stepped through the opening that he had made, and close after him stepped Tiki-pu!

Tiki-pu was grown tall and strong—he was even handsome; but for all that, his old master recognized him and saw with an envious foreboding that under his arms he carried many rolls and stretchers and portfolios, and other belongings of his craft. Clearly Tiki-pu was coming back into the world, and was going to be a great painter.

Down the garden path came Wio-wani, and Tiki-pu walked after him. Tiki-pu was so tall that his head stood well over Wio-wani's shoulders—old man and young man together made a handsome pair.

How big Wio-wani grew as he walked down the avenues of his garden and into the foreground of his picture! And how big the brick in his hand! And ah, how angry he seemed!

Wio-wani came right down to the edge of the picture-frame and held up the brick. "What did you do that for?" he asked.

"I . . . didn't!" Tiki-pu's old master was beginning to reply; and the lie was still rolling on his tongue when the weight of the brick-bat, hurled by the stout arm of Wio-wani, felled him. After that he never spoke again. That brickbat, which he himself had reared, became his own tombstone.

Just inside the picture-frame stood Tiki-pu, kissing the wonderful hands of Wio-wani, which had taught him all their skill. "Goodbye, Tiki-pu," said Wio-wani, embracing him tenderly. "Now I am sending my second self into the world. When you are tired and want rest, come back to me: old Wio-wani will take you in."

Tiki-pu was sobbing, and the tears were running down his cheeks as he stepped out of Wio-wani's wonderfully painted garden, and stood once more upon earth. Turning, he saw the old man walking away along the path towards the little door under the palace-wall. At the door Wio-wani turned back and waved his hand for the last time. Tiki-pu still stood watching him. Then the door opened and shut, and Wio-wani was gone. Softly as a flower the picture seemed to have folded its leaves over him.

Tiki-pu leaned a wet face against the picture and kissed the door in the palace-wall which Wio-wani had painted so beautifully. "O Wio-wani, dear master," he cried, "are you there?"

He waited and called again, but no voice answered him.

Howard Pyle – Frank Stockton

HOW BOOTS BEFOOLED THE KING

By HOWARD PYLE

ONCE upon a time there was a king who was the wisest in all of the world. So wise was he that no one had ever befooled him, which is a rare thing, I can tell you. Now, this king had a daughter who was as pretty as a ripe apple, so that there was no end to the number of lads who came asking to marry her. Every day there were two or three of them dawdling around the house, so that at last the old king grew tired of having them always about.

So he sent word far and near that whoever should befool him might have the princess and half of the kingdom to boot, for he thought that it would be a wise man indeed who could trick him. But the king also said, that whoever should try to befool him and fail, should have a good whipping. This was to keep foolish fellows away.

The princess was so pretty that there was no lack of lads who came to have a try for her and half of the kingdom, but every one of these went away with a sore back and no luck.

Now, there was a man who was well off in the world, and who had three sons, the first was named Peter, and the second was named Paul. Peter and Paul thought themselves as wise as anybody in all of the world, and their father thought as they did.

As for the youngest son, he was named Boots. Nobody thought anything of him except that he was silly, for he did nothing but sit poking in the warm ashes all of the day.

One morning Peter spoke up and said that he was going to the town to have a try at befooling the king, for it would be a fine thing to have a princess in the family. His father did not say no, for if anybody was wise enough to befool the king, Peter was the lad.

So, after Peter had eaten a good breakfast, off he set for the town, right foot foremost. After a while he came to the king's house and—rap! Tap! tap!—he knocked at the door.

Well; what did he want?

Oh! he would only like to have a try at befooling the king.

Very good; he should have his try. He was not the first one who had been there that morning, early as it was.

So Peter was shown in to the king. "Oh, look!" said he. "Yonder are three black geese out in the courtyard!"

But no, the king was not to be fooled so easily as all that. "One goose is enough to look at at a time," said he; "take him away and give him a whipping!"

And so they did, and Peter went home bleating like a sheep.

One day Paul spoke up. "I should like to go and have a try for the princess, too," said he.

Well, his father did not say no, for Paul was the more clever.

So off went Paul as merrily as a duck in the rain. By and by he came to the castle, and then he, too, was brought before the king just as Peter had been.

"Oh, look!" said he. "Yonder is a crow sitting in the tree with three white stripes on his back!"

But the king was not so silly as to be fooled in that way. "Here is a Jack," said he, "who will soon have more stripes on his back than he will like. Take him away and give him his whipping!"

Then it was done as the king had said, and Paul went away home bawling like a calf.

One day up spoke Boots. "I should like to go and have a try for the pretty princess, too," said he.

At this they all stared and sniggered. What! he go where his clever brothers had failed, and had nothing to show for the trying but a good beating? What had come over the lout! Here was a pretty business, to be sure! That was what they all said.

But all of this rolled away from Boots like water from a duck's back. No matter, he would like to go and have a try like the others. So he begged and begged until his father was glad to let him go to be rid of his teasing, if nothing else.

Then Boots asked if he might have the old tattered hat that hung back of the chimney.

Oh, yes, he might have that if he wanted it, for nobody with good wits was likely to wear such a thing.

So Boots took the hat, and after he had brushed the ashes from his shoes set off for the town, whistling as he went.

The first body whom he met was an old woman with a great load of earthenware pots and crocks on her shoulders.

"Good day, mother," said Boots.

"Good day, son," said she.

"What will you take for all of your pots and crocks?" said Boots.

"Three shillings," said she.

"I will give you five shillings if you will come and stand in front of the king's house, and do thus and so when I say this and that," said Boots.

Oh, yes! she would do that willingly enough.

So Boots and the old woman went on together, and presently came to the king's house. When they had come there, Boots sat down in front of the door and began bawling as loud as he could—"No, I will not! I will not do it, I say! No, I will not do it!"

So he kept on, bawling louder and louder until he made such a noise that, at last, the king himself came out to see what all the hubbub was about. But when Boots saw him he only bawled out louder than ever, "No, I will not! I will not do it, I say!"

"Stop! stop!" cried the king. "What is all this about?"

"Why," said Boots, "everybody wants to buy my cap, but I will not sell it! I will not do it, I say!"

"But, why should anybody want to buy such a cap as that?" said the king.

"Because," said Boots, "it is a fooling cap and the only one in all the world."

"A fooling cap!" said the king. For he did not like to hear of such a cap as that coming into the town. "Hum-m-m-m! I should like to see you fool somebody with it. Could you fool that old body yonder with the pots and the crocks?"

"Oh, yes! That is easily enough done," said Boots, and without

more ado he took off his tattered cap and blew into it. Then he put
it on his head again and bawled out, "Break pots! break pots!"

No sooner had he spoken these words than the old woman jumped
up and began breaking and smashing her pots and crocks as though
she had gone crazy. That was what Boots had paid her five shillings
for doing, but of it the king knew nothing. "Hui!" said he to himself. "I must buy that hat from the fellow or he will fool the princess
away from me for sure and certain." Then he began talking to Boots
as sweetly as though he had honey in his mouth. Perhaps Boots
would sell the hat to him?

Oh, no! Boots could not think of such a thing as selling his fooling cap.

Come, come, the king wanted that hat, and sooner than miss
buying it he would give a whole bag of gold money for it.

At this Boots looked up and looked down, scratching his head.
Well, he supposed he would have to sell the hat some time, and the
king might as well have it as anybody else. But for all that he did
not like parting with it.

So the king gave Boots the bag of gold, and Boots gave the king
the old tattered hat, and then he went his way.

After Boots had gone the king blew into the hat and blew into the
hat, but though he blew enough breath into it to sail a big ship, he
did not befool so much as a single titmouse. Then, at last, he began
to see that the fooling cap was good on nobody else's head but
Boots's; and he was none too pleased at that, you may be sure.

As for Boots, with his bag of gold he bought the finest clothes
that were to be had in the town, and when the next morning had
come he started away bright and early for the king's house. "I have
come," said he, "to marry the princess, if you please."

At this the king hemmed and hawed and scratched his head. Yes,
Boots had befooled him sure enough; but, after all, he could not give
up the princess for such a thing as that. Still, he would give Boots
another chance. Now, there was the high-councilor, who was the
wisest man in all the world. Did Boots think that he could fool him
also?

Oh, yes! Boots thought that it might be done.

Very well; if he could befool the high-councilor so as to bring him to the castle the next morning against his will, Boots should have the princess and the half of the kingdom; if he did not do so he should have his beating. Then Boots went away, and the king thought that he was rid of him now for good and all.

As for the high-councilor, he was not pleased with the matter at all, for he did not like the thought of being fooled by a clever rogue, and taken here and there against his will. So when he had come home, he armed all of his servants with blunderbusses, and then waited to give Boots a welcome when he should come.

But Boots was not going to fall into any such trap as that! No indeed! Not he! The next morning he went quietly and bought a fine large meal-sack. Then he put a black wig over his beautiful red hair, so that no one might know him. After that he went to where the high-councilor lived, and when he had come there he crawled inside of the sack, and lay just beside the door of the house.

By and by came one of the maid servants to the door, and there lay the great meal-sack with somebody in it.

"Ach!" cried she. "Who is there?"

But Boots only said, "Sh-h-h-h-h!"

Then the serving maid went back into the house, and told the high-councilor that one lay outside in a great meal-sack, and that all that he said was, "Sh-h-h-h-h!"

So the councilor went himself to see what it was all about. "What do you want here?" said he.

"Sh-h-h-h-h!" said Boots. "I am not to be talked to now. This is a wisdom-sack, and I am learning wisdom as fast as a drake can eat peas."

"And what wisdom have you learned?" said the councilor.

Oh! Boots had learned wisdom about everything in the world. He had learned that the clever scamp who had fooled the king yesterday was coming with seventeen tall men to take the high-councilor, willy-nilly, to the castle that morning.

When the high-councilor heard this, he fell to trembling till his teeth rattled in his head. "And have you learned how I can get the better of this clever scamp?" said he.

Oh, yes! Boots had learned that easily enough.

So, good! Then if the wise man in the sack would tell the high-councilor how to escape the clever rogue the high-councilor would give the wise man twenty dollars.

But no, that was not to be done; wisdom was not bought so cheaply as the high-councilor seemed to think.

Well, the councilor would give him a hundred dollars then.

That was good! A hundred dollars were a hundred dollars. If the councilor would give him that much he might get into the sack himself, and then he could learn all the wisdom that he wanted, and more besides.

So Boots crawled out of the sack, and the councilor paid his hundred dollars and crawled in.

As soon as he was in all snug and safe, Boots drew the mouth of the sack together and tied it tightly. Then he flung sack, councilor, and all over his shoulder, and started away to the king's house, and anybody who met them could see with half an eye that the councilor was going against his will.

When Boots came to the king's castle he laid the councilor down in the goose-house, and then he went to the king.

When the king saw Boots again, he bit his lips with vexation. "Well," said he, "have you fooled the councilor?"

"Oh, yes!" says Boots. "I have done that."

And where was the councilor now?

Oh, Boots had just left him down in the goose-house. He was tied up safe and sound in a sack, waiting till the king should send for him.

So the councilor was sent for, and when he came the king saw at once that he had been brought against his will.

"And now may I marry the princess?" said Boots.

But the king was not willing for him to marry the princess yet. No! no! Boots must not go so fast. There was more to be done yet. If he would come tomorrow morning he might have the princess and welcome, but he would have to pick her out from among four-score other maids just like her; did he think that he could do that?

Oh, yes! Boots thought that that might be easy enough to do.

So, good! Then come tomorrow; but he must understand that if he failed he should have a good whipping, and be sent packing from the town.

So off went Boots, and the king thought that he was rid of him now, for he had never seen the princess, and how could he pick her out from among eighty others?

But Boots was not going to give up so easily as all that! No, not he! He made a little box, and then he hunted up and down until he had caught a live mouse to put into it.

When the next morning came he started away to the king's house, taking his mouse along with him in the box.

There was the king, standing in the doorway, looking out into the street. When he saw Boots coming toward him he made a wry face. "What!" said he. "Are you back again?"

Oh, yes. Boots was back again. And now if the princess was ready he would like to go and find her, for lost time was not to be gathered again like fallen apples.

So off they marched to a great room, and there stood eighty-and-one maidens, all as much alike as peas in the same dish.

Boots looked here and there, but, even if he had known the princess, he could not have told her from the others. But he was ready for all that. Before anyone knew what he was about, he opened the box, and out ran the little mouse among them all. Then what a screaming and a hubbub there was! Many looked as though they would have liked to swoon, but only one of them did so. As soon as the others saw what had happened, they forgot all about the mouse, and ran to her and fell to fanning her and slapping her hands and chafing her temples.

"This is the princess," said Boots.

And so it was.

After that the king could think of nothing more to set Boots to do, so he let him marry the princess as he had promised, and have half of the kingdom to boot.

That is all of this story—

Only this: It is not always the silliest one that sits kicking his feet in the ashes at home.

KING STORK

By HOWARD PYLE

With Illustration by THE AUTHOR

THERE was a drummer marching along the high-road—forward march!—left, right!—tramp, tramp tramp!—for the fighting was done, and he was coming home from the wars. By and by he came to a great wide stream of water, and there sat an old man as gnarled and as bent as the hoops in a cooper shop. "Are you going to cross the water?" said he.

"Yes," says the drummer, "I am going to do that if my legs hold out to carry me."

"And will you not help a poor body across?" says the old man.

Now, the drummer was as good-natured a lad as ever stood on two legs. "If the young never gave a lift to the old," says he to himself, "the wide world would not be worth while living in." So he took off his shoes and stockings, and then he bent his back and took the old man on it, and away he started through the water—splash!

But this was no common old man whom the drummer was carrying, and he was not long finding that out, for the farther he went in the water the heavier grew his load—like work put off until tomorrow—so that, when he was half-way across, his legs shook under him and the sweat stood on his forehead like a string of beads in the hop-window. But by and by he reached the other shore, and the old man jumped down from his back.

"Phew!" says the drummer, "I am glad to be here at last!"

And now for the wonder of all this: The old man was an old man no longer, but a splendid tall fellow with hair as yellow as gold. "And who do you think I am?" said he.

But of that the drummer knew no more than the mouse in the haystack, so he shook his head, and said nothing.

"I am king of the storks, and here I have sat for many days; for the wicked one-eyed witch who lives on the glass hill put it upon me for a spell that I should be an old man until somebody should carry me over the water. You are the first to do that, and you shall not lose by it. Here is a little bone whistle; whenever you are in trouble just blow a turn or two on it, and I will be by to help you.'

Thereupon King Stork drew a feather cap out of his pocket and clapped it on his head, and away he flew, for he was turned into a great, long, red-legged stork as quick as a wink.

But the drummer trudged on the way he was going, as merry as a cricket, for it is not everybody who cracks his shins against such luck as he had stumbled over, I can tell you. By and by he came to the town over the hill, and there he found great bills stuck on the walls. They were all proclamations. And this is what they said:

The princess of that town was as clever as she was pretty; that was saying a great deal, for she was the handsomest in the whole world. ("Phew! but that is a fine lass for sure and certain," said the drummer.) So it was proclaimed that any lad who could answer a question the princess would ask, and would ask a question the princess could not answer, and would catch the bird that she would be wanting, should have her for his wife and half of the kingdom to boot. ("Hi! but here is luck for a clever lad," says the drummer.) But whoever should fail in any one of the three tasks should have his head chopped off as sure as he lived. ("Ho! but she is a wicked one for all that," says the drummer.)

That was what the proclamation said, and the drummer would have a try for her; "for," said he, "it is a poor fellow who cannot manage a wife when he has her"—and he knew as much about that business as a goose about churning butter. As for chopping off heads, he never bothered his own about that; for, if one never goes out for fear of rain one never catches fish.

Off he went to the king's castle as fast as he could step, and there he knocked on the door, as bold as though his own grandmother lived there.

But when the king heard what the drummer had come for, he took out his pocket-handkerchief and began to wipe his eyes, for he had a soft heart under his jacket, and it made him cry like anything to see another coming to have his head chopped off, as so many had done before him. For there they were, all along the wall in front of the princess's window, like so many apples.

But the drummer was not to be scared away by the king's crying a bit, so in he came, and by and by they all sat down to supper—he and the king and the princess. As for the princess, she was so pretty that the drummer's heart melted inside of him, like a lump of butter on the stove—and that was what she was after. After a while she asked him if he had come to answer a question of hers, and to ask her a question of his, and to catch the bird that she should set him to catch.

"Yes," said the drummer, "I have come to do that very thing." And he spoke as boldly and as loudly as the clerk in church.

"Very well, then," says the princess, as sweet as sugar candy, "just come along tomorrow, and I will ask you your question."

Off went the drummer; he put his whistle to his lips and blew a turn or two, and there stood King Stork, and nobody knows where he stepped from.

"And what do you want?" says he.

The drummer told him everything, and how the princess was going to ask him a question tomorrow morning that he would have to answer, or have his head chopped off.

"Here you have walked into a pretty muddle, and with your eyes open," says King Stork, for he knew that the princess was a wicked enchantress, and loved nothing so much as to get a lad into just such a scrape as the drummer had tumbled into. "But see, here is a little cap and a long feather—the cap is a dark-cap, and when you put it on your head one can see you no more than so much thin air. At twelve o'clock at night the princess will come out into the castle garden and will fly away through the air. Then throw your leg over the feather, and it will carry you wherever you want to go; and if the princess flies fast it will carry you as fast and faster."

"Dong! Dong!" The clock struck twelve, and the princess came out of her house; but in the garden was the drummer waiting for her with the dark-cap on his head, and he saw her as plain as a pike-staff. She brought a pair of great wings which she fastened to her shoulders, and away she flew. But the drummer was as quick with his tricks as she was with hers; he flung his leg over the feather which King Stork had given him, and away he flew after her, and just as fast as she with her great wings.

By and by they came to a huge castle of shining steel that stood on a mountain of glass. And it was a good thing for the drummer that he had on his cap of darkness, for all around outside of the castle stood fiery dragons and savage lions to keep anybody from going in without leave.

But not a thread of the drummer did they see; in he walked with the princess, and there was a great one-eyed witch with a beard on her chin, and a nose that hooked over her mouth like the beak of a parrot.

"Uff!" said she. "Here is a smell of Christian blood in the house."

"Tut, mother!" says the princess. "How you talk! Do you not see that there is nobody with me?" For the drummer had taken care that the wind should not blow the cap of darkness off of his head, I can tell you. By and by they sat down to supper, the princess and the witch, but it was little the princess ate, for as fast as anything was put on her plate the drummer helped himself to it, so that it was all gone before she could get a bite.

As fast as anything was put on her plate, the drummer helped himself to it.

"Look, mother!" she said. "I eat nothing, and yet it all goes from my plate; why is that so?" But that the old witch could not tell her, for she could see nothing of the drummer.

"There was a lad came today to answer the question I shall put to him," said the princess. "Now what shall I ask him by way of a question?"

"I have a tooth in the back part of my head," said the witch, "and it has been grumbling a bit; ask him what it is you are thinking about, and let it be that."

Yes, that was a good question for sure and certain; and the princess would give it to the drummer tomorrow, to see what he had to say for himself. As for the drummer, you can guess how he grinned, for he heard every word that they said.

After a while the princess flew away home again, for it was nearly the break of day, and she must be back before the sun rose. And the drummer flew close behind her, but she knew nothing of that.

The next morning up he marched to the king's castle and knocked at the door, and they let him in.

There sat the king and the princess, and lots of folks besides. Well, had he come to answer her question? That was what the princess wanted to know.

Yes, that was the very business he had come about.

Very well, this was the question, and he might have three guesses at it: What was she thinking of at that minute?

Oh, it could be no hard thing to answer such a question as that, for lasses' heads all ran upon the same things more or less; was it a fine silk dress with glass buttons down the front that she was thinking of now?

No, it was not that.

Then, was it of a good stout lad like himself for a sweetheart, that she was thinking of?

No, it was not that.

No? Then it was the bad tooth that had been grumbling in the head of the one-eyed witch for a day or two past, perhaps.

Dear, dear! but you should have seen the princess's face when she heard this! Up she got and off she packed without a single word, and the king saw without the help of his spectacles that the drummer had guessed right. He was so glad that he jumped up and down and snapped his fingers for joy. Besides that, he gave out that bonfires should be lighted all over the town, and that was a fine thing for the little boys.

The next night the princess flew away to the house of the one-eyed witch again, but there was the drummer close behind her just as he had been before.

"Uff!" said the one-eyed witch. "Here is a smell of Christian blood, for sure and certain." But all the same, she saw no more of the drummer than if he had never been born.

"See, mother," said the princess, "that rogue of a drummer answered my question without winking over it."

"So," said the old witch, "we have missed for once, but the second time hits the mark; he will be asking you a question tomorrow, and here is a book that tells everything that has happened in the world, and if he asks you more than that he is a smart one and no mistake."

After that they sat down to supper again, but it was little the princess ate, for the drummer helped himself out of her plate just as he had done before.

After a while the princess flew away home, and the drummer with her.

"And, now, what will we ask her that she cannot answer?" said the drummer; so off he went back of the house, and blew a turn or two on his whistle, and there stood King Stork.

"And what will we ask the princess," said he, "when she has a book that tells her everything?"

King Stork was not long in telling him that: "Just ask her so and so and so and so," said he, "and she would not dare to answer the question."

Well, the next morning there was the drummer at the castle all in good time; and, had he come to ask her a question? that was what the princess wanted to know.

Oh, yes, he had come for that very thing.

Very well, then, just let him begin, for the princess was ready and waiting, and she wet her thumb, and began to turn over the leaves of her Book of Knowledge.

Oh, it was an easy question the drummer was going to ask, and it needed no big book like that to answer it. The other night he dreamed that he was in a castle all built of shining steel, where there lived a witch with one eye. There was a handsome bit of a lass there who was as great a witch as the old woman herself, but for the life of him he could not tell who she was; now perhaps the princess could make a guess at it.

There the drummer had her as tight as a fly in a bottle, for she did not dare to let folks know that she was a wicked witch like the one-eyed one; so all she could do was to sit there and gnaw her lip. As for the Book of Knowledge, it was no more use to her than a fifth wheel under a cart.

But if the king was glad when the drummer answered the princess's question, he was twice as glad when he found she could not answer his.

All the same, there is more to do yet, and many a slip betwixt the cup and the lip: "The bird I want is the one-eyed raven," said the princess, "Now bring her to me if you want to keep your head off of the wall yonder."

Yes; the drummer thought he might do that as well as another thing. So off he went back of the house to talk to King Stork.

"Look," said King Stork, and he drew a net out of his pocket as fine as a cobweb and as white as milk; "take this with you when you go with the princess to the one-eyed witch's house tonight, throw it over the witch's head, and then see what will happen. Only, when you catch the one-eyed raven you are to wring her neck as soon as you lay hands on her, for if you don't it will be the worse for you."

Well, that night off flew the princess just as she had done before, and off flew the drummer at her heels, until they came to the witch's house, both of them.

"And did you take his head this time?" said the witch.

No, the princess had not done that, for the drummer had asked such and such a question, and she could not answer it; all the same, she had him tight enough now, for she had set it as a task upon him that he should bring her the one-eyed raven, and it was not likely he would be up to doing that. After that the princess and the one-eyed witch sat down to supper together, and the drummer served the princess the same trick that he had done before, so that she got hardly a bite to eat.

"See," said the old witch when the princess was ready to go, "I will go home with you tonight, and see that you get there safe and sound." So she brought out a pair of wings, just like those the princess had, and set them on her shoulders, and away both of them flew with the drummer behind. So they came home without seeing a soul, for the drummer kept his cap of darkness tight upon his head all the while.

"Good night," said the witch to the princess, and "Good night" said the princess to the witch, and the one was for going one way and the other the other. But the drummer had his wits about him sharply enough, and before the old witch could get away he flung the net that King Stork had given him over her head.

Hi! but you should have been there to see what happened; for it was a great one-eyed raven, as black as the inside of the chimney, that he had in his net.

Dear, dear, how it flapped its wings and struck with its great beak! But that did no good, for the drummer just wrung its neck, and there was an end of it.

The next morning he wrapped it up in his pocket-handkerchief and off he started for the king's castle, and there was the princess waiting for him, looking as cool as butter in the well, for she felt sure the drummer was caught in the trap this time.

"And have you brought the one-eyed raven with you?" she said.

"Oh, yes," said the drummer, and here it was wrapped up in this handkerchief.

But when the princess saw the raven with its neck wrung, she gave a great shriek and fell to the floor. There she lay and they had to pick her up and carry her out of the room.

But everybody saw that the drummer had brought the bird she had asked for, and all were as glad as glad could be. The king gave orders that they should fire off the town cannon, just as they did on his birthday, and all the little boys out in the street flung up their hats and caps and cried, "Hurrah! Hurrah!"

But the drummer went off back of the house. He blew a turn or two on his whistle, and there stood King Stock. "Here is your dark-cap and your feather," says he, "and it is I who am thankful to you, for they have won me a real princess for a wife."

"Yes, good," says King Stork, "you have won her, sure enough, but the next thing is to keep her; for a lass is not cured of being a witch as quickly as you seem to think, and after one has found one's eggs one must roast them and butter them into the bargain. See now, the princess is just as wicked as ever she was before, and if you do not keep your eyes open she will trip you up after all. So listen to what I tell you. Just after you are married, get a great bowl of fresh milk and a good, stiff switch. Pour the milk over the princess when you are alone together, and after that hold tight to her and lay on the switch, no matter what happens, for that is the only way to save yourself and to save her."

Well, the drummer promised to do as King Stork told him, and by and by came the wedding-day. Off he went over to the dairy and got a fresh pan of milk, and out he went into the woods and cut a stout hazel switch, as thick as his finger.

As soon as he and the princess were alone together he emptied the milk all over her; then he caught hold of her and began laying on the switch for dear life.

It was well for him that he was a brave fellow and had been to the wars, for, instead of the princess, he held a great black cat that glared at him with her fiery eyes, and growled and spat like any-thing. But that did no good, for the drummer just shut his eyes and laid on the switch harder than ever.

Then—puff!—instead of a black cat it was like a great, savage wolf, that snarled and snapped at the drummer with its red jaws; but the drummer just held fast and made the switch fly, and the wolf scared him no more than the black cat had done.

So out it went, like a light of a candle, and there was a great snake that lashed its tail and shot out its forked tongue and spat fire. But no; the drummer was no more frightened at that than he had been at the wolf and the cat, and, dear, dear! how he dressed the snake with his hazel switch.

Last of all, there stood the princess herself. "Oh, dear husband!"

she cried, "let me go, and I will promise to be good all the days of my life."

"Very well," says the drummer, "and that is the tune I like to hear."

That was the way he gained the best of her, whether it was the bowl of milk or the hazel switch, for afterwards she was as good a wife as ever churned butter; but what did it is a question that you will have to answer for yourself. All the same, she tried no more of her tricks with him, I can tell you. And so this story comes to an end, like everything else in the world.

THE STOOL OF FORTUNE

By HOWARD PYLE

Illustrations by THE AUTHOR

ONCE upon a time there came a soldier marching along the road, kicking up a little cloud of dust at each step—as strapping and merry and bright-eyed a fellow as you would wish to see in a summer day. Tramp! tramp! tramp! he marched, whistling as he jogged along, though he carried a heavy musket over his shoulder and though the sun shone hot and strong and there was never a tree in sight to give him a bit of shelter.

At last he came in sight of the King's Town and to a great field of stocks and stones, and there sat a little old man as withered and brown as a dead leaf, and clad all in scarlet from head to foot.

"Ho! soldier," said he, "are you a good shot?"

"Aye," said the soldier, "that is my trade."

"Would you like to earn a dollar shooting off your musket for me?"

"Aye," said the soldier, "that is my trade also."

"Very well, then," said the little man in red, "here is a silver button to drop into your gun instead of a bullet. Wait you here, and about sunset there will come a great black bird flying. In one claw it carries a feather cap and in the other a round stone. Shoot me the silver button at that bird, and if your aim is good it will drop the feather cap and the pebble. Bring them to me to the great town-gate and I will pay you a dollar for your trouble."

"Very well," said the soldier, "shooting my gun is a job that fits me like an old coat." So, down he sat and the old man went his way.

Well, there he sat and sat and sat and sat until the sun touched the rim of the ground, and then, just as the old man said, there came flying a great black bird as silent as night. The soldier did not tarry to look or to think. As the bird flew by, up came the gun to his shoulder, squint went his eye along the barrel—Puff! Bang!—

I vow and declare that if the shot he fired had cracked the sky he

277

could not have been more frightened. The great black bird gave a yell so terrible that it curdled the very blood in his veins and made his hair stand upon end. Away it flew like a flash—a bird no longer, but a great, black demon, smoking and smelling most horribly of brimstone, and when the soldier gathered his wits, there lay the feather cap and a little, round, black stone upon the ground.

"Well," said the soldier, "it is little wonder that the old man had no liking to shoot at such game as that." And thereupon he popped the feather cap into one pocket and the round stone into another, and shouldering his musket marched away until he reached the towngate, and there was the old man waiting for him.

"Did you shoot the bird?" said he.

"I did," said the soldier.

"And did you get the cap and the round stone?"

"I did."

"Then here is your dollar."

"Wait a bit," said the soldier, "I shot greater game that time than I bargained for, and so it's ten dollars and not one you shall pay me before you lay finger upon the feather cap and the little stone."

"Very well," said the old man, "here are ten dollars."

"Ho! ho!" thought the soldier, "is that the way the wind blows?" —"Did I say ten dollars?" said he; "'twas a hundred dollars I meant."

At that the old man frowned until his eyes shone green. "Very well," said he, "if it is a hundred dollars you want, you will have to come home with me, for I have not so much with me." Thereupon he entered the town with the soldier at his heels.

Up one street he went and down another, until at last he came to a great, black, ancient, ramshackle house; and that was where he lived. In he walked without so much as a rap at the door, and so led the way to a great room with furnaces and books and bottles and jars and dust and cobwebs, and three grinning skulls upon the mantel-piece, each with a candle stuck atop of it, and there he left the soldier while he went to get the hundred dollars.

The soldier sat him down upon a three-legged stool in the corner and began staring about him; and he liked the looks of the place as little as any he had seen in all of his life, for it smelled musty and dusty, it did: the three skulls grinned at him, and he began to think that the little old man was no better than he should be. "I wish," says he, at last, "that instead of being here I might be well out of my scrape and in a safe place."

Now the little old man in scarlet was a great magician, and there was little or nothing in that house that had not some magic about it, and of all things the three-legged stool had been conjured the most. "I wish that instead of being here I might be well out of my scrape, and in a safe place." That was what the soldier said; and hardly had the words left his lips when—whisk! whir!—away flew the stool through the window, so suddenly that the soldier had only just time enough to grip it tight by the legs to save himself from falling. Whir! whiz!—away it flew like a bullet. Up and up it went —so high in the air that the earth below looked like a black blanket spread out in the night; and then down it came again, with the soldier still gripping tight to the legs, until at last it settled as light as a feather upon a balcony of the king's palace; and when the soldier caught his wind again he found himself without a hat, and with hardly any wits in his head.

There he sat upon the stool for a long time without daring to move, for he did not know what might happen to him next. There he sat and sat, and by-and-by his ears got cold in the night air, and then he noticed for the first time that he had lost his headgear, and bethought himself of the feather cap in his pocket. So out he drew it and clapped it upon his head, and then—lo and behold!—he found he had become as invisible as thin air—not a shred or a hair of him could be seen. "Well!" said he. "Here is another wonder, but I am safe now at any rate." And up he got to find some place not so cool as where he sat.

He stepped in at an open window, and there he found himself in a beautiful room, hung with cloth of silver and blue, and with chairs and tables of white and gold; dozens and scores of waxlights shone like so many stars, and lit every crack and cranny as bright as day, and there at one end of the room upon a couch, with her eyelids closed and fast asleep, lay the prettiest princess that ever the sun shone upon. The soldier stood and looked and looked at her, and looked and looked at her, until his heart melted within him like soft butter, and then he kissed her.

"Who is that?" said the princess, starting up, wide-awake, but not a soul could she see, because the soldier had the feather cap upon his head.

"Who is that?" said she again; and then the soldier answered, but without taking the feather cap from his head.

"It is I," said he, "and I am King of the Wind, and ten times greater than the greatest of kings here below. One day I saw you walking in your garden and fell in love with you, and now I have come to ask you if you will marry me and be my wife?"

"But how can I marry you," said the princess, "without seeing you?"

"You shall see me," said the soldier, "all in good time. Three days from now I will come again, and will show myself to you, but just now it cannot be. But if I come, will you marry me?"

"Yes, I will," said the princess, "for I like the way you talk—that I do!"

Thereupon the soldier kissed her and said good-bye, and then stepped out of the window as he had stepped in. He sat him down upon his three-legged stool. "I wish," said he, "to be carried to such and such a tavern." For he had been in that town before, and knew the places where good living was to be had.

Whir! whiz! Away flew the stool as high and higher than it had flown before, and then down it came again, and down and down until it lit as light as a feather in the street before the tavern

oor. The soldier tucked his feather cap in his pocket, and the three-
egged stool under his arm, and in he went and ordered a pot of
eer and some white bread and cheese.

Meantime, at the king's palace was such a gossiping and such a
ubbub as had not been heard there for many a day; for the pretty
rincess was not slow in telling how the invisible King of the Wind
ad come and asked her to marry him; and some said it was true
nd some said it was not true, and everybody wondered and talked,
nd told their own notions of the matter. But all agreed that three
ays would show whether what had been told was true or no.

As for the soldier, he knew no more how to do what he had prom-

ed to do than my grandmother's cat; for where was he to get
lothes fine enough for the King of the Wind to wear? So there he
at on his three-legged stool thinking and thinking, and if he had
nown all that I know he would not have given two turns of his wit
pon it. "I wish," says he, at last—"I wish that this stool could help
ne now as well as it can carry me through the sky. I wish," says he,
that I had a suit of clothes such as the King of the Wind might
eally wear."

The wonders of the three-legged stool were wonders indeed!

Hardly had the words left the soldier's lips when down came
omething tumbling about his ears from up in the air; and what

should it be but just such a suit of clothes as he had in his mind—all crusted over with gold and silver and jewels.

"Well," says the soldier, as soon as he had got over his wonder again, "I would rather sit upon this stool than any I ever saw." And so would I, if I had been in his place, and had a few minutes to think of all that I wanted.

So he found out the trick of the stool, and after that wishing and having were easy enough, and by the time the three days were ended the real King of the Wind himself could not have cut a finer figure. Then down sat the soldier upon his stool, and wished himself at the king's palace. Away he flew through the air, and by-and-by there he was, just where he had been before. He put his feather cap upon his head, and stepped in through the window, and there he found the princess with her father, the king, and her mother, the queen, and all the great lords and nobles waiting for his coming; but never a stitch nor a hair did they see of him until he stood in the very midst of them all. Then he whipped the feather cap off of his head, and there he was, shining with silver and gold and glistening with jewels—such a sight as man's eyes never saw before.

"Take her," said the king, "she is yours." And the soldier looked so handsome in his fine clothes that the princess was as glad to hear those words as any she had ever listened to in all her life.

"You shall," said the king, "be married tomorrow."

"Very well," said the soldier. "Only give me a plot of ground to build a palace upon that shall be fit for the wife of the King of the Wind to live in."

"You shall have it," said the king, "and it shall be the great parade ground back of the palace, which is so wide and long that all my army can march round and round in it without getting into its own way; and that ought to be big enough."

"Yes," said the soldier, "it is." Thereupon he put on his feather cap and disappeared from the sight of all as quickly as one might snuff out a candle.

He mounted his three-legged stool and away he flew through the air until he had come again to the tavern where he was lodging. There he sat him down and began to churn his thoughts, and the butter he made was worth the having, I can tell you. He wished for a grand palace of white marble, and then he wished for all sorts of things to fill it—the finest that could be had. Then he wished for servants in clothes of gold and silver, and then he wished for fine horses and gilded coaches. Then he wished for gardens and orchards and lawns and flower-plats and fountains, and all kinds and sorts of things, until the sweat ran down his face from hard thinking and wishing. And as he thought and wished, all the things he thought and wished for grew up like soap-bubbles from nothing at all.

Then, when day began to break, he wished himself with his fine clothes to be in the palace that his own wits had made, and away he flew through the air until he had come there safe and sound.

But when the sun rose and shone down upon the beautiful palace and all the gardens and orchards around it, the king and queen and all the court stood dumb with wonder at the sight. Then, as they stood staring, the gates opened, and out came the soldier riding in his gilded coach with his servants in silver and gold marching beside him, and such a sight the daylight never looked upon before that day.

Well, the princess and the soldier were married, and if no couple had ever been happy in the world before, they were then. Nothing was heard but feasting and merrymaking, and at night all the sky was lit with fireworks. Such a wedding had never been before, and all the world was glad that it had happened.

That is, all the world but one; that one was the old man dressed in scarlet that the soldier had met when he first came to town. While all the rest were in the hubbub of rejoicing, he put on his thinking-cap, and by-and-by began to see pretty well how things lay, and that, as they say in our town, there was a fly in the milk-jug. "Ho, ho!" thought he. "So the soldier has found out all about the three-legged stool, has he? Well, I will just put a spoke into his wheel for him." And so he began to watch for his chance to do the soldier an ill turn.

Now, a week or two after the wedding, and after all the gay doings had ended, a grand hunt was declared, and the king and his new son-in-law and all the court went to it. That was just such a

chance as the old magician had been waiting for; so the night before
the hunting-party returned he climbed the walls of the garden, and
so came to the wonderful palace that the soldier had built out of
nothing at all, and there stood three men keeping guard so that no
one might enter.

But little that troubled the magician. He began to mutter spells
and strange words, and all of a sudden he was gone, and in his
place was a great black ant, for he had changed himself into an ant.
In he ran through a crack of the door (and mischief has got into
many a man's house through a smaller hole for the matter of that).
In and out ran the ant through one room and another, and up and
down and here and there, until at last in a far-away part of the magic
palace he found the three-legged stool, and if I had been in the
soldier's place I would have chopped it up into kindling-wood after
I had gotten all that I wanted. But there it was, and in an instant
the magician resumed his own shape. Down he sat him upon the
stool. "I wish," said he, "that this palace and the princess and all
who are within it, together with its orchards and its lawns and its
gardens and everything, may be removed to such and such a country,
upon the other side of the earth."

And as the stool had obeyed the soldier, so everything was done
now just as the magician said.

The next morning back came the hunting-party, and as they rode
over the hill—lo and behold!—there lay stretched out the great
parade ground in which the king's armies used to march around and
around, and the land was as bare as the palm of my hand. Not a
stick or a stone of the palace was left; not a leaf or a blade of the
orchards or gardens was to be seen.

The soldier sat as dumb as a fish, and the king stared with eyes
and mouth wide open. "Where is the palace, and where is my
daughter?" said he, at last, finding words and wit.

"I do not know," said the soldier.

The king's face grew as black as thunder. "You do not know?"
he said. "Then you must find out. Seize the traitor!" he cried.

But that was easier said than done, for, quick as a wink, as they
came to lay hold of him, the soldier whisked the feather cap from

his pocket and clapped it upon his head, and then they might as well have hoped to find the south wind in winter as to find him.

But though he got safe away from that trouble he was deep enough in the dumps, you may be sure of that. Away he went, out into the wide world, leaving that town behind him. Away he went, until by-and-by he came to a great forest, and for three days he traveled on and on—he knew not whither. On the third night, as he sat beside a fire which he had built to keep him warm, he suddenly bethought himself of the little round stone which had dropped from the bird's claw, and which he still had in his pocket. "Why should it not also help me," said he, "for there must be some wonder about it." So he brought it out, and sat looking at it and looking at it, but he could make nothing of it for the life of him. Nevertheless, it might have some wishing power about it, like the magic stool. "I wish," said the soldier, "that I might get out of this scrape." That is what we have all wished many and many a time in a like case; but just now it did the soldier no more good to wish than it does good for the rest of us. "Bah!" said he. "It is nothing but a black stone after all." And then he threw it into the fire.

Puff! Bang! Away flew the embers upon every side, and back tumbled the soldier, and there in the middle of the flame stood just such a grim, black being as he had one time shot at with the silver button.

As for the poor soldier, he just lay flat on his back and stared with eyes like saucers, for he thought that his end had come for sure.

"What are my lord's commands?" said the being, in a voice that shook the marrow of the soldier's bones.

"Who are you?" said the soldier.

"I am the spirit of the stone," said the being. "You have heated it in the flame, and I am here. Whatever you command I must obey."

"Say you so?" cried the soldier, scrambling to his feet. "Very well, then, just carry me to where I may find my wife and my palace again."

Without a word the spirit of the stone snatched the soldier up, and flew away with him swifter than the wind. Over forest, over field, over mountain and over valley he flew, until at last, just at the crack of day, he set him down in front of his own palace gate in the far country where the magician had transported it.

After that the soldier knew his way quickly enough. He clapped his feather cap upon his head and into the palace he went, and from one room to another, until at last he came to where the princess sat weeping and wailing, with her pretty eyes red from long crying.

Then the soldier took off his cap again, and you may guess what sounds of rejoicing followed. They sat down beside each other, and after the soldier had eaten, the princess told him all that had happened to her; how the magician had found the stool, and how he had transported the palace to this far-away land; how he came every day and begged her to marry him—which she would rather die than do.

To all this the soldier listened, and when she had ended her story he bade her dry her tears, for, after all, the jug was only cracked, and not past mending. Then he told her that when the sorcerer came again that day she should say so and so and so and so, and that he would be by to help her with his feather cap upon his head.

After that they sat talking together as happy as two turtle-doves, until the magician's foot was heard on the stairs. And then the soldier clapped his feather cap upon his head just as the door was opened.

"Snuff, snuff!" said the magician, sniffing the air. "Here is a smell of Christian blood."

"Yes," said the princess, "that is so; there came a peddler today, but after all he did not stay long.'

"He'd better not come again," said the magician, "or it will be the worse for him. But tell me, will you marry me?"

"No," said the princess. "I shall not marry you until you can prove yourself to be a greater man than my husband."

"Pooh!" said the magician, "that will be easy enough to prove; tell me how you would have me do so and I will do it."

"Very well," said the princess, "then let me see you change yourself into a lion. If you can do that I may perhaps believe you to be as great as my husband."

"It shall," said the magician, "be as you say." He began to mutter spells and strange words, and then all of a sudden he was gone, and in his place there stood a lion with bristling mane and flaming eyes—a sight fit of itself to kill a body with terror.

"That will do!" cried the princess, quaking and trembling at the sight, and thereupon the magician took his own shape again.

"Now," said he, "do you believe that I am as great as the poor soldier?"

"Not yet," said the princess, "I have seen how big you can make yourself, now I wish to see how little you can become. Let me see you change yourself into a mouse."

"So be it," said the magician, and began again to mutter his spells. Then all of a sudden he was gone just as he was gone before, and in his place was a little mouse sitting up and looking at the princess with a pair of eyes like glass beads.

But he did not sit there long. This was what the soldier had planned for, and all the while he had been standing by with his feather hat upon his head. Up he raised his foot, and down he set it upon the mouse.

Crunch!—that was an end of the magician.

After that all was clear sailing; the soldier hunted up the three-legged stool and down he sat upon it, and by dint of no more than just a little wishing, back flew palace and garden and all through the air again to the place whence it came.

I do not know whether the old king ever believed again that his son-in-law was the King of the Wind; anyhow, all was peace and friendliness thereafter, for when a body can sit upon a three-legged stool and wish to such good purpose as the soldier wished, a body is just as good as a king, and a good deal better, to my mind.

THE EMERGENCY MISTRESS

By FRANK R. STOCKTON

JULES VATERMANN was a woodcutter, and a very good one. He always had employment, for he understood his business so well, and was so industrious and trustworthy, that everyone in the neighborhood where he lived, who wanted wood cut, was glad to get him to do it.

Jules had a very ordinary and commonplace life until he was a middle-aged man, and then something remarkable happened to him. It happened on the twenty-fifth of January, in a very cold winter. Jules was forty-five years old, that year, and he remembered the day of the month, because in the morning, before he started out to his work, he had remarked that it was just one month since Christmas.

The day before, Jules had cut down a tall tree, and he had been busy all morning sawing it into logs of the proper length and splitting it up and making a pile of it.

When dinner time came around, Jules sat down on one of the logs and opened his basket. He had plenty to eat—good bread and sausage, and a bottle of beer, for he was none of your poor wood-cutters.

As he was cutting a sausage, he looked up and saw something coming from behind his wood-pile.

At first, he thought it was a dog, for it was about the right size for a small dog, but in a moment he saw it was a little man. He was a little man indeed, for he was not more than two feet high. He was dressed in brown clothes and wore a peaked cap, and he must have been pretty old, for he had a full white beard. Although otherwise warmly clad, he wore on his feet neither shoes nor stockings, and came hopping along through the deep snow as if his feet were very cold.

When he saw this little old man, Jules said never a word. He merely thought to himself: "This is some sort of fairy man."

But the little old person came close to Jules, and drawing up one foot, as if it was so cold that he could stand on it no longer, he said:

"Please, sir, my feet are almost frozen."

"Oh, ho!" thought Jules, "I know all about that. This is one of the fairy-folks who come in distress to a person, and who, if that person is kind to them, make him rich and happy; but if he turns them away, he soon finds himself in all sorts of misery. I shall be very careful." And then he said aloud: "Well, sir, what can I do for you?"

"That is a strange question," said the dwarf. "If you were to walk by the side of a deep stream, and were to see a man sinking in the water, would you stop and ask him what you could do for him?"

"Would you like my stockings?" said Jules, putting down his knife and sausage, and preparing to pull off one of his boots. "I will let you have them."

"No, no!" said the other. "They are miles too big for me."

"Will you have my cap or my scarf in which to wrap your feet and warm them?"

"No, no!" said the dwarf. "I don't put my feet in caps and scarfs."

"Well, tell me what you would like," said Jules. "Shall I make a fire?"

"No, I will not tell you," said the fairy-man. "You have kept me standing here long enough."

Jules could not see what this had to do with it. He was getting very anxious. If he were only a quick-witted fellow, so as to think of exactly the right thing to do, he might make his fortune. But he could think of nothing more.

"I wish, sir, that you would tell me just what you would like for your cold feet," said Jules, in an entreating tone, "for I shall be very glad to give it to you, if it is at all possible."

"If your ax were half as dull as your brain," said the dwarf, "you would not cut much wood. Good day!"—and he skipped away behind the wood-pile.

Jules jumped up and looked after him, but he was gone. These fairy people have a strange way of disappearing.

Jules was not married, and had no home of his own. He lived with a good couple who had a little house and an only daughter, and that was about the sum of their possessions. The money Jules paid for his living helped them a little, and they managed to get along. But they were quite poor.

Jules was not poor. He had no one but himself to support, and he had laid by a sum of money to live on when he should be too old to work.

But you never saw a man so disappointed as he was that evening as he sat by the fire after supper.

He had told his family all about his meeting with the dwarf, and lamented again and again that he had lost such a capital chance of making his fortune.

"If I could only have thought what it was best to do!" he said again and again.

"I know what I should have done," said Selma, the only daughter of the poor couple, a girl about eleven years old.

"What?" asked Jules, eagerly.

"I should have just snatched the little fellow up, and rubbed his feet and wrapped them in my shawl until they were warm," said she.

"But he would not have liked that," said Jules. "He was an old man and very particular."

"I would not care," said Selma; "I wouldn't let such a little fellow stand suffering in the snow, and I wouldn't care how old he was."

"I hope you'll never meet any of these fairy people," said Jules. "You'd drive them out of the country with your roughness, and we might all whistle for our fortunes."

Selma laughed and said no more about it.

Every day after that, Jules looked for the dwarf-man, but he did not see him again. Selma looked for him, too, for her curiosity had been much excited; but as she was not allowed to go out to the woods in the winter, of course, she never saw him.

But, at last, summer came; and, one day, as she was walking by a little stream which ran through the woods, whom should she see, sitting on the bank, but the dwarf-man! She knew him in an instant from Jules's descriptions. He was busily engaged in fishing, but he did not fish like anyone else in the world. He had a short pole, which was floating in the water, and in his hand he held a string which was fastened to one end of the pole.

When Selma saw what the old fellow was doing, she burst out laughing. She knew this was not very polite, but she could not help it.

"What's the matter," said he, turning quickly toward her.

"I'm sorry I laughed at you, sir," said Selma, "but that's no way to fish."

"Much you know about it," said the dwarf. "This is the only way to fish. You let your pole float, with a piece of bait on a hook fastened to the big end of your pole. Then you fasten a line to the little end. When a fish bites, you haul in the pole by means of the string."

"Have you caught anything yet?" asked Selma.

"No, not yet," replied the dwarf.

"Well, I'm sure I can fish better than that. Would you mind letting me try a little while?"

"Not at all—not at all!" said the dwarf, handing the line to Selma. "If you think you can fish better than I can, do it by all means."

Selma took the line and pulled in the pole. Then she unfastened the hook and bait which was on the end of the pole, and tied it to the end of the line, with a little piece of stone for a sinker. She then took up the pole, threw in the line, and fished like common people. In less than a minute she had a bite, and, giving a jerk, she drew out a fat little fish as long as her hand.

"Hurrah!" cried the little old man, giving a skip in the air; and then, turning away from the stream, he shouted, "Come here!"

Selma turned around to see whom he was calling, and she perceived another gnome, who was running toward them. When he came near, she saw that he was much younger than the fisher-gnome.

"Hello!" cried the old fellow. "I've caught one."

Selma was amazed to hear this. She looked at the old gnome,

who was taking the fish off the hook, as if she were astonished that he could tell such a falsehood.

"What is this other person's name?" said she to him.

"His name," said the old gnome, looking up, "is Class 60, H."

"Is that all the name he has?" asked Selma, in surprise.

"Yes. And it is a very good name. It shows just who and what he is."

"Well, then, Mr. Class 60, H," said Selma, "that old—person did not catch the fish. I caught it myself."

"Very good! Very good!" said Class 60, H, laughing and clapping his hands. "Capital! See here!" said he, addressing the older dwarf, and he knelt down and whispered something in his ear.

"Certainly," said the old gnome. "That's just what I was thinking of. Will you mention it to her? I must hurry and show this fish while it is fresh,"—and, so saying, he walked rapidly away with the little fish, and the pole and tackle.

"My dear Miss," said Class 60, H, approaching Selma, "would you like to visit the home of the gnomes—to call, in fact, on the Queen Dowager of all the Gnomes?"

"Go down underground, where you live?" asked Selma. "Would it be safe down there, and when could I get back again?"

"Safe, dear Miss! Oh, perfectly so! And the trip will not take you more than a couple of hours. I assure you that you will be back in plenty of time for supper. Will you go, if I send a trusty messenger for you? You may never have another chance to see our country."

Selma thought that this was very probable, and she began to consider the matter.

As soon as Class 60, H, saw that she was really trying to make up her mind whether or not to go, he cried out:

"Good! I see you have determined to go. Wait here five minutes and the messenger will be with you," and then he rushed off as fast as he could run.

"I didn't say I would go," thought Selma, "but I think I will."

In a few minutes Selma heard a deep voice behind her say: "Well, are you ready?"

Turning suddenly, she saw, standing close to her, a great black bear!

Frightened dreadfully, she turned to run, but the bear called out: "Stop! You needn't be frightened. I'm tame."

The surprise of hearing a bear speak overcame poor Selma's terror; she stopped, and looked around.

"Come back," said the bear; "I will not hurt you in the least. I am sent to take you to the Queen Dowager of the Gnomes. I don't mind your being frightened at me. I'm used to it. But I am getting a little tired of telling folks that I am tame," and he yawned wearily.

"You are to take me?" said Selma, still a little frightened, and very certain that, if she had known a bear was to be sent for her, she never would have consented to go.

"Yes," said the bear. "You can get on my back and I will give you a nice ride. Come on! Don't keep me waiting, please."

There was nothing to be done but to obey, for Selma did not care to have a dispute with a bear, even if he were tame, and so she got upon his back, where she had a very comfortable seat, holding fast to his long hair.

The bear walked slowly but steadily into the very heart of the forest, among the great trees and rocks. It was so lonely and solemn here that Selma felt afraid again.

"Suppose we were to meet with robbers," said she.

"Robbers," said the bear, with a laugh. "That's good! Robbers, indeed! You needn't be afraid of robbers. If we were to meet any of them, you would be the last person they'd ever meet."

"Why?" asked Selma.

"I'd tear 'em all into little bits," said the bear, in a tone which quite restored Selma's confidence, and made her feel very glad that she had a bear to depend upon in those lonely woods.

It was not very long before they came to an opening in a bank of earth, behind a great tree. Into this the bear walked, for it was wide enough, and so high that Selma did not even have to lower her head as they passed in. They were now in a long winding passage, which continually seemed as if it were just coming to an end, but which turned and twisted, first one way and then another, and always kept going down and down. Before long they began to meet gnomes, who very respectfully stepped aside to let them pass. They now went through several halls and courts, cut in the earth, and directly, the bear stopped before a door.

"You get off here," said the bear; and, when Selma had slid from his back, he rose up on his hind legs and gave a great knock with the iron knocker on the door. Then he went away.

In a moment the door opened, and there stood a little old gnome woman, dressed in brown, and wearing a brown cap.

"Come in!" she said; and Selma entered the room. "The Queen Dowager will see you in a few minutes," said the little old woman. "I am her housekeeper. I'll go and tell her you're here, and, meantime, it would be well for you to get your answers ready, so as to lose no time."

Selma was about to ask what answers she meant, but the housekeeper was gone before she could say a word.

The room was a curious one. There were some little desks and stools in it, and in the center stood a great brown ball, some six or seven feet in diameter. While she was looking about at these things, a little door in the side of the ball opened, and out stepped Class 60, H.

"One thing I didn't tell you," he said hurriedly. "I was afraid if I mentioned it you wouldn't come. The Queen Dowager wants a governess for her grandson, the Gnome Prince. Now, please don't say you can't do it, for I'm sure you'll suit exactly. The little fellow has had lots of teachers, but he wants one of a different kind now. This is the schoolroom. That ball is the globe where he studies his geography. It's only the under part of the countries that he has to know about, and so they are marked out on the inside of the globe. What they want now is a special teacher, and after having come here, and had the Queen Dowager notified, it wouldn't do to back out, you know."

"How old is the Prince?" asked Selma.

"About seventy-eight," said the gnome.

"Why, he's an old man," cried Selma.

"Not at all, my dear Miss," said Class 60, H. "It takes a long time for us to get old. The Prince is only a small boy; if he were a human boy, he would be about five years old. I don't look old, do I?"

"No," said Selma.

"Well, I'm three hundred and fifty-two, next Monday. And as for Class 20, P—the old fellow you saw fishing—he is nine hundred and sixty."

"Well, you are all dreadfully old, and you have very funny names," said Selma.

"In this part of the world," said the other, "all gnomes, except those belonging to the nobility and the royal family, are divided into classes, and lettered. This is much better than having names, for you know it is very hard to get enough names to go around, so that everyone can have his own. But here comes the housekeeper," said Class 60, H, retiring very quickly into the hollow globe.

"Her Majesty will see you," said the housekeeper; and she conducted Selma into the next room, where on a little throne, with a high back and rockers, sat the Queen Dowager. She seemed rather smaller than the other gnomes, and was very much wrinkled and wore spectacles. She had white hair, with little curls on each side, and was dressed in brown silk.

She looked at Selma over her spectacles.

"This is the applicant?" said she.

"Yes, this is she," said the housekeeper.

"She looks young," remarked the Queen Dowager.

"Very true," said the housekeeper, "but she cannot be any older at present."

"You are right," said Her Majesty; "we will examine her."

So saying, she took up a paper which lay on the table, and which seemed to have a lot of items written on it.

"Get ready," said she to the housekeeper, who opened a large blank-book and made ready to record Selma's answers.

The Queen Dowager read from the paper the first question:

"What are your qualifications?"

Selma, standing there before the little old queen and this little old housekeeper, was somewhat embarrassed, and a question like this did not make her feel any more at her ease. She could not think what qualifications she had. As she did not answer at once, the Queen Dowager turned to the housekeeper and said:

"Put down, 'Asked, but not given.'"

The housekeeper put that down, and then she jumped up and looked over the list of questions.

"We must be careful," said she, in a whisper, to the Queen Dowager, "what we ask her. It won't do to put all the questions to her. Suppose you try number 'Twenty-eight'?"

"All right," said Her Majesty; and, when the housekeeper had sat down again by her book, she addressed Selma and asked:

"Are you fond of children?"

"Yes, ma'am," said Selma.

"Good!" cried the Queen Dowager. "An admirable answer."

And the housekeeper nodded and smiled at Selma, as if she were very much pleased.

"'Eighty-two' would be a good one to ask next," suggested the housekeeper.

Her Majesty looked for "Eighty-two," and read it out:

"Do you like pie?"

"Very much, ma'am," said Selma.

"Capital! Capital!" said Her Majesty. "That will do. I see no need of asking her any other questions. Do you?" said she, turning to the housekeeper.

"None whatever," said the other. "She answered all but one, and that one she really didn't miss."

"There is no necessity for any further bother," said the Queen Dowager. "She is engaged."

And then she arose from the throne and left the room.

"Now, my dear girl," said the housekeeper. "I will induct you into your duties. They are simple."

"But I should like to know," said Selma, "if I'm to stay here all the time. I can't leave my father and mother—"

"Oh, you won't have to do that," interrupted the housekeeper. "You will take the Prince home with you."

"Home with me?" exclaimed Selma.

"Yes. It would be impossible for you to teach him properly here

We want him taught Emergencies—that is, what to do in case of various emergencies which may arise. Nothing of the kind ever arises down here. Everything goes on always in the usual way. But on the surface of the earth, where he will often go when he grows up, they are very common, and you have been selected as a proper person to teach him what to do when any of them occur to him. By the way, what are your terms?"

"I don't know," said Selma. "Whatever you please."

"That will suit very well—very well indeed," said the housekeeper. "I think you are just the person we want."

"Thank you," said Selma; and just then a door opened and the Queen Dowager put in her head.

"Is she inducted?" she asked.

"Yes," said the housekeeper.

"Then here is the Prince," said the Queen Dowager, entering the room and leading by the hand a young gnome about a foot high. He had on a ruffled jacket and trousers, and a little peaked cap. His royal grandmother led him to Selma.

"You will take him," she said, "for a session of ten months. At the end of that time we shall expect him to be thoroughly posted in emergencies. While he is away, he will drop all his royal titles and be known as Class 81, Q. His parents and I have taken leave of him. Good-bye!"

And she left the room, with her little handkerchief to her eyes.

"Now then," said the housekeeper, "the sooner you are off, the better. The bear is waiting."

So saying, she hurried Selma and the Prince through the school-room, and, when they opened the door, there stood the bear, all ready. Selma mounted him, and the housekeeper handed up the Prince, first kissing him good-bye. Then off they started.

The Prince, or, as he must now be called, Class 81, Q, was a very quiet and somewhat bashful little fellow; and, although Selma talked a good deal to him on the way, he did not say much. The bear carried them to the edge of the woods, and then Selma took him up in her arms and ran home with him.

It may be well supposed that the appearance of their daughter with the young gnome in her arms greatly astonished the worthy cottagers, and they were still more astonished when they heard her story.

"You must do your best, my dear," said her mother, "and this may prove a very good thing for you, as well as for this little master here."

Selma promised to do as well as she could, and her father said he would try and think of some good emergencies, so that the little fellow could be well trained.

Everybody seemed to be highly satisfied, even Class 81, Q, himself, who sat cross-legged on a wooden chair, surveying everything about him; but when Jules Vatermann came home, he was very much dissatisfied, indeed.

"Confound it!" he said, when he heard the story. "I should have done all this. That should have been my pupil, and the good luck should have been mine. The gnome-man came first to me, and, if he had waited a minute, I should have thought of the right thing to do. I could teach that youngster far better than you, Selma. What do you know about emergencies?"

Selma and her parents said nothing. Jules had been quite cross-grained since the twenty-fifth of January, when he had met the gnome, and they had learned to pay but little attention to his fault-finding and complaining.

The little gnome soon became quite at home in the cottage, and grew very much attached to Selma. He was quiet, but sensible and bright, and knew a great deal more than most children of five. Selma did not have many opportunities to educate him in her peculiar branch. Very commonplace things generally happened in the cottage.

One day, however, the young gnome was playing with the cat, and began to pull her tail. The cat, not liking this, began to scratch Class 81, Q. At this, the little fellow cried and yelled all the more fiercely. But Selma, who ran into the room on hearing the noise, was equal to the emergency. She called out, instantly:

"Let go of his tail!"

The gnome let go, and the cat bounded away.

The lesson of this incident was then carefully impressed on her pupil's mind by Selma, who now thought that she had at last begun to do her duty by him.

A day or two after this, Selma was sent by her mother on an errand to the nearest village. As it would be dark before she returned, she did not take the little gnome with her. About sunset, when Jules Vatermann returned from his work, he found the youngster playing by himself in the kitchen.

Instantly, a wicked thought rushed into the mind of Jules, Snatching up the young gnome, he ran off with him as fast as he could go. As he ran, he thought to himself:

"Now is my chance. I know what to do, this time. I'll just keep this young rascal and make his people pay me a pretty sum for his ransom. I'll take him to the city, where the gnomes never go, and leave him there, in safe hands, while I come back and make terms. Good for you, at last, Jules!"

So on he hurried as fast as he could go. The road soon led him into a wood, and he had to go more slowly. Poor little Class 81, Q, cried and besought Jules to let him go, but the hard-hearted wood-cutter paid no attention to his distress.

Suddenly, Jules stopped. He heard something, and then he saw something. He began to tremble. A great bear was coming along the road, directly toward him!

What should he do? He could not meet that dreadful creature. He hesitated but a moment. The bear was quite near, and, at the first growl it gave, Jules dropped the young gnome and turned and ran away at the top of his speed. The bear started to run after him, not noticing little Class 81, Q, who was standing in the road; but as he passed the dwarf, who had never seen any bear except the tame one which belonged to the gnomes, and who thought this animal was his old friend, the little fellow seized him by the long hair on his legs and began to climb up on his back.

The bear, feeling some strange creature on him, stopped and looked around. The moment the young gnome saw the fiery eyes and the glittering teeth of the beast, he knew he had made a mistake; this was no tame bear.

The savage beast growled, and, reaching back as far as he could, snapped at the little fellow on his back, who quickly got over on the other side. Then the bear reached back on that side, and Class 81, Q, was obliged to slip over again. The bear became very angry, and turned around and around in his efforts to get at the young gnome, who was nearly frightened to death. He could not think what in the world he should do. He could only remember that, in a great emergency—but not quite as bad a one as this—his teacher had come to his aid with the counsel, "Let go of his tail." He would gladly let go of the bear's tail, but the bear had none—at least, none that he could see. So what was he to do? "Let go of his tail!" cried the poor little fellow to himself. "Oh, if he only had a tail!"

Before long the bear himself began to be frightened. This was something entirely out of the common run of things. Never before in his life had he met with a little creature who stuck to him like that. He did not know what might happen next, and so he ran as hard as he could toward his cave. Perhaps his wife, the old mother-bear, might be able to get this thing off. Away he dashed, and, turning sharply around a corner, little Class 81, Q, was jolted off, and was glad enough to find himself on the ground with the bear running away through the woods.

The little fellow rubbed his knees and elbows, and, finding that he was not at all hurt, set off to find the cottage of his friend, Selma, as well as he could. He had no idea which way to go, for the bear had turned around and around so often that he had become quite bewildered. However, he resolved to trudge along, hoping to meet some one who could tell him how to go back to Selma.

After a while, the moon rose, and then he could see a little better; but it was still quite dark in the woods, and he was beginning to be very tired, when he heard a noise as if someone was talking. He went toward the voice, and soon saw a man sitting on a rock by the roadside.

When he came nearer, he saw that the man was Jules, who was wailing and moaning and upbraiding himself.

"Ah me!" said the conscience-stricken woodcutter, "Ah me! I am a wretch indeed. I have given myself up into the power of the Evil ne. Not only did I steal that child from his home and from the ood people who have always befriended me, but I have left him to devoured by a wild beast of the forest. Whatever shall I do? atan himself has got me in his power, through my own covetous- ss and greed. How—oh, how—can I ever get away from him?"

The little gnome had now approached quite close to Jules, and, inning up to him, he said: "Let go of his tail!"

If the advice was good for him in an emergency, it might be ood for others. Jules started to his feet and stood staring at the oungster he had thought devoured.

"Whoever would have supposed," said he at last, "that a little eathen midget like that, born underground, like a mole, would ever ome to me and tell me my Christian duty. And he's right, too. atan would never have got hold of me if I hadn't been holding to im all these months, hoping to get some good by it. I'll do it, my oy. I'll let go of his tail, now and forever." And, without thinking ask Class 81, Q, how he got away from the bear, he took him up his arms and ran home as fast as he could.

During the rest of the young gnome's stay with Selma, he had everal other good bits of advice in regard to emergencies, but none at was of such general application as this counsel to let go of a at's tail, or the tail of anything else that was giving him trouble.

At the expiration of the session, the Queen Dowager was charmed ith the improvement in her grandson. Having examined him in egard to his studies, she felt sure that he was now perfectly able to ke care of himself in any emergency that might occur to him.

On the morning after he left, Selma, when she awoke, saw lying n the floor the little jacket and trousers of her late pupil. At first, he thought it was the little fellow himself; but when she jumped p and took hold of the clothes, she could not move them. They ere filled with gold.

That was the pay for the tuition of Class 81, Q.

OLD PIPES AND THE DRYAD

By FRANK R. STOCKTON

A MOUNTAIN brook ran through a little village. Over th
brook there was a narrow bridge, and from the bridge
footpath led out from the village and up the hillside to the cottag
of Old Pipes and his mother.

For many, many years Old Pipes had been employed by the vi
lagers to pipe the cattle down from the hills. Every afternoon, a
hour before sunset, he would sit on a rock in front of his cottag
and play on his pipes. Then all the flocks and herds that were gra
ing on the mountains would hear him, wherever they might happe
to be, and would come down to the village—the cows by the easie
paths, the sheep by those not quite so easy, and the goats by the stee
and rocky ways that were hardest of all.

But now, for a year or more, Old Pipes had not piped the cattl
home. It is true that every afternoon he sat upon the rock and playe
upon his familiar instrument, but the cattle did not hear him. H
had grown old, and his breath was feeble. The echoes of his cheerfu
notes, which used to come from the rocky hill on the other side o
the valley, were heard no more; and twenty yards from Old Pipe
one could scarcely tell what tune he was playing. He had becom
somewhat deaf, and did not know that the sound of his pipes wa
so thin and weak, and the cattle did not hear him. The cows, th
sheep, and the goats came down every afternoon as before, but thi
was because two boys and a girl were sent up after them. The vil
lagers did not wish the good old man to know that his piping wa
no longer of any use; so they paid him his little salary every month
and said nothing about the two boys and the girl.

Old Pipes' mother was, of course, a great deal older than he wa
and was as deaf as a gate—posts, latch, hinges and all—and sh
never knew that the sound of her son's pipe did not spread over al
the mountain-side and echo back strong and clear from the opposit
hills. She was very fond of Old Pipes, and proud of his piping

302

d as he was so much younger than she was, she never thought of
m as being very old. She cooked for him, made his bed, and
ended his clothes; and they lived very comfortably on his little
lary.

One afternoon, at the end of the month, when Old Pipes had
ished his piping, he took his stout staff and went down the hill
the village to receive the money for his month's work. The path
emed a great deal steeper and more difficult than it used to be; and
d Pipes thought that it must have been washed by the rains and
eatly damaged. He remembered it as a path that was quite easy to
averse either up or down. But Old Pipes had been a very active
an, and as his mother was so much older than he was, he never
ought of himself as aged and infirm.

When the Chief Villager had paid him, and he had talked a
tle with some of his friends, Old Pipes started to go home. But
en he had crossed the bridge over the brook, and gone a short
stance up the hillside, he became very tired, and sat down upon
stone. He had not been sitting there half a minute when along
me two boys and a girl.

"Children," said Old Pipes, "I'm very tired tonight, and I don't
lieve I can climb up this steep path to my home. I think I shall
ve to ask you to help me."

"We will do that," said the boys and the girl, quite cheerfully.
en one boy took him by the right hand and the other by the left,
ile the girl pushed him in the back. In this way he went up the
ll quite easily, and soon reached his cottage door. Old Pipes gave
ch of the three children a copper coin, and then they sat down for
ew minutes' rest before starting back to the village.

"I'm sorry that I tired you so much," said Old Pipes.

"Oh, that would not have tired us," said one of the boys, "if we
d not been so far today after the cows, the sheep, and the goats.
ey rambled high up on the mountain, and we never before had
ch a time in finding them."

"Had to go after the cows, the sheep, and the goats!" exclaimed
d Pipes. "What do you mean by that?"

The girl, who stood behind the old man, shook her head, put

her hand on her mouth, and made all sorts of signs to the boy t
stop talking on this subject; but he did not notice her, and prompt
answered Old Pipes.

"Why, you see, good sir," said he, "that as the cattle can't he:
your pipes now, somebody has to go after them every evening t
drive them down from the mountain, and the Chief Villager h:
hired us three to do it. Generally it is not very hard work, but t
night the cattle had wandered far."

"How long have you been doing this?" asked the old man.

The girl shook her head and clapped her hand on her mout
more vigorously than before, but the boy went on.

"I think it is about a year now," he said, "since the people fir
felt sure that the cattle could not hear your pipes, and from that tir
we've been driving them down. But we are rested now, and will g
home. Good night, sir."

The three children then went down the hill, the girl scolding t
boy all the way home. Old Pipes stood silent a few moments, an
then went into his cottage.

"Mother," he shouted, "did you hear what those children said:

"Children!" exclaimed the old woman. "I did not hear them.
did not know there were any children here."

Then Old Pipes told his mother, shouting very loudly to mak
her hear, how the two boys and the girl had helped him up the hil
and what he had heard about his piping and the cattle.

"They can't hear you?" cried his mother. "Why, what's the matt
with the cattle?"

"Ah, me!" said Old Pipes. "I don't believe there's anything th
matter with the cattle. It must be with me and my pipes that the
is something the matter. But one thing is certain: if I do not earn th
wages the Chief Villager pays me, I shall not take them. I shall g
straight to the village and give back the money I received today

"Nonsense!" cried his mother. "I'm sure you've piped as we
as you could, and no more can be expected. And what are we to c
without the money?"

"I don't know," said Old Pipes. "But I'm going down to th
village to pay it back."

The sun had now set; but the moon was shining very brightly on the hillside, and Old Pipes could see his way very well. He did not take the same path by which he had gone before, but followed another, which led among the trees upon the hillside, and, though longer, was not so steep.

When he had gone about halfway, the old man sat down to rest, leaning his back against a great oak tree. As he did so, he heard a sound like knocking inside the tree, and then a voice distinctly said:

"Let me out! let me out!"

Old Pipes instantly forgot that he was tired, and sprang to his feet. "This must be a Dryad tree!" he exclaimed. "If it is, I'll let her out."

Old Pipes had never, to his knowledge, seen a Dryad tree, but he knew there were such trees on the hillsides and the mountains, and that Dryads lived in them. He knew, too, that in the summer time, on those days when the moon rose before the sun went down, a Dryad could come out of her tree if anyone could find the key which locked her in and turn it. Old Pipes closely examined the trunk of the tree, which stood in the full moonlight. "If I see that key," he said, "I shall surely turn it." Before long he perceived a piece of bark standing out from the tree, which appeared to him very much like the handle of a key. He took hold of it, and found he could turn it quite around. As he did so, a large part of the side of the tree was pushed open, and a beautiful Dryad stepped quickly out.

For a moment she stood motionless, gazing on the scene before her—the tranquil valley, the hills, the forest, and the mountain-side, all lying in the soft, clear light of the moon. "Oh, lovely! lovely!" she exclaimed. "How long it is since I have seen anything like this!" And then, turning to Old Pipes, she said: "How good of you to let me out! I am so happy and so thankful that I must kiss you, you dear old man!" And she threw her arms around the neck of Old Pipes, and kissed him on both cheeks. "You don't know," she then went on to say, "how doleful it is to be shut up so long in a tree. I don't mind it in the winter, for then I am glad to be sheltered, but in summer it is a rueful thing not to be able to see all the beauties of the world. And it's ever so long since I've been let out. People so seldom come this way, and when they do come at the right time they either don't hear me, or they are frightened and run away. But you, you dear old man, you were not frightened, and you looked and looked for the key, and you let me out, and now I shall not have to go back till winter has come and the air grows cold. Oh, it is glorious! What can I do for you to show you how grateful I am?"

"I am very glad," said Old Pipes, "that I let you out, since I see that it makes you so happy. But I must admit that I tried to find the key because I had a great desire to see a Dryad. But if you wish to do something for me, you can, if you happen to be going down toward the village."

"To the village!" exclaimed the Dryad. "I will go anywhere for you, my kind old benefactor."

"Well, then," said Old Pipes. "I wish you would take this little bag of money to the Chief Villager, and tell him that Old Pipes cannot receive pay for the services which he does not perform. It is now more than a year that I have not been able to make the cattle hear me when I piped to call them home. I did not know this until tonight, but now that I know it I cannot keep the money, and so I send it back." So handing the little bag to the Dryad, he bade her good night, and turned toward his cottage.

"Good night," said the Dryad. "And I thank you over and over and over again, you good old man!"

Old Pipes walked toward his home, very glad to be saved the fatigue of going all the way down to the village and back again. "To be sure," he said to himself, "this path does not seem at all steep, and I can walk along it very easily, but it would have tired me dreadfully to come up all the way from the village, especially as I could not have expected those children to help me again." When he reached home, his mother was surprised to see him so soon.

"What!" she exclaimed, "have you already come back? What did the Chief Villager say? Did he take the money?"

Old Pipes was just about to tell her that he had sent the money to the village by a Dryad, when he suddenly reflected that his mother would be sure to disapprove such a proceeding, and so he merely said he had sent it by a person whom he had met.

"And how do you know that the person will ever take it to the Chief Villager?" cried his mother. "You will lose it, and the villagers will never get it. Oh, Pipes! Pipes! When will you be old enough to have ordinary common sense?"

Old Pipes considered that as he was already seventy years of age he could scarcely expect to grow any wiser, but he made no remark on this subject, and saying that he doubted not that the money would go safely to its destination, he sat down to his supper. His mother scolded him roundly, but he did not mind it, and after supper he went out and sat on a rustic chair in front of the cottage to look at the moonlit village, and to wonder whether or not the Chief Villager really received the money. While he was doing these two things, he went fast asleep.

When Old Pipes left the Dryad, she did not go down to the village with the little bag of money. She held it in her hand, and thought about what she had heard.

"This is a good and honest old man," she said, "and it is a shame that he should lose this money. He looked as if he needed it, and I don't believe the people in the village will take it from one who has served them so long. Often, when in my tree, have I heard the sweet notes of his pipes. I am going to take the money back to him." She did not start immediately, because there were so many beautiful things to look at. But after a while she went up to the cottage, and finding Old Pipes asleep in his chair, she slipped the little bag into his coat pocket, and silently sped away.

The next day Old Pipes told his mother that he would go up the mountain and cut some wood. He had a right to get wood from the mountain, but for a long time he had been content to pick up the dead branches which lay about his cottage. Today, however, he felt so strong and vigorous that he thought he would go and cut some fuel that would be better than this. He worked all the morning, and when he came back he did not feel at all tired, and had a very good appetite for his dinner.

Now, Old Pipes knew a good deal about Dryads, but there was one thing which, although he had heard, he had forgotten. This was that a kiss from a Dryad makes a person ten years younger. The people of the village knew this, and they were very careful not to let any child of ten years or younger go into the woods where the Dryads were supposed to be, for if they should chance to to be kissed by one of these tree-nymphs, they would be set back so far that they would cease to exist. A story was told in the village that a very bad boy of eleven once ran away into the woods, and had an adventure of this kind, and when his mother found him he was a little baby of one year old. Taking advantage of her opportunity, she brought him up more carefully than she had done before, and he grew to be a very good boy indeed.

Now Old Pipes had been kissed twice by the Dryad, once on each cheek, and he therefore felt as vigorous and active as when he was a hale man of fifty. His mother noticed how much work he was doing, and told him that he need not try in that way to make up for the loss of his piping wages, for he would only tire himself out, and get sick. But her son answered that he had not felt so well for years, and that he was quite able to work. In the course of the afternoon, Old Pipes, for the first time that day, put his hand in his coat-pocket, and there, to his amazement, he found the little bag of money. "Well, well!" he exclaimed, "I am stupid indeed! I really thought that I had seen a Dryad, but when I sat down by that big oak tree I must have gone to sleep and dreamed it all, and then I came home thinking I had given the money to a Dryad, when it was in my pocket all the time. But the Chief Villager shall have the money, I shall not take it to him today, but tomorrow I wish to go to the village to see some of my old friends, and then I shall give up the money."

Towards the close of the afternoon, Old Pipes, as had been his custom for so many years, took his pipes from the shelf on which they lay, and went out to the rock in front of the cottage.

"What are you going to do?" cried his mother. "If you will not consent to be paid, why do you pipe?"

"I am going to pipe for my own pleasure," said her son. "I am used to it, and I do not wish to give it up. It does not matter now whether the cattle hear me or not, and I am sure that my piping will injure no one."

When the good man began to play upon his favorite instrument he was astonished at the sound that came from it. The beautiful notes of the pipes sounded clear and strong down into the valley, and spread over the hills, and up the sides of the mountain beyond, while, after a little interval, an echo came back from the rocky hill on the other side of the valley.

"Ha, ha!" he cried. "What has happened to my pipes? They must have been stopped up of late, but now they are as clear and good as ever."

Again the merry notes went sounding far and wide. The cattle on the mountain heard them, and those that were old enough remembered how these notes had called them from their pastures every evening, and they started down the mountain, the others following.

The merry notes were heard in the village below, and the people were much astonished thereby. "Why, who can be blowing the pipes of Old Pipes?" they said. But as they were all very busy, no one went up to see. One thing however, was plain enough: the cattle were coming down the mountain. So the two boys and the girl did not have to go after them, and had an hour for play, for which they were very glad.

The next morning Old Pipes started down to the village with his money, and on the way he met the Dryad. "Oh! ho!" he cried. "Is that you? Why, I thought my letting you out of the tree was nothing but a dream."

"A dream!" cried the Dryad. "If you only knew how happy you have made me, you would not think it merely a dream. And has it not benefited you? Do you not feel happier? Yesterday I heard you playing beautifully on your pipes."

"Yes, yes," cried he. "I did not understand it before, but I see it all now. I have really grown younger. I thank you, I thank you, good Dryad, from the bottom of my heart. It was the finding of the money in my pocket that made me think it was a dream."

"Oh, I put it in when you were asleep," she said, laughing, "because I thought you ought to keep it. Good-bye, kind, honest man. May you live long, and be as happy as I am now."

Old Pipes was greatly delighted when he understood that he was.

really a younger man. But that made no difference about the money, and he kept on his way to the village. As soon as he reached it, he was eagerly questioned as to who had been playing his pipes the evening before, and when the people heard that it was himself, they were very much surprised. Thereupon Old Pipes told what had happened to him, and then there was greater wonder, with hearty congratulations and hand-shakes, for Old Pipes was liked by every one. The Chief Villager refused to take his money, and although Old Pipes said that he had not earned it, everyone present insisted that, as he could now play on his pipes as before, he should lose nothing because, for a time, he was unable to perform his duty. So Old Pipes was obliged to keep his money, and after an hour or two spent in conversation with his friends, he returned to his cottage.

There was one individual, however, who was not at all pleased with what had happened to Old Pipes. This was an Echo-dwarf who lived on the hills on the other side of the valley, and whose duty it was to echo back the notes of the pipes whenever they could be heard. There were a great many other Echo-dwarfs on these hills, some of whom echoed back the songs of maidens, some the shouts of children, and others the music that was often heard in the village. But there was only one who could send back the strong notes of the pipes of Old Pipes, and this had been his sole duty for many years. But when the old man grew feeble, and the notes of his pipes could not be heard on the opposite hills, this Echo-dwarf had nothing to do, and he spent his time in delightful idleness; and he slept so much and grew so fat that it made his companions laugh to see him walk.

On the afternoon on which, after so long an interval, the sound of the pipes was heard on the echo hills, this dwarf was fast asleep behind a rock. As soon as the first notes reached them, some of his companions ran to wake him. Rolling to his feet, he echoed back the merry tune of Old Pipes. Naturally, he was very much annoyed and indignant at being thus obliged to give up his life of comfortable leisure, and he hoped that this pipe-playing would not occur again.

But this afternoon he was awake and listening, and, sure enough, at the usual hour along came the notes of the pipes, as clear and strong as they had ever been, and he was obliged to work as long as Old Pipes played. The Echo-dwarf was very angry. He had supposed, of course, that the pipe playing had ceased forever, and he felt that he had a right to be indignant at being thus deceived. He was so much disturbed that he made up his mind to go and try to find out whether this was to be a temporary matter or not. He had plenty of time, as the pipes were played but once a day, and he set off early in the morning for the hill on which Old Pipes lived. It was hard work for the fat little fellow, and when he had crossed the valley and had gone some distance into the woods on the hillside, he stopped to rest, and in a few minutes the Dryad came tripping along.

"Ho, ho!" exclaimed the dwarf. "What are you doing here? And how did you get out of your tree?"

"Doing!" cried the Dryad. "I am being happy, that's what I am doing. I was let out of my tree by the good old man who plays the pipes to call the cattle down from the mountain, and it makes me happier to think that I have been of service to him. I gave him two kisses of gratitude, and now he is young enough to play his pipes as well as ever."

The Echo-dwarf stepped forward, his face pale with passion. "Am I to believe," he said, "that you are the cause of this great evil that has come upon me? That you are the wicked creature who has again started this old man upon his career of pipe-playing? What have I done that you should have condemned me for years to echo the notes of those wretched pipes?" At this the Dryad laughed loudly.

"What a funny little fellow you are!" she said. "Anyone would think you had been condemned to toil from morning till night, while what you really have to do is merely to imitate for half an hour every day the merry notes of Old Pipes' piping. Fie upon you, Echo-dwarf! You are lazy and selfish, and that is what is the matter with you. Instead of grumbling at being obliged to do a little wholesome work, which is less, I am sure, than that of any other Echo-dwarf upon the rocky hillside, you should rejoice at the good fortune of the old man who has regained so much of his strength and vigor. Go home and learn to be just and generous, and then you may be happy."

"Insolent creature!" shouted the dwarf, as he shook his fat little fist at her. "I'll make you suffer for this. You shall find out what it is to heap injury and insult upon one like me, and to snatch from him the repose that he has earned by long years of toil." And shaking his head savagely, he hurried back to the rocky hillside.

Every afternoon the merry notes of the pipes of Old Pipes sounded down into the valley and over the hills and up the mountain-side, and every afternoon, when he had echoed them back, the little dwarf grew more and more angry with the Dryad. Each day, from early morning till it was time for him to go back to his duties upon the rocky hillside, he searched the woods for her. He intended, if he met her, to pretend to be very sorry for what he had said, and he thought he might be able to play a trick upon her which would revenge him well. One day, while thus wandering among the trees, he met Old Pipes. The Echo-dwarf did not generally care to see or to speak to ordinary people, but now he was so anxious to find the object of his search that he stopped and asked Old Pipes if he had seen the Dryad. The piper had not noticed the little fellow, and he looked down on him with some surprise.

"No," he said. "I have not seen her, and I have been looking everywhere for her."

"You!" cried the dwarf. "What do you wish with her?"

Old Pipes then sat down on a stone, so that he should be nearer the ear of his small companion, and he told what the Dryad had done for him. When the Echo-dwarf heard that this was the man whose pipes he was obliged to echo back every day, he would have slain him on the spot had he been able. But as he was not able, he merely ground his teeth and listened to the rest of the story.

"I am looking for the Dryad now," Old Pipes continued, "on account of my aged mother. When I was old myself, I did not notice how very aged my mother was; but now it shocks me to see how feeble and decrepit her years have caused her to become, and I am looking for the Dryad to ask her to make my mother younger, as she made me."

The eyes of the Echo-dwarf glistened. Here was a man who might help him in his plans.

"Your idea is a good one," he said to Old Pipes, "and it does you honor. But you should know that a Dryad can make no person younger but one who lets her out of her tree. However, you can manage the affair very easily. All you need do is to find the Dryad, tell her what you want, and request her to step into her tree and be shut up for a short time. Then you will go and bring your mother to the tree, she will open it, and everything will be as you wish. Is not this a good plan?"

"Excellent!" cried Old Pipes. "I will go instantly and search more diligently for the Dryad."

"Take me with you," said the Echo-dwarf. "You can easily carry me on your strong shoulders, and I shall be glad to help you in any way that I can."

"Now, then," said the little fellow to himself, as Old Pipes carried him rapidly along, "if he persuades the Dryad to get into a tree— and she is quite foolish enough to do it—and then goes away to bring his mother, I shall take a stone or a club and I will break off the key of that tree, so nobody can ever turn it again. Then Mistress Dryad will see what she brought upon herself by her behavior to me."

Before long they came to the great oak tree in which the Dryad had lived, and, at a distance, they saw that beautiful creature herself coming toward them.

"How excellently well everything happens!" said the dwarf. "Put me down, and I will go. Your business with the Dryad is more important than mine, and you need not say anything about my having suggested your plan to you. I am willing that you should have all the credit of it yourself."

Old Pipes put the Echo-dwarf upon the ground, but the little rogue did not go away. He concealed himself between some low, mossy rocks, and he was so much of their color that you would not have noticed him if you had been looking straight at him.

When the Dryad came up, Old Pipes lost no time in telling her about his mother, and what he wished her to do. At first the Dryad answered nothing, but stood looking very sadly at Old Pipes.

"Do you really wish me to go into my tree again?" she said. "I should dreadfully dislike to do it, for I don't know what might happen. It is not at all necessary, for I could make your mother younger at any time if she would give me the opportunity. I had already thought of making you still happier in this way, and several times I have waited about your cottage, hoping to meet your aged mother; but she never comes outside, and you know a Dryad cannot enter a house. I cannot imagine what put this idea into your head. Did you think of it yourself?"

"No, I cannot say that I did," answered Old Pipes. "A little dwarf whom I met in the woods proposed it to me."

"Oh," cried the Dryad, "now I see through it all. It is the scheme of that vile Echo-dwarf—your enemy and mine. Where is he? I should like to see him."

"I think he has gone away," said Old Pipes.

"No, he has not," said the Dryad, whose quick eyes perceived the Echo-dwarf among the rocks. "There he is. Seize him and drag him out, I beg of you."

Old Pipes perceived the dwarf as soon as he was pointed out to him, running to the rocks, he caught the little fellow by the leg and pulled him out.

"Now, then," cried the Dryad, who had opened the door of the great oak, "just stick him in there, and we will shut him up. Then I shall be safe from his mischief for the rest of the time I am free."

Old Pipes thrust the Echo-dwarf into the tree. The Dryad pushed the door shut. There was a clicking sound of bark and wood, and no one would have noticed the big oak ever had an opening in it.

"There," said the Dryad. "Now we need not be afraid of him. And I assure you, my good piper, that I shall be very glad to make your mother younger as soon as I can. Will you not ask her to come out and meet me?"

"Of course I will," cried Old Pipes. "I will do it without delay."

Then, the Dryad by his side, he hurried to his cottage. But when he mentioned the matter to his mother, the old woman became very angry indeed. She did not believe in Dryads; and if they really did exist, she knew they must be witches and sorceresses, and she would have nothing to do with them. If her son had ever allowed himself to be kissed by one of them he ought to be ashamed of himself. As to its doing him the least bit of good, she did not believe a word of it. He felt better than he used to feel, but that was very common. She had sometimes felt that way herself, and she forbade him ever to mention a Dryad to her again.

That afternoon Old Pipes, feeling very sad that his plan in regard to his mother had failed, sat down upon the rock and played upon his pipes. The pleasant sounds went down the valley and up the hills and mountain, but, to the great surprise of some persons who happened to notice the fact, the notes were not echoed back from the rocky hillside, but from the woods on the side of the valley where Old Pipes lived.

The next day many of the villagers stopped in their work to listen to the echo of the pipes coming from the woods. The sound was not as clear and strong as it used to be when it was sent back from the rocky hillside, but it certainly came from among the trees. Such a thing as an echo changing its place in this way had never been heard of before, and nobody was able to explain how it could have happened. Old Pipes, however, knew very well that the sound came from the Echo-dwarf shut up in the great oak tree. The sides of the tree were thin, the sound of the pipes could be heard through them, and the dwarf was obliged by the laws of his being to echo back those notes whenever they came to him. But Old Pipes thought he might get the Dryad in trouble if he let anyone know that the Echo-dwarf was shut up in the tree, and so he wisely said nothing about it.

One day the two boys and a girl who had helped Old Pipes up the hill were playing in the woods. Stopping near the great oak tree, they heard a sound of knocking within it, and then a voice plainly said: "Let me out! let me out!"

For a moment the children stood still in astonishment and then one of the boys exclaimed: "Oh, it is a Dryad, like the one Old Pipes found! Let's let her out!"

"What are you thinking of?" cried the girl. "I am the oldest of all, and I am only thirteen. Do you wish to be turned into crawling babies? Run! run! run!"

And the two boys and the girl dashed down into the valley as fast as their legs could carry them. There was no desire in their youthful hearts to be made younger than they were. For fear that their parents might think it well that they should commence their careers anew, they never said a word about finding the Dryad tree.

As the summer days went on, Old Pipes' mother grew feebler and feebler. One day when her son was away, for he now frequently went into the woods to hunt or fish, or down into the valley to work, she arose from her knitting to prepare the simple dinner. But she felt so weak and tired that she was not able to do the work to which she had been so long accustomed. "Alas! alas!" she said, "the time has come when I am too old to work. My son will have to hire some one to come here and cook his meals, make his bed, and mend his clothes. Alas! alas! I had hoped that as long as I lived I should be able to do these things. But it is not so. I have grown utterly worthless, and somone else must prepare the dinner for my son. I wonder where he is." And tottering to the door, she went outside to look for him. She did not feel able to stand, and reaching the rustic chair, she sank into it quite exhausted, and soon fell asleep.

The Dryad, who had often come to the cottage to see if she could find an opportunity of carrying out Old Pipes' affectionate design, now happened by, and seeing that the much-desired occasion had come, she stepped up quietly behind the old woman and gently kissed her on each cheek, and then as quietly disappeared.

In a few minutes the mother of Old Pipes awoke, and looking up at the sun, she exclaimed: "Why, it is almost dinner time! My son will be here presently, and I am not ready for him." And rising to her feet, she hurried into the house, made the fire, set the meat and vegetables to cook, laid the cloth, and by the time her son arrived the meal was on the table.

"How a little sleep does refresh one!" she said to herself, as she was bustling about. She was a woman of very vigorous constitution, and at seventy had been a great deal stronger and more active than her son was at that age. The moment Old Pipes saw his mother, he knew that the Dryad had been there. But while he felt as happy as a king, he was too wise to say anything about her.

"It is astonishing how well I feel today!" said his mother. "And either my hearing has improved or you speak much more plainly than you have done of late."

The summer days went on and passed away, the leaves were falling from the trees, and the air was becoming cold.

"Nature has ceased to be lovely," said the Dryad, "and the night winds chill me. It is time for me to go back into my comfortable quarters in the great oak. But first I must pay another visit to the cottage of Old Pipes."

She found the piper and his mother sitting side by side on the rock in front of the door. The cattle were not to go to the mountain any more that season, and he was piping them down for the last time. Loud and merrily sounded the pipes of Old Pipes, and down the mountain-side came the cattle, the cows by the easiest paths, the sheep by those not quite so easy, and the goats by the most difficult ones among the rocks, while from the great oak tree were heard the echoes of the cheerful music.

"How happy they look, sitting there together!" said the Dryad. "And I don't believe it will do them a bit of harm to be still younger." And moving up quietly behind them, she first kissed Old Pipes on his cheek, and then his mother.

Old Pipes who had stopped playing, knew what it was, but he did not move, and said nothing. His mother, thinking that her son had kissed her, turned to him with a smile and kissed him in return. Then she arose and went into the cottage, a vigorous woman of sixty, followed by her son, erect and happy, and twenty years younger than herself.

The Dryad sped away to the woods, shrugging her shoulders as she felt the cool evening wind.

When she reached the great oak, she turned the key and opened the door. "Come out," she said to the Echo-dwarf, who sat blinking within. "Winter is coming on, and I want the comfortable shelter of my tree for myself. The cattle have come down from the mountain for the last time this year, the pipes will no longer sound, and you can go to your rocks and have a holiday until next spring."

Upon hearing these words the dwarf skipped quickly out, and the Dryad entered the tree and pulled the door shut after her. "Now, then," she said to herself, "he can break off the key if he likes. It does not matter to me. Another will grow out next spring. And although the good piper made me no promise, I know that when the warm days arrive next year, he will come and let me out again."

The Echo-dwarf did not stop to break the key of the tree. He was too happy at being released to think of anything else, and he hastened as fast as he could to his home on the rocky hillside.

The Dryad was not mistaken when she trusted in the piper. When the warm days came again he went to the oak tree to let her out. But, to his sorrow and surprise, he found the great tree lying upon the ground. A winter storm had blown it down, and it lay with its trunk shattered and split. And what became of the Dryad, no one ever knew.

Hans Christian Andersen

THE PRINCESS ON THE PEA

By HANS CHRISTIAN ANDERSEN

THERE was once a Prince who wanted to marry a Princess; but she was to be a *real* princess. So he traveled about, all through the world, to find a real one, but everywhere there was something in the way. There were princesses enough, but whether they were *real* princesses he could not quite make out: there was always something that did not seem quite right. So he came home again, quite sad: for he wished so much to have a real princess.

One evening a terrible storm came on. It lightened and thundered, the rain streamed down; it was quite fearful! Then there was a knocking at the town gate, and the old King went out to open it.

It was a Princess who stood outside the gate. But, mercy! how she looked, from the rain and the rough weather! The water ran down from her hair and her clothes; it ran in at the points of her shoes, and out at the heels; and yet she declared that she was a real princess.

"Yes, we will soon find that out," thought the old Queen. But she said nothing, only went into the bedchamber, took all the bedding off, and put a pea on the flooring of the bedstead; then she took twenty mattresses and laid them upon the pea, and then twenty eider-down beds upon the mattresses. On this the Princess had to lie all night. In the morning she was asked how she had slept.

"Oh, miserably!" said the Princess. "I scarcely closed my eyes all night long. Goodness knows what was in my bed. I lay upon something hard, so that I am black and blue all over. It is dreadful!"

Now they saw that she was a real princess, for through the twenty mattresses and the twenty eider-down beds she had felt the pea. No one but a real princess could be so delicate.

So the Prince took her for a wife, for now he knew that he had a true princess; the pea was put in the museum, and it is there now, unless somebody carried it off. Look you, this is a true story.

THE ELFIN MOUND

By HANS CHRISTIAN ANDERSEN

SEVERAL large-lizards were running quickly into the cleft of an old tree; they could understand each other perfectly, for they all spoke the lizard language.

"What a noise there is in the old Elfin mound!" said one of the Lizards. "What a rumbling and uproar! For two nights I have not been able to close my eyes, and might just as well have had a tooth-ache, for then I certainly should not have slept."

"There is a something going on there," said the other Lizard. "They let the mound stand on four red poles till the crowing of the cock, to have it thoroughly aired; and the Elfin damsels have learnt new dances, in which there is some stamping. Something's going on."

"Yes; I have spoken to an earthworm of my acquaintance," said the third Lizard. "The Earthworm came direct from the mound, where day and night he had been rummaging about in the ground. He had heard a good deal; for he can see nothing, poor wretch, but eavesdropping and listening he understands to perfection. Visitors are expected at the Elfin mound; visitors of rank, but who they were, the Earthworm either would not or could not say. All the Jacks-o'-the-lantern have been ordered to prepare a procession by torchlight; and all the silver and gold, of which there is plenty in the Elfin mound, will be polished and laid in the moonshine."

"But who can the strangers be?" said all the Lizards. "What can be going on? Listen! What a humming and buzzing!"

At the same instant the Elfin mound opened, and an elderly Elfin damsel, without a back, but for the rest very respectably dressed, came tripping forth. It was the old Elfin King's housekeeper; she was distantly related to him, and wore an amber heart on her fore-head. Her feet were so nimble—trip—trap—trip—trap!—how she skipped along, right away to the moor to the Night-raven!

"You will be invited to the Elfin mound, and that tonight," said she. "But would you not do us a great favor, and take charge of the invitations? As you do not give parties yourself, you must do us this service. Strangers of high rank are coming to us: magicians of no small importance, let me tell you; and so the old Elfin King wants to show himself off to advantage."

"Who is to be invited?" asked the Night-raven.

"Why, to the grand ball everybody may come; men even, if they do but speak in their sleep, or are able to do something in our way. But the principal banquet is to be very select: those of the first rank only are to be invited. I have had a long discussion with the Elfin King; for, according to my notions, we cannot even ask ghosts. The Sea-god and his daughters must be invited first; 'tis true, they don't much like coming on dry land, but they will have probably a wet stone to sit upon, or maybe something better still; and then, I think, they will not refuse for this once. We must have the old Mountain Dwarfs of the first class, with tails; the Elf of the Brook, and the Brownie; and then, I think, we must not omit the Swart Elf, and the Skeleton Horse: they belong, it is true, to the clergy, who are not of our sort; however, 'tis their office, and they are, moreover, nearly related to us, and are continually paying us visits."

"Caw!" said the Night-raven, and flew away to invite the company.

The Elfin maidens were already dancing on the Elfin mound: they danced with long shawls, woven of haze and moonshine; and to all who like this sort of dancing, it seems pretty. In the center of the Elfin mound was the great hall, splendidly ornamented; the floor was washed with moonshine, and the walls were rubbed with witches' fat, so that they shone in the light like tulip leaves. In the kitchen there was a great quantity of frogs among the dishes; adders' skins, with little children's fingers inside; salad of mushroom-seed; wet mice's snouts and hemlock; beer, from the brewery of the old Witch of the Moor; sparkling saltpeter wine from a grave-cellar— all very substantial eating: rusty nails and church-window glass were among the delicacies and kickshaws.

The old Elfin King had his golden crown polished with powdered slate-pencil. It was the pencil of the head-scholar; and to obtain this one is very difficult for the Elfin King.

They hung up the curtains in the bedchamber, and fastened them with adder spittle. It was a humming and a buzzing mound!

"Now we must perfume the place with singed hair and pigs' bristles; and then I think I shall have done my share of the business," said the little Elfin damsel.

"Dear papa," said the least of the daughters, "shall I now know who the high visitors are?"

"Well, then," said he, "I suppose I must tell you. Two of my daughters are to show themselves off, in order to get married. Two will certainly be married. The aged Mountain Elf of Norway, who lives in the old Dovrefield, and possesses many craggy castles, and a gold-mine, too—which is a better thing than one imagines—is coming here with his two sons; and they are to choose themselves wives. The hoary Elf is an honest old Norwegian, merry and straight forward. I have known him since many a long day, when we drank together to better acquaintance and good fellowship. He came here to fetch his wife—she is dead now—who was the daughter of the Rock-king. Oh, how I long to see the old northern Elf! His sons, people say, are coarse, blustering fellows; but maybe one wrongs them, and when older, they will improve."

"And when will they come?" asked his daughter.

"That depends on wind and weather," said the Elfin King. "They travel economically; they will come here by water. I wish they would go through Sweden; but the old gentleman has no inclination that way. He does not keep pace with the time, and that I can't bear."

At the same moment two Jacks-o'-the-lantern came hopping in, one faster than the other, and for that reason one was first.

"They're coming! They're coming!" cried they.

"Give me my crown; and let me stand in the moonshine," said the Elfin King.

The daughters held up their long shawls and bowed to the earth.

There stood the hoary Mountain Elf, with a crown of hardened icicles and polished fir-cones on his head, and wrapped up in a mantle of fir, and boots of the same. His sons, on the contrary, went with open throats, for they disdained the cold.

"Is that a mound?" asker the lesser of the youths, pointing to the Elfin home. "In Norway we call such a thing a hole."

"Boy," said the father, "a mound rises upward, and a hole goes inward. Have you no eyes in your head?"

Now they went in to the Elfin mound, where there was very choice company, certainly; and had come together with such speed, one might have thought they had been borne thither on the breeze; however, the arrangements for everyone were neat and pretty. The sea-folk sat at table in large water-butts; and they said they felt just as if they were at home. All observed good manners at the table, except the two little Norwegian Mountain Elves, who put their feet on the board, for they thought that all they did was becoming.

"Take your feet away from the plates," said the old Elf; and then they obeyed, although not immediately. They tickled the ladies next them with fir-cones; then they pulled off their boots, to be more at their ease, and gave them to the ladies to hold for them; but their father was very different. He told about the proud Norwegian rocks, and of the waterfalls, which, covered with foam, dashed downwards, raging and roaring like thunder; he told about the salmon, that leaps up against the falling waters, when the Spirit of the flood plays on her golden harp. He related about the clear winter nights, when the bells on the sledges jingle, and the youths run with flaming torches over the smooth ice, which is so transparent that they could see how affrighted the fishes were beneath their feet. He, indeed, could recount so that one saw and heard the things he described; when, huzza! all of a sudden, the old Elf gave one of the Elfin damsels a smacking kiss; and yet they were not even distantly related.

The Elfin maidens were now to dance, simple as well as stamping dances; and then came the most difficult one of all, the so-called "Dance out of the dance." Confound it! their legs grew so long, one did not know which was the beginning nor which was the end: one could not distinguish legs from arms; all was twirling about in the air like sawdust; and they went whizzing round to such a degree the Skeleton Horse grew quite sick, and had to leave the table.

"Brrrrr!" said the gray-headed Elf, "that's a regular Highland fling. But what can they do besides spin about like a whirlwind?"

"That you shall see," said the King, calling the youngest of his daughters. She was as delicate and fair as moonlight, and was the daintiest of all the sisters. She put a white wand in her mouth, and vanished. That was her art.

But the old Mountain Elf said, this was an art he should not at all like in his wife, nor did he think his sons would, either.

The other could walk beside her own self, as though she had a shadow, which is a thing Elves never have.

The third one's talent was of a very different kind; she had learned in the brewery of the Witch of the Moor, and she knew how to lard alder-wood with glowworms.

"She would make a good housewife," said the Mountain Elf, blinking, for he did not at all like drinking so much.

Then came the fourth Elfin maiden; she had a large golden harp, and when she touched the first string, everybody lifted up the left foot, for the Elves are all left-sided; and when she touched the next, everybody was forced to do whatever she pleased.

"That is a dangerous damsel," said the Mountain Elf; but both his sons went out of the Elfin mound, for they were tired of it.

"What can the next daughter do?" asked the old Elf.

"I have learned to love the Norwegians," said she, " and I will not marry unless I can go to Norway."

But the youngest of the sisters whispered into the old Elf's ear, "She only says that, because she has heard, in an old Norwegian rhyme, that when even the world is at an end, the rocks of Norway will stand firm; and that's the reason she wants to go there, for she is greatly afraid of death."

"Ho, ho!" said the old Elf, "that's the way the wind blows, it is? But what can the seventh and last do?"

"The sixth comes before the seventh," said the Elfin King.

"I can do nothing but tell people the truth," said she. "No one troubles about me; I have enough to do to get my shroud ready."

Now came the seventh and last. And what could she do? She could tell as many fairy tales as she chose.

"Here are my five fingers," said the old Mountain Elf. "For each one tell me a story."

And the Elfin maiden took hold of him by the wrist, and he laughed till he was choked; and when she came to the finger

at wore a golden ring, just as if it knew that matrimony was going
n, the old Elf said, "Hold fast what you have! The hand is yours!
will take you myself to wife!"

And the Elfin maiden said that the fairy tale to the ring-finger,
nd to the little finger, were wanting.

"Oh, we'll hear them in winter," said the old Elf; "and about
ie fir tree, too, and about the birch, and the gifts of the wood-
ymphs, and about the crackling frost. You shall have opportunities
nough of telling stories, for no one understands that yonder. And
iere we will sit in our rocky dwelling, where the pine-torch is burn-
ig, and where we drink mead out of the golden horns of the old
Norwegian kings; I got some as a present from the Water-spirit.
nd when we are sitting so together, Garbo will come to pay us a
isit, and he will sing to you all the songs of the mountain maidens.
How merry we shall be! The salmon will leap in the waterfall, and
ash against the walls of rock; but he will not be able to come in to
s, after all! Yes, yes; one leads a happy and comfortable life in dear
ld Norway! But where are the boys?"

Why, they were running about the fields, blowing out the wills-o'-
ie-wisp that were coming quite orderly in a procession of torches.

"What's all this harum-scarum about?" said the old Elf. "I have
aken a stepmother for you; now you may choose a wife, too."

But they said they liked speechifying and boon companionship
etter, and had no taste for matrimony; and so they made speeches,
ossed off their glasses, and turned them topsy-turvy, to show that
hey were quite empty. They then pulled off their coats, and lay
lown on the table to sleep. But the old Elf danced round the room
vith his young bride, and exchanged boots with her; for that is
nuch more genteel than exchanging rings.

"The cock is crowing!" said the elderly damsel who attended to
he housekeeping, "We must now bolt the shutters, lest the sun
hould spoil our complexions."

And then the mound closed. The Lizards ran about and up and
lown the cleft tree, and one said to the other, "How much I like the
ld Mountain Elf!" "I like the merry boys better," said the Earth-
vorm; but then he could not see, poor wretch!

THE TINDER-BOX

By HANS CHRISTIAN ANDERSEN

THERE came a Soldier marching along the high road—*one, two! one, two!* He had a knapsack on his back and a saber by his side, for he had been in the wars, and now he wanted to go home. And on the way he met with an old Witch: she was very hideous, and her under lip hung down upon her breast. She said, "Good evening, Soldier. What a fine sword you have, and what a big knapsack! You're a proper soldier! Now you shall have as much money as you like to have."

"I thank you, you old Witch!" said the Soldier.

"Do you see that great tree?" quoth the Witch; and she pointed to a tree which stood beside them. "It's quite hollow inside. You must climb to the top, and then you'll see a hole, through which you can let yourself down and get deep into the tree. I'll tie a rope round your body, so that I can pull you up again when you call me."

"What am I to do down in the tree?" asked the Soldier.

"Get money," replied the Witch. "Listen to me. When you come down to the earth under the tree, you will find yourself in a great hall; it is quite light, for above three hundred lamps are burning there. Then you will see three doors; these you can open, for the keys are hanging there. If you go into the first chamber, you'll see a great chest in the middle of the floor; on this chest sits a dog, and he's got a pair of eyes as big as two teacups. But you need not care for that. I'll give you my blue-checked apron, and you can spread it out upon the floor; then go up quickly and take the dog, and set him on my apron; then open the chest, and take as many shillings as you like. They are of copper: if you prefer silver, you must go into the second chamber. But there sits a dog with a pair of eyes as big as mill wheels. But do not you care for that. Set him upon my apron, and take some of the money. And if you want gold, you can have that too—in fact, as much as you can carry—if you go into the third chamber. But the dog that sits on the money-chest there has two eyes as big as round towers. He is a fierce dog, you may be sure; but you needn't be afraid. Only set him on my apron, and he won't hurt you; and take from the chest as much gold as you like."

"That's not so bad," said the Soldier. "But what am I to give you, you old Witch? For you will not do it for nothing, I fancy."

"No," replied the Witch, "not a single shilling will I have. You shall only bring me an old Tinder-box which my grandmother forgot when she was down there last."

"Then tie the rope round my body," cried the Soldier.

"Here it is," said the Witch, "and here's my blue-checked apron."

Then the Soldier climbed up into the tree, let himself slip down into the hole, and stood, as the Witch had said, in the great hall where the three hundred lamps were burning.

Now he opened the first door. Ugh! there sat the dog with eyes as big as teacups, staring at him. "You're a nice fellow!" exclaimed the Soldier; and he set him on the Witch's apron, and took as many copper shillings as his pockets would hold, and then locked the chest, set the dog on it again, and went into the second chamber. Aha! there sat the dog with eyes as big as mill wheels.

"You should not stare so hard at me," said the Soldier; "you might strain your eyes." And he set the dog upon the Witch's apron. And when he saw the silver money in the chest, he threw away all the copper money he had, and filled his pockets and his knapsack with silver only. Then he went into the third chamber. Oh, but that was horrid! The dog there really had eyes as big as towers, and they turned round and round in his head like wheels.

"Good evening!" said the Soldier; and he touched his cap, for he had never seen such a dog as that before. When he had looked at him a little more closely, he thought, "That will do," and lifted him down to the floor, and opened the chest. Mercy! what a quantity of gold was there! He could buy with it the whole town, and the sugar sucking-pigs of the cake woman, and all the tin soldiers, whips, and rocking-horses in the whole world. Yes, that was a quantity of money! Now the Soldier threw away all the silver coin with which he had filled his pockets and his knapsack, and took gold instead: yes, all his pockets, his knapsack, his boots, and his cap were filled, so that he could scarcely walk. Now indeed he had plenty of money. He put the dog on the chest, shut the door, and then called up through the tree, "Now pull me up, you old Witch."

"Have you the Tinder-box?" asked the Witch.

"Plague on it!" exclaimed the Soldier. "I had clean forgotten that." And he went and brought it.

The Witch drew him up, and he stood on the high road again, with his pockets, boots, knapsack, and cap full of gold.

"What are you going to do with the Tinder-box?" asked the Soldier.

"That's nothing to you," retorted the Witch. "You've had your money; just give me the Tinder-box."

"Nonsense!" said the Soldier. "Tell me directly what you're going to do with it or I'll draw my sword and cut off your head."

"No!" cried the Witch.

So the Soldier cut off her head. There she lay! But he tied up all his money in her apron, took it on his back like a bundle, put the Tinder-box in his pocket, and went straight off toward the town.

That was a splendid town! And he put up at the very best inn, and asked for the finest rooms, and ordered his favorite dishes, for now he was rich, as he had so much money. The servant who had to clean his boots certainly thought them a remarkably old pair for such a rich gentleman: but he had not bought any new ones yet. The next day he procured proper boots and handsome clothes. Now our Soldier had become a fine gentleman; and the people told him of all the splendid things which were in their city, and about the King, and what a pretty Princess the King's daughter was.

"Where can one get to see her?" asked the Soldier.

"She is not to be seen at all," said they all together; "she lives in a great copper castle, with a great many walls and towers round about it; no one but the King may go in and out there, for it has been prophesied that she shall marry a common soldier, and the King can't bear that."

"I should like to see her," thought the Soldier; but he could not get leave to do so. Now he lived merrily, went to the theater, drove in the King's garden, and gave much money to the poor; and this was very kind of him, for he knew from old times how hard it is when one has not a shilling. Now he was rich, had fine clothes, and gained many friends, who all said he was a rare one, a true cavalier; and that pleased the Soldier well. But as he spent money every day and never earned any, he had at last only two shillings left; and he was obliged to turn out of the fine rooms in which he had dwelt, and had to live in a little garret under the roof, and clean his boots for himself, and mend them with a darning needle. None of his friends came to see him, for there were too many stairs to climb.

It was quite dark one evening, and he could not even buy himself a candle, when it occurred to him that there was a candle end in the Tinder-box which he had taken out of the hollow tree into which the Witch had helped him. He brought out the Tinder-box and the candle end; but as soon as he struck fire and the sparks rose up from the flint, the door flew open, and the dog who had eyes as big as a couple of teacups, and whom he had seen in the tree, stood before him, and said: "What are my lord's commands?"

"What is this?" said the Soldier. "That's a famous Tinder-box, if I can get everything with it that I want! Bring me some money," said he to the dog; and *whisk!* the dog was gone, and *whisk!* he was back again, with a great bag full of shillings in his mouth.

Now the Soldier knew what a capital Tinder-box this was. If he struck it once, the dog came who sat upon the chest of copper money; if he struck it twice, the dog came who had the silver; and if he struck it three times, then appeared the dog who had the gold. Now the Soldier moved back into the fine rooms, and appeared again in handsome clothes; and all his friends knew him again, and cared very much for him indeed.

Once he thought to himself: "It is a very strange thing that one cannot get to see the Princess. They all say she is very beautiful; but what is the use of that, if she has always to sit in the great copper castle with the many towers? Can I not get to see her at all? Where is my Tinder-box?" And so he struck a light, and *whisk!* came the dog with eyes as big as teacups.

"It is midnight certainly," said the Soldier, "but I should very much like to see the Princess, only for one little moment."

And the dog was outside the door directly, and, before the Soldier thought it, came back with the Princess. She sat upon the dog's back and slept; and everyone could see she was a real princess, for she was so lovely. The Soldier could not refrain from kissing her, for he was a thorough soldier. Then the dog ran back again with the Princess. But when morning came, and the King and Queen were drinking tea, the Princess said she had had a strange dream, about a dog and a soldier—that she had ridden upon the dog, and the soldier had kissed her.

"That would be a fine history!" said the Queen.

So one of the old court ladies had to watch the next night by the Princess's bed, to see if this was really a dream, or what it might be.

The Soldier had a great longing to see the lovely Princess again; so the dog came in the night, took her away, and ran as fast as he could. But the old lady put on water boots, and ran just as fast after him. When she saw that they both entered a great house, she thought, "Now I know where it is;" and with a bit of chalk she drew a great cross on the door. Then she went home and lay down, and the dog came up with the Princess; but when he saw that there was a cross drawn on the door where the Soldier lived, he took a piece of chalk too, and drew crosses on all the doors in the town. And that was cleverly done, for now the lady could not find the right door, because all the doors had crosses upon them.

In the morning early came the King and the Queen, the old court lady and all the officers, to see where it was the Princess had been. "Here it is!" said the King, when he saw the first door with a cross upon it. "No, my dear husband, it is there!" said the Queen, who descried another door which also showed a cross. "But there is one, and there is one!" said all, for wherever they looked there were crosses on the doors. So they saw that search would avail them nothing.

But the Queen was an exceedingly clever woman, who could do more than ride in a coach. She took her great gold scissors, cut a piece of silk into pieces, and made a neat little bag; this bag she filled with fine wheat flour, and tied it on the Princess's back; and when that was done, she cut a little hole in the bag, so that the flour would be scattered along all the way which the Princess should take.

In the night the dog came again, took the Princess on his back, and ran with her to the Soldier, who loved her very much, and would gladly have been a prince, so that he might have her for his wife. The dog did not notice at all how the flour ran out in a stream from the castle to the windows of the Soldier's house, where he ran up the wall with the Princess. In the morning the King and the Queen saw well enough where their daughter had been, and they took the Soldier and put him in prison.

There he sat. Oh, but it was dark and disagreeable there! And they said to him, "Tomorrow you shall be hanged." That was not amusing to hear, and he had left his Tinder-box at the inn. In the morning he could see, through the iron grating of the little window, how the people were hurrying out of the town to see him hanged. He heard the drums beat and saw the soldiers marching. All the people were running out, and among them was a shoemaker's boy with leather apron and slippers, and he galloped so fast that one of his slippers flew off, and came right against the wall where the Soldier sat looking through the iron grating.

"Halloo, you shoemaker's boy! You needn't be in such a hurry," cried the Soldier to him. "It will not begin till I come. But if you will run to where I lived, and bring me my Tinder-box, you shall have four shillings; but you must put your best leg foremost."

The shoemaker's boy wanted to get the four shillings, so he went and brought the Tinder-box, and—we shall hear what happened.

Outside the town a great gallows had been built, and round it stood the soldiers and many hundred thousand people. The King and Queen sat on a splendid throne, opposite to the judges and the whole council. The Soldier already stood upon the ladder; but as they were about to put the rope around his neck, he said that before a poor criminal suffered his punishment an innocent request was always granted to him. He wanted very much to smoke a pipe of tobacco, and it would be the last pipe he would smoke in the world. The King would not say "No" to this; so the Soldier took his Tinder-box, and struck fire. One—two—three!—and there suddenly stood all the dogs—the one with eyes as big as teacups, the one with eyes as large as mill-wheels, and the one whose eyes were as big as round towers.

"Help me now, so that I may not be hanged," said the Soldier.

And the dogs fell upon the judges and all the council, seized one by the leg and another by the nose, and tossed them all many feet into the air, so that they fell down and were all broken to pieces.

"I won't!" cried the King; but the biggest dog took him and the Queen, and threw them after the others. Then the soldiers were afraid, and the people cried, "Little Soldier, you shall be our king, and marry the beautiful Princess!"

So they put the Soldier into the King's coach, and all the three dogs darted on in front and cried "Hurrah!" and the boys whistled through their fingers, and the soldiers presented arms. The Princess came out of the copper castle, and became Queen, and she liked that well enough. The wedding lasted a week, and the three dogs sat at the table, too, and opened their eyes wider than ever at all they saw.

THE UGLY DUCKLING

By HANS CHRISTIAN ANDERSEN

IT was so glorious out in the country; it was summer; the corn-fields were yellow, the oats were green, the hay had been put up in stacks in the green meadows, and the stork went about on his long red legs, and chattered Egyptian, for this was the language he had learned from his good mother. All around the fields and meadows were great forests, and in the midst of these forests lay deep lakes. Yes, it was right glorious out in the country. In the midst of the sunshine there lay an old farm, with deep canals about it, and from the wall down to the water grew great burdocks, so high that little children could stand upright under the loftiest of them. It was just as wild there as in the deepest wood, and here sat a Duck upon her nest; she had to hatch her ducklings; but she was almost tired out before the little ones came; and then she so seldom had visitors. The other ducks liked better to swim about in the canals than to run up to sit down under a burdock, and cackle with her.

At last one eggshell after another burst open. "Piep! Piep!" it cried, and in all the eggs there were little creatures that stuck out their heads.

"Quack! quack!" they said; and they all came quacking out as fast as they could, looking all round them under the green leaves; and the mother let them look as much as they chose, for green is good for the eye.

"How wide the world is!" said all the young ones, for they certainly had much more room now than when they were in the eggs.

"D'ye think this is all the world?" said the mother. "That stretches far across the other side of the garden, quite into the parson's field; but I have never been there yet. I hope you are all together," and she stood up. "No, I have not all. The largest egg still lies there. How long is that to last? I am really tired of it." And she sat down again.

"Well, how goes it?" asked an old Duck who had come to pay her a visit.

"It lasts a long time with that one egg," said the Duck who sat there. "It will not burst. Now, only look at the others; are they not the prettiest little ducks one could possibly see? They are all like their father; the rogue, he never comes to see me."

"Let me see the egg which will not burst," said the old visitor. "You may be sure it is a turkey's egg. I was once cheated in that way, and had much anxiety and trouble with the young ones, for they are afraid of the water. Must I say it to you, I could not get them to venture in. I quacked and I clacked, but it was no use. Let me see the egg. Yes, that's a turkey's egg. Let it lie there; and teach the other children to swim."

"I think I will sit on it a little longer," said the Duck. "I've sat so long now that I can sit a few days more."

"Just as you please," said the old Duck; and she went away.

At last the great egg burst. "Piep! piep!" said the little one, and crept forth. It was very large and very ugly. The Duck looked at it. "It's a very large duckling," said she; "none of the others look like that: can it really be a turkey chick? Well, we shall soon find out. It must go into the water, even if I have to thrust it in myself."

The next day it was bright, beautiful weather; the sun shone on all the green trees. The Mother-Duck went down to the canal with all her family. Splash! she jumped into the water. "Quack! quack!" she said, and one duckling after another plunged in. The water closed over their heads, but they came up in an instant, and swam capitally; their legs went of themselves, and they were all in the water. The ugly gray Duckling swam with them.

"No, it's not a turkey," said she; "look how well it can use its legs, and how straight it holds itself. It is my own child! On the whole it's quite pretty, if one looks at it rightly. Quack! quack! come with me, and I'll lead you out into the great world, and present you in the duck yard; but keep close to me, so that no one may tread on you; and take care of the cats!"

And so they came into the duck yard. There was a terrible riot going on in there, for two families were quarreling about an eel's head, and the cat got it after all.

"See, that's how it goes in the world!" said the Mother-Duck; and she whetted her beak, for she too wanted the eel's head. "Only use your legs," she said. "See that you can bustle about, and bow your heads before the old Duck yonder. She's the grandest of all here; she's of Spanish blood—that's why she's so fat; and d'ye see? she has a red rag round her leg; that's something particularly fine, and the greatest distinction a duck can enjoy; it signifies that one does not want to lose her, and that she's to be known by the animals and by men too. Shake yourselves—don't turn in your toes; a well-brought-up duck turns its toes quite out, just like father and mother —so! Now bend your necks and say 'Quack!'"

And they did so: but the other ducks round about looked at them, and said quite boldly—"Look there! Now we're to have these hanging on, as if there were not enough of us already! And—fie!—how that Duckling yonder looks; we won't stand that!" And one duck flew up at it, and bit it in the neck.

"Let it alone," said the mother; "it does no harm to anyone."

"Yes, but it's too large and peculiar," said the Duck, who had bitten it; "and therefore it must be put down."

"Those are pretty children that the mother has there," said the old Duck with the rag round her leg. "They're all pretty but that one; that was rather unlucky. I wish she could bear it over again."

"That cannot be done, my lady," replied the Mother-Duck. "It is not pretty, but it has a really good disposition, and swims as well as any other; yes, I may even say, it swims better. I think it will grow up pretty, and become smaller in time; it has lain too long in the egg, and therefore is not properly shaped." And then she pinched it in the neck, and smoothed its feathers. "Moreover it is a drake," she said, "and therefore it is not of so much consequence. I think he will be very strong: he makes his way already."

"The other ducklings are graceful enough," said the old Duck. "Make yourself at home; and if you find an eel's head, you may bring it to me."

And now they were at home. But the poor Duckling which had crept last out of the egg, and looked so ugly, was bitten and pushed and jeered, as much by the ducks as by the chickens.

"It is too big!" they all said. And the turkey-cock, who had been born with spurs, and therefore thought himself an emperor, blew himself up like a ship in full sail, and bore straight down upon it; then he gobbled and grew quite red in the face. The poor Duckling did not know where it should stand or walk; it was quite melancholy because it looked ugly, and was the butt of the whole duck yard.

So it went on the first day; and afterwards it became worse and worse. The poor Duckling was hunted about by everyone; even its brothers and sisters were quite angry with it, and said, "If the cat would only catch you, you ugly creature!" And the mother said, "If you were only far away!" and the ducks bit it, and the chickens beat it, and the girl who had to feed the poultry kicked at it with her foot.

Then it ran and flew over the fence, and the little birds in the bushes flew up in fear.

"That is because I am so ugly!" thought the Duckling; and it shut its eyes, but flew on farther; and so it came out into the great moor, where the wild ducks lived. Here it lay the whole night long; and it was weary and downcast.

Toward morning the wild ducks flew up, and looked at their new companion.

"What sort of a one are you?" they asked; and the Duckling turned in every direction, and bowed as well as it could. "You are remarkably ugly!" said the Wild Ducks. "But that is nothing to us, so long as you do not marry into our family."

Poor thing! It certainly did not think of marrying, and only hoped to obtain leave to lie among the reeds and drink some of the swamp water.

Thus it lay two whole days; then came thither two wild geese, or, properly speaking, two wild ganders. It was not long since each had crept out of an egg, and that's why they were so saucy.

"Listen, comrade," said one of them. "You're so ugly that I like you. Will you go with us, and become a bird of passage? Near here, in another moor, there are a few sweet lovely wild geese, all unmarried, and all able to say 'Rap?' You've a chance of making your fortune, ugly as you are."

"Piff, paff!" resounded through the air; and the two ganders fell down dead in the swamp, and the water became blood red. "Piff! paff!" it sounded again, and the whole flock of wild geese rose up from the reeds. And then there was another report. A great hunt was going on. The sportsmen were lying in wait all round the moor, and some were even sitting up in the branches of the trees, which spread far over the reeds. The blue smoke rose up like clouds among the dark trees, and was wafted away across the water; and the hunting dogs came—splash, splash!—in to the swamp, and the rushes and the reeds bent down on every side. That was a fright for the poor Duckling! It turned its head, and put it under its wing; but at that moment a frightful great dog stood close by the Duckling. His tongue hung far out of his mouth, and his eyes gleamed horrible and ugly; he thrust out his nose close against the Duckling, showed his sharp teeth and—splash, splash!—on he went, without seizing it.

"Oh, Heaven be thanked!" sighed the Duckling. "I am so ugly, that even the dog does not like to bite me!"

And so it lay quite quiet, while the shots rattled through the reeds and gun after gun was fired. At last, late in the day, all was still; but the poor Duckling did not dare to rise up; it waited several hours before it looked round, and then hastened away out of the moor as fast as it could. It ran on over field and meadow; there was such a storm raging that it was difficult to get from one place to another.

Toward evening the Duck came to a little miserable peasant's hut. This hut was so dilapidated that it did not itself know on which side it should fall; and that's why it remained standing. The storm whistled round the Duckling in such a way that the poor creature was obliged to sit down, to stand against it; and the wind blew worse and worse. Then the Duckling noticed that one of the hinges of the door had given way, and the door hung so slanting that the Duckling could slip through the crack into the room; which is what it did.

Here lived a woman, with her Cat and her Hen. And the Cat, whom she called Sonnie, could arch his back and purr, he could even give out sparks; but for that one had to stroke his fur the wrong way. The Hen had quite little short legs, and therefore she was called Chickabiddy Shortshanks; she laid good eggs, and the woman loved her as her own child.

In the morning the strange Duckling was at once noticed, and the Cat began to purr and the Hen to cluck.

"What's this?" said the woman, and looked all round; but she could not see well, and therefore she thought the Duckling was a fat duck that had strayed. "This is a rare prize!" she said. "Now I shall have duck's eggs. I hope it is not a drake. We must try that."

And so the Duckling was admitted on trial for three weeks; but no eggs came. And the Cat was master of the house, and the Hen was the lady, and always said "We and the world!" for she thought they were half the world, and by far the better half. The Duckling thought one might have a different opinion, but the Hen would not allow it.

"Can you lay eggs?" she asked.

"No."

"Then will you hold your tongue!"

And the Cat said, "Can you curve your back, and purr, and give out sparks?"

"No."

"Then you will please have no opinion of your own when sensible folks are speaking."

And the Duckling sat in a corner and was melancholy; then the fresh air and the sunshine streamed in; and it was seized with such a strange longing to swim on the water, that it could not help telling the Hen of it.

"What are you thinking of?" cried the Hen. "You have nothing to do, that's why you have these fancies. Lay eggs, or purr, and they will pass over."

"But it is so charming to swim on the water," said the Duckling, "so refreshing to let it close above one's head, and to dive down to the bottom."

"Yes, that must be a mighty pleasure, truly," quoth the Hen. "I fancy you must have gone crazy. Ask the Cat about it—he's the cleverest animal I know—ask him if he likes to swim on the water, or to dive down: I won't speak about myself. Ask our mistress, the old

woman; no one in the world is cleverer than she. Do you think she
has any desire to swim, and to let the water close above her head?"

"You don't understand me," said the Duckling.

"We don't understand you? Then pray who is to understand you?
You surely don't pretend to be cleverer than the Cat and the woman
—I won't say anything of myself. Don't be conceited, child, and
thank your Maker for all the kindness you have received. Did you
not get into a warm room, and have you not fallen into company
from which you may learn something? But you are a chatterer, and
it is not pleasant to associate with you. You may believe me, I speak
for your good. I tell you disagreeable things, and by that one may
always know one's true friends! Only take care that you learn to lay
eggs, or to purr, and give out sparks!"

"I think I will go out into the wide world," said the Duckling.

"Yes, do go," replied the Hen.

And so the Duckling went away. It swam on the water, and
dived, but it was slighted by every creature because of its ugliness.

Now came the autumn. The leaves in the forest turned yellow and
brown; the wind caught them so that they danced about, and up in
the air it was very cold. The clouds hung low, heavy with hail and
snowflakes, and on the fence stood the raven, crying, "Croak! croak!"
for mere cold; yes, it was enough to make one feel cold to think of
this. The poor little Duckling certainly had not a good time. One
evening—the sun was just setting in his beauty—there came a whole
flock of great, handsome birds out of the bushes; they were dazzlingly white, with long, flexible necks; they were swans. They uttered a very peculiar cry, spread forth their glorious great wings, and
flew away from that cold region to warmer lands, to fair open lakes.
They mounted so high, so high! And the ugly Duckling felt quite
strangely as it watched them. It turned round and round in the
water like a wheel, stretched out its neck toward them, and uttered
such a strange, loud cry as frightened itself. Oh! it could not forget
those beautiful, happy birds; and so soon as it could see them no
longer, it dived down to the very bottom, and when it came up
again, it was quite beside itself. It knew not the name of those birds,
and knew not whither they were flying; but it loved them more than

it had ever loved any one. It was not at all envious of them. How could it think of wishing to possess such loveliness as they had? It would have been glad if only the ducks would have endured its company—the poor, ugly creature!

And the winter grew cold, very cold! The Duckling was forced to swim about in the water, to prevent the surface from freezing entirely; but every night the hole in which it swam about became smaller and smaller. It froze so hard that the icy covering crackled again; and the Duckling was obliged to use its legs continually to prevent the hole from freezing up. At last it became exhausted, and lay quite still, and thus froze fast into the ice.

Early in the morning a peasant came by, and when he saw what had happened, he took his wooden shoe, broke the ice-crust to pieces, and carried the Duckling home to his wife. Then it came to itself again. The children wanted to play with it; but the Duckling thought they wanted to hurt it, and in its terror fluttered up into the milk pan, so that the milk spurted down into the room. The woman clasped her hands, at which the Duckling flew down into the butter tub, and then into the meal barrel and out again. How it looked then! The woman screamed, and struck at it with the fire tongs; the children tumbled over one another in their efforts to catch the Duckling; and they laughed and they screamed! Well it was that the door stood open, and the poor creature was able to slip out between the shrubs into the newly-fallen snow—there it lay quite exhausted.

But it would be too melancholy if I were to tell all the misery and care which the Duckling had to endure in the hard winter. It lay out on the moor among the reeds, when the sun began to shine again and the larks to sing: it was a beautiful spring.

Then all at once the Duckling could flap its wings: they beat the air more strongly than before, and bore it strongly away; and before it well knew how all this happened, it found itself in a great garden, where the elder trees smelt sweet, and bent their long green branches down to the canal that wound through the region. Oh, here it was so beautiful, such a gladness of spring! And from the thicket came three glorious white swans; they rustled their wings, and swam lightly on the water. The Duckling knew the splendid creatures, and felt oppressed by a peculiar sadness.

"I will fly away to them, to the royal birds! And they will beat me, because I, that am so ugly, dare to come near them. But it is all the same. Better to be killed by *them* than to be pursued by ducks, and beaten by fowls, and pushed about by the girl who takes care of the poultry yard, and to suffer hunger in winter!" And it flew out into the water, and swam toward the beautiful swans: these looked at it, and came sailing down upon it with outspread wings. "Kill me!" said the poor creature, and bent its head down upon the water, expecting nothing but death. But what was this that it saw in the clear water? It beheld its own image; and, lo! it was no longer a clumsy dark-gray bird, ugly and hateful to look at, but a—swan!

It matters nothing if one is born in a duck yard, if one has only lain in a swan's egg.

It felt quite glad at all the need and misfortune it had suffered, now it realized its happiness in all the splendor that surrounded it. And the great swans swam round it, and stroked it with their beaks.

Into the garden came little children, who threw bread and corn into the water; and the youngest cried, "There is a new one!" and the other children shouted joyously, "Yes, a new one has arrived!" And they clapped their hands and danced about, and ran to their father and mother; and bread and cake were thrown into the water; and they all said, "The new one is the most beautiful of all! So young and handsome!" and the old swans bowed their heads before him.

Then he felt quite ashamed, and hid his head under his wings, for he did not know what to do; he was so happy, and yet not at all proud. He thought how he had been persecuted and despised; and now he heard them saying that he was the most beautiful of all birds. Even the elder tree bent its branches straight down into the water before him, and the sun shone warm and mild. Then his wings rustled, he lifted his slender neck, and cried rejoicingly from the depths of his heart—

"I never dreamed of so much happiness when I was the Ugly Duckling!"

THE FIR-TREE

By HANS CHRISTIAN ANDERSEN

OUT in the woods stood a nice little Fir-tree. The place he had was a very good one: the sun shone on him; as to fresh air, there was enough of that, and round him grew many large-sized comrades, pines as well as firs. But the little Fir wanted so very much to be a grown-up tree.

He did not think of the warm sun and of the fresh air; he did not care for the little cottage-children that ran about and prattled when they were in the woods looking for wild strawberries. The children often came with a whole pitcher full of berries, or a long row of them threaded on a straw, and sat down near the young Tree and said, "Oh, how pretty he is! What a nice little fir!" But this was what the Tree could not bear to hear.

At the end of a year he had shot up a good deal, and after another year he was another long bit taller; for with fir-trees one can always tell by the shoots how many years old they are.

"Oh, were I but such a high tree as the others are!" sighed he. "Then I should be able to spread out my branches, and with the tops to look into the wide world! Then would the birds build nests among my branches; and when there was a breeze, I could bend with as much stateliness as the others!"

Neither the sunbeams, nor the birds, nor the red clouds which morning and evening sailed above, gave the little Tree any pleasure.

In winter, when the snow lay glittering on the ground, a hare would often come leaping along, and jump right over the little Tree. Oh, that made him so angry! But two winters were past, and in the third the Tree was so large that the hare was obliged to go round it. "To grow and grow, to get older and be tall," thought the Tree— "that, after all, is the most delightful thing in the world!"

In autumn the woodcutters always came and felled some of the largest trees. This happened every year; and the young Fir-tree, that had now grown to a very comely size, trembled at the sight; for the magnificent great trees fell to the earth with noise and cracking, the branches were lopped off, and the trees looked long and bare: they were hardly to be recognized; and then they were laid in carts, and the horses dragged them out of the wood.

Where did they go to? What became of them?

In spring when the Swallows and the Storks came, the Tree asked them, "Don't you know where they have been taken? Have you not met them anywhere?"

The Swallows did not know anything about it; but the Stork looked musing, nodded his head, and said: "Yes; I think I know; I met many ships as I was flying hither from Egypt; on the ships were magnificent masts, and I venture to assert that it was they that smelt so of fir. I may congratulate you, for they lifted themselves on high most majestically!"

"Oh, were I but old enough to fly across the sea! But how does the sea look in reality? What is it like?"

"That would take a long time to explain," said the Stork, and with these words off he went.

"Rejoice in thy growth!" said the Sunbeam. "Rejoice in thy vigorous growth, and in the fresh life that moveth within thee!"

And the Wind kissed the Tree, and the Dew wept tears over him; but the Fir understood it not.

When Christmas came, quite young trees were cut down; trees which often were not even as large or of the same age as this Fir-tree, who could never rest, but always wanted to be off. These young trees, and they were always the finest-looking, retained their branches; they were laid on carts, and the horses drew them out of the wood.

"Where are they going to?" asked the Fir. "They are not taller than I; there was one indeed that was considerably shorter—and why do they retain all their branches? Whither are they taken?"

"We know! We know!" chirped the Sparrows. "We have peeped in at the windows in the town below! We know whither they are taken! The greatest splendor and the greatest magnificence one can imagine await them. We peeped through the windows, and saw them planted in the middle of the warm room, and ornamented with the most splendid things—with gilded apples, with ginger-bread, with toys, and many hundred lights!"

"And then?" asked the Fir-tree, trembling in every bough. "And then? What happens then?"

"We did not see anything more; it was incomparably beautiful."

"I would fain know if I am destined for so glorious a career," cried the Tree, rejoicing. "That is still better than to cross the sea! What a longing do I suffer! Were Christmas but come! I am now tall, and my branches spread like the others that were carried off last year! Oh, were I but already on the cart! Were I in the warm room with all the splendor and magnificence! Yes, then something better, something still grander, will surely follow, or wherefore should they thus ornament me? Something better, something still grander, *must* follow—but what? Oh, how I long, how I suffer! I do not know myself what is the matter with me!"

"Rejoice in our presence!" said the Air and the Sunlight. "Rejoice in thy own fresh youth!"

But the Tree did not rejoice at all; he grew and grew, and was green both winter and summer. People that saw him said, "What a fine tree!" and toward Christmas he was one of the first that was cut down. The ax struck deep into the very pith; the tree fell to the earth with a sigh: he felt a pang—it was like a swoon; he could not think of happiness, for he was sorrowful at being separated from his home, from the place where he had sprung up. He well knew that he should never see his dear old comrades, the little bushes and flowers around him, any more; perhaps not even the birds! The departure was not at all agreeable.

The Tree only came to himself when he was unloaded in a court-yard with the other trees, and heard a man say, "That one is splendid! We don't want the others." Then two servants came in rich livery and carried the Fir-tree into a large and splendid drawing-room. Portraits were hanging on the walls, and near the white porcelain stove stood two large Chinese vases with lions on the covers. There, too, were large easy-chairs, silken sofas, large tables full of picture books, and full of toys worth hundreds and hundreds of crowns—at least the children said so. And the Fir-tree was stuck upright in a cask that was filled with sand; but no one could see that it was a cask, for green cloth was hung all round it, and it stood on a large gayly-colored carpet. Oh, how the tree quivered! What was to happen? The servants, as well as the young ladies, decorated it. On one branch there hung little nets cut out of colored paper, and each net was filled with sugar-plums; and among the other boughs gilded apples and walnuts were suspended, looking as though they had grown there, and little blue and white tapers were placed among the leaves. Dolls that looked for all the world like men—the Tree had never beheld such before—were seen among the foliage, and at the very top a large star of gold tinsel was fixed. It was really splendid—beyond description splendid.

"This evening!" said they all. "How it will shine this evening!"

"Oh," thought the Tree, "if the evening were but come! If the tapers were but lighted! And then I wonder what will happen! Perhaps the other trees from the forest will come to look at me! Perhaps the sparrows will beat against the window-panes! I wonder if I shall take root here, and winter and summer stand covered with ornaments!"

He knew very much about the matter! But he was so impatient, that for sheer longing he got a pain in his back, and this with trees is the same thing as a headache with us.

The candles were now lighted. What brightness! What splendor! The Tree trembled so in every bough that one of the tapers set fire to the foliage. It blazed up splendidly.

"Help! help!" cried the young ladies, and they quickly put out the fire.

Now the Tree did not even dare tremble. What a state he was in! He was so uneasy lest he should lose something of his splendor, that he was quite bewildered amidst the glare and brightness; when suddenly both folding doors opened, and a troop of children rushed in as if they would upset the Tree. The older persons followed quietly; the little ones stood quite still. But it was only for a moment; then they shouted so that the whole place reëchoed; they danced round the Tree, and one present after the other was pulled off.

"What are they about?" thought the Tree. "What is to happen

now!" And the lights burned down to the very branches, and as they burned down they were put out one after the other, and then the children had permission to plunder the Tree. So they fell upon it with such violence that all its branches cracked; if it had not been fixed firmly in the cask, it would certainly have tumbled down.

The children danced about with their beautiful playthings: no one looked at the Tree except the old nurse, who peeped between the branches; but it was only to see if there was a fig or an apple left that had been forgotten.

"A story! a story!" cried the children, drawing a little fat man toward the Tree. He seated himself under it, and said, "Now we are in the shade, and the Tree can listen, too. But I shall tell only one story. Now which will you have: that about Ivedy-Avedy, or about Klumpy-Dumpy who tumbled downstairs, and yet after all came to the throne and married the princess?"

"Ivedy-Avedy," cried some; "Klumpy-Dumpy," cried the others. There was such a bawling and screaming!—the Fir-tree alone was silent, and he thought to himself, "Am I not to bawl with the rest? —Am I to do nothing whatever?" for he was one of the company, and had done what he had to do.

And the man told about Klumpy-Dumpy that tumbled down, who notwithstanding came to the throne, and at last married the princess. And the children clapped their hands, and cried out, "Oh, go on! Do go on!" They wanted to hear about Ivedy-Avedy, too, but the little man only told them about Klumpy-Dumpy. The Fir-tree stood quite still and absorbed in thought: the birds in the wood had never related the like of this: "Klumpy-Dumpy fell downstairs, and yet he married the princess! Yes, yes, that's the way of the world!" thought the Fir-tree, and believed it all, because the man who told the story was so good-looking. "Well, well! who knows, perhaps I may fall downstairs, too, and get a princess as wife!" And he looked forward with joy to the morrow, when he hoped to be decked out again with lights, playthings, fruits, and tinsel.

"I won't tremble tomorrow!" thought the Fir-tree. "I will enjoy to the full all my splendor! Tomorrow I shall hear again the story of Klumpy-Dumpy, and perhaps that of Ivedy-Avedy, too." And the whole night the Tree stood still and in deep thought.

In the morning the servant and the housemaid came in. "Now then the splendor will begin again," thought the Fir. But they dragged him out of the room, and up the stairs into the loft; and here in a dark corner, where no daylight could enter, they left him. "What's the meaning of this?" thought the Tree. "What am I to do here? What shall I hear now, I wonder?" And he leaned against the wall, lost in reverie. Time enough had he, too, for his reflections; for days and nights passed on, and nobody came up; and when at last somebody did come, it was only to put some great trunks in a corner out of the way. There stood the Tree quite hidden; it seemed as if he had been entirely forgotten.

" 'Tis now winter out-of-doors!" thought the Tree. "The earth is hard and covered with snow; men cannot plant me now, and therefore I have been put up here under shelter till the springtime comes! How thoughtful that is! How kind man is, after all! If it only were not so dark here, and so terribly lonely! Not even a hare. And out in the woods it was so pleasant when the snow was on the ground, and the hare leaped by; yes—even when he jumped over me; but I did not like it then. It is really terribly lonely here!"

"Squeak! squeak!" said a little Mouse at the same moment, peeping out of his hole. And then another little one came. They snuffed about the Fir-tree, and rustled among the branches.

"It is dreadfully cold," said the Mouse. "But for that, it would be delightful here, old Fir, wouldn't it?"

"I am by no means old," said the Fir-tree. "There's many a one considerably older than I am."

"Where do you come from," asked the Mice; "and what can you do?" They were so extremely curious. "Tell us about the most beautiful spot on the earth. Have you never been there? Were you never in the larder, where cheeses lie on the shelves, and hams hang from above; where one dances about on tallow candles; that place where one enters lean, and comes out again fat and portly?"

"I know no such place," said the Tree. "But I know the wood, where the sun shines, and where the little birds sing." And then he told all about his youth; and the little Mice had never heard the like before; and they listened and said: "Well, to be sure! How much you have seen! How happy you must have been!"

"I!" said the Fir-tree, thinking over what he had himself related. "Yes, in reality those were happy times." And then he told about Christmas Eve, when he was decked out with cakes and candles.

"Oh," said the little Mice, "how fortunate you have been, old Fir-tree!"

"I am by no means old," said he. "I came from the wood this winter; I am in my prime, and am only rather short for my age."

"What delightful stories you know!" said the Mice. And the next night they came with four other little Mice, who were to hear what the Tree recounted; and the more he related, the more plainly he remembered all himself; and it appeared as if those times had really been happy times. "But they may still come—they may still come. Klumpy-Dumpy fell downstairs, and yet he got a princess!" and he thought at the moment of a nice little Birch-tree growing out in the woods: to the Fir, that would be a real charming princess.

"Who is Klumpy-Dumpy?" asked the Mice. So then the Fir-tree told the whole fairy tale, for he could remember every single word of it; and the little Mice jumped for joy up to the very top of the Tree. Next night two more Mice came, and on Sunday two Rats, even; but they said the stories were not interesting, which vexed the little Mice; and they, too, now began to think them not so very amusing.

"Do you know only one story?" asked the Rats.

"Only that one," answered the Tree. "I heard it on my happiest evening; but I did not then know how happy I was."

"It is a very stupid story! Don't you know one about bacon and tallow candles? Can't you tell any larder stories?"

"No," said the Tree.

"Then good-bye," said the Rats; and they went home.

At last the little Mice stayed away also; and the Tree sighed: "After all, it was very pleasant when the sleek little Mice sat around me and listened to what I told them. Now that, too, is over. But I will take good care to enjoy myself when I am brought out again."

But when was that to be? Why, one morning there came a number of people and set to work in the loft. The trunks were moved, the tree was pulled out and thrown down on the floor, but a man drew him toward the stairs, where the daylight shone.

"Now a merry life will begin again," thought the Tree. He felt the fresh air, the first sunbeam—and now he was out in the court-yard. All passed so quickly, there was so much going on around him, that the Tree quite forgot to look to himself. The court adjoined a garden, and all was in flower; the roses hung so fresh and odorous over the balustrade, the lindens were in blossom, the Swallows flew by, and said "Quirre-vit! my husband is come!" but it was not the Fir-tree that they meant.

"Now, then, I shall really enjoy life," said he, exultingly, and spread out his branches; but, alas! they were all withered and yellow. It was in a corner that he lay, among weeds and nettles. The golden star of tinsel was still on the top of the Tree, and glittered in the sunshine.

In the courtyard some of the merry children were playing who had danced at Christmas round the Fir-tree, and were so glad at the sight of him. One of the youngest ran and tore off the golden star.

"Only look what is still on the ugly old Christmas tree!" said he, trampling on the branches, so that they all cracked beneath his feet.

And the Tree beheld all the beauty of the flowers, and the freshness in the garden; he beheld himself, and wished he had remained in his dark corner in the loft; he thought of his first youth in the wood, of the merry Christmas Eve, and of the little Mice who had listened with so much pleasure to the story of Klumpy-Dumpy.

"'Tis over—'tis past!" said the poor Tree. "Had I but rejoiced when I had reason to do so! But now 'tis past, 'tis past!"

And the gardener's boy chopped the Tree into small pieces; there was a whole heap lying there. The wood flamed up splendidly under the large brewing copper, and it sighed so deeply! Each sigh was like a shot.

The boys played about in the court, and the youngest wore the gold star on his breast which the Tree had had on the happiest evening of his life. However, that was over now—the tree gone, the story at an end. All, all was over; every tale must end at last.

THE CONSTANT TIN SOLDIER

By *HANS CHRISTIAN ANDERSEN*

T HERE were once five-and-twenty tin soldiers; they were all brothers, for they had all been born of one old tin spoon. They shouldered their muskets, and looked straight before them; their uniform was red and blue, and very splendid. The first thing they had heard in the world, when the lid was taken off their box, had been the words "Tin soldiers!" These words were uttered by a little boy, clapping his hands; the soldiers had been given to him, for it was his birthday; and now he put them upon the table. Each soldier was exactly like the rest; but one of them had been cast last of all, and there had not been enough tin to finish him; but he stood as firmly upon his one leg as the others on their two; and it was just this soldier who became remarkable.

On the table on which they had been placed stood many other playthings, but the toy that attracted most attention was a neat castle of cardboard. Through the little windows one could see straight into the hall. Before the castle some little trees were placed round a little looking-glass, which was to represent a clear lake. Waxen swans swam on this lake, and were mirrored in it. This was all very pretty; but the prettiest of all was a little lady, who stood at the open door of the castle; she was also cut out in paper, but she had a dress of the clearest gauze, and a little narrow blue ribbon over her shoulders, that looked like a scarf; and in the middle of this ribbon was a shining tinsel rose, as big as her whole face. The little Lady stretched out both her arms, for she was a dancer, and then she lifted one leg so high that the Tin Soldier could not see it at all, and thought that, like himself, she had but one leg.

"That would be the wife for me," thought he; "but she is very grand. She lives in a castle, and I have only a box, and there are five-and-twenty of us in that. It is no place for her. But I must try to make acquaintance with her."

And then he lay down at full length behind a snuffbox which

was on the table; there he could easily watch the little dainty lady, who continued to stand on one leg without losing her balance.

When the evening came, all the other tin soldiers were put into their box, and the people in the house went to bed. Now the toys began to play at "visiting," and at "war," and "giving balls." The tin soldiers rattled in their box, for they wanted to join, but could not lift the lid. The Nut-cracker threw somersaults, and the Pencil amused itself on the table; there was so much noise that the Canary woke up, and began to speak too, and even in verse. The only two who did not stir from their places were the Tin Soldier and the Dancing Lady; she stood straight up on the point of one of her toes, and stretched out both her arms: and he was just as enduring on his one leg; and he never turned his eyes away from her.

Now the clock struck twelve—and, bounce!—the lid flew off the snuffbox; but there was not snuff in it, but a little black goblin.

"Tin Soldier," said the Goblin, "don't stare at things that don't concern you." But the Tin Soldier pretended not to hear him.

"Just you wait till tomorrow!" said the Goblin.

But when the morning came, and the children got up, the Tin Soldier was placed in the window; and whether it was the Goblin or the draught that did it, all at once the window flew open, and the Soldier fell, head over heels, out of the third story. That was a terrible passage! He put his leg straight up, and struck with his helmet downward, and his bayonet between the paving-stones.

The servant-maid and the little boy came down directly to look for him, but though they almost trod upon him they could not see him. If the Soldier had cried out, "Here I am!" they would have found him; but he did not think it fitting to call out loudly, because he was in uniform.

Now it began to rain; the drops soon fell thicker, and at last it came down in a stream. When the rain was past, two boys came by.

"Just look!" said one of them. "There lies a tin soldier. He must come out and ride in the boat."

And they made a boat out of a newspaper, and put the Tin Soldier in the middle of it; and so he sailed down the gutter, and the two boys ran beside him and clapped their hands. Goodness preserve us! How the waves rose in that gutter, and how fast the stream ran! But then it had been a heavy rain. The paper boat rocked up and down, and sometimes turned round so rapidly that the Tin Soldier trembled; but he remained firm, and never changed countenance, and looked straight before him, and shouldered his musket. All at once the boat went into a long drain, and it became as dark as if he had been in his box.

"Where am I going now?" he thought. "Yes, yes, that's the Goblin's fault. Ah! if the little Lady only sat here with me in the boat, it might be twice as dark for what I should care."

Suddenly there came a great water rat, who lived under the drain. "Have you a passport?" said the Rat. "Give me your passport."

But the Tin Soldier kept silence, and only held his musket tighter.

The boat went on, but the Rat came after it. Hu! how he gnashed his teeth, and called out to the bits of straw and wood—"Hold him! Hold him! He hasn't paid toll—he hasn't shown his passport!"

But the stream became stronger and stronger. The Tin Soldier could see the bright daylight where the arch ended; but he heard a roaring noise, which might well frighten a bolder man. Only think —just where the tunnel ended, the drain ran into a great canal; and for him, that would have been as dangerous as for us to be carried down a great waterfall.

Now he was already so near it that he could not stop. The boat was carried out, the poor Tin Soldier stiffening himself as much as he could, and no one could say that he moved an eyelid. The boat whirled round three or four times, and was full of water to the very edge—it must sink. The Tin Soldier stood up to his neck in water, and the boat sank deeper and deeper, and the paper was loosened more and more; and now the water closed over the Soldier's head. Then he thought of the pretty little Dancer, and how he should never see her again; and it sounded in the Soldier's ears:

"Farewell, farewell, thou warrior brave,
Die shalt thou this day."

And now the paper parted, and the Tin Soldier fell out; but at that moment he was snapped up by a great fish.

Oh, how dark it was in that fish's body! It was darker yet than in the drain tunnel; and then it was very narrow, too. But the Tin Soldier was unmoved, and lay at full length, shouldering his musket.

The fish swam to and fro; he made the most wonderful movements, and then became quite still. At last something flashed through him like lightning. The daylight shone quite clear, and a voice said aloud, "The Tin Soldier!" The fish had been caught, carried to market, bought, and taken into the kitchen, where the cook cut him open with a large knife. She seized the Soldier round the body with both her hands, and carried him into the room, where all were anxious to see the remarkable man who had traveled about in the inside of a fish; but the Tin Soldier was not at all proud. They placed him on the table, and there—no! What curious things may happen in the world! The Tin Soldier was in the very room in which he had been before! He saw the same children, and the same toys stood upon the table; and there was the pretty castle with the graceful little Dancer. She was still balancing herself on one leg, and held the other extended in the air. She was faithful, too. That moved the Tin Soldier: he was very near weeping tin tears, but that would not have been proper. But they said nothing to each other.

Then one of the little boys took the Tin Soldier and flung him into the stove. He gave no reason for doing this. It must have been the fault of the Goblin in the snuffbox.

The Tin Soldier stood there quite illuminated, and felt a heat that was terrible; but whether this heat proceeded from the real fire or from love he did not know. The colors had quite gone off from him; but whether that had happened on the journey, or had been caused by grief, no one could say. He looked at the little Lady, she looked at him, and he felt that he was melting; but he stood firm, shouldering his musket. Then suddenly the door flew open, and the draught of air caught the Dancer, and she flew like a sylph just into the stove to the Tin Soldier, and flashed up in a flame, and then was gone! Then the Tin Soldier melted down into a lump, and when the servant-maid took the ashes out next day, she found him in the shape of a little tin heart. But of the Dancer nothing remained but the tinsel rose, and that was burned as black as a coal.

THE SWINEHERD

By HANS CHRISTIAN ANDERSEN

THERE was once a poor Prince; he had a kingdom that was very small; still it was quite large enough to marry upon; and he wished to marry.

It was certainly rather cool of him to say to the Emperor's daughter, "Will you have me?" But so he did; for his name was renowned far and wide; and there were a hundred Princesses who would have answered, "Thank you." But see what she said. Now we will hear.

By the grave of the Prince's father there grew a rose tree—a most beautiful rose tree; it blossomed only once in every five years, and even then bore only one flower, but that was a rose that smelt so sweet as to make one forget all cares and sorrows.

And furthermore, the Prince had a nightingale, who could sing in such a manner that it seemed as though all sweet melodies dwelt in her little throat. So the Princess was to have the rose and the nightingale; and they were accordingly put into large silver caskets, and sent to her.

The Emperor had them brought into a large hall, where the Princess was playing at "making calls," with the ladies of the court; they never did anything else, and when she saw the caskets with the presents, she clapped her hands for joy.

"Ah, if it were but a little pussycat!" exclaimed she; then out came the beautiful rose.

"Oh, how prettily it is made!" said all the court ladies.

"It is more than pretty," said the Emperor; "it is charming!"

But the Princess touched it, and was almost ready to cry.

"Fie, papa!" said she. "It is not made at all; it is natural!"

"Fie!" cried all the court ladies. "It is natural!"

"Let us see what is in the other casket, before we get into a bad humor," proposed the Emperor. So the Nightingale came forth, and sang so delightfully that at first no one could say anything ill-humored of it.

354

"Superbe! Charmant!" exclaimed the ladies; for they all used to chatter French, each one worse than her neighbor.

"How much the bird reminds me of the musical box that belonged to our blessed Empress!" remarked an old Knight. "Ah, yes! It is the very same tone, the same execution."

"Yes! yes!" said the Emperor, and he wept like a little child.

"I will still hope that it is not a real bird," said the Princess.

"Yet it is a real bird," said those who had brought it.

"Well, then, let the bird fly," returned the Princess; and she positively refused to see the Prince.

However, he was not to be discouraged; he daubed his face over brown and black; pulled his cap over his ears, and knocked at the door.

"Good day, Emperor!" said he. "Can I have employment at the palace?"

"Oh, there are so many that want a place!" said the Emperor. "Well, let me see, I want some one to take care of the pigs, for we have a great many of them."

So the Prince was appointed "Imperial Swineherd." He had a dirty little room close by the pigsty; and there he sat the whole day, and worked. By the evening, he had made a pretty little saucepan. Little bells were hung all around it; and when the pot was boiling, these bells tinkled in the most charming manner, and played the old melody:

"Ah! thou dearest Augustine!
All is gone, gone, gone!"

But what was still more curious, whoever held his finger in the smoke of this saucepan, immediately smelt all the dishes that were cooking on every hearth in the city: this, you see, was something quite different from the rose.

Now the Princess happened to walk that way; and when she heard the tune, she stood quite still, and seemed pleased; for she could play "Dearest Augustine"; it was the only piece she knew, and she played it with one finger.

"Why, there is my piece!" said the Princess. "That Swineherd must certainly have been well educated! Here! Go in and ask him the price of the instrument."

And so one of the court ladies must run in; however, she drew on wooden slippers first.

"What will you take for the saucepan?" inquired the lady.

"I will have ten kisses from the Princess," said the swineherd.

"Mercy on us!" said the lady.

"Yes, I cannot sell it for less," said the swineherd.

"Well, what does he say?" asked the Princess.

"I cannot tell you, really," replied the lady; "it is too bad!"

"Then you can whisper it!" So the lady whispered it.

"He is an impudent fellow!" said the Princess, and she walked on; but when she had gone a little way, the bells tinkled so prettily—

> "Ah thou dearest Augustine!
> All is gone, gone, gone!"

"Stay!" said the Princess. "Ask him if he will have ten kisses from the ladies of my court."

"No, thank you!" answered the swineherd. "Ten kisses from the Princess, or I keep the saucepan myself."

"That must not be, either!" said the Princess; "But do you all stand before me, that no one may see us."

And the court ladies placed themselves in front of her, and spread out their dresses; and so the Swineherd got ten kisses, and she got the saucepan.

It was delightful! The saucepan was kept boiling all the evening, and the whole of the following day. They knew perfectly well what was cooking at every fire throughout the city, from the chamberlain's to the cobbler's; the court ladies danced, and clapped their hands.

"We know who has soup and who has pancakes for dinner today, who has cutlets, and who has eggs. How interesting!"

And "How interesting!" said the Lord Steward's wife.

"Yes, but keep my secret, for I am an Emperor's daughter."

"Mercy on us," said they all.

The Swineherd—that is to say, the Prince, for no one knew that he was other than an ill-favored swineherd—let not a day pass without working at something; he at last constructed a rattle, which, when it was swung around, played all the waltzes and jig-tunes which have ever been heard since the creation of the world.

"Ah, that is *superbe!*" said the Princess when she passed by; "I have never heard prettier compositions! Go in and ask him the price of the instruments; but I won't kiss him!"

"He will have a hundred kisses from the Princess!" said the court lady who had been in to ask.

"I think he is crazy!" said the Princess, and walked on; but when she had gone a little way, she stopped again. "One must encourage art," said she; "I am the Emperor's daughter. Tell him, he shall, as on yesterday, have ten kisses from me and may take the rest from the ladies of the court."

"Oh, but we should not like that at all!" said the court ladies.

"What are you muttering?" asked the Princess; "if I can kiss him, surely you can! Remember, I give you your food and wages." So the court ladies were obliged to go to him again.

"A hundred kisses from the Princess," said he, "or else let everyone keep his own."

"Stand around!" said she; and all the ladies stood round her whilst the kissing was going on.

"What can be the reason for such a crowd close by the pigsty?" said the Emperor, who happened just then to step out on the balcony. He rubbed his eyes and put on his spectacles. "They are the ladies of the court; there is some play going on. I must go down and see what they are about!" So he pulled up his slippers at the heel, for he had trodden them down.

Heh, there! What a hurry he is in.

As soon as he had got into the courtyard, he moved very softly, and the ladies were so much engrossed with counting the kisses that all might go on fairly, that they did not perceive the Emperor. He rose on his tiptoes.

"What is all this?" said he, when he saw what was going on, and he boxed the Princess's ears with his slipper, just as the Swineherd was taking the eighty-sixth kiss.

"Off with you!" cried the Emperor, for he was very angry; and both Princess and Swineherd were thrust out of the city.

The Princess now stood and wept, the Swineherd scolded, and the rain poured down.

"Oh, how miserable I am!" said the Princess. "If I had but married the handsome young Prince! Ah, how unfortunate I am!"

And the Swineherd went behind a tree, washed the black-and-brown color from his face, threw off his dirty clothes, and stepped forth in his princely robes; he looked so noble that the Princess could not help bowing before him.

"I am come to despise thee," said he. "Thou wouldst not have an honorable prince! Thou couldst not prize the rose and the nightingale, but thou wast ready to kiss the Swineherd for the sake of a trumpery plaything. Now thou hast thy deserts!"

He then went back to his own little kingdom, and shut the door of his palace in her face. Now she might well sing:

"Ah! thou dearest Augustine!
All is gone, gone, gone!"

THE NIGHTINGALE

By *HANS CHRISTIAN ANDERSEN*

Illustration by V. PEDERSEN

IN China, you must know, the Emperor is a Chinaman, and all whom he has about him are Chinamen, too. It happened a good many years ago, but that's just why it's worth while to hear the story, before it is forgotten. The Emperor's palace was the most splendid in the world; it was made entirely of porcelain, very costly, but so delicate and brittle that one had to take care how one touched it. In the garden were to be seen the most wonderful flowers, and to the costliest of them silver bells were tied, which sounded, so that nobody should pass by without noticing the flowers. Yes, everything in the Emperor's garden was admirably arranged. And it extended so far, that the gardener himself did not know where the end was. If a man went on and on, he came into a glorious forest with high trees and deep lakes. The wood extended straight down to the sea, which was blue and deep; great ships could sail to and fro beneath the branches of the trees; and in the trees lived a Nightingale, which sang so splendidly that even the poor Fisherman, who had many other things to do, stopped still and listened, when he had gone out at night to throw out his nets, and heard the Nightingale.

"How beautiful that is!" he said; but he was obliged to attend to his property, and thus forgot the bird. But when in the next night the bird sang again, and the Fisherman heard it, he exclaimed again, "How beautiful that is!"

From all the countries of the world travelers came to the city of the Emperor and admired it, and the palace, and the garden, but when they heard the Nightingale, they said, "That is the best of all!"

And the travelers told of it when they came home; and the learned men wrote many books about the town, the palace, and the garden. But they did not forget the Nightingale; that was placed highest of all; and those who were poets wrote most magnificent poems about the Nightingale in the wood by the deep lake.

The books went through all the world, and a few of them once came to the Emperor. He sat in his golden chair, and read, and read: every moment he nodded his head, for it pleased him to peruse the masterly descriptions of the city, the palace, and the garden. "But the Nightingale is the best of all!"—it stood written there.

"What's that?" exclaimed the Emperor. "I don't know the Nightingale at all! Is there such a bird in my empire, and even in my garden? I've never heard of that. To think that I should have to learn such a thing for the first time from books!"

And hereupon he called his Cavalier. This Cavalier was so grand that if any one lower in rank than himself dared to speak to him, or to ask him any question, he answered nothing but "P!"—and that meant nothing.

"There is said to be a wonderful bird here called a Nightingale!" said the Emperor. "They say it is the best thing in all my great empire. Why have I never heard anything about it?"

"I have never heard him named," replied the Cavalier. "He has never been introduced at court."

"I command that he shall appear this evening, and sing before me," said the Emperor. "All the world knows what I possess, and I do not know it myself!"

"I have never heard him mentioned," said the Cavalier. "I will seek for him. I will find him."

But where was he to be found? The Cavalier ran up and down all the staircases, through halls and passages, but no one among all those whom he met had heard talk of the Nightingale. And the Cavalier ran back to the Emperor, and said that it must be a fable invented by the writers of books.

"Your Imperial Majesty cannot believe how much is written that is fiction, besides something that they call the black art."

"But the book in which I read this," said the Emperor, "was sent to me by the high and mighty Emperor of Japan, and therefore it cannot be a falsehood. I will hear the Nightingale! It must be here this evening! It has my imperial favor; and if it does not come, all the court shall be trampled upon after the court has supped!"

V. Pedersen

Death sat upon his chest, and had put on his golden crown.

[See page 366]

"Tsing-pe!" said the Cavalier; and again he ran up and down all the staircases, and through halls and corridors; and half the court ran with him, for the courtiers did not like being trampled upon.

Then there was a great inquiry after the wonderful Nightingale, which all the world knew excepting the people at court.

At last they met with a poor little girl in the kitchen, who said: "The Nightingale? I know it well; yes, it can sing gloriously. Every evening I get leave to carry my poor sick mother the scraps from the table. She lives down by the strand, and when I get back and am tired, and rest in the wood, then I hear the Nightingale sing. And then the water comes into my eyes, and it is just as if my mother kissed me!"

"Little Kitchen Girl," said the Cavalier, "I will get you a place in the kitchen, with permission to see the Emperor dine, if you will lead us to the Nightingale, for it is announced for this evening."

So they all went out into the wood where the Nightingale was accustomed to sing; half the court went forth. When they were in the midst of their journey a cow began to low.

"Oh!" cried the court pages, "now we have it! That shows a wonderful power in so small a creature! I've certainly heard it before."

"No, those are cows lowing!" said the little Kitchen Girl. "We are a long way from the place yet."

Now the frogs began to croak in the marsh. "Glorious!" said the Court Preacher. "I hear it—it sounds like little church bells."

"No, those are frogs!" said the little Kitchen-maid. "But now I think we shall soon hear it."

And then the Nightingale began to sing.

"That is it!" exclaimed the little Girl. "Listen, listen! and yonder it sits." And she pointed to a little gray bird up in the boughs.

"Is it possible?" cried the Cavalier. "I should never have thought it looked like that! How simple it looks! It must certainly have lost its color at seeing such grand people around."

"Little Nightingale!" called the little Kitchen-maid, quite loudly. "Our gracious Emperor wishes you to sing before him."

"With the greatest pleasure!" replied the Nightingale, and began to sing most delightfully.

"It sounds just like glass bells!" said the Cavalier. "And look at its little throat, how it's working! It's wonderful that we had never heard it before. That bird will be a great success at court."

"Shall I sing once more before the Emperor?" asked the Nightingale, for it thought the Emperor was present.

"My excellent little Nightingale," said the Cavalier, "I have great pleasure in inviting you to a court festival this evening, when you shall charm his Imperial Majesty with your beautiful singing."

"My song sounds best in the greenwood!" replied the Nightingale; still it came willingly when it heard what the Emperor wished.

The place was festively adorned. The walls and the flooring, which were of porcelain, gleamed in the rays of thousands of golden lamps. The most glorious flowers, which could ring clearly, had been placed in the passages. There was a running to and fro, and a thorough draught, and all the bells rang loudly.

In the midst of the great hall, where the Emperor sat, a golden perch had been placed, on which the Nightingale was to sit. The whole court was there, and the little Cook-maid had got leave to stand behind the door, as she had now received the title of a real court cook. All were in full dress, and all looked at the little gray bird, to which the Emperor nodded.

And the Nightingale sang so gloriously that the tears came into the Emperor's eyes, and the tears ran down over his cheeks; and then the Nightingale sang still more sweetly—that went straight to the heart. The Emperor was so pleased that he said the Nightingale should have his golden slipper to wear round its neck. But the Nightingale declined, saying it had already received a sufficient reward.

"I have seen tears in the Emperor's eyes—that is the real treasure to me. An emperor's tears have a peculiar power. I am rewarded enough!" And then it sang again with a sweet, glorious voice.

"That's the most amiable coquetry I ever saw!" said the ladies who stood round about, and then they took water in their mouths to gurgle when anyone spoke to them. They thought they should be nightingales, too. And the lackeys and chambermaids reported they were satisfied, too; and that was saying a good deal, for they are the most difficult to please. The Nightingale achieved a real success.

It was now to remain at court, to have its own cage, with liberty to go out twice every day and once at night. Twelve servants were appointed when the Nightingale went out, each of whom had a silken string fastened to the bird's leg, which they held very tight. There was really no pleasure in an excursion of that kind.

The whole city spoke of the wonderful bird, and when two people met, one said nothing but "Nightin," and the other said "gale"; and then they sighed, and understood one another. Eleven peddlers' children were named for the bird, but not one of them could sing a note.

One day the Emperor received a large parcel, on which was written "The Nightingale."

"There we have a new book about this celebrated bird," he said.

But it was not a book, but a little work of art, contained in a box: an artificial nightingale, which was to sing like a natural one, and was brilliantly ornamented with diamonds, rubies, and sapphires. So soon as the artificial bird was wound up, he could sing one of the pieces that he really sang, and then his tail moved up and down, and shone with silver and gold. Round his neck hung a little ribbon, and on that was written, "The Emperor of China's Nightingale is poor compared to that of the Emperor of Japan."

"That is capital!" said they all, and he who had brought the artificial bird immediately received the title, Imperial Head-Nightingale-Bringer.

"Now they must sing together; what a duet that will be!"

And so they had to sing together; but it did not sound very well, for the real Nightingale sang in its own way, and the artificial bird sang waltzes. "That's not his fault," said the Play-master; "he's quite perfect, and very much in my style."

Now the artificial bird was to sing alone. He had just as much success as the real one, and then it was much handsomer to look at— it shone like bracelets and breastpins.

Three-and-thirty times over did it sing the same piece, and yet was not tired. The people would gladly have heard it again, but the Emperor said that the living Nightingale ought to sing something now. But where was it? No one had noticed that it had flown away out of the open window, back to the greenwood.

"But what is become of that?" said the Emperor.

And all the courtiers abused the Nightingale, and declared that it was a very ungrateful creature.

"We have the best bird after all," said they.

And so the artificial bird had to sing again, and that was the thirty-fourth time that they had listened to the same piece. For all that, they did not know it quite by heart, for it was so very difficult. And the Play-master praised the bird particularly; yes, he declared that it was better than a nightingale, not only with regard to its plumage and the many beautiful diamonds, but inside as well.

"For you see, ladies and gentlemen, and above all, your Imperial Majesty, with a real nightingale one can never calculate what is coming, but in this artificial bird everything is settled. One can explain it; one can open it, and make people understand where the waltzes come from, how they go, and how one follows up another."

"Those are quite our own ideas," they all said.

And the speaker received permission to show the bird to the people on the next Sunday. The people were to hear it sing too, the Emperor commanded; and they did hear it, and were as much pleased as if they had all got tipsy upon tea, and they all said, "Oh!" and held up their forefingers and nodded. But the poor Fisherman, who had heard the real Nightingale, said:

"It sounds pretty enough, and the melodies resemble each other, but there's something wanting, though I know not what!"

The real Nightingale was banished from the country and empire. The artificial bird had its place on a silken cushion close to the Emperor's bed; all the presents it had received, gold and precious stones, were ranged about it; in title it had advanced to be the High Imperial After-Dinner-Singer, and in rank, to number one on the left hand; for the Emperor considered that side the most important on which the heart is placed, and even in an emperor the heart is on the left side; and the Play-master wrote a work of five-and-twenty volumes about the artificial bird; it was very learned and very long, full of the most difficult Chinese words; but yet all the people declared that they had read it, and understood it, for fear of being considered stupid, and having their bodies trampled on.

So a whole year went by. The Emperor, the court, and all the other Chinese knew every little twitter in the artificial bird's song by heart. But just for that reason it pleased them best—they could sing with it themselves, and they did so. The street boys sang, "Tsi-tsi-tsi-glug-glug!" and the Emperor himself sang it, too.

But one evening, when the artificial bird was singing its best, and the Emperor lay in bed listening to it, something inside the bird said, "Whizz!" Something cracked. "Whir-r-r!" All the wheels ran round, and then the music stopped.

The Emperor immediately sprang out of bed, and caused his body physician to be called; but what could *he* do? Then they sent for a watchmaker, and after a good deal of talking and investigation, the bird was put into something like order; but the Watchmaker said that the bird must be carefully treated, for the barrels were worn, and it would be impossible to put new ones in in such a manner that the music would go. There was a great lamentation; only once in a year was it permitted to let the bird sing, and that was almost too much. But then the Play-master made a little speech, full of heavy words, and said this was just as good as before—and so of course it was as good as before.

Now five years had gone by, and a real grief came upon the whole nation. The Chinese were really fond of their Emperor; and now he was ill, and could not, it was said, live much longer. Already a new Emperor had been chosen, and the people stood out in the street and asked the Cavalier how their old Emperor did.

"P!" said he, and shook his head.

Cold and pale lay the Emperor in his great gorgeous bed; the whole court thought him dead, and each one ran to pay homage to the new ruler. The chamberlains ran out to talk it over, and the ladies' maids had a great coffee party. All about, in all the halls and passages, cloth had been laid down so that no footstep could be heard, and therefore it was quiet there, quite quiet. But the Emperor was not dead yet: stiff and pale he lay on the gorgeous bed with the long velvet curtains and the heavy gold tassels; high up, a window stood open, and the moon shone in upon the Emperor and the artificial bird.

The poor Emperor could scarcely breathe; it was just as if something lay upon his chest; he opened his eyes, and then he saw that it was Death who sat upon his chest, and had put on his golden crown, and held in one hand the Emperor's sword and in the other his beautiful banner. And all around, from among the folds of the splendid velvet curtains, strange heads peered forth: a few very ugly, the rest quite lovely and mild. These were the Emperor's bad and good deeds, that stood before him now that Death sat on his heart.

"Do you remember this?" whispered one to the other. "Do you remember that?" and then they told him so much that the perspiration ran from his forehead.

"I did not know that!" said the Emperor. "Music! music! the great Chinese drum!" he cried. "So that I need not hear all they say!"

And they continued speaking, and Death nodded like a Chinaman to all they said.

"Music! music!" cried the Emperor. "You little precious golden bird, sing, sing! I have given you gold and costly presents; I have even hung my golden slipper around your neck—sing now, sing!"

But the bird stood still; no one was there to wind him up, and he could not sing without that; but Death continued to stare at the Emperor with his great hollow eyes, and it was quiet, fearfully quiet.

Then there sounded from the window, suddenly, the most lovely song. It was the little live Nightingale, that sat outside on a spray. It had heard of the Emperor's sad plight, and had come to sing to him of comfort and hope. And as it sang the specters grew paler and paler; the blood ran quicker and more quickly through the Emperor's weak limbs; and even Death listened, and said,

"Go on, little Nightingale, go on!"

"But will you give me that splendid golden sword? Will you give me that rich banner? Will you give me the Emperor's crown?"

And Death gave up each of these treasures for a song. And the Nightingale sang on and on; and it sang of the quiet churchyard where the white roses grow, where the elder-blossom smells sweet, and where the fresh grass is moistened by the tears of survivors. Then Death felt a longing to see his garden, and floated out at the window in the form of a cold, white mist.

"Thanks! Thanks!" said the Emperor. "You heavenly little bird! I know you well. I banished you from my country and empire, and yet you have charmed away the evil faces from my couch, and banished Death from my heart! How can I reward you?"

"You have rewarded me!" replied the Nightingale. "I drew tears from your eyes when I sang the first time—I shall never forget that. Those are the jewels that rejoice a singer's heart. But now sleep, and grow fresh and strong again. I will sing you something."

And it sang, and the Emperor fell into a sweet slumber. Ah! how mild and refreshing that sleep was! The sun shone upon him through the windows when he awoke refreshed and restored; not one of his servants had yet returned, for they all thought he was dead; only the Nightingale still sat beside him and sang.

"You must always stay with me," said the Emperor. "You shall sing as you please; and I'll break the artificial bird into a thousand pieces."

"Not so," replied the Nightingale. "It did well as long at it could; keep it as you have done till now. I cannot build my nest in the palace to dwell in it, but let me come when I feel the wish; then I will sit in the evening on the spray yonder by the window, and sing you something, so that you may be glad and thoughtful at once. I will sing of those who are happy and of those who suffer: I will sing of good and of evil that remain hidden round about you. The little singing bird flies far around, to the poor fisherman, to the peasant's roof, to everyone who dwells far away from you and from your court. I love your heart more than your crown, and yet the crown has an air of sanctity about it. I will come and sing to you—but one thing you must promise me."

"Everything!" said the Emperor; and he stood there in his imperial robes, which he had put on himself, and pressed the sword which was heavy with gold to his heart.

"One thing I beg of you: tell no one that you have a little bird who tells you everything. Then it will go all the better."

And the Nightingale flew away.

The servants came in to look to their dead Emperor, and—yes, there he stood, and the Emperor said "Good morning!"

SOURCES OF STORIES IN VOLUME II

The Magic Fishbone, by Charles Dickens. Frederick Warne & Company, Inc.

The Story of the Four Little Children Who Went Round the World, from Nonsense Books, by Edward Lear. Little, Brown & Company.

Living in Wales: The Gardener and the White Elephants, from The Spider's Palace, by Richard Hughes. Harper & Brothers.

Prince Rabbit, from Number Two Joy Street. D. Appleton-Century Company.

The Pumpkin Giant, from The Pot of Gold, by Mary E. Wilkins. Lothrop, Lee and Shepard Company.

How They Broke Away to Go to the Rootabaga Country, from Rootabaga Stories, by Carl Sandburg. Harcourt, Brace & Company, Inc.

Uncle Remus, from Uncle Remus, His Songs and His Sayings, by Joel Chandler Harris. D. Appleton-Century Company.

The Ouphe of the Wood, from Stories Told to a Child, by Jean Ingelow. Little, Brown & Company.

Brownie and the Cook, from The Adventures of a Brownie, by Dinah Maria Mulock Craik. G. P. Putnam's Sons.

The Greedy Shepherd, from Granny's Wonderful Chair, by Frances Browne. E. P. Dutton & Company, Inc.

The Light Princess, by George Macdonald. The Macmillan Company.

The Seller of Dreams: The Lost Half-Hour, from The Firelight Fairy Book, by Henry Beston. Little, Brown & Company.

The Dutch Cheese, by Walter de la Mare. Alfred A. Knopf, Inc.

A Tale of Three Tails, from Tales of Silver Lands, by Charles J. Finger. Doubleday, Doran & Company, Inc.

The Seventh Princess, from Italian Peepshow, by Eleanor Farjeon. Frederick A. Stokes.

The Two Youths Whose Father Was under the Sea, from The Big Tree of Bunlahy, by Padraic Colum. The Macmillan Company.

The Stone Lion, from Tales from Timbuktu, by Constance Smedley. Harcourt, Brace & Co.

Aladdin: Ali Baba, from The Children's Book, by Horace E. Scudder. Houghton Mifflin.

A Chinese Fairy Tale, from Moonshine and Clover, by Laurence Housman. Harcourt, Brace & Company, Inc.

How Boots Befooled the King: King Stork, from The Wonder Clock, by Howard Pyle. Harper & Brothers.

The Stool of Fortune, from Twilight Land, by Howard Pyle. Harper & Brothers.

The Emergency Mistress, from The Floating Prince, by Frank R. Stockton. Charles Scribner's Sons.

Old Pipes and the Dryad, from The Queen's Museum, by Frank R. Stockton. Charles Scribner's Sons.

The Princess on the Pea, from Stories and Tales, by Hans Christian Andersen. Houghton Mifflin Co. The other Andersen Stories from Wonder Stories, Told for Children, by Hans Christian Andersen, Houghton Mifflin Co.